ARENA

BY MAURICE GHNASSIA

NOVELS

Foule aux Dames
Un Dimanche pour Pleurer

THEATRE

Les Fugitifs

ARENA

A NOVEL BY
Maurice Ghnassia

INTRODUCTION BY

JÉRÔME CARCOPINO

OF THE ACADÉMIE FRANÇAISE

New York • The Viking Press

Copyright © 1969 by Maurice Ghnassia
All rights reserved

First published in 1969 by The Viking Press, Inc.
625 Madison Avenue, New York, N.Y. 10022

Published simultaneously in Canada by
The Macmillan Company of Canada Limited

Library of Congress catalog card number: 69-15659

Printed in U.S.A. by Vail-Ballou Press, Inc.

TRANSLATED FROM THE FRENCH

To the memory of Esther Karsenty-Ghnassia
and Frank Facciolo

and to Louisa, Noëlle, Barbara, and Patrick

INTRODUCTION

By Jérôme Carcopino

of the Académie Française

I have been asked to write a few lines, by way of introduction to Maurice Ghnassia's novel based on the lives of Spartacus and Crassus.

How could I decline this honor when confronted with so admirable a work? Yet how can I restrict myself to a few lines?

I have never read Saurin's play (*Spartacus*, 1760), but Ghnassia's most immediate predecessors * have twisted men and events so as to make their fiction fit their political views; those who went before had written at a time when criticism had as yet neither formalized its methods nor asserted its rights.

Therefore, I am convinced that Maurice Ghnassia is the first novelist to have focused a scholarly and passionate intelligence upon the study of the times in which his characters lived, so that he might attempt to bring them alive once more out of the psychological environment which shaped their souls and the political and social conditions surrounding the course of events that made Spartacus immortal. I feel justified in stating that no other author has been better nor so powerfully able to fuse the

* Arthur Koestler, *The Gladiators*, 1939; Howard Fast, *Spartacus*, 1951.

modern aesthetics of novel construction with the respect for history.

His imagination has breathed life into the data the writers of antiquity handed down to us; it has not modified their substance, changed their meaning, or altered their colors.

Without any doubt, Maurice Ghnassia intended, as was his right—indeed, his duty—not to distort the past by drawing parallels as facile as they are fallacious between it and the present, which will very shortly become irrelevant, but to bring out of the past those values and accents which apply for all times.

In this, he magnificently succeeded.

Ghnassia first mentioned his project to me in 1953; his vast knowledge of the subject had already impressed me. Now, finished fifteen years later, his work is so readable and has such impact that it should be of great value to enlightened readers as well as to students of this period of Roman history and of political science. At any rate, we must wish it the fine success it deserves.

The simplicity, restraint, and clarity of the style may tend to overshadow the author's admirable penetration into his subject; they are the product of a fine mastery of language and a profound knowledge of the material. In some fifteen pages, the two principal characters are established against the troubled background of fifteen skillfully drawn years of Roman history (88–73 B.C.): Spartacus amidst the clash of the armies of Mithridates and Sulla, and Crassus in his flight from the reprisals of Marius and Cinna.

Alexander's message, the arrival at Capua, the gladiatorial fights, the Saturnalia, the power and precision of the descriptions of the landscapes, the atmosphere of the games, and the streets, are all passages of rare quality. This same high quality is also found in other sections. All of them are worth quoting: the scene at the house of the Prince of the Senate; the development of Alba; Polla's appeal at the seashore; Crassus' friend, Alexander—to whom Plutarch devoted but a short paragraph—who is so engaging, so powerful, that we regretfully part company with him each time as the chapters run along. But is this not already revealing too much?

In the unfolding of this story, the outcome is a foregone conclusion and the destiny of Spartacus inescapably fixed. And yet, the novel emerges as an epic with a brilliantly constructed plot and as a history of ideas shown through the confrontations of the characters. Faced with the burning questions of the moment, all the characters are forced to make choices. Whatever its nature, each crisis is total, the confrontation is constant. Each character is the confidant of another: they are a set of mirrors. The characters come alive, and the author's presence vanishes.

Throughout the story, fresh insights, historical truths, new dimensions appear, and the characters' actual problems become clear to us, finally freeing Spartacus and Crassus from the partisan or nostalgic portraits and the mythological dust which until now has gathered over their names.

As Jules Romains did in *Le Dictateur,* so Maurice Ghnassia has pitted the noblest aspirations of the few against the instincts that drive the many; the initial purity—luminous as dawn—against the compromises and shortcomings, the ultimate defeats, which inevitably follow; the exaltation of the ideal—its diamond immediately marred by a material too tough to fashion—against the disillusionments of reality.

But Ghnassia never loses sight of these perpetual conflicts, which are the very tragedies of mankind and which give to his work its greatest emotive power, nor of the fact that he chose the first century before our era, in a time at once so akin to and so far from our own. And it is his constant concern that the human truths for which, without any rhetoric, he is so eloquent a spokesman, should never be unfaithful to the Roman truth of two thousand years ago. Thus, Maurice Ghnassia is the author of a great novel. It is authentically historical, and for this the historian in me congratulates him and expresses his sincere gratitude.

AUTHOR'S NOTE

As Jérôme Carcopino remarks in his Introduction, the War of Spartacus has aroused the interest of several authors in the last two hundred years. Why write a novel on a subject that has already been explored several times? Well, there are many examples of works based on the same subject. It suffices to mention only two names and dozens of titles come to mind—Thomas Beckett and Joan of Arc. But in this case there are also other reasons. During the German occupation of France, curfew was early. I used all my time in the evening to read. But since I did not care for the Germans' and their collaborators' "new" literature, I turned back to my own pre–World War II books and logically went back to the classics—the French, first. And because I had always been interested in Roman history, I also reread Cicero's *Letters to Atticus,* Plutarch's *Lives,* Appian's *Civil Wars* and Gustave Bloch's and Jérôme Carcopino's *Roman History.* In the last three studies, I paused a long time and reread avidly everything pertaining to the revolt of Spartacus. Unfortunately, there was not much material covering it.

In the meantime, the German occupation of my country was

going on. When it became necessary to "take the maquis," as we used to say in those days, I went up the mountains, but I carried my Cicero, Appian, Plutarch and Bloch-Carcopino books in my knapsack everywhere I went.

In the Resistance group to which I belonged, we lived just the same way runaways and guerrilleros have lived throughout the world for thousands of years. However, the few differences that separated the maquis fighters from Spartacus' fugitives and the ordinary legionary soldiers were huge—we had shoes, matches, and aspirin. Our weaponry was the same as our enemy's; so was Spartacus'. We had machine guns, guns, rifles and grenades; the Germans did, too. Spartacus had lances, swords and shields; so did the legionaries. We had to eat roots, sometimes several days in a row, and we engaged in combat.

There was no glamour about life in the maquis. It was a dangerous, slippery, tricky, sometimes disgusting and sometimes grand adventure. One rarely survived one's mistake. Man was at his best and at his worst. There has never been anything romantic, glamorous, colorful or *nice* about fighting man to the death, regardless of the engaging posters, the pretexts given, the flowers of rhetoric or the artful use of the camera. The necessity of the encounter may sometimes be or seem to be *legitimate,* but its absolute conclusion is never justifiable. Man's death by man is always scandalous.

My books had become my closest companions, under any weather, for three and a half years. I understood more and more Spartacus' problems at every engagement, in every dangerous situation, during every difficult moment, and specially all the time that we went without food. I knew his problems; we were living them. It also appeared to me that the lives of Spartacus and Crassus included parallel elements, particularly disturbing, which the authors of antiquity and our contemporary historians Bloch and Carcopino had neglected to bring out.

By 1953, eight years after World War II, my notes on the period were covered with dust. I was writing novels, doing translations; I was also busy with jazz music for radio productions and with the dubbing of foreign films. And then Dien Bien Phu and Algeria became the background of our daily lives; they were disturbing and bloody reminders of the guerrilla warfare of World War II and some events of two thousand years ago.

The name for our century could well be "the century of hecatombs." At the end of the nineteenth century, the split of France into two camps over the Dreyfus case gave a symbolical start to the splits that were to take place in many nations. My country was split another time at the end of the Algerian War—in broad lines, there were two Frances, the France of de Gaulle and the France of Sartre. With World War I, Spain, Hitler's genocide and World War II, the atomic bomb and the wars of liberation, more than forty million people have died violent deaths—not to mention the Congolese, Indo-Pakistani, South African, Indonesian, and Nigerian bloodbaths of people torn by civil wars.

So, some fifteen years ago, when I saw in Paris the novels of my most recent predecessors on Spartacus, I read them and a deep astonishment dominated all my reactions—the two well-known writers had used the historical events as a springboard to express their political convictions. But the subject of the War of Spartacus remained; they had not exhausted it. I thought there was something else to do with it in this century of hecatombs—so, I have tried.

M.G.

ARENA

"Genuine charity demands sacrifice for the good of the species—it is hard, it is full of self-overcoming, because it needs human sacrifice. And this pseudo humaneness called Christianity wants it established that no one should be sacrificed."

—Friedrich Nietzsche,
The Will to Power

"The true point of view on all things is that of the most dispossessed; the executioner may be unaware of what he is doing; the victim unexceptionably experiences his suffering, his death; the truth of oppression is the oppressed himself."

—Jean-Paul Sartre,
Les Communistes et la paix

ARENA

PROLOGUE

The speck burst from the haze like a bolide. It grew, inanimate between sky and fog, swelled further, and then opened out into a vertical flutter; beneath the flat orange sun of the late autumn afternoon, the wing idled and ceased to move; the bird glided, drifted downward, skimmed the poplars along the Hebrus, and chose to alight with little pointed steps on the roof of a hut, supported askew by beams covered with brown moss. Its eye scanned the water. Horses were approaching, the gull turned its head.

The company had advanced under cover of a forest that ended before the last foothills of the Rhodope. The centurion raised his arm and two decurions at once spurred their horses; the officer pointed to two men lying on a hillside in the middle of a flock of sheep. Weapons clanked as the flock was surrounded. One of the men awoke. He attempted to get up, but was stopped by the end of a soldier's lance; the man was unarmed. The soldier prodded the other shepherd, who made a sudden turn, and his head struck against the Roman's leg armor. The shepherd's mouth gaped in surprise. "Up!" The two men got up. Some legionaries came toward the younger shepherd, but the older one grabbed the first soldier's arm, twisted it behind his back, and shoved his knee into his loins, breaking his arm as he fell. He then seized his young companion by the shoulder and drew him to his side, but a lance struck the older man in the back and pierced his chest. He fell to his knees. His hand slid down the young shepherd's arm as far as the fingers, which he pressed for a moment; he fell forward and in a faint voice uttered a name "Spartacus!" A legionary set a foot on his back to pry the lance out, and the Romans went off with the sheep in a cloud of yellow dust.

Tied by his hands to the saddle of a horse with some other prisoners, the shepherd turned to look at his dead companion; a whiplash struck him on the neck, another straightened his legs which had buckled beneath him, and a third got him to walk on.

Beneath a sky tormented by the horizontal rays of the sun falling behind Samothrace, there stretched the great reddened patch of the Lake of Stentor, formed by the mouth of the Hebrus before it slips into the Aegean Sea. In front of the mist slowly covering the dunes, the western sky cast ominous purple reflections on helmets, breastplates, and weapons. On the other side of the lake, Archelaus' old house was in flames. Far ahead, on the right bank, raising another cloud of yellow dust, another column of red and white tunics, other prisoners, other sheep were moving off in the direction of the sea.

The shepherd-prisoner eyed the legionaries, their light uniforms, the way they rode, stiffly, with the reins tight on the horses' necks. The dust made him cough; he spat. For the first time since awakening, he closed his mouth; the surprise was gone. Up above, his face against the grass of the hillock, the man was stretched out; a trickle of blood had flowed from his back as far as the nape of his neck and come to a stop beneath his white hair. Lower down, from his observation post, the gull watched the river flow by.

From the banks of the Hebrus, adding each day to the number of its Odrysian prisoners, the company made its way up toward Philippopolis, crossed Macedonia, went down through Thessaly, and stopped at Demetrias, a Roman strongpoint on the Pelasgic Gulf. There, the prisoners were subjected to a rigorous regimen.

In a few months the weak were dead, but the strong were transformed into Roman soldiers with a level of physical fitness so high that they had to be employed at construction work, made to go on long marches and forced to dig ditches which were only to be filled in the next day to avoid the evils of idleness while keeping the men in good shape. Thus did the winter go by for Spartacus, who had suddenly become a soldier in an auxiliary corps of the Roman army.

In the spring of that year, 87 B.C., Rome's trade and expansion were brought to a standstill by the recent fall of Delos to the King of Pontus, Mithridates VI Eupator, who, at a time when the stability of the Roman Empire was threatened from within by Marius and Cinna, had made the most of a situation already undermined in Asia by the arrogant, grasping foreign policy of the Senate. Mithridates, protected in the rear by his recent conquests and the natural fortress of his immense Kingdom of Pontus, was also master of the Black Sea, the Thracian Bosphorus, the Aegean, and the entire Hellenic East. And now, from the Greek coast, across the Ionian Sea, he was threatening the whole of Italy.

To stop the King of Pontus from advancing and to quell his ambitions, the Senate sent Cornelius Sulla to war against him. He landed in Epirus with a mere five legions, consisting of twenty thousand infantry and five thousand cavalry, to pit against the all-powerful Mithridates, who could launch a thousand ships in a few hours, raise three or four hundred thousand infantry and forty thousand cavalry, and had more than a hundred scythe-chariots manned by his Sarmatian mercenaries. Sulla's position seemed hopelessly vulnerable. On arriving at Demetrias, he looked into the physical condition of the bands raised in Thrace from among the Odrysians, whose numbers included Spartacus. He absorbed them into his army and went down through Thessaly, along the Aegean coastline. When he reached Chersonesus, he left the auxiliary corps of Odrysians there to guard the straits of Euboea and marched on Athens. He spent the rest of the year in front of the Long Walls in a vain attempt to take the Piraeus. When winter came, Sulla had also lost all contact with Rome, where Cinna had betrayed him.

At nightfall, in normal times, before the night life of the City began, dogs, cats, and rats would clear the major part of the garbage from the streets of Rome, and as soon as the first stalls opened, well before dawn, they would disappear, sometimes leaving a few victims behind them. But at the end of this particular day, December 31, 87, the animals had searched in vain: the inhabitants themselves had been fighting over the scraps for the past week. At the beginning of this particularly harsh winter, even the howling of wolves had been heard. Now the Romans waited, cowering in homes, trembling with cold and fear in the silence of the City.

As if to end this year in another bloodbath, Marius and Cinna, lusting for revenge, were going to enter Rome as if it were enemy territory and slaughter the nobles in this last episode of a civil war in which the antagonists were the two consuls Sulla had nominated before embarking at Brundisium: the democrat Cinna and the noble Octavius.

Violence had first arisen when, under the leadership of Sulla, the nobles had set fire to houses, defended their privileges amidst the bloody street fighting, and restored the Senate's authority, which had been challenged by the revolutionary party of Sulpicius and Marius.

A second time, as soon as Sulla had embarked for the East to fight Mithridates, Cinna had taken advantage of his absence to suggest that the people recall from exile all the Marianists Sulla had banished. But he failed to inform his fellow consul Octavius of his decision. Octavius, faithful to his public charge and completely loyal to the Senate, had entered Rome with mercenaries who had been armed by the nobles. After further carnage, he had again restored the Senate's authority, banished Cinna and the tribunes who had joined him in the struggle, and ordered the election of a new consul.

The third outbreak of violence occurred after Marius returned from Africa. He landed in Etruria, opened the prisons, recruited a legion of volunteers, and joined Cinna, who had agreed to let him take over command of the war in Asia in exchange for his help against Octavius. In pursuing their social war against the aristocrats, the two men had enlisted the help of the Etrurians and Samnites and had brutally cut Rome's lines of supply. A fierce battle with the Senate's army ensued under a hot summer sun, resulting in heavy losses which were multiplied still further by the ravages of the plague. Victorious, Marius and Cinna had withdrawn with their troops, who were becoming difficult to restrain, but they had induced them to wait for winter to return to the attack. Powerless, the Senate had then offered to surrender Rome on condition that the enemy refrain from reprisals. But the victors had not replied: all the atrocities were about to follow.

Appearing from all sides, Marius' prisoners from Etruria and Cinna's serfs from Samnium began the slaughter. At a street corner three fleeing Romans had halted; they talked quickly in undertones. The eldest, L. Licinius Crassus, the censor, pale, breathing with difficulty, signaled briefly to his two companions to move on. Seeing them hurry away, the old man covered his head with a flap of his toga, slit his veins, and waited for death against the wall. The invaders were drawing nearer. Silent and swift, with torches in their hands, the first Barbarians were already entering a house at the end of the street, in the van of the main body.

Surprised by another group, the censor's two sons retraced their steps. A lance struck the slower deep below the shoulder; he was overtaken and killed. The other, Marcus, discarded his cloak as he ran. He advanced with a powerful stride, sword in hand. He stumbled over a body and fell between two empty baskets; he waited in the shadow of the market, recovering his breath. He was seized with nausea: the body on the ground was his father's. He turned about, ready to come out of the shadow, but some men were coming in his direction. A group passed by, carrying a woman who had fainted; a Barbarian followed more slowly, carrying a torch. Crassus crouched in wait for a moment; under his blow, the Barbarian fell without a sound. Crassus slit his throat and dragged him between the baskets, where he wrapped himself in his victim's clothes; with precision in his haste, he dirtied his face, neck, and hands, took up the lighted torch, and without any hindrance got out of Rome through the Porta Collina, where at last he stopped.

The City looked white and clean in the cold of the night. Here and there a building was ablaze; torches would momentarily light up a narrow street or wall. The tremor of the City arose from the ground vibrating beneath the rush and roar of the invaders and the mad flight of their victims. Murder and rape were taking place in the stench of burning grease of the torches and the sulphur-colored veil that now covered the City. Windows, suddenly lit by several torches, revealed the silhouettes of men in the act of butchering others; a moment later, all was darkness again. Other windows lit up, flashing the same scene, then immediately plunged again into darkness. A tremor now was shaking Crassus as if his limbs had caught it from the ground. He raised his eyes; stars shone through a rent in the clouds. He shivered. His teeth clenched, his body shaken, his eyes wet with tears, he looked one last time at the city where his father and brother had just fallen under the blows of the Marianists. He hurried away.

With three friends he had come across in his flight, Crassus reached a small villa situated on high ground between the Via Appia and the Via Latina. It was raining. A well-kept road led up toward his father's property. Soon, among the trees, he saw the villa's marble statues gleaming in the moonlight and the rain. Crassus went around the house until he reached the kitchen, where a light was shining. "Mamita!" He waited a moment. "Mamita!" He was about to go in when a little white-haired bondwoman opened the kitchen door; a smell of grilled peppers made its way to him. He relaxed.

"Marcus? Is that you?"

Crassus came out of the shadows. He rushed forward and kissed the bondwoman.

"Are you alone, Mamita?"

"In the kitchen, yes. You're cold, my son. Come near the fire."

Marcus gestured to his friends to follow him. "Where is Alexander?"

"In his room, my son."

In the kitchen, the slave, Mamita, lit a small oil lamp and held it up to the men's faces. "Cats. Wet cats. Give them a room, Marcus. Go and change and then come and eat."

"No, Mamita. We don't have time. I'm going to see Alexander.

In a small room filled with Latin and Greek manuscripts,

Alexander was asleep on some large cushions, under several blankets. Crassus sat down beside him. Alexander opened his eyes and immediately shut them again. "I need you, professor," said Crassus. Alexander opened his eyes. They embraced. "I need you," Crassus repeated. "You must leave this house with Mamita and the servants."

"Marius?"

"Yes. The censor and my brother have both been killed. The pack are after me. I don't know where to go. . . ."

Alexander got up and shivered. Like Crassus, he had short hair, but his was white. He put on a gown and began to run on one spot, marking time, listening as Crassus explained the situation. Suddenly he came up to his friend. "Spain," Alexander said.

"Why Spain?"

"Because your father is known there. You made some friends there during his praetorship. Remember Vibius? You talked to me a lot about him. Spain is the only country where you'll be able to wait for a while without danger. But stay in hiding. Now that Marius and Cinna have seized power, anyone might be tempted to hand your head over to them for the slightest reward. I'll let you know when you can come back. Don't move before that. But you must send word to me, at my house in Rome, as to where you have taken refuge."

"In Rome!"

"Yes, the enemy never looks under his own windows."

In the kitchen Mamita had heated some milk and honey; when Crassus and Alexander arrived, she served it to the five men in large goblets. They drank in silence. Crassus kissed Mamita. "Take good care of her, Alexander; she makes honey-milk almost as well as I do."

Mamita smiled sadly. "Are you going away for long, my son?"

"I don't know."

"Then, I'd better pour some water."

Crassus smiled. "I'll be back, Mamita."

The slave smiled through her tears and caressed the fugitive's face. "I know that you'll be back, my son. But I want you to turn around when I call, and then I'll pour the water."

Crassus clasped her once more, embraced Alexander, and went

out with his companions. Mamita was weeping. Alexander put his arm around the bondwoman's shoulders and drew her outside. She had a water-jug in her hand. "Marcus!" she called. He looked back: she poured a little water. She called him three times. Three times he looked back and watched her pour the water. "Now, my son, the way home is clean for you," murmured Mamita. Crassus raised his arm for the last time and went off to the slaves' yard, where he called for two sturdy Nubians by name; they selected twelve of their fellow countrymen for him and quickly got them ready for the journey. Crassus took a last look at the villa and joined the little group, as it disappeared into the night.

In Spain, Crassus met some friends who had also fled from Rome. He found them in a nervous state, as if Marius and Cinna were pursuing them only twenty paces away, and took them with him. Following Alexander's instructions, he hid in a cave on the estate of his friend, Vibius Pacianus. From there, Crassus sent a slave to Vibius to explain the situation. Vibius immediately agreed to take care of him and his friends and slaves, ordering the steward of his domain to see that his people prepared a meal for them every day, placed it near the cave, and then discreetly went away. The cave was not far from the sea; the two steep slopes that formed it by meeting at their base concealed an entrance so narrow as to be invisible to anyone unaware of its existence. Very high-ceilinged, the cave hid within its depths recesses which interconnected and opened out into galleries. It was an ideal retreat for Crassus. He did not have to do without either water or light; a spring rose at the foot of the rock and the natural fissures in the stone allowed sufficient light; the air was pure and free of dampness. Crassus sent two Nubians to Alexander in Rome to let him know where he had taken refuge.

Every day Vibius' steward brought the men in the cave all necessary supplies without ever seeing them or knowing who they were, while they always saw him as they kept a lookout posted for his arrival. The meals he provided were abundant and not without a certain delicacy, and Vibius, being truly eager to treat Crassus with all the warmth of his friendship, took into account the youthful desires of his invisible guest. He selected two beautiful slave girls and took them to the seashore. There, he showed them the way and bade them enter the cave without fear. Seeing them arrive, Crassus' friends thought for a moment that they had been discovered, but the women, following Vibius' instructions to the letter, said they were looking for a master hidden in the cave. Understanding his friend's thoughtfulness, Crassus invited the two girls in.

Crassus lived in that cave for three years. One spring evening, while he was running on the beach at some distance from his companions who were bathing, a colossal Nubian appeared before him. "Lord Crassus?" he asked. Crassus froze. "I've brought you a message from Lord Alexander," the slave said excitedly, handing him a papyrus roll wrapped in cloth.
Crassus recognized him as one of the two slaves he had sent to Alexander. "Where is your companion?"
"Lord Alexander explains," said the Nubian, pointing to the roll.
Crassus went back to the group who were bathing. "News from Rome!" he shouted. They all ran after him into the cave. Before settling down to read, Crassus saw that the Nubian was fed. He stayed beside his slave during the entire meal and had him describe his journey; but, despite this great honor, the exhausted Nubian fell asleep. Crassus covered him and then went up with his friends to the gallery which was his own room. By the light of an oil lamp Crassus opened the letter.

Rome, March 25, 671 *

Marcus, my friend:
As I promised you, I took Mamita to my house in Rome. It is easier to shut yourself off here than in the provinces, and as I am not of noble rank I have been left in peace. Mamita gets up early and probably goes to sleep after me. To help pass the time, I have taught her to read, write, and add. She even knows a little Greek! We seldom go out into the City, which we detest. One day I shall tell you about Rome, certainly the dirtiest city in the world.

* 83 B.C.

> Marcus, the moment has come for you to avenge the murder of your father and brother and, eventually, to play your part in this country.
> You went away on the day before the calends of January. The next day, as I learned from my friend C——on arriving here, Marius and Cinna took up their consulships without convening an electoral assembly, as you might guess. They immediately had their predecessors hurled from the top of the Tarpeian Rock; their bodies were still lying there when we arrived, left to the dogs, the rats, the wolves, and the birds. . . . Then, inciting the people to dedicate themselves to the manhunt, and letting loose the murderous fury of their gangs, Marius and Cinna started in by sentencing all their enemies to death, "so as," they said, "to insure peace!" The names of all their enemies, as well as those of their relatives and friends, were posted. Sulla's name headed the list of proscribed "public enemies." His house and goods were seized, but his wife managed to flee with her children. Your name and those of your unfortunate relatives were also on the lists. The fate of the proscribed has been frightful. Their names have been expunged from the community, they have been killed on sight in the streets, their heads displayed in the Forum, their progeny declared infamous, and their possessions sold at auction. . . . But seventeen days after you left, Marius died. The official report: pleurisy!

"Marius is dead!" Crassus exclaimed. Lamps were lit. The exclamation was followed by cries of joy, the cries of joy by songs, and wine began to flow. Crassus calmly resumed his reading.

> Let us now turn to Sulla's campaign against Mithridates. It is important that you know the gist of this, because you will probably be coming back to fight under his banner. Sulla laid siege to Athens and stormed it (calends of March, 668 *), took the Piraeus a fortnight later, and in less than two months more succeeded in what seemed impossible: he drove Mithridates from Greece! But Mithridates immediately replied with a powerful offensive against him, and here

---

* 86 B.C.

is something that you will appreciate, with your taste for legendary exploits. Sulla had to do something to raise the morale of his legionaries, now without sandals and their food kits empty after several days' marching; so he faced the enemy at the head of his troops, shouting, "Soldiers! If you are asked where you left your general, say, 'At Orchomenus!'" And Sulla defeated Mithridates again in Boeotia. That was in the fall of 668. Mithridates also found himself threatened by Cinna's two legions, which had crossed the Thracian Bosphorus and attacked him in Bithynia, determined to overtake Sulla and wrest his gains from him. This enterprise nearly succeeded, but the leader—one Fimbria—thought more of destroying Mithridates in order to annex his kingdoms than of bringing him into subjection (as your peers of the aristocracy wanted—acting solely, as you know, in the interests of a Rome saturated with conquests in any case). One can only assume that this traditional policy coincided with the interests and views of Sulla, for he quickly set out for Macedonia and crossed Thrace * again, to begin his negotiations with Mithridates' lieutenants during the winter of 668–669 †, then with the King himself, whom he met at Dardanus in August, 669. Mithridates came to terms, and Fimbria, who was left with nothing more to defend for Cinna, unless he were to take on both Sulla and Mithridates, committed suicide at Pergamum while his two legions passed to Sulla's command.

Sulla took up residence at Ephesus, on the Aegean coast of Asia, where he investigated the trials of some local traitors, and he wrote a letter to the Senate announcing his intention to revenge the persecutions which his family had endured. After this, he left Fimbria's two legions with Lucullus (his wife's nephew) so as to restore order in the neighboring regions of Pontus; he thereupon left again for Greece, accompanied by his wife and the bulk of his troops, while one

* On crossing the Hebrus, Spartacus recognized his native land and deserted the Odrysian troops to hide in the woods which bordered the Lake of Stentor, at the mouth of the river.
† 86–85 B.C.

legion alone recrossed the Hellespont with instructions to regroup in Euboea, where Sulla and his wife Metella spent last winter *, resting and attending some ceremonies given in their honor, as well as becoming initiated into the mysteries and supervising the packing of their trunks, which contained, among other precious objects, the manuscripts of Aristotle.

I'm falling asleep; I'll leave the rest for tomorrow.

Sulla's legion, which took the land route back to Greece after crossing the Hellespont, marched in easy stages, hunting a bit, sleeping a lot, sending patrols out here and there, in any case appreciating this vacation granted by their great general. One of these reconnaissance groups rode up along the Hebrus to try to capture a bandit who was said to have stolen some cattle and herded them on to the foothills of the Rhodope.

After his desertion, Spartacus had returned home, where he had recaptured a few head of cattle from the Roman administrators of his country, which had been declared pacified. On finding himself surrounded, he fought furiously and owed his life only to the fact that the patrol acted with great calm. Although, like the other Odrysians, he had contributed to Sulla's Greek victories, he now found himself in the unwelcome position of having to act as servant to his former comrades-in-arms until their arrival in Euboea where, with several hundred other slaves, he was thrown into a pit guarded by Barbarians who had volunteered for the job, which brought a few extra denarii in pay.

Rome, March 26

As soon as he heard that Sulla had dictated peace terms in the East to Mithridates, Cinna was concerned about what was happening to his expeditionary force. When he learned of Fimbria's suicide and the incorporation of his two legions into those of Sulla, Cinna began to make preparations for war. He mobilized a fleet in Sicily and raised treasure, troops, and victuals, but just as he was about to land in Illyria, in the middle of a storm, he was murdered by his own men.

---

* 84–83 B.C.

"Cinna is dead!" Crassus cried out. "Murdered!" But this time nobody reacted, for everyone in the cave was asleep.

> The command of Cinna's troops then passed into the hands of one Carbo and the two consuls for that year [*], Scipio and Norbanus; if they landed, they would have to fight Lucullus. His mind at ease on that score, but in a hurry to satisfy his vengeance, Sulla, incalculably rich in treasure, left Euboea, carrying off a booty of several thousand slaves crammed with his army into more than fifteen hundred ships.
>
> Sulla has just landed at Brundisium with forty thousand soldiers, who are by now fanatically loyal to him. Immediately, several nobles who were in open rebellion against the consuls offered to cooperate with him.
>
> That is what you must do.
>
> Young Pompey, for example, has raised and equipped three legions at his own expense in Picenum (where he has many clients) and has just turned one of them over to Sulla. Is this the beginning of military dictatorship? I am afraid so! In any case, the time has come for you to leave Spain. Try to muster two or three thousand volunteers, an entire legion if you can, to meet Sulla at Brundisium. You will have to go through Mauretania because Liguria and Etruria are not safe. You must move quickly!
>
> As I am convinced that you will not hesitate for one moment, I have taken the liberty of sending one of your Nubians to Sulla with a message assuring him of your loyalty and informing him of your arrival. I know that your father's death will grieve him.
>
> Mamita and I are awaiting you impatiently.
>
> Best wishes,
Alexander
>
> P.S. Mamita told me this morning that you used to walk with your arms folded when you were little. "That means he'll be rich," she added. You now know something of your future and you will probably believe in Mamita's prediction because you are just as superstitious as your nurse.

[*] 83 B.C.

The following morning, Crassus left the cave. With the help of his friend Pacianus, he recruited on the spot a legion of volunteers, crossed Mauretania, and met Sulla at Brundisium, where the General cordially welcomed him. Sulla defeated Norbanus and disarmed Scipio; Pompey gave chase to Carbo, who was forced to retreat to Africa; and Crassus crushed the last Marianist troops in Rome on November 1, 82, in front of that very same Porta Collina through which he had had to flee the City five years earlier. The next day, Sulla was in control. He had signed the peace treaty in the East and brought his country's second civil war to an end. He had a large army at his disposal as well as all his gold from Asia: everyone acknowledged his supremacy—even Metellus and Pompey, for, although they had greatly contributed to the defeat of the Marianists by organizing the resistance at home, unlike Sulla, they did not have the consular title nor the defeat of Mithridates to their credit. Absolute master, sharing his victory with none, Sulla founded an imperial regime on the strength of his prestige, his military might, and his financial resources.

The day after his victory, Sulla proscribed all his enemies, and there was a rush for the spoils—the nobles giving vent to their resentment against the Marianists and the poor dividing up the booty.

Alexander spent that evening with Crassus, who was still flushed with his victory. Reminding him of a passage in the message he had sent, Alexander said, "You see, it's the beginning of personal power, of military dictatorship." But Crassus was no longer thinking of anything but revenge.

After having two second-raters elected to the consulship for 81, thus respecting the old electoral forms to preserve appearances, Sulla bathed Italy in the blood of his victims. Anyone at all was free to claim the reward of twelve thousand denarii promised to informers and killers. At the time of the public auctions which followed the confiscation of the assets of the proscribed, Crassus first recovered his parents' villa and then laid the foundation of a fortune which, in a short while, was to make him the most opulent of Roman magnates. Often, the lists of the proscribed were lengthened by someone's name merely because the greed of an informer had been aroused by the victim's wealth. By threatening landowners with having their names put on the fatal lists, Crassus was able to acquire desirable properties for a few denarii; afterwards, he denounced the owners. In charge of these proscriptions in the south, he hunted down the rich in order to lay hands on their fortunes, which they in turn had sometimes acquired through previous proscriptions. But Sulla grew weary of so much greed and withdrew the authority from Crassus, who did not seem to be affected by this demotion; his vengeance had been satisfied, and, having made his fortune, he now spent his time consolidating and increasing it.

ARENA

I

The slaves shut up in the dungeons of Brundisium did not spend all their time in these cold, foul-smelling pits. They were given the most varied kinds of work, until the time when Sulla might decide their fate. Spartacus had been assigned to clearing away the rubble of buildings gutted by fire along the Appian Way on the outskirts of town. That evening, an unpleasant surprise was in store for him and his fellow slaves; during the day, another shipment of slaves had arrived from Greece. Since there were no other lockups for them, they had been crammed into the same underground holes. Before going in, the slaves received their daily ration: a dish of lentils and a goblet of water. Spartacus followed in when his turn came, carrying his lentils and goblet. Pushing ahead as he was pushed from behind, he reached the spot he had made his own since his arrival at the prison. A very young girl was lying there, wide-eyed. Spartacus sat down. As he downed his lentils, he watched her. A material which must once have been a colorful palla reached down to her feet; she was wearing fine leather sandals, tied high about her ankle, the gift of a mistress, probably. She was frightened. Her arms held close to her sides did not deceive Spartacus, for her hands clenched on the woolen material betrayed the apprehension which he could also read in her eyes. She felt that he was looking at her, and turned her head toward him pertly, then away again. Spartacus ate slowly. When he had finished, everyone seemed to be asleep. He remained seated a moment more, and then in his turn lay down on his side. The slave girl was looking at him. Dark locks fell over her broad rounded forehead; she had large green eyes that fear and ill-treatment had made hollow. Big white teeth shone through her thick lips. Spartacus ran his hand over her face, closing her eyes. She opened them again. She looked at the Thracian, peered into his eyes, and something like relaxation came over her face; her breathing seemed to become more regular, she closed her eyes. During the night, she was a bit restless. She awakened; her long black hair was covering Spartacus' shoulder. A draft of cold air was coming down the long corridor. At that moment, the moonlight exposed all its length. She looked at Spartacus as he slept and laid her head on his shoulder, her hand outstretched against the Thracian's broad chest. Without opening his eyes, he placed his hand on hers; she nestled a bit closer to him. When the guards came to rouse the slaves with cracks of their whips, the girl's whole arm was resting on Spartacus' chest. The Thracian moved gently aside and whispered to her, "Get up!" She opened her eyes. As soon as she recognized him, her fear was gone. She got up and walked out behind the wretched group of slaves. A hot, heavy rain was falling from the sky, which was still dark. Spartacus took his mate's hand and had her walk in front of him. In the evening, he fed her.

Too exhausted to speak, in this way they lived alongside each other for several months, night and day, without ever exchanging a word. When peace came, the dictator ordered the slaves to be sent to Rome, where they were to be sold.

On this day of the nones of July 79, the inhabitants of Rome were in a state of great agitation. The heat by itself might have been bearable—even though it accentuated the stenches of fish, rancid oils, meat, and cesspools, which, for want of any wind over the lazy Tiber, hung the more heavily in the streets—Sulla had declared in the open Forum that he was ready to answer to anyone for all the blood that had been shed for Rome. In the silence that followed this declaration, he had abdicated—dismissed his lictors and his guard, and walked home like any ordinary citizen, alone in the crowd, undauntedly exposing his back to anyone's dagger. Giving way to Pompey, who had betrayed him in his own interest, Sulla thus unexpectedly stood aside with dignity, avoiding surrender and renouncing the violent solution which would inevitably have led to a third civil war.

Agitation was therefore at its height amid the population who had been brought into the streets by three causes: the heat, Sulla's declaration and subsequent abdication, and the arrival from Brundisium of the slaves from the East; to say nothing of the bath hour, which added still further to the urban confusion as everyone tried to force his way toward his favorite bath in the narrow, hot, foul-smelling streets.

As the long column of slaves approached from the East, it was the stench which first alerted them to the proximity of the City, for the sun shining in their eyes would have made it impossible for them to see it.

To the slaves, Rome, on the left bank of the Tiber, was first of all that high defensive wall of tuff blocks before which Hannibal had been forced to turn away his assault. Then, the level plain swarming with soldiers, gleaming with helmets, weapons, and shields, the flat stretch between the Tiber and the Janiculum: the Campus Martius. The wall surrounding the City at that time encompassed the Capitoline Hill, the edge of the Esquiline, the Velabrum, and the two humps of the Aventine; it had recently been extended at this place by the consuls to better fend off the attacks of Cinna.

Coming nearer, the slaves saw that what they had at first taken for the shadow of a cloud on the Campus Martius was in fact a group of new dwellings. The outbreak of civil war nine years earlier had created a great influx of people returning to Rome to seek shelter with the insurgents. Close to half a million people then lived within a Rome whose area reached barely four hundred acres. Confronted with these huddled masses, Sulla two years before had opened a part of the Campus Martius to the urban plebs and they had wasted no time in building. Architects drew up their plans, streets were laid out, houses went up, and the City was thus expanded through works which, while rebuilding on the ruins, reduced unemployment and kept idle minds busy. On the Esquiline Hill a shrine was being raised to Hercules. New streets had just been planned: the Via Vittoria, from the Velabrum to the Palatine; the Via Palatina, from the Forum to the Palatine; and the Via Capitolina, from the Forum to the Capitol. The old Forum itself had been given more air, altered through new pavements of tuff, brick, and shards. Rome was spreading, reaching down toward the Tiber . . .

As they came to this new area, Spartacus' young girl companion was walking in front of the Thracian. He grasped her shoulder. She did not turn back, but her hand rose to take hold of his. She stroked it. Spartacus withdrew his hand. Taking advantage of a local commotion, he managed to outwit the guards. The slave girl saw him slip quickly in front of a butcher's display from which he stole a knife; he cut his bonds and disappeared into the crowd.

In a moment Spartacus left the parade ground of the Campus Martius to follow a cloth merchant whose cart was blocked by a large litter inlaid with specular stone. He slipped under the cart and pulled off a piece of material that was hanging down. Standing in front of his mule, the merchant was shouting himself hoarse trying to clear a passage. Spartacus made his way out through the dense cluster of legs pressed against the side of the cart, quickly flung the stolen goods around his shoulders, and let it fall like a pallium. Though it was nearly setting, the sun was still warm; many of the strollers had covered their heads with a flap of their togas; Spartacus did likewise and entered Rome at the point where the bustle was the greatest. All the nations of the earth came together here, under the arcades, in the congestion of the streets, and at the entrances to buildings. Spartacus, jostled and himself jostling, forced his way through to the Porta Esquilina, on the opposite side of the City, where he stole a mule and rode off on it. He skirted the City and reached the Via Flaminia. He went on all night long; at daybreak, he was in Umbria. Sleeping by day, advancing and stealing his food by night, he reached the Adriatic coast and crossed the Rubicon. From there, the roads being virtually empty, he was able to move by day, and he got to

Illyria, which he followed down its coast, crossed the land of the Scordisci, and, at the beginning of January 78, was once again at the foot of the Rhodope. He went on down as far as the Propontis, on which he embarked below Byzantium with a band of Cilician pirates. They entered the Black Sea, which they crossed in every direction before deciding on the promising shores of Pontus. But there, they were arrested and sent to the quarries of Mount Paryadres; Spartacus and a few of the more fortunate ones were escorted to the heights of the mountain, whose forests were a source of ship timber. For two years, Spartacus was alternately woodman and carpenter. He derived a certain amount of pleasure from working on these heights, which reminded him of his own country, until the collapse of a quarry buried a crew of miners, and the woodcutters were impressed into a relief squad in which Spartacus spent an entire year. He escaped from it with some of his old Cilician comrades. By way of Armenia Minor and Galatia, they reached Phrygia, where they fell into the hands of legionaries, who took them back to Pergamum.

Five years after leaving Brundisium for Rome, Spartacus was crossing the Aegean Sea again, passing the Cyclades, going up the Ionian Sea, entering the Adriatic, and once more landing at Brundisium. He and a load of slaves were immediately set on the road to Rome.

As the City was already very crowded and the column of slaves a sizable one, it had been decided that the slave market might be held in front of the new living quarters built on the Campus Martius. Brokers immediately went into action, bribing the guards so as to be given priorities. The lanistae—promoters of gladiatorial contests—from every province, many accompanied by their messengers, had rushed there for purchases. The soldiers grouped the slaves in two ranks while awaiting the arrival of the commissioners. And then some children began to run between the two ranks, carrying the messages of the brokers; the market was under way.

The first line of slaves, composed of entire families, was soon sold to landowners whose fields had lain fallow during the civil wars or been plundered as the armies passed through. Families were much in demand, the woman and children for the farm chores, the men and youths for work in the fields, and, not wanting to be separated, they would not try to run away.

The second line consisted of girls, women, and men, who would be sold in job lots to speed up their disposal. The men were gauged for their strength and professional skills, the girls and women for specific jobs. They were selected also, like the men, for their age and looks.

Lentulus Baliatus, an important lanista of Capua, walked along the file, guided by his runners who pointed out the best lots to him. At the moment, they were leading him toward one group which was dominated by the head of a Black. He looked at the men, evaluating them; next to the Black, an almost naked slave was squatting on his heels, his arms hanging loosely at his sides, his palms turned toward the sky, his eyelids lowered, waiting. Baliatus made a sign; the runner had the man stand up, but his eyes remained lowered. He was a good inch taller than the Black. A murmur of admiration ran through the buyers who crowded around him. Baliatus' runners attempted to hold them back, drowning their bids with loud shouts and offering bribes to the commissioners to wait for Baliatus to make up his mind. The lanista screwed up his eyes and smiled, stroking his short black beard. He prodded his whip handle into the belly of the man, who raised his eyes. Baliatus' runners kept urging the commissioners to hold off, swearing they had been there first.

"Your name?" said Baliatus.

"Spartacus."

He had changed a great deal since that day in the fall of 88 when, on the banks of the Hebrus, his father had been murdered before his eyes. Almost fifteen years had gone by. His forehead was higher; his black hair was longer and knotted high on his head and low between his shoulders. His body, although twice as heavy, gave the impression of being slim. His muscles had developed considerably, accentuating the delicacy of the harmonious joints connecting the limbs; his face had lost the indecisive lines of adolescence during the violent training with the legions, the forced marches, the felling of the high timber stands of Mount Paryadres, and the toil in the mines. The long raised slits of his eyes gave his face the look of an eastern Asiatic, but, despite the high-knotted black hair pulling back the temples, which might have added to the deception, the blue of the iris, the straight nose, and the bronzed skin brought the mysterious, perplexing origin of that intense face a whole continent westward. A fine scar—perhaps from a sword thrust which only a quick backward movement had held to a mere slice of the tip—drew a straight line that started from the left deltoid muscle, bypassed the armpit, and almost horizontally crossed half the width of the chest; it came to a stop at the apex of the flat triangle of his breastbone, which made the bone stand out from his powerful chest like a pennant.

Baliatus overlooked none of these details, while behind him the buyers kept shoving each other to get a better look at Spartacus, who waited with downcast eyes. Along with the Black, the Thracian completed a lot of twenty-four male slaves. Baliatus indicated agreement to his runners, who made payment to the commissioners amid their noisy objections. The slaves were immediately surrounded and tied together in pairs. Lifted by two Syrians, Lentulus Baliatus was seated on the back of a poor mule that almost disappeared under his enormous body. The setting sun left behind a red river in the sky, which was quickly clouding over in the east; Baliatus flipped a flap of his cloak over his head and gave the signal to set off. Six Syrian porters surrounded him to brush aside the crowd of beggars in front and protect him from the jostling from behind. In his train came the slaves, surrounded by guards. Once out of Rome, Baliatus switched from his mule to a large litter carried by eight of his Syrians, but it was too late to venture very far along the Appian Way. As night fell, Baliatus stopped three leagues outside the City at an inn where he took a bath and had supper. He went to sleep wrapped in his pallium. Before dawn, the small troop resumed its journey; by evening, Baliatus was beyond Antium. As on the day before, he bathed and dined, and went to sleep in his clothes.

In a corner of the inn courtyard, the slaves were eating. The Black was lying on his side, near Spartacus; the Thracian was eating in small mouthfuls. The Black eyed him.

"You not hungry?" he asked.
"Sure I am."
"You don't eat fast."
"No."

Spartacus was seated with his legs straight in front of him, his back resting against the wall.

"You know where we're going?" asked the Black.

"No."

"To Capua. Ever been there?"

"No."

"Well, I have," said a Samnite who was lying behind the Black.

The Black turned to him. "Is it big?" he asked.

"No. Four or five times smaller than Rome."

"Still far?"

"Three or four days away."

During the third day of their journey, Baliatus made a halt at Terracina, where he took delivery of a hundred slaves and a large consignment of arms that were piled up in chests on several wagons. The lanista dealt directly with the vendors and paid them in cash. Two days later, during the afternoon, Baliatus and his slaves arrived at Capua.

For a long time, Capua had enjoyed a reputation of which its inhabitants were extremely proud: between Genoa and Reggio, it was the most delightful resort in the country, the favorite vacation spot for Roman aristocracy and wealthy merchants. Watered by the Volturno, whose peaceful stream was ideal for the development of fisheries, river traffic, and bathing, Capua was queen of the coastal plain of Campania, which surrounded it like a jewel case. Protected from cold winds by the Apennines to the north and east and by the body of the Sorrento peninsula to the southeast, while the rains from the Tyrrhenian Sea showered their blessings on it from the west, Campania was covered with abundant vegetation, sumptuous villas, and prospering farms; from Pompeii to Suessa Aurunca, the olive groves were thick, the timber stands of the Apennines furnished wood for ships, and, in the Volturno basin, orchards, pasture lands, and vineyards alternated like the notes of an octave in a victory chant of nature. Lined with poplars, aspen upstream and white near the city and downstream, the Volturno made its way to the sea a few leagues farther on. The proximity of that river mouth afforded the Capuans spices and rare oils from the East, leathers and pelts from Africa, wheat from Sicily, and throughout the year fresh supplies of slave labor.

During these peaceful years in the province of Campania, Capua was a happy, fulfilled city. There was some unemployment, to be sure, but regular benefits were paid by public assistance, and the unemployed and their families were fed; they were also poorly housed, and lived wretchedly, but since slaves were available, well-to-do Capuans would reason, why hire citizens whose labor would have been so much more expensive! "And, anyway, there is the Volturno," they would say. "If the unemployed want to work, all they have to do is fish." And years went by. And, as in any well-protected, peaceful city growing rich on its tourist trade, pigeons easily found food in the gardens, on the public squares, around the circus, in front of shops, and on window sills. Solemn, going about in full safety with the majesty of the obese, haughtily nodding their approval at every step, the pigeons held sway in this city whose inhabitants took them for a divine symbol of prosperity. Along the river, the pigeons democratically shared their authority with lively, vigilant squirrels which, whatever the season, approached to accept food from the hands of children or old people. Capuans, whether owners of a shop, a farm, or an inn, tended naturally in this temperate and fertile region to linger in the bath, tarry at table, lengthen their siestas. So it was in the midst of pigeons and squirrels that the future gladiators went through a sleeping Capua.

Lentulus Baliatus had bought a block of buildings near the south side of the city. He had closed off all the windows facing the streets surrounding it and demolished the buildings contained within the square; in the middle of the wall exposed to the south, the lanista had had a large opening made, leading inward to a well-kept field used by the gladiators as a training ground. This free space was surrounded by high palisades, along which guards kept a day-and-night watch. This opening in the wall also gave access to a wide yard, at the end of which was the gladiators' refectory. Until the heavy door devised by Baliatus would be ready for closing the mess hall, relays of four guards were always on duty in front of the opening.

On his arrival at the training school, Baliatus rushed across the yard as quickly as his corpulence would allow and burst into the carpentry shop. A guard was kissing a girl while the slave carpenters worked busily away.

"Well, what about that door?" Baliatus barked as he came in.

The guard roughly pushed the girl away, and she immediately started sweeping the floor. Baliatus gave her a big smack on the rump; she groaned at the blow, but went right on sweeping. The guard was swatted over the head with a plank, and everyone laughed. Even the guard. The guard most of all. To all of them, obviously, Baliatus' behavior was a sign of his good mood. The joiner, a sturdy Greek slave, bent down to check the evenness of a chamfer he was planning. While examining the board, he answered the lanista, "You want a very heavy door, master, a door as heavy as a wall . . . but you'd like to have it finished as fast as an ordinary bedroom door!"

"You've been at it for two weeks," replied Baliatus as he ran his hand over the new chamfer.

"I can't finish it without hinges, fittings, a lock . . ."

"Don't you have any more?"

"Sure I do. But not for a door like this. Any one of these planks would be heavy enough to rip off the hinges that I have!"

"So?"

"I'll have to make them myself at the forge."

"Good."

Baliatus went down at the end of the plank and closed one eye to squint at the chamfer. He gave a slight groan as he stood up again. "When you finish this door, you'll come and see a load of wood I just got. I want you to build me a very wide bed. . . . When will you have the hinges finished?"

"I don't know. I have to find . . . I don't know."

Baliatus screwed up his eyes. He went toward the Greek and said to him in an almost friendly tone, "Watch out. There may be a joiner in the new bunch. You're very easy to replace."

"There may be ten joiners among them, master, maybe a hundred. But they'll need special hinges if you want to see your door in place. And special hinges take time."

Baliatus shrugged his shoulders. "All right. Hurry up." He left the carpentry shop and went back toward his new slaves, with hurried little steps. His red cloak was so broad that his legs barely ruffled its old folds whose fresh big grease-stains were caked with the dust picked up on the road. He took a whip from one of the guards, ordering the new slaves to be lined up in two lines. Baliatus shouted, "Women on the left!" He made a first selection among them: the prettiest ones were sent to the baths; the others, less shapely or unappealing to the taste of the lanista, were left to the discretion of a camp overseer who would assign them tasks. Then Baliatus turned to the men. He waved two wretched, elderly creatures away from the hundred-odd men he had bought at Terracina, and kept all the rest. He motioned to them to follow him. The column was quite ragged, and the guards got it into shape with light lashings on the shoulders and backs. Behind Baliatus, the human herd went through the refectory and came out on the training ground.

Among the abundantly puffing and sweating gladiators, one in particular, a one-eyed retiarius—clearly a Samnite, as evidenced by his choice of weapons, the trident and net—was noticeable for his wild shouts and powerful blows. All the other gladiators were silent, shifting around rapidly, slipping under their opponents' nets, and even more quickly straightening up in order to strike. The men who followed each other in opposing the Samnite found that all their feints were useless—none of their tricks took him in. The one-eyed man's net flew out, speedy, all-enveloping, implacable, at the very instant when the other gladiator was off balance and could not duck. Spartacus, like his companions, noticed the Samnite immediately. While Baliatus discussed matters with the trainers, the slaves tried to make out what was being said about them. Among them were robbers, murderers, common-law criminals who had escaped from prison, prisoners of war of all nationalities whose countries had fallen before the onslaught of the Roman legions. Unable to catch a single word of the orders the lanista was whispering to the trainers, the captives turned their attention to the gladiators who, realizing they were watched, fought with redoubled skill. Spartacus observed each of them attentively. The one-eyed Samnite had kept his net and discarded his trident for a heavy mace bristling with spikes. A mirmillo armed with a small round shield and a long sica—the kind of curved dagger used especially by Thracians—was now training with him. Warding off the mace-blows beneath his shield, he was simulating sica-thrusts to the belly and thighs. The Samnite maneuvered around the mirmillo, swinging his mace back and forth at ground level. All of a sudden, just as the mirmillo, behind his shield, was about to sweep a slashing blow at the Samnite's legs, while his mace was to the rear, the net came down and trapped him from head to toe. The one-eyed man pulled in his net and sent the mirmillo to the ground head first, while he raised his mace ready to crush him. The net-fighter did not complete his stroke, but burst into a huge laugh that drowned out the murmurs of admiration from the ranks of the newcomers.

The Samnite showed enormous economy of movement in his steps. As Spartacus watched him, he saw the reason as soon as the other straightened up, feeling that he had trained enough. He had short, thick legs, a broad pelvis, and a heavy torso. When he passed in front of Spartacus to go and put down his mace and net, the Thracian could hear his strained breathing. The thumb of the left hand in which he held the net was missing. Spartacus also noticed his neck, a wide, short triangle set on round shoulders. He was still watching him when the stroke of a lash cut across his back. Spartacus turned around. The instructor who had struck him had already gone off. Baliatus was hurrying back to the refectory.

One of the instructors spoke: "The master brought you here to work. You are our pupils. We are going to make gladiators of you. We will feed and train you. You are lucky: here, each one fights with his favorite weapons. So as to put up a better fight, of course." He laughed. Some of the gladiators who had come closer laughed with him. "We're not interested in making you into lousy butchers; we want solid gladiators," the instructor continued. "I won my freedom in the arena. You can do the same if you work hard. But you are dogs. If you win several times, you don't want freedom; you want the easy life you have here. If you win!" All the instructors snickered. "We are going to help you get to know your weapons and those of your opponents." He smiled in the direction of his instructor-friends, and went on: "Your names won't be put in the hopper until you are good and ready for combat." He laughed with his mouth open. He had no teeth left. The instructors laughed with him.

"All the gladiators you saw training are veterans; fighters who all have more than a hundred victories to their credit. Several of them have more than five hundred. They're the best gladiators in the world. They'll come and watch you train in two weeks; the week after that, you'll have to be ready to fight."

He moved away a bit. "And now, you'll file past the weapons baskets; take the ones you know best and we'll see at once how you handle them."

The column moved off and each one chose his weapons. Spartacus, last in line, found nothing to his liking left in the baskets. An instructor came toward him. "Couldn't you find what you wanted?"

"No."

"What are your weapons?"

"Sica and buckler."

The instructor looked into all the baskets and came back to Spartacus.

"What else are you good with?"

Spartacus insisted: "I want a sica."

"I'll find one for you. What are your other weapons?"

Spartacus glanced around at all the newcomers. There was no variety in the weapons: the Samnites had a net and trident, or a mace; the others, Thracians, Greeks, Bithynians, Asiatics, and even some Capuans, had opted for the sica and buckler which were the usual weapons of the Thracians.

"Well?" The instructor was getting impatient. "What other weapons?"

"Hatchet and lash."

The instructor looked at Spartacus, openmouthed. "Hatchet and lash!"

Spartacus, who had not raised his eyes, did not repeat his choice. The instructor glanced around and came close to the Thracian. He took him by the arm. "You want to get yourself killed?"

"No."

The instructor spoke lower still. "I've seen lots of men go

through here; I've seen a lot who didn't want to fight. I taught them how to handle the sword and the shield, the mace, the lance, the trident, the net. They had something to defend themselves with. But I can't help you if you ask me for weapons that I've never used! And especially, ones that I've never fought against!"

Spartacus looked at him without replying and lowered his eyes. The instructor tried to catch his eyes again, but the Thracian kept them lowered.

"What's your name?"

"Spartacus."

"Where are you from?"

"From Thrace."

"There are two Thracians here; old-timers. They fight with the sica and buckler."

"That's what I asked for," Spartacus said calmly.

"I don't have any more. You'll have to . . . We'll have to wait until the end of the first fights to get some back."

"Then I'll take the hatchet and lash."

"I won't be able to teach you anything with those."

Spartacus did not reply.

"Very well," said the trainer with irritation. "You don't want a lance? A net? A mace? A trident? That's all I've got!"

"No."

"You'll get what you want."

He went back toward the gladiators who had mingled with the newcomers. The one-eyed retiarius joined them. The instructor went up to him, and Spartacus could see he was talking about him. The Samnite gave a great laugh and went off toward the refectory. An instructor lined up the newcomers, and passed before them, inspecting how they held their weapons. They all handled them properly. Baliatus knew how to choose his men. And he was too good a customer to the pirates for them to sell him more than two or three unserviceable men in a hundred-lot.

"What you are to do here is train, not kill, each other," the instructor told the newcomers. "You are to strike at each other without landing your blows, so as to learn the possible parries against different weapons."

He placed the men face to face—a retiarius opposite a mirmillo—and one of them, since Spartacus was unarmed, found himself alone. He had a trident and a net. One of the gladiators set himself opposite him with a sica and buckler. He was one of the two Thracians the trainer had talked about. At a sign from the instructor, the first two newcomers went fiercely at each other. The trainer stopped them short with lash strokes on the back.

"You can kill each other in the arena. Here, you're only training. Start over."

When the third pair were working out, the one-eyed Samnite came back smiling, bringing a hatchet and a lash. As he passed behind the instructor, he said something to him and the other looked at the weapons. "Keep it up," the instructor shouted to the pupils, "keep training," and he walked over to Spartacus, followed by the Samnite, who gave the weapons to the Thracian. The latter put down the hatchet and took the lash. Its leather was flexible, well-plaited, and tipped with a short iron point; a guard's lash. Spartacus picked up the hatchet and turned toward the tree he was leaning against. He took the tip of the lash between two fingers and removed it from the leather with a series of light hatchet strokes. He examined the handle, put the hatchet down again, and cracked the leather thong, which seemed to suit him with its six- or seven-foot length. The gladiators had now left the newcomers in the sole care of the instructors; their attention was drawn by the sharp crack of the leather, and they went over toward Spartacus. The Thracian then picked up the hatchet. It was short; the handle was quite slender and the blade double-edged. Spartacus took it in his right hand and walked a few steps away. The gladiators moved away from the tree. Spartacus tested the weight of the hatchet and then threw it at the tree. His move had been fantastically fast; the hatchet spun with a swoosh and the point of the blade drove true into the tree. Spartacus had scarcely moved in letting go of the weapon. The Samnite and the trainer, who had smiled when they saw the Thracian test the weight of the weapon, were still trying to take back that smile as Spartacus came to retrieve his hatchet. He carefully removed it from the tree, and slid his nail along the blade. Then he took the lash in his left hand; its tip was on the ground, in front of him. He gave a slight inward flick of the wrist. The tip flipped over and curled back and up until it reached his hand; the Thracian spread two fingers and grasped the whole roll. That was all. The men were no longer talking. They knew that a formidable opponent would be entering the arena with them.

"Who do you want to train with?" asked the trainer.

"Alone," said Spartacus without raising his eyes from his weapons. "And chop some wood with a heavy ax."

The trainer shrugged his shoulders. He tried to find something to say that would give him an advantage. He said halfheartedly: "You can chop all the wood you like; we need some in the kitchen every day. . . . But you won't stand a chance against a net and pitchfork." And he went off to watch the newcomers. The gladiators also moved away, and Spartacus started to look for something on the ground. Near a tree, he found a flat stone; he sat down in the shade and began to sharpen the hatchet.

Thus did several days go by: Spartacus chopping wood, taking care of his weapons, running a lot, whether marking time or around the field. The first day, everyone had burst out laughing when they saw him run. One of the trainers had yelled to him: "In the arena, Spartacus, you're not supposed to run, you're supposed to stand and fight." The gladiators had laughed even louder. Spartacus had not answered; he had continued to run, lengthening his strides a bit more.

Looking at his future opponents, he had noticed two retiarii among the newcomers: one Celt and one Samnite. The Celt, Gannicus, was athletic; a little heavy, but fast. He had big blue eyes and a flattened nose. His black hair was cut straight along the nape of his neck. He was putting up a strong fight, skillfully handling a long chain with a heavy spiked mace at the end of it. In his left hand he had a net. The Samnite, Capito, was tall, broad, and armed with three weapons: a short sica through his belt, a trident, and a net. He was completely hairless and his pale blue lashless eyes gave him a spent, sleepy look. The blows that Capito struck were sometimes off the mark, but they were quick and powerful.

One evening, while all the gladiators were on their way to the mess hall, the instructors lined them up in the school entrance-yard. Between the veterans and the newcomers who kept arriving at the ludus ten or more at a time, they now numbered over five hundred. The chief instructor announced that two hundred fighters would be required for the next day. "That's just fine," said Blamma, the one-eyed Samnite, "I need the money." He shook with a loud laugh. "My women cost me plenty!"

All the old-timers stepped out of the ranks and, according to the rules of the school, selected their adversaries. Spartacus noticed that two of his fellow countrymen were the first to choose. One of the newcomers, scrawny and stooped, told the instructor that he was not yet ready to fight. The instructor brushed off the sickly slave. "Oh, you'll never be ready to fight. So, you might as well go tomorrow; that way, you won't cost us as much." And, as the man just stood there, the instructor swiped at him with his lash, which the other thought he could avoid by ducking, but the leather slashed across his face; the man walked off crying silently, his hands over his eyes.

A Greek pirate hesitated for a long time in front of Spartacus and then chose Gannicus; the Greek usually carried his weapons in his belt: two broad blades, flat and straight, with double edges. He was tall, well-proportioned, and agile. Several more veterans went past Spartacus without choosing him. Capito was selected in his turn. Finally, when the instructors had counted out one hundred and ninety-eight fighters, the Samnite came forward. It was accepted practice in the ludus that the best gladiator, the one who got the biggest rewards from the crowd and the lanista, should be the last one to pick, taking the toughest opponent, willingly left to him by the other veterans who had little taste for finding themselves overmatched. The Samnite went straight to the instructor. "The hatchet man," he said. Spartacus raised his eyes for a moment. He saw that the two men were exchanging a smile.

ARENA

II

On the eve of the gladiatorial contests, when the lanistae had completed their negotiations with the aediles representing the notables who sponsored the fights, it was customary that a banquet be held for the next day's fighters. Baliatus had not been stingy. Having made a top-price deal for fights in which more than half of his men would be killed, he had prepared a feast for the gladiators in the mess hall. Those who were not scheduled to fight the next day had had to eat quickly and be locked up in their quarters well ahead of their usual time. On the heavy mess tables, oil lamps were burning, lighting the low gray vaults. At this point in the preparation for the contests, visits by the public were allowed. Prostitutes came in to make dates with the famous gladiators whose chances of winning seemed certain. Wealthy homosexuals, attracted by the physiques of the gladiators, as well as others, less rich and in direct competition with the prostitutes, also tried to make dates with them for the evening after the games. There was a crowd of bookmakers, too, who came to assess the men's physical conditions and to discuss among themselves the chances of each man in order to be able, at the crack of dawn, to start taking bets at the entrances to the circus.

Blamma, the one-eyed Samnite, attracted by far the largest crowd. There was a young nobleman accompanying a woman, copiously doused with perfume, whose noble birth was evident from the way she wore her long stola with the gold-embroidered instita on its border; a long belt knotted high at the side of her dazzling dress emphasized her firm, full breasts. Her blond hair was held by a simple red band tied at the nape of the neck; in her hand she carried a peacock-feathered fan, behind which, at the moment, she was hiding her face. She nudged her companion's arm. "Blamma," said the young nobleman, "you have been granted freedom and the great palm of victory fifteen times. You . . ."

"Seventeen times, milord."

"Seventeen times! My apologies, Blamma. But tell me, you are rich, why don't you give up the arena?"

Blamma swallowed a large chunk of meat before replying. "Women, my master; women eat up everything that I earn."

The young woman laughed behind her fan. Pushing her companion aside, she went up to the one-eyed Samnite and gave him a long kiss right on the mouth. She laughed again and looked about her; the onlookers stepped out of her way as she stopped behind Capito, who was facing Spartacus. Her young companion followed her, carrying her green parasol. The Thracian, who had not been watching, was eating in small mouthfuls, forgoing the spiced meats. The woman looked at him for a long time. Spartacus went on eating as if she did not exist; yet, he could not be unaware of her presence, for everyone was silently watching her. "Who's he fighting?" she asked her companion.

"Me," Blamma replied.

The woman made a disappointed face; she tossed her head and quickly left the refectory.

Seated between Spartacus and the veteran who had selected him as his opponent, the newcomer who had been lashed across the face was stuffing himself with food. A kind of stupefaction had overcome him. He was no longer afraid, it appeared. There was perhaps a share of fatalism in his resignation. Suddenly, after drinking, he got up and looked straight ahead of him. The Thracian grabbed his arm and flung him against a wall, where he sat vomiting onto his knees. On an order from the guards, some slaves came and lifted up the still-vomiting man, and dragged him outside.

A coach came in to tell the married gladiators that their wives had assembled in the yard. The Samnite, along with many others, got up and went out. At that point Gannicus, the athletic Celt, leaned toward Spartacus, who was eating at his right. "Aren't you hungry?" he asked.

"Sure I am."

"It doesn't look it."

Spartacus went on eating his small mouthfuls without answering. Gannicus took him by the shoulder and whispered into his ear. "Do you want to escape?" Spartacus went on eating; his face was blank. Gannicus leaned toward him again. "When we leave the mess hall, come walk with me," he said, and bit into a big chunk of meat. Spartacus raised his eyes and saw that the Celt was watching him. A moment later, when the other Thracian and Capito came in and sat down again, Gannicus whispered to them. The Celt got up; a short while later, Spartacus followed him.

Watched by two guards, some of the gladiators were strolling in the yard. Spartacus unconcernedly sauntered toward the tree under which Gannicus had sat down; he lay down beside him. His hands behind his head, without moving, Gannicus explained: "Last night, one of the veterans asked me whether I wanted to escape. I agreed to his plan. This evening, they put our weapons in the fighters' dormitory. Ours. The weapons of the men who aren't fighting tomorrow are in the coaches' dormitory. Before the fights, escape won't be possible. There'll be guards everywhere and they'll take our weapons from us. Afterward, they may take us to the bathhouse. See it there? It's the red shed near the exit. To the left, there's the coaches' dormitory. After our bath, instead of going to the mess hall, we'll take the weapons from the coaches' dorm by going through a door in the bathhouse entranceway. On the training field, one of the veterans will be waiting for our signal to bring the others in to arm themselves."

Gannicus had spoken quickly. The guards were already coming for them. Gannicus got up. "Understand?"

"Yes."

A guard was coming close.

"Coming?"

"Maybe."

Gannicus looked at him. Spartacus got up. Gannicus followed him. They joined the guard and, with the other fighters, went to their dormitory. Gannicus came to lie beside Spartacus. They spoke in whispers. "Why maybe?"

"What?"

"Why do you say maybe you'll come?"

"Because maybe I'll be dead."

Gannicus took his eyes off the door for a moment so as to look at the Thracian. "Who are you fighting?"

"The one-eyed Samnite."

"With the mace and net?"

"Yes."

"Did you see him training?"

"Yes. But a real fight is something else again."

"Of course. Are you scared?"

"No. Who are you fighting?"

"The big hairless Greek. Sica and buckler."

Spartacus closed his eyes. Gannicus said something more, but Spartacus had fallen asleep.

Daylight filtered into the dormitory through the narrow opening at ceiling level. The men were no longer asleep; they were thinking of the fights. Some of them, paralyzed with fear, were curled up, moaning and clutching at their stomachs. Blamma looked at Spartacus, who was asleep; the Thracian seemed perfectly relaxed, his head on his right arm. The Samnite turned uneasily on his side, trying to relax. When the guards came in, Spartacus was still asleep. Gannicus put his hand on his shoulder. The Thracian opened his eyes. A coach came in behind the guards. "Up!" he shouted. Those who were most fearful of the fights had to be struck before they got up. The two hundred gladiators were taken out to the training field. The old-timers immediately formed a group without prearrangement. The novices silently watched them, with teeth clenched. A cart drawn by two mules and covered with a thick cloth came through the archway of the ludus. A guard stopped it near the gladiators, who came up one by one to take a gold-embroidered purple chlamys from Sidon, fastened at the neck with a clip, which each of them was to wear. With flicks of their whips, the guards and coaches dressed up the ranks, and then the head coach gave the signal to move. The gladiators marched barehanded, followed by slaves carrying the weapons in large baskets.

On these days of the munus, the streets of Capua were all but deserted, most of the inhabitants having gone to the circus. In military formation, the gladiators marched out of the school. Guards of the Capuan cohort surrounded them to escort them among the belated Capuans hurrying toward the circus. The gladiators went through the arcades, past the perfume shops and the dyers', and reached the now deserted market place. Once past the market, despite the guards who tried to make a path for them, the gladiators advanced with more difficulty. In the narrow streets, at the approaches to the circus where the din was at its height, the crowds grew thicker and thicker. While the entrances to the circus had been kept fairly clear, the streets were so crowded that it took the gladiators almost an hour to cover a stretch which at that time of day, if there had been no games, they could have walked in a few minutes. It was a day for thieves and beggars. For prostitutes, too, who were the most adept at getting through the crowds. They were surrounded by their bodyguard of procurers, anxious to preserve their property in good condition, who were not reluctant to either threaten or beat off any daring ones who took advantage of the crush to touch them. Insults filled the air, fights broke out; here and there, a young woman or an old man fainted. Yet, despite the shouting and kicking, the crowd on the whole remained rather calm. Less jaded than the Romans, the Capuans did not so often get an opportunity to spend a full day exclusively devoted to gladiatorial contests.

From the humblest to the richest, all went to the circus decked out in their finest togas. Class distinctions faded in the common passion for the games. In Rome as in Capua, where unemployment was rife, leisure was kept under control only by the public dole, and the circus games served as a diversion to unrest. After noon, from one end of the year to the other, Capuan workers had little to do. In order that they might not spend their free time dangerously talking politics, a subject their impoverished condition would inevitably have led them to, the games were used to take their minds off their troubles, indulge their passions, divert their energies, and provide a wholesome distraction from all other activities. The Senate, knowing that an idle man is a sleeping rebel whose awakening can often be perilous, fed the Roman, kept the Capuan busy, entertained them at circuses. As long as the diversions lasted, the power and control of the Senate over the masses—whose tenements dangerously surrounded the palaces—were secure, in Campania as well as in Latium.

When Pompey was in Spain, covering himself with glory in the war against Sertorius, Crassus, after building the most colossal Roman fortune of the age, was using it as a springboard for his political ambitions. Having made a friend—and a client—of the propraetor of the province of Campania, he had invested a fortune preparing this festive week for the Capuans. That day, the gladiatorial fights were to be the climax.

Erected on a slight dip in the land just outside the city, the Capuan circus was of vast proportions. Nine hundred feet long, four hundred and fifty wide, its stone stands rose in three tiers beneath which every kind of trader in Capua set up shop, from the caterer of roasts to the prostitute. At the end of each day of games, gangs of slaves cleaned the stands and the arena after the spectators had left. Spectators, in some cases, had to be thrown out, for they would come with supplies of food for the whole week, hoping to be able to sleep in their seats to keep their places. Others, who did not live in Capua, spent their nights under the arcades or along the walls of the circus.

Theatrical performances and, above all, races had attracted fans from the nearby provinces. The animal day, which came before the gladiatorial fights, had been especially popular: Mesopotamian lions, Nubian hippopotamuses, Hyrcanian tigers, elephants, bulls—all had gone down by the dozens in one great bloodbath. All week long, the circus had been jammed to the breaking point; in fact, the day before, it had actually cracked under the charge of the enraged mastodons, and if the spectators had not been so engrossed in the show, panic might have broken out in the north hemicycle and spread to the rest of the forty thousand watchers. To crown this scene of carnage, the last day had been reserved for the local gladiators.

ARENA

III

At the approach to the circus, the appearance of the one-eyed Samnite brought shouts of joy. At the doors, the hinge-pins moaned under the thrust of the crowd. Inside, the gladiators were greeted by a single roar from the multitude, which rose as one man on seeing them; but, since the propraetor had not yet arrived, the coaches quickly led their men down into one of the basements. It ran the length of the building above the wild animals which lack of time had kept from the games the day before. Their strong scent rose within the dark vaults and mixed with that of the blood shed the day before. The impatient spectators stamping and clapping, the beasts roaring in the basements, and the crowd rumbling outside the circus combined into a sort of powerful panting, taking on deafening proportions in the corridors and adding further to the panic of the weaker gladiators and to the tension of the veterans, impatient to get back into the arena, weapons in hand.

And while the panic and the tension increased in the rumbling vaults, while the additional stench from the urine and excrement uncontrollably discharged from the helpless bowels of over-excited men and beasts filled the men's lungs, turned their stomachs, and caused them to fall vomiting in long roaring spasms, Marcus Licinius Crassus was making his entrance, handsome, elegant, perfumed, onto the podium where the propraetor was modestly awaiting him; with one arm raised, the other stretched toward Crassus, he received the ovation of the crowd and, by his gesture, transmitted it to the one who so generously was treating the people to a last day of entertainment, one final bloodbath—human this time.

At the invitation of the propraetor, Crassus moved toward him, and the cheering, which seemed to have reached its peak, grew still louder to welcome him. Forty thousand chests roared his name to the sky: *"Crassus!"* And the startled pigeons fled from the arena and the roof of the stands.

In the basement, the coaches were conferring. They decided the gladiators would have to have some air while awaiting the signal for the fights.

They shook the fighters. The narrow basement into which they had been crowded was faintly lighted by a ray of sun falling at some distance on the stairs. In this half-light, there was silence among the gladiators, caught between the rumble of the beasts and that of the crowd. From time to time, a man vomited. They were all pale and tense. To relieve his feelings, perhaps, or to try to relax, one of them would suddenly scream. Spartacus remained seated, his feet under his thighs, his arms hanging limp, the palms of his hands turned toward the dark sweating vault alive with insects. From time to time, some of them fell, victims of a silent, unseen fight. The Thracian, with his head to one side, appeared to be staring at his hands; in fact, his eyes were closed. Those among his companions whose eyes were neither glazed with fright nor clouded with nausea looked at him, possibly envious of his seeming calm.

The coaches shook the fighters. They lined up tensely. In two ranks—their bearing much less relaxed than when they had arrived, their purple and gold chlamyses now soiled—they went up the stairs. They entered the arena, blinded by the sun and startled by the heat accumulated within the bowl of the circus and reflected by the white sand. A wild shout welcomed them; the excited animals gave a furious reply.

The best seats—on a level with the podium—were the boxes which faced each other across the narrowest part of the arena. The box occupied by the propraetor, Crassus, and their retinues, was about twelve feet above the field, with the sun at its back. The gladiators filed past, to the applause of the crowd, and squads of slaves then came in to clean the arena into which spectators had thrown fruit peels, bones, pebbles, and even fish spines. Dragging big rakes, then fine nets, the slaves cleared away all the rubbish, while the inspection and distribution of weapons began. A strident voice, coming from the upper terrace where the poorer spectators stood, elbowing each other for a better vantage point, suddenly rent the air.

"Start the fights!"

The voice had a strong accent of Bruttium, whose inhabitants, after more than a century, still had the unenviable reputation of having surrendered to Hannibal without having put up a fight. Another voice, this one powerful, responded from the opposite standing-room area.

"Back to your mountain, there, Hannibal!"

The crowd burst into a roar of laughter that spread to the podium and was followed by a general move forward: the head coach, who had sent the gladiators back to the basement, was now arriving before the propraetor's box. He saluted with his right hand and waited. The propraetor stood up. The crowd silently imitated him. He raised his right arm, from which hung a white towel.

"People of Capua!" he shouted. "My noble and generous friend, General Marcus Licinius Crassus, makes an offering of these fights to the immortal gods to assuage their wrath and bring peace to your dead!"

In silence, the crowd waved their handkerchiefs and the ends of their shawls in signs of pious gratitude. The propraetor's hand was still raised; he was staring straight in front of him, with a short, deep wrinkle on his brow. He wore an embroidered Tyrian toga draped over his scarlet tunic; in his left hand he held an ivory baton surmounted by an eagle taking flight, and on his head he wore a heavy crown of gold leaves. At the sound of the trumpet, the aedile threw the white towel into the arena and, like a living idol, came back to sit on his ivory chair beside a smiling

Crassus, while there began a tuneless piece of music in which grating flutes merged with the trumpets, and horns with the hydraulic organ. The first ten gladiators came running in: the games had begun.

The gladiators saluted with their right hands. In pairs, they began to feel each other out while a fever of excitement crept down from the standing room to the seats below. Very quickly, some of the men fell, ludicrous little red spots on a yellow rectangle bordered with multicolored yelling rows of spectators. As at the chariot races, excited neighbors were making bets with each other. Almost fifty gladiators fell in this manner during the hot spring morning.

At the midday intermission, Crassus asked that the common-law prisoners sentenced to die the next day for their crimes be sent out together. More than a hundred of them were pushed out onto the sand. Two of them were drawn aside, one armed and the other unarmed, with no more protection than a tunic. The death of both of them was as inevitable as their bravery was futile, for the armed prisoner, who was certain to kill the unarmed man, was then disarmed in his turn in favor of another, the same sword being used for all of them. In less than an hour, all the prisoners were dead, the noonday festivities were over, and the carnage exhaled its vapors through clouds of incense.

The arena was strewn with lacerated bodies, and a team of masked slaves then ran out toward the fallen men, making sure they were dead by giving them great mallet blows on the head. The undertaker's men, the libitinarii, then carried off the bodies on stretchers and threw them into the dark gallery where the remaining gladiators, about to go into the arena, were waiting. Groups of ten appeared in rapid succession, urged on by their long wait and by the crowd, now seized with a murderous frenzy, yelling at them, "Hit him! Kill him! Brain him!" Each wound brought a reaction from the mob which was concerned about its bets; savage shouts of glee rose up whenever the one they had bet against started to stagger. And then, suddenly, the groups of ten stopped coming out.

On the freshly raked arena, beneath the now-scorching afternoon sun, two pairs of fighters walked toward the podium: two Greek mirmillos against two retiarii, Gannicus and Capito. The two Greeks wore brown-fabric leg-coverings, tied around their legs with strings; they were armed like Thracians, with the curved sica, the round buckler, and the murma, a helmet with a sea fish carved on it. Facing them were Capito, the Samnite retiarius, carrying a trident and net, and Gannicus, the Celt, armed with the spiked mace and net. After the traditional salute to the praetorian box, Capito ran off toward the center of the arena, at the same time watching what his opponent was doing. Behind the fence, the thrashers were getting ready to drive him out to the fight, but Capito had now stopped and was waiting for his adversary. The latter, confused for a moment, had run out behind him. When he was ten paces away, Capito pretended to start running away again. The Greek sprang rapidly after him, but Capito sidestepped and threw his net as he turned; the Greek had anticipated this and passed under the net while he lunged with his arm holding the sica. Capito reversed his field, as he dragged his spread net; the Greek leaped after him. Without turning, Capito hastened his pace. The Greek was still behind him, closing in. Then, suddenly, Capito sidestepped, spreading his net at the very moment when the Greek leaped with upraised sica. On seeing the net, he flattened himself in the air, with arms outspread, to avoid entrapment. But whether he was caught in the net or not no longer mattered; Capito's trident was even then going through his back. No longer able to go on fighting, bleeding abundantly, the Greek dropped his sica; rolling over on his back, he raised his left hand as if to beg for mercy. The crowd had not even had time to react before the Samnite's trident struck him again. The masked slaves crushed the Greek's skull with a mallet blow. His body was being carried off as the cheer rose from the stands. Capito did not salute, but ran back to the basement.

The other Greek, a bald giant, had stabbed Gannicus' left arm with a thrust of his sica. Now the Greek was driving the retiarius toward the podium as he swept the air in front of him with great strokes of the sica. The crowd was screaming with joy. Gannicus' net, which the Celt had not brought back in front of him as he retreated, dragged dangerously on the sand. He had now narrowed his big blue eyes, almost closed them. Coming confidently closer and closer, the Greek swiftly raised his sica;

Gannicus started to raise his mace. The dagger traced a red slice on Gannicus' left shoulder; the Celt swung his mace, dodging another sica thrust as he fell to his knees. The mace hooked around the Greek's wrist and Gannicus pulled. The sica flew out of the hand of the Greek, who was coming forward with his shield raised. Gannicus rolled over on his left side. As the center spike of the small buckler passed within an inch of his head, Gannicus seized the Greek's ankle and brought him down. Gannicus was already on his feet. He ran off, leaving his net. When he turned around, the quick, silent Greek was almost upon him. He had retrieved his sica; Gannicus succeeded in dodging the full force of the blow, but the dagger caught him in the side. He fell to one knee. The crowd screamed. The sica was about to strike him mortally this time; it was coming down on him, when the Greek suddenly let it go. With his head, Gannicus had butted him in the lower belly. His adversary clutched at his genitals with a cry and fell to his knees, his face in the sand. Gannicus got back up and smashed his head with a blow of the mace. A gasp of surprise rose from the stands at this unexpected turn of events; but already a squad of slaves was turning over the blood-stained sand while others were dragging the body away.

When Gannicus got back to the other gladiators, one of the coaches gave him a slight pat on the shoulder. Gannicus pushed him away so violently that he was knocked back against the wall of the dark corridor. Nobody spoke. The head coach sent another group of eight men out to fight. Spartacus, his back against a wall, watched Gannicus sit down, streaming with sweat, his teeth clenched, and shaken with a furious tremor. The head coach, two steps up, was watching the gladiators in the arena. Shouts arose from time to time, startling Gannicus, who had closed his eyes. Capito, unscathed, joined the trainer. A quick, sharp, crushing noise; a roar from the crowd rolled beneath the vaults. Two men came back, blood-soaked, victorious. They sat down next to each other, opposite Gannicus, whose eyes were still closed. Two brothers, probably twins, they had suffered almost identical wounds, high on the left thigh. They were trying to catch their breath through their mouths, eyes closed, perhaps reliving their fights. Still another man came back, reeling, his hands on his chest. When he saw the others, he almost smiled. "I had spared him . . . the last time!" he said in a gasp. A little blood bubbled on his lips. He turned as he fell, dead.

The coach, who had turned around at his entrance, looked at the others. "No quarter for the losers!" he said, and he went on watching the last two fighters.

"Get your whip ready, Thracian!"

Spartacus raised his eyes; it was the one-eyed Samnite who had just spoken to him. The coach turned around. "No. You'll go up last, with . . ." A single shout arose from the crowd, drowning out the trainer's words. Two fighters were brought back into the corridor; they had simultaneously struck each other a mortal blow. One of them still had the sword in his belly. They were thrown alongside the dead gladiators, whom teams of naked, blood-red libitinarii were methodically stripping, from their helmets to their sandals. Some of the gladiators had carried money, or jewels, on them. Those in charge of stripping, sorting, transporting the corpses, and cleaning the arena and corridors, shared in this booty, while the weapons and clothes were returned to Baliatus; refurbished, cleaned up, they could be used again another time. The libitinarii were now working in a pool of blood. Bending over their victims, quick and precise, they unerringly tossed the helmets, weapons, and clothing on the proper salvage piles and—with a mechanical gesture—shoved the sticky bodies toward a team who stacked them beneath the stairs with the other naked bodies, oozing blood and sometimes still uttering death rattles . . .

The impatience of the crowd was reaching a hysterical pitch. They were yelling for the Samnite: "Blamma! Blamma! Blamma!"

The trainer sent out a group of four. The crowd screamed its disappointment: "Blamma! Blamma! Blamma!" The four men fought to the accompaniment of shouts of "Blamma! Blamma!"

The Samnite turned toward Spartacus, and snapped, "Get your whip ready, Thracian!"

"It's ready," Spartacus said as he got up.

Gannicus opened his eyes. The last man came back, slightly wounded on the left cheek, one eye closed.

"Blamma! Blamma!" roared the crowd.

The slaves assigned to clean up brought back two bodies that they threw at the feet of the weapons- and clothing-salvagers. One of the twins started to vomit. Besides Blamma and Spartacus, there was now only one other pair left: two Thracians.

"Spartacus!"

The Thracian went over to Gannicus, who had called to him. "Listen!" Spartacus bent down close to the Celt. "Hit him when he swings his mace back."

Spartacus straightened up. "I'll see," he said. Gannicus called again: "Blamma!" The Samnite, smiling, excited, was listening to the crowd call for him. Spartacus took his whip in his left hand and wiped his right hand before picking up the hatchet. Gannicus called as loud as he could to make the Samnite hear him over the uproar. "Blamma!"

As he was about to go out, the Samnite turned around.

"Good-bye," said Gannicus.

The Samnite started toward Gannicus, but the coach pushed him into the arena. A long cheer greeted him.

It was customary for the opponent to come into the arena from the opposite side of the stairs. When Spartacus set foot on the sand, there was a short, surprised silence, immediately followed by laughter and jeers. "A hatchet and whip!" "He's crazy!" But it seemed that Spartacus did not care about making a spectacular entrance; one hand shading his eyes, which were nearly closed, he stood still, adjusting to the glare of the sun on the rectangle of sand. The multicolored crowd was making a mad din; thinking they were being cheated by having Spartacus pitted against the overwhelming Samnite, they were demanding another opponent for their hero.

Baliatus arrived, surrounded by four bodyguards. He went up to the trainer. "Give one of the Thracians to the Samnite." The coach jumped out on the field and went to speak to Blamma; he then ran toward one of the Thracians who was walking toward the center and gave him his instructions. The Thracian turned and looked at Spartacus. This change in the program had taken only a few seconds. Spartacus, still motionless at the head of the stairs, was informed in turn. Now his eyes were wide open; he set his weapons down on the ground and rubbed his hands in the sand, picked up his weapons again, and in his turn walked toward the center. The Thracian he was due to fight was lined up with the others before the podium, saluting the propraetor's box. Spartacus came forward, his head slightly tilted to one side. While walking toward the box, he turned his head toward the sun for a moment and continued calmly forward. About twenty paces away from the others, he stopped and drew himself up. A brief silence followed by murmurs passed over the circus like the rustling of wings. The man with the whip was not saluting! The three fighters who had been waiting for him turned around as one. Very erect, his face turned toward the upper tiers, Spartacus waited. His body suddenly seemed to be twice its size. The head coach started running toward him. "Go salute the praetor!" he shouted. As Spartacus did not move, the coach ran toward the box. "Noble praetor . . . This gladiator is new at the school; he is not acquainted with the rules of the circus."

"His name?"

"Spartacus."

The name ran through the stands. In a few moments, all the spectators knew it.

"Very well, go ahead!" said the propraetor.

The coach went back to the stairway, the propraetor gave the signal. The Samnite turned toward one of the Thracians, the other Thracian toward Spartacus. The Thracian was not equipped with the sica of his compatriots, but with a long sword and a buckler, a flat, wide helmet and leg coverings. In spite of his helmet, as he turned around the sun caught him by surprise, and he quickly raised his sword hand toward his eyes, pretending to adjust his helmet to mislead Spartacus; while doing this, about ten paces away, he tried to get around his opponent. Spartacus lowered his chin and hunched his shoulders while slightly spreading his arms. In the distance, behind his opponent, whom he allowed to advance a little, he could see the Samnite swinging his mace up and down, back and forth . . . When the Thracian had the sun at his side, Spartacus quickly took two steps forward. His opponent did the same but slowly, then took two more very quick steps and lunged with his sword; behind his buckler, only his eyes and legs could be seen. Spartacus dodged by taking one step back and turned toward the sun. The Thracian took advantage of this to move forward and thrust again with his sword, withdrawing his arm behind the buckler as quickly as it had emerged. Along his slightly flexed body, Spartacus began swinging his arms slowly, back and forth. He took a step forward. The other thrust out his arm. The whip shot out like a serpent's tongue and wound around the sword rather high on the hilt. Spartacus pulled. Trying to keep his balance, the man for a moment raised the arm holding the buckler. Immediately afterward, he was once again protected behind the shield, but he stepped back and fell on one side, dead. Someone screamed. The whole crowd stood up. They had seen nothing except the flash of the sun on the buckler when it had been raised. At that very moment, Spartacus had completed his move: he pulled the sword away with the whip by stepping to the side, as if he had repeated this motion a hundred times under identical conditions, almost without looking; the hatchet had landed in the man's chest, beneath the heart, and come out again as the buckler came down to protect the Thracian a fraction of a second too late.

At first there was silence in the crowd, then a single shout, bursting from every chest, screamed Spartacus' name into the sky.

"I didn't see a thing!" the propraetor said to Crassus. "Never saw a thing!"

In the corridor, Gannicus had joined Capito to watch the whip man in combat. Baliatus leaned toward the coach: "I never saw a thing!"

"Neither did I," answered the other.

No one had seen it. But there was the man, dead. Everyone looked back at his blood a second time to make sure. The spectators, who had had eyes only for the Samnite and were delightedly savoring his cruel methods, knew that he was prolonging their homicidal pleasure by smashing his opponent little by little with increasingly brutal mace-blows. So the audience had for the first time glanced at the other two fighters when they were closing in. And then, all of a sudden, one of them had fallen. Hearing the cheers of the crowd yelling the name of Spartacus, the Samnite decided quickly to put an end to the affair. Spartacus was slowly walking toward the corridor. The Samnite looked in his direction a second, dodged a sword thrust, and flung out his net almost at ground level. It opened out as it rose and while the

Thracian was stepping back the mace struck him in the legs. Swinging around again, another powerful swipe pinned the buckler against the Thracian's chest, and a third swing of the mace smashed his face. The amazed crowd was still standing and shouting Spartacus' name as Blamma, unscathed and glinting with sweat, came over to salute the propraetor. The Samnite was on his way back to the corridor, when a new wave swept through the spectators.

"Spartacus-Blamma! . . . Spartacus-Blamma! . . . Spartacus-Blamma! . . ."

It was inevitable; the crowd was demanding the climax. This final fight would give them a hero for the day—as Baliatus had foreseen and feared. "Not today. I can gross a great gate with those two," he said to the coach. But already, bounding out of the propraetorian box, two decurions of the Capuan cohort were running across the arena. Spartacus was leaning against a wall. Gannicus and Capito, standing near him, were saying nothing.

Seeing the decurions arrive, the coach said, "You'll have to go up again, Spartacus." At that moment, the Samnite was coming into the shade of the foul-smelling corridor; the smells of urine, excrement, vomit, and sweat were now mingled with those of blood and heaped corpses.

"Get away! Back to the camp!" Baliatus was wailing.

Too late. The decurions were there.

"The praetor wants to see your last two gladiators," one of them told the coach.

"You'll have to go back up," the coach said to the two fighters.

The Samnite did not wait; he ran up the stairs. The crowd was calling, "Spartacus! Spartacus!" and stamping and clapping. The decurions were waiting. Spartacus picked up his weapons and went back up the stairs. As he had the first time, he stopped at the top, laid down his weapons, and rubbed his hands in the sand. The crowd yelled his name once more and now watched every one of his motions. Spartacus rubbed the handles of his weapons with sand. The Samnite, on the other hand, had gone back to salute the propraetor and then turned around. He set down his weapons and wiped his forehead. Spartacus made note of the way the shadows fell on the arena and walked toward its center. As in the preceding fight, going against all the rules of the circus, he stopped before reaching the center and waited for his opponent to join him. All he wore was a red subligar tied at one side of his waist. He was fighting with naked legs and torso, while his companions, on the contrary, had protected as much of themselves as possible without hindering their movements. Blamma, for instance, wore on his chest a sort of goatskin sack with a hole cut for the neck and held around the waist by a string knotted over the loins. He wore a broad licium that hid his genitals and covered his thighs, as well as leg guards tied below the knees and at the ankles.

In the crowd, bets were going up. There was continual scuffling for better vantage points in the standing area. Blamma picked up his weapons and, in the suddenly silent circus, he was perhaps the only person who was moving. As he walked slowly toward Spartacus, he spread the arm holding the net and began to swing his mace. Spartacus turned and took up his position with his back to the sun. Blamma had to squint to follow the Thracian who was now in the large rectangular shadow cast by the podium. Blamma moved forward toward the left, either to get into the shadow or to maneuver Spartacus out of it; but the Thracian stood his ground, following the Samnite only by turning his head toward the right. Blamma got into the shade. He stopped there a moment, then walked toward Spartacus, who was facing him. The distance between them lessened rapidly, fifteen, fourteen, thirteen, twelve paces . . . His muscles relaxed, Spartacus stood motionless. The Samnite was perspiring freely under the goatskin clinging to his belly. Eleven, ten, nine, eight paces . . . Blamma took one step more, and then moved his foot back, thrusting forward the arm that held the net. A woman cried out; Spartacus did not move. The muscles of his left arm had merely tautened: Blamma had not let loose his net. In the same move following this feint, the Samnite leaped two paces, casting out his net, which unfurled. Spartacus slightly flexed his right leg and the lash struck out, slicing the air with a short hiss. It struck the dangerous net which had so suddenly spread above the Thracian. Instead of coming down on Spartacus, the net crumpled, pinched from top to bottom by the end of the whip. The lash rolled back under the fingers of Spartacus, who had not moved—but the heavy mace was now coming down to the accompaniment of a yell. Spartacus leaped under Blamma's arm and turned up behind the Samnite, who swung about in his thrust and swept at Spartacus' legs. The Thracian avoided the awful blow only by jumping over the mace which quickly completed its orbit. Spartacus' feet were barely back on the ground when the net was again unfurling above his head. To avoid it, Spartacus was forced to retreat and Blamma struck what was certainly one of his favorite blows, as someone in the crowd yelled, "Now!" The mace having gathered its full speed in a complete swing, Blamma had cast the net sideways, as he turned, and the mace followed, rising rapidly from left to right. The crowd roared, "Kill!" The stroke had been beautifully planned. On one side, the unfurled net in its full width, blown out, ready to snap shut; on the other, coming in with lightning speed, the mace as big as a head, bristling with sharp spikes. The blow seemed impossible to parry. Spartacus stopped the sweep of the mace by catching the chain in the crook formed by the handle and blade of his hatchet. At the same time, his left arm flung out the lash. The weight of the mace carried the Samnite forward while its chain wound around the hatchet handle and the net came down without effect along Spartacus' left arm. The crowd was on its feet, howling with delight. The two men collided and both jumped back at once, pulling back at both the mace and the hatchet, but the two weapons were stuck together. Blamma and Spartacus had the same idea at the same time; they both rushed at each other to be able to pull apart even faster and free their weapons.

The crowd had become one savage, roaring mass. The two men, their arms taut with the effort, their legs flexed, were now tugging without moving. While he pulled, the Samnite was gathering in his net with a deft finger, mesh by mesh. When it was half in, he swung it at Spartacus' head, more to distract the Thracian from his effort than with any hope of catching him in it. Since there was not enough space between them for such a maneuver, the net struck Spartacus on the neck. Without letting go of his lash, he grabbed the net and, tugging suddenly at both mace and net, landed his knee in Blamma's gut. Blamma groaned, but still did not let go. However, the blow had told on him, and his resistance weakened. Spartacus let go of the net and unfurled his lash behind him. It went whistling out to whip the face of the one-eyed man, leaving a diagonal line of blood in its trace. Raging and yelling, the Samnite let go of his net and seized the mace-chain in both hands. Pivoting on the spot with an amazing display of strength, he made Spartacus swing around at the end of the radius formed by the hatchet and mace. Spartacus' hand was slipping. He had to let go of the hatchet. While the Samnite swung completely around, Spartacus bent down and picked up a handful of sand in his right hand. The Samnite, facing him again, stepped quickly aside and came back armed with the hatchet and mace, which he had gotten apart. The lash whistled and cut Blamma's face from the opposite direction. The Samnite made a wild lunge with the hatchet, but it did not reach its mark. He threw it into the distance and gathered up his net; the lash bit into his back, unprotected by the goatskin. Blamma quickly straightened up and swung the mace. Spartacus jumped to evade it and threw his handful of sand into Blamma's eye. The Samnite roared. Covered with sand and blood, he began to swing around, and, protected by the mace circling before him, he wiped his face. He gave a great yell and flung his net, but Spartacus was not there; he was running over to his hatchet. Blamma followed him. When he got within twenty paces of Spartacus, the sun blinded his eye already burned by the sand and he did not see the Thracian throw his hatchet. The weapon whistled as it hurtled through the air and landed bolt upright in the Samnite's breast.

Already possessed of a furious excitement, the crowd howled, "Kill him, Spartacus!" The blow had brought Blamma to his knees. He got back to his feet, came closer to the Thracian, and swung the mace wildly, but still with great force. Spartacus easily avoided it and began to walk toward the corridor, watching Blamma walk behind him, gasping, with the hatchet in his chest. His face and neck covered with blood, sand, and sweat, the Samnite was coming at him, terrifyingly. Spartacus stopped; guards were coming toward him armed with whips and tridents to force him back to the fight. He watched Blamma approach, his arms spread, his eye almost closed, his face contorted. Spartacus was twice struck with a strap, in an effort to spur him back, but he did not move. Blamma took two more steps. "Kill me quick!" he said in a last gasp. The Thracian ran toward Blamma, seized the hatchet handle and pulled it out. The blood spurted over Spartacus; in the same swing, Spartacus had raised the hatchet and split the skull of the Samnite, who fell.

Already, the three guards were upon him; it was obvious that they had been ordered to put an end to Spartacus. The Thracian was suddenly a changed man. His calm had disappeared. Snarling with rage, he stepped over Blamma, unleashed his lash, and sent the first guard's trident flying; the hatchet swung out, hurtled, and landed in the man's nose, crushing the bones. The man fell backward without a sound, his hands over his eyes. The second had only a whip. Spartacus picked up Blamma's mace and snapped out his lash; a line of blood crossed the guard's face, a second snap knocked the whip out of his hand. The man came forward and picked up Blamma's net. Spartacus crushed his shoulder with a stroke of the mace. The third guard raised his trident; the mace crushed his chest. Spartacus looked about him, wild, pale, bathed in blood from head to foot. And suddenly, all the spectators were on their feet, shouting the Thracian's name, "*Spartacus!*"

Slaves carrying baskets were now walking toward the victorious Thracian while the libitinarii transported the corpses and cleaned the arena. The slaves tendered him their baskets filled with silver plates, gold pieces, bracelets, bottles of perfume, brightly colored pieces of yard goods . . .

And the shouts continued: "*Spartacus! Spartacus!*"

The Thracian had let his arms fall to his sides. The coaches came running toward him, with towels in their hands. The praetorian box emptied and the crowd discussed the fights, yelling its delight and admiration for Spartacus. Somber, turned inward, the Thracian stood looking at the baskets laden with gifts.

The munus was over, Spartacus was the hero of the day. He turned his back on the baskets, the coaches, the crowds; solemnly, slowly, he headed back toward the corridor to join his fellows.

The sun was setting. In the streets, on the way back, people were shouting Spartacus' name; women threw him flowers. Frightened children cried as he went by. Gannicus came over to the Thracian and put his arm around his shoulder as if to congratulate him. He whispered very softly to him, "Don't forget, after the bath!"

Spartacus looked at him. "I haven't forgotten."

After the bath, night had fallen. A Cilician and a Celt who had decided to leave without awaiting the others came out of the baths and went into the coaches' dormitory. The weapons were gone! When they tried to come out, guards were waiting for them. Someone had talked. They were chained and thrown into a pit to await their fate. Wounded, sick, exhausted, the other gladiators were surrounded and led off to their dormitory where they were given a ration of tepid water and a large dish of boiled cereal. Spartacus drank all of his water and immediately fell asleep.

ARENA

IV

In this early summer of 73 B.C., Marcus Licinius Crassus was perhaps the only man in all of Italy with no call to make before daybreak. But, the power of a lord being measured by the size of his clientele, he would have tarnished his reputation if he had preferred his bed to his humming swarm of clients. He received complaints from some, confidences from others, and greetings from all, and his daily gifts to each of his regular retainers were helpful to lawyers without cases, teachers without pupils, as well as artists without commissions—for whom the six sesterces a day that Crassus gave them were, for the most part, their only income. Those citizens who were privileged to know a craft, and especially to have the good luck to exercise it, added the magnate's gifts to their salaries; so as not to arrive late at their employers', they first ran over to collect their grants before dawn. The clients were expected to appear in togas—as clean as possible—and this obligation was a further burden to their meager budgets. However, their patron graciously gave them a new one each year in addition to his New Year's present.

From freed slave to great lord, everyone was bound to someone more powerful than he by obligations comparable to those which former slaves continued to owe the masters who had freed them. Each one, therefore, appeared at the house of his patron and patiently awaited his turn, which was decided not by their order of arrival but by their social importance: praetors before tribunes, knights before ordinary citizens, and the freeborn before the manumitted.

Crassus never failed to receive his clients in person, to invite them from time to time to his table, or to help them by his gifts and aid. Some patrons distributed food baskets, especially in cases where the clients lacked the bare necessities and cash might go for gaming or bets, rather than for food. The richest patrons, after having received their clients, went off in their turn as clients to visit those richer than they. The humblest of paterfamilias made several visits, so as to accumulate several grants of victuals or money. Since everyone knew someone richer than himself, it was not unusual to see a man recently freed go as a client to one freed earlier. Still others, hoping to receive more generous grants, dragged with them their pregnant or ailing wives, their sickly children, mothers, brothers or sisters, or even their whole families.

Crassus was the only man to have no patron, for there was none in Italy who could be counted wealthier than he. The praetor, the propraetor, and the commander of the guard were clients of his, along with many other administrators and officers who had their own clientele.

Lentulus Baliatus, the lanista, also had a large clientele to support, and undoubtedly his wealth would not have permitted him to make visits, but his profession compelled him to seek out favors from aediles and other high-placed personages. Some of these officials exacted very high prices for their favors; others who were rich enough to sponsor games and often in need of Baliatus' gladiators at reasonable terms, were glad to lavish their favors on him.

On this particular morning, Baliatus got up before dawn and went to the home of Crassus, who greeted him most courteously. Crassus made an agreement with the promoter to put on four gladiatorial contests a month during the summer season. Both men found it to their advantage: by giving both bread and games to the Capuans, Crassus gained in popularity; while Baliatus, receiving contraband slaves on whom he paid no taxes, could sell his gladiators at lower prices than the other lanistae, and Crassus could close his eyes to the illegal provenance of the fighters, since he occupied no administrative office.

With the deal concluded for four contests a month, Baliatus hurried off to the school where his own clients were awaiting him. After their visit, he went to his room and sent for one of his new slave girls. He stretched out on cushions and ate some fruit while waiting. The curtain parted and a guard pushed a young woman into the room; Baliatus looked at her and smiled.

"Tell me your name, little flower."

"Polla."

He arose with difficulty and came behind her. Very close. He slipped his hands under the slave's arms, cupped her breasts and bit her on the neck. The slave wrenched free and turned furiously on Baliatus, her lips drawn back, her teeth clenched. Baliatus went for a leather strap hanging near his bed and came back toward the slave girl. He gave her a lash on her shoulder; a trickle of blood appeared and Baliatus lumbered over to her. He toppled her over on the cushions and tried to find her mouth; crushed beneath his weight, she turned her head away and bit the lanista on the shoulder. Baliatus sprang up, howling. Two guards rushed in. "To the kitchens!" he yelled, as he gripped his shoulder. "To the gladiators' kitchens, and send me Alba!" The guards went out, pushing the slave girl before them. "And send up another woman!" Baliatus called again, amid his groans.

During the following month, Baliatus received six hundred more slaves in hundred-lots. After a few days of training, they were sent into the circus each week. Since the near-escape, the camp rules forbade any mingling between the newcomers and the veterans until they met in the arena. The ranks of the veterans were steadily decreasing; out of two hundred, half had been lost in the last three contests. Their weapons had been taken away, and all training was forbidden to them. They never saw the sun any more except when they were taken from the dormitory to the mess hall or to the circus.

It was the day before the last June contests. The pre-fight banquet was now given only for the newcomers, the old-timers getting their evening meal in midafternoon.

Dressed in rags, Alba and Polla came into the mess hall from the kitchens, carrying platters which they put on the tables. Alba came close to Polla and stroked her face. "How beautiful you are!" she said. "Where are you from?"

"Thrace."

Alba took her hand and led her to a bench. The mess hall was empty; the guards, knowing the two women were alone in the kitchens, had gone to sit under the trees near the stream. In the middle of the yard, the Cilician and the Celt, who had been arrested in the coaches' dormitory, had been crucified. Their bodies, burned by the sun, rotting, hung pitifully amid the buzzing of thousands of flies. Alba and Polla looked at them, empty-eyed.

"How old are you, Polla?"

"I don't know."

Alba turned her head and stroked her hair. "Where were you bought?"

"In Rome."

Baliatus suddenly came into the mess hall, surrounded by guards. "Alba!" he shouted. Polla fled into the kitchen. "Well?" He carelessly let the handle of his whip slide along Alba's back.

"She hasn't told me anything yet, master."

He shoved the whip handle into her chest. "If you don't know something within the hour, you will be whipped." He went out, followed by the guards. Alba joined Polla in the kitchens. She took her arm. "Why won't you give in?"

Polla breathed out, in a whisper, "Because I don't want to."

Alba was almost crying. "You don't know what you're saying, Polla. Look at me."

Polla looked into Alba's anxious face. Alba went on. "I don't know my age, but I'm not old. When I got here . . ." Polla was avoiding Alba's eyes, so Alba roughly turned her around, gripping her shoulders. "Look at me! When I got here, I was a little girl. He didn't make any propositions; he just raped me and sent me to the kitchens!" Alba began to cry quietly, her teeth clenched. "You see what I've become! And I may be younger than you!" Polla stroked Alba's face. "I can't," she said softly. Alba was sobbing. Her eyes lowered, she whispered, "If you give in, he'll set you free." Polla freed herself from Alba's hands; she took a dish and went into the mess hall. Alba ran behind her. "He's done it before."

"Sure, that's what they all say!" Polla replied without turning around.

Some gladiators came into the mess hall. Some guards stayed for a moment in front of the opening and then moved away. The men sat down, somber, silent, while Polla went from the kitchens to the mess hall, bringing the dishes. Alba took an empty pitcher and began to follow Polla. "But you'll be free, Polla. Free!" Polla placed a plate on a table, near Spartacus. Alba set the pitcher down and took Polla's arm. The gladiators were watching them. Alba was shaking Polla.

"Do you hear me? Free!"

Polla looked at her. "I don't know what freedom is, Alba. Do you?"

"No . . . But I know . . . freedom is everything! Everything!"

"Baliatus isn't the first one to promise it to me."

Spartacus looked up at Polla. All the men were now listening to these women talking about freedom in front of them, on the eve of the fights. "Nor the last!" Polla added. She leaned against a wall behind Spartacus and the Thracian turned his head to look at her.

"Would you give in, under the same conditions?"

Alba laughed through her tears. "Oh, me! . . . I was taken without being given any chance!" Some of the gladiators broke into laughter. With emotion, Polla came close to her, but Alba moved quickly aside. "How do I have to tell it to you?" she screamed. "You'll be free! *Free!*"

Polla lowered her head. "Free, Alba, and dirty. Very dirty." She took an empty plate from the table and walked toward the kitchens.

Alba followed her; she whispered, "Look, it wouldn't be anything new for you, would it? Baliatus . . . Baliatus wouldn't be the first one!"

Polla shook her head.

"So," Alba replied in a very sweet, almost tender, voice, "as long as there were others!"

"Of course, there were others. But they were no freer than I was!"

"What difference does that make?"

Polla answered very quietly, as if to herself, "All the difference, all the difference in the world. . . ."

"As far as that goes, they're all the same."

Polla looked at her a moment, absently. "Oh!" she lowered her head. "I don't know."

"Well, I do know. Freemen or slaves, it makes no difference here," said Alba, patting her belly. "It's here," she added, pointing to her forehead.

"Maybe . . . Maybe you're right. I don't know . . . I don't know any more. I . . . I gave myself freely to the ones that I knew . . . I was looking . . . for some appeasement; they were too, I guess."

Alba seemed to be moved. She smiled a sad smile and said in a little voice, "Well . . . That's good, if you found it." Polla quickly covered her face with her hands and shook her head.

Baliatus burst into the mess hall. Polla looked up, eyed him a moment, and ran toward the back of the kitchen. Baliatus took one step toward her, and then stopped. Polla waited, panting. She had seized a heavy, pointed skewer. She was waiting. Baliatus shrugged his shoulders and attempted a laugh. He threw a half-eaten apple on the table of the gladiators, who sat watching him, with closed faces. No one touched the apple. Alba was looking at Baliatus as he advanced upon her, his whip under his arm. She backed up against the wall and covered her head with her arms, anticipating a blow.

"Let her choose a man!" Baliatus barked. "Explain the rules of the school to her."

He walked out under the watchful eyes of the gladiators, spoke for a moment to the guards, and went away. Alba slowly straightened up and went to the kitchen. "You have to choose a gladiator. One of those who're going to fight. If he comes back, you belong to him. To him alone. If he doesn't come back—and, one day, he won't—then, you'll be like me: you'll be there any time for anyone who wants to take you."

Polla did not move, her hand still tensed on the skewer. Alba came over to her. "Come on . . . You have to choose now." Alba took the skewer and put it down on a fly-covered meatboard. They went back into the mess hall; the gladiators had heard the lanista; they were looking at the two women. A few of them got up from the table and went to sit at the back of the refectory. Polla walked straight to the first one, took his face in her hands, gazed at him, then went on. The length of the bench, she stared into the eyes of each man. At the end of the table, Spartacus was eating, watching Polla come close; there were still three gladiators on this side before she got to Spartacus. She was about to put her hand on the shoulder of one of them when she saw the Thracian. The man she had been about to choose raised his head; it was scar-covered Gannicus. He was at least twice as old as Polla. He took her hand between two of his fingers. "Don't look at me, Polla. I have a daughter, somewhere in Gaul; I hope she's like you." Polla smiled at him and went on to the next one. She looked at Spartacus again and passed the man by. She took the Thracian's face in her hands and gazed at it at length. She ran her fingers over Spartacus' lips and then tenderly through his hair. "I slept on your shoulder . . . I remember. I walked before you as far as Rome. You got away!"

Spartacus smiled a brief, sad smile. "Yes. You slept next to me, at Brundisium."

The guards came in. Alba ran to Polla. "Hurry up!"

"I've chosen," Polla said. She ran a finger over the Thracian's mouth. "You!"

The guards shoved the gladiators out into the central gangway. Spartacus watched Polla as he went off. Alba took Polla by the shoulders and said, "Come on!" Polla followed her, docilely, absently.

Some cooks came in, followed by slaves and Capuan citizens, the curious who had come to see the banquet of the new gladiators. Polla and Alba cleared the tables and lighted the lamps.

Late that night, after the feast, Alba and Polla crossed the yard. As they went by the old-timers' dormitory, where Spartacus was asleep, Polla stopped. Alba urged her gently on. "I didn't recognize him at first," said Polla.

"If you'd only been able to put up with Baliatus a little, you could have been freed."

"They caught him again!" Polla was murmuring. "They caught him again. . . ."

Before daybreak, the veterans were assembled in the mess hall to avoid contact with the newcomers until contest time. Baliatus intended to sell every last man he had; to make his point, he had had the Cilician and the Celt crucified. The turn of the other veterans would come if they did not get killed fighting, but he figured he could still make a profit on them. Despite their lack of training, their deprivations, and mistreatment, the ranks of the veterans were holding up. Spartacus remained the betting favorite, along with Gannicus and Capito.

That morning, Baliatus got rid of his clientele in a hurry through a distribution of food baskets that had been prepared the day before. Then he went into the mess hall and had the veterans draw lots. "When you're all dead, I'll feel a lot better!" he barked at them irritably. "You'll fight each other first, and then the winners can take on the newcomers." Spartacus' opponent was a Greek who fought with the net and trident. As soon as Baliatus was out of the mess hall, the Greek walked over to the Thracian.

"Kill me right off, Spartacus."

"You have to put up a fight, Fortis."

The Greek glanced around him. The others were gloomy, tense. Fortis took Spartacus by the arm. "I don't want to fight any more!"

"Neither do I," said Spartacus, without raising his eyes. "But we have to!"

"Why?"

"To stay alive," said the Thracian, barely above a whisper.

While Alba was keeping the guard distracted, Polla went into the mess hall; Spartacus had his back to the entrance. She ran to the kitchens and looked out at him. Fortis had grabbed Spartacus by the shoulders and was shaking him. "To stay alive? What for, Spartacus? For what life?"

"Yours," said the Thracian. "You have nothing else, but you do have your life. Fight to keep it."

"You're going to kill me."

"I'm going to fight for my life, Fortis."

"It comes to the same thing!"

Spartacus grasped the Greek's hands and calmly removed them from his shoulders without apparent effort. He smiled a sad smile. "I won't start the fight."

"Neither will I," Fortis replied.

Spartacus looked at him for a moment, trying to meet his eyes. "Yes, you will. You'll strike the first blows."

Fortis collapsed on a table, his head on his arms. Just as Spartacus was coming over to put his hand on his shoulder, Fortis suddenly got up and ran toward the kitchens. Seeing the Greek come toward the door, Polla stepped aside. Fortis grabbed a skewer and ran back into the mess hall. Spartacus looked at Fortis and the weapon with surprise. Fortis was going from one gladiator to the next, yelling, "I don't want to fight! Kill me! Kill me!" Two of the gladiators seized hold of him and took the skewer. Puzzled, Spartacus went toward the kitchens. At the threshold, he gave a long look inside. Polla flattened herself against the wall. Spartacus stood there thoughtfully for a moment and then came back to the table.

"I don't want to fight any more! I don't want to fight any more!" Fortis was screaming as he struggled.

The guards came in and dressed the lines up with lash strokes. Spartacus went out, holding Fortis by the arm; Polla ran toward the door. She remained there a long time, leaning against the jamb. Alba went by several times. Polla did not even notice her. Intense, her hands clenched behind her, she kept repeating in a monotone, "Come back! Come back! Come back! . . ."

With the gladiators gone for the day, the kitchen and mess hall were empty. Evening came. Polla had fallen asleep, crouched against the doorjamb. Alba came and woke her. She took her to one of the cells reserved for couples, where Polla sat down, to wait again. The silent and greatly diminished ranks of the gladiators came back about midnight; the guards took them directly to their dormitories. A moment later, Spartacus came out, escorted by two guards, who led him to the couples' quarters. Spartacus had to bend down to go into the low cell. When the door was closed behind him, Spartacus moved forward on his knees. The tamped-earth floor was damp. A ray of moonlight came in through a narrow diagonal slit near the ceiling. The Thracian got to the opposite wall and looked around. He could not see Polla crouching in the darkest corner. Moaning softly, he lay down. Polla went to him on her knees and lay down at his side; she put her head on his chest. Spartacus' moans stopped. As she stroked Spartacus' arm, Polla suddenly drew back. Accustomed to the darkness of the cell, she could see his wound. Still on her knees, she went and fetched a ladle that still had a little water in it. She washed the wound and gave Spartacus to drink. Tenderly, she stroked the Thracian's face. "Your arm . . . Does it hurt?"

Without opening his eyes, Spartacus answered, "Yes, there." He pointed to his belly.

"You're wounded in the stomach!" Polla brought her hand to her mouth, in fright.

"There were a hundred of us," Spartacus said. "Now, there are only a handful left. It hurts . . . there!"

Polla pressed close to him; Spartacus stroked her hair.

"Spartacus, they scare me!" She looked at him. "Baliatus, the guards—they scare me!"

Spartacus raised his wounded arm and took her face in his hand. "Don't be afraid of them. When you meet them, look into their eyes. They're the ones who are afraid. Not you. You're just tired. Do you hear me? You're not scared, just tired . . . All of us are tired."

"Aren't you ever scared, Spartacus?" Polla asked in a whisper.

"Sure. I was scared until this morning . . . I've been scared every day, as far back as I can remember. I've been scared I wouldn't find what I wanted the most. . . . I want to go home, back to the country where I was born. Yes, that's what I want the most; to go back there. I want to use my strength for myself, for you, for the ones they make me kill. . . . To use my strength against evil."

Polla was listening. She was trembling. "I don't know any more whether I'm cold or scared," she said, as if to herself. "But . . . how do you know? . . ."

"I know," he said. His voice was grave and tender. He seemed to have caught his breath again. "I know," he said. "What makes us suffer is evil. I was scared just as long as I hadn't found out. . . . Now, I know."

He was stroking her hair; the moonlight glinted on it and in the depths of Polla's green eyes as she intently gazed at him. "You will get everything you want, Spartacus. I can read it on your face, in your eyes." She took his head, placed it gently on the ground and, slipping her arm under his waist, laid her head on Spartacus' belly. "Where were you bought?"

"In Rome . . . How about you?"

"In Rome. Have you ever been free?"

"Yes."

Polla raised her head, but asked no questions. She laid her head gently back on the Thracian's belly.

"That was so long ago!" he said.

Neither of them was used to talking. Their words came out as if thrown and they listened to them, a little surprised at their sound, at hearing themselves speak, at communicating. Or perhaps it was the tone they had selected in the silence, the solitude, and the night that surprised them. The warm tone of confidence. "I believe I had a good life then." Spartacus stopped. He ran his hand through Polla's hair. The dull sound of large drops of rain surprised them. They listened for a moment. Their coop suddenly lit up and the heavy, furious rumble broke out, very near. It was like a signal to all the other sounds of the night: the heavy rain increased, the trees came to life, and a scent of laved sand arose, wet, and was immediately followed, wafted on the wind, by the more subtle, almost tender, aroma of leaves still hot with sun and reviving in the rain. "Yes, I think I had a good life. I spoke to the sheep all day long. I didn't see anyone but them! I told them everything. When I was tired of being alone, I shouted as loud as I could and my shouts rolled off the mountainsides. . . . When I went very high up, I could see the sea, far, far away . . ." Spartacus broke off. When he resumed, his voice had changed, become hard and cold. "They came and took me away. My father was holding me by the arm; they killed him. They took the sheep away, too. To get back home, I ran away from their army; they caught me again. I met you at Brundisium and I escaped in Rome; I crossed the mountains, I got back home, but I couldn't stay there. They caught me again much later and I was sold in Rome, to Baliatus. . . . I've never stopped fighting!" Spartacus was still lying down, his eyes turned toward the narrow opening. "Your head keeps my belly warm," he said. He turned his head. "Why are you looking at me like that?"

"I feel better now."

"So do I."

She pressed her lips against the hollow of his hand. "I see a snake coiled around your face; that's a sign of strength."

Spartacus propped himself up on an elbow to look at her. "You've been initiated into the mysteries of Bacchus! My mother saw that snake, too, when I was born. He must have grown big by now!" Polla laughed. Her laugh rolled out, short, light, round, full. They looked at each other, surprised, moved, and Polla threw herself into Spartacus' arms. She laughed through her tears on his shoulder. "You said you were scared until this morning. Why this morning?"

Spartacus did not answer immediately. He was listening to the sounds of the storm. "This morning," he said, "there was a gladiator who refused to fight, Fortis."

"Yes, I saw him. I was in the kitchens. I . . . I didn't dare talk to you before the fight."

"You saw, he found a weapon!"

"Yes. The meat pin?"

Spartacus was sitting up, his back to the wall; he had taken Polla by the shoulders, and was whispering, rapidly. "I had never thought about the kitchen tools. Are there many of them?"

"Yes."

"Cleavers? Hooks? Skewers?"

"Yes."

Spartacus' eyes narrowed. He murmured, "Good. Very good."

"What are you going to do with them?"

"I don't know yet. . . . I'll tell you when the time comes."

"You plan to fight the guards?"

"We're going to get out of here."

He had spoken so low that Polla was not sure she had understood. When the meaning of the words finally made its way to her, she leaned forward, terrified, covering her mouth, to say, "What are you saying?"

"We have nothing to lose," said Spartacus. "And nothing to hope for if we stay here. Nothing! Nothing but death! . . . We have to get out of here, it's the only thing to do."

Polla bit her lower lip, her forehead wrinkled with worry. "But . . . how?"

"I don't know. Listen, less than a month ago, there were two hundred of us in my dormitory; we were planning a break, but someone talked. They took our weapons away. Tonight, the only ones left are Gannicus, Capito, me, and a few other veterans. The newcomers are being killed at the rate of almost a hundred a week! We have to get out! Fast!"

Polla was now calm again. She had listened to him intently, with eyes lowered. Now, she was looking at him, a bit sadly. She grasped his hand. "And . . . then?"

"Then?"

"After we get out, what?"

Spartacus leaned toward her. "We'll go home, to our own country."

"To Thrace?"

"Yes."

"What about the others?"

"Them? Well . . . they're Celts, Germans; they'll go back home, too, they'll do as they like. . . . But first we have to get out of here. Afterward, everything will be easy. So easy . . ."

ARENA

V

The next day, Spartacus came out of his cell with Polla. While she headed for the kitchens, the Thracian joined Gannicus, Capito, and those who were left of the group of veteran gladiators in their dormitory. He stepped aside with Gannicus. "I'm going to make a break."

"How?" the Celt asked calmly.

Spartacus spoke for a moment, then signaled to Capito; the conversation went on with the Samnite joining in.

In the afternoon, they were taken to the mess hall. The door leading to the training field had still not been put up. The newcomers were working out. In the distance, guards were sleeping in the shade of a wall. In front of the door leading to the yard, which remained open, two guards walked their posts without conviction. As soon as the gladiators were in, Spartacus ran to the kitchens, followed by Gannicus and Capito. They came back armed with several skewers and cleavers. Polla and Alba were following them. Several gladiators got up when they saw them. Gannicus signaled to them not to say anything and posted himself at one side of the door, with Capito on the other. Spartacus called out: "Guard!"

A guard ran up and came in sword in hand. Gannicus plunged his skewer into his back and the guard fell without a sound. Capito quickly pulled him aside and took his sandals, Gannicus his helmet and leggings, Spartacus his sword. They resumed their positions and went through the operation again. "Guard!"

Another guard came up and suffered the same fate. At Spartacus' third call, no one came. He stuck his head out; the yard was empty. The Thracian turned toward the other gladiators, who gathered around him.

"If you want to get out, take your weapons from the kitchens."

Everyone came back more or less well armed; those who had found nothing else carried either a stool held by one leg or a heavy tray.

"Now what?" Capito asked.

"We're going out. The guards and coaches are out on the field with the novices. There are probably a few guards at the entrance, along the fence. Hurry, before the newcomers come this way."

Gannicus was about to go out.

"Wait!" Spartacus said. "Put on one of the guards' tunics and keep an eye on those who are near the wall."

Gannicus stripped one of the guards and went out. As he walked back, he said, "They're drinking. Some of them are sleeping."

Spartacus turned toward the others. "We have to go out of the mess hall as if we were escorted by guards; from a distance, they'll see us marching in formation and won't suspect a thing." He turned toward the two women. "Have you eaten?"

"I couldn't," said Polla.

Alba had eaten.

"Take something along," Spartacus told Polla. "You have to eat."

"A fine time to eat!" Capito exclaimed. "Are you hungry?"

"Yes," Spartacus said, "always."

"He's thinking about food! Know what I'm thinking about? Freedom. Freedom . . . right out there!" Capito, with a big grin, was pointing to the door in front of which Gannicus was still keeping watch.

"Freedom is a lot farther than that," said Spartacus. And, as

Gannicus came by, "What are the guards doing, Gannicus?"

"They're singing. Quite a few of them are asleep," he repeated. Spartacus turned toward Polla. "Just keep close behind me."

"Yes."

The Thracian took Alba by the arm. "Will you be strong enough to run? To fight?"

Alba seemed rooted to the spot. "It's that door," she said. "Afterward I think I'll find the strength. . . . I'll have to. But it's that door!"

Spartacus took her hand and put his arm around Polla's shoulder. "Look. The door is open. It always has been. You go through it twenty times a day!" He stepped forward with Polla, but Alba remained where she was, unable to move. "I can't! I can't!" she said, desperately.

But the gladiators could not wait any longer; under the leadership of Gannicus who was wearing the dead guard's tunic and helmet, they were already lining up in the yard. Spartacus gently pushed Polla out and Capito placed her between the ranks. Spartacus turned and said softly, "Come, Alba!" At the same time, he held his hands out to her.

"Spartacus!" Capito called.

"Come, Alba!" the Thracian repeated.

Alba put her hands in his. Spartacus guided her slowly across the threshold, as one helps a child to walk. Alba threw herself into his arms, breaking into mingled sobs and laughter. Spartacus carried her as far as the ranks, which were already getting under way. "I really did make a fuss," Alba was saying, "about nothing at all."

Spartacus left her within the ranks and ran up the length of the column. He turned around. The novices were still training on the other side of the refectory. To the right, under the trees, some of the guards were singing; they had been drinking. The column speeded up when it got near the exit. A dozen guards were sitting in front of the gate. They raised their heads toward Gannicus who walked toward the first of them. The guard was opening his mouth; he did not get a chance to speak. The struggle lasted only a few seconds. The guards had not even had time to get to their feet; now they were lying in a pool of blood. The gladiators shoved them aside. At this time of the afternoon in the scorching heat—with no games scheduled, a few hours before bath time—the Capuans had no reason to be anywhere near the distant streets around the gladiators' camp, where under any circumstances all commerce was forbidden. Marching faster and faster, then running, the group of fugitives went down a first street, leading south. Spartacus, Gannicus, and Capito kept the pace under control. When they reached an intersection, they halted the column; on the ground a child was playing with a big red-furred cat. He looked up at the men and said to his cat, "Look at the gladiators!" Spartacus turned around; he stood a head taller than all the others. "Don't run!" he told them. "If we must fight . . ." They resumed their march. Coming up the now-straggling ranks of the column, Polla took up a place beside Spartacus. As they arrived at another street corner, one startled woman exclaimed at seeing them. Another woman came out of a courtyard, straightened a strand of her hair and exclaimed in turn. A cookshop owner, in his stain-covered apron, carving fork in hand, watched them openmouthedly, pinned to the spot.

The fugitives invaded his shop and came out armed with knives, skewers, cleavers, long meat hooks. The cook watched them go off, sitting on the ground before his shop; he suddenly jumped up, waving his fork, and started to run after the fugitives. "Help! I've been robbed! Help!"

The shouting was now increasing, announcing the arrival of this silent, fierce troop, dressed in bloodstained rags. When the fugitives reached the marketplace, some twenty guards of the local cohort came out of the inns. The fugitives swiftly attacked them, without giving them time to recover from their surprise, and crushed them almost without slowing down. The Capuans' siesta had been irretrievably interrupted by the time the guards marched out of the city through the South Gate. Rudely awakened from their naps, their stomachs still heavy with their noonday meals, the men marched out in an ugly mood.

On the way, some thirty of the fugitives armed themselves further by looting a weapons convoy destined for a neighboring gladiators' school. But still all of the escapees were not armed. There were seventy-three of them; ten or so still had only sticks, skewers, or cleavers. The looting of the convoy had slowed their progress and allowed the guards to get closer. There were a little over two hundred soldiers. Gannicus saw them. The fugitives kept going for a while, but Spartacus drew them up at a bend in the road. Gannicus and Capito took half the troop and went to hide behind the bushes. Spartacus went on with the remainder. The guards reached the bend at the double, out of breath; at their head, their commander could see Spartacus' section marching up the middle of the road. Two of the fugitives had a moment's hesitation; they threw away their weapons and ran over to the guards who butchered them without listening to them. The young commander shouted an order. The guards deployed, surrounding the group, which had halted. The commander had chosen the only possible tactic. He gave another order and the battle was on. Gannicus, Capito, and their section charged, killing from behind. Inside, the circle of soldiers was closing in dangerously. The fugitives were having trouble finding room to strike back. Spartacus succeeded in breaking out on one flank and was suddenly face to face with Gannicus' men. Taking a mace from the hands of a fallen man, and now having all the room he needed, he swung it quickly around him, opening another gap toward the middle. The guards retreated, relieving the section in the middle which charged while Gannicus' men continued to harry the flanks. The commander found himself at the head of a squad of about twenty, separated from his main body. He gave another order. In vain. His men, encircled in small groups, had no chance of escaping the slaughter. Throwing off his helmet, he started to run away, followed by his group of survivors. There was nothing more he could do. Giving no quarter, the fugitives were cutting down his encircled command. Spartacus turned toward him. About fifty paces apart, they were facing each other. Two guards ran toward the Thracian; Spartacus flung his mace without apparent effort, almost without moving. The first one was hit in the chest, dragging the other down with him. For a moment, Spartacus gazed at the young helmetless, disarmed commander. On the road, the battle was still going on; picking up his mace, he ran to the aid of Gannicus, who was now surrounded.

The young commander watched the scene, mouth agape, powerless, fascinated. The Thracian was cutting his men down with rapid, well-aimed blows of the mace. Among the encircled guards, someone recognized him and called out his name: "Spartacus! It's Spartacus!" There was a brief lull in the fighting and those among the guards who could get away ran toward their commander; those who stayed and fought were slaughtered on the spot.

Without any hurry, the fugitives took the weapons, sandals, leggings, helmets, and shields of the guards they had brought down. The commander was perplexed. He looked at his wounded, demoralized men; out of two hundred, he had barely fifty left. And they were in a sad state. Now, the fugitives were armed, and marching upon him. To make a stand would be suicidal for his little troop. The commander ordered retreat. As he turned and ran, he saw that his men had not waited for him.

Spartacus stopped the pursuers. "Where are you running to?" he yelled. The men looked at him. He shouted, "Now we're much better armed. If they attack us, we can defend ourselves." The fugitives came back and bunched around him, shouting for joy. "Look what we did with a lot of sticks and skewers," Spartacus went on, pointing to the guards lying in their own blood. "Now let's get away from the city; let's find a safe place." He looked about him. In the distance, the dark mass of Vesuvius stood out, its steep, slippery slopes covered with wild vines. He pointed in that direction and the column moved off, walking, jumping, running. On the way, they looted and burned a farm which the slaves who were working it did not try to defend. Two of them asked the fugitives where they were going. "Over there!" one of them said, pointing to Vesuvius. The two slaves joined them. Gannicus asked them why they were leaving their companions. "To go back home, to Gaul."

"Whose farm is that?" asked Spartacus.

"Whose are any of the farms around here?" answered the slave. "Crassus'. This one and all the others."

In front of the gate of the latifundium, Spartacus looked up; the sun was setting in the sea. Without a word, he set off again, with Polla and Alba at his sides. Everyone fell in behind. The moon was shining high above when they reached the foot of Vesuvius.

ARENA

VI

Once back in Capua, the commander of the local guard called at the praetor's. He was informed that the magistrate had been invited to the estate of General Crassus, at Suessa Aurunca, nine leagues northwest of Capua. It was a long ride, and night was falling. The commander dispatched a messenger to announce that he would call next morning and sent for Lentulus Baliatus. Thereupon he took every necessary precaution, ordering the city gates closed and guarded by some thirty militiamen and citizen-volunteers who would be paid a few denarii for the night watch.

The lanista came an hour later, breathless, perspiring, looking appalled. The commander had just finished his bath; slaves were bustling about him, making his bed, setting the table.

"What an honor for humble Baliatus," said the lanista with a bow. "What . . . What do you wish from me, Lord Galba?"

"Humble Baliatus!"

The commander picked up a whip and poked the promoter's fat belly. "Your vanity is as great as your belly."

"They killed more than twenty of my guards!" Baliatus moaned, holding his stomach.

"They killed a hundred and fifty of mine!" Galba thundered. "Why weren't you prepared for this escape?"

"But, milord, I never even thought of it. An escape, indeed! I have guards! They would have warned me!"

"Well, where were your wonderful guards today?"

"On the training field, milord. The escapees killed the other ones, the ones who were guarding the gate."

The commander was pacing, a towel wrapped around his waist. He went and poured himself a glass of wine and gulped it down. "It's always the same story with you lanistae."

"Yes, milord," said Baliatus.

"Yes, milord . . . Yes, milord . . ." The commander once again shoved the whip handle into the fat belly. "No matter how the insurrection comes about, it's never possible to find the true causes. How many escapees are there?"

"Seventy-three, milord. And two women."

"And who is that man—that Spartacus?"

"My finest gladiator, milord."

"Where does he come from?"

"Thrace . . . I think."

"Where did you buy him?"

"In Rome."

"Did you declare him?"

"Of course, milord, most certainly."

"Nothing certain about it at all!" Galba shouted. "I know you never declare the consignments of slaves that land on the coast."

"There's nothing illegal about them, milord."

The commander advanced on Baliatus, who backed up against the wall, and shoved his whip hard into the belly of the lanista, who gasped for breath. "No, there's nothing illegal about them, lanista. Quite the contrary. But there is a head tax on every one of them. When was the last time you paid it?"

"I . . . I couldn't say, milord," said Baliatus, sweating profusely.

The commander shoved the whip further in. The lanista opened his mouth, gasping for breath.

"Oh yes, you can say, Baliatus; you're going to tell me right away!"

Baliatus was breathing with difficulty. "I . . . I made a special agreement with . . . with the lord who sponsors the games."

The commander withdrew his whip. He paced up and down a moment and came back to the lanista. "I'm keeping my eye on you, Baliatus. As soon as the lord you refer to stops sponsoring the games, I'll be around to inspect your school."

"Yes, milord." With downcast eyes, Baliatus went on, "Lord Galba, I should feel most honored if . . . if you were to consent to call on me every day . . . early in the morning."

The commander blanched. Baliatus waited with downcast eyes, his hands clasped over his belly. Galba smiled briefly. "The duties of my office do not permit me to go out early in the morning, lanista. But you might send me one of your guards with . . ."

"Yes, certainly . . . that's a very good idea, milord. I'll send you a guard, starting tomorrow morning."

The commander sat down at the table, and a slave immediately served him.

"I won't be home tomorrow morning, lanista; but your guard can just leave his . . . message."

"Yes, milord."

The commander waved his hand and Baliatus backed out through the door, bowing and scraping as he went.

Before daybreak, the commander left Capua for Suessa Aurunca, accompanied by ten guards. When he got there, Crassus was bathing in his pale pink marble pool; it was rectangular, with shallow steps on both sides leading down into highly perfumed water. The slender marble columns surrounding it supported the vault of a portico decorated with a mosaic depicting the funeral of Patroclus. To the right, the portico turned in front of the west façade of the villa; on this façade, all the potentialities of blue had been explored in a monochrome mosaic design, without any subject, made up of simple horizontal stripes. The stripes started at the top of the vault with the palest blue and ended in deep blue at the bottom of the wall; the floor began with the same sustained blue, graduating to pale blue at the foot of the columns and going back through the scale to deep blue at the edge of the pool. At the south, the portico opened on to a festival of flowers which seemed conscious of their importance in the design of the garden. The light seemed to be coming from within the flower bed, from the flowers themselves, generously reflected by the petals for all to enjoy. And the flowers looked like proudly adorned ladies, gathered for some kind of silent contest. They looked inspired. They had talent. In order better to bring out the luxuriousness of color in the flower bed without disturbing the eye, the floor mosaic of the galleria was of the same pure white as the columns. To the east, the mosaic of the vault depicted the farewell of Hector and Andromache and the floor was wrought in the same blue stripes as faced the façade of the villa. The galleria opened on to the sea that could be heard rolling at the bottom of a hill on which rows of olive, orange, and lemon trees stretched as far as the eye could see. To the north, finally, along the entire width of the pool, surmounting three shallow steps several paces wide, were three arches designed by Alexander for his friend Crassus: on either side, a narrow raised arch framing a sculpture of Crassus' father and brother; in the center, a much wider semicircular arch shining with the name of Flora in long wrought-gold lettering.

A gentle breeze was blowing from the south. It was nearly noon, everything seemed asleep within the domain. Most of the slaves were in the fields, while the household servants were busy in the kitchens, housecleaning, or secretly snatching an hour's rest in the shade of the barns. The birds seemed to be flustered by the noise of a scraper polishing a slab somewhere in the right wing of the villa.

A young slave came running out of the house; he went along the portico in front of the façade and down the steps leading to the water. Crassus looked at him. "Lord Cnaeus Baebius Galba, commander of the guard."

Crassus swam over to the slave. "I'll see him here."

He came out of the water. His chest was covered with black hair. His legs and thighs, too. Crassus was then forty-two years old. A trace of plumpness was threatening at his waist and, despite fine proportions, the over-all line was rather heavy. He glanced at his belly and rapidly ran his hands over it. Crassus was tall. Over six feet. His rectangular face was handsome, but there was something amiss; short, curly hair ill concealed a scar that cut his forehead straight along the whole hairline, from temple to temple. His thick black eyelashes fell vertically over his eyes, like curtains, making Crassus hold his head back in order to see. With its high forehead, the nose slender between the eyes but broad and bulging at the base, the thick lips but small mouth, the prominent frontal arch further accentuated by thick eyebrows, his face expressed a singular combination of barbarism and culture, passion and intelligence, refinement and brutality. His tutor, Alexander, had taught him Greek literature and the art of eloquence, courses which his father the censor had strictly supervised. Thanks to his brother, Crassus also excelled at hunting, archery, and javelin throwing, rode bareback for hours at a time, and swam powerfully, with his broad, muscular shoulders and slender legs—perhaps too slender in proportion to his torso.

Crassus came out of the water. A naked little boy with black curly hair came over to him, carrying a red-and-white robe and a pair of matching sandals. Crassus did not put them on. He started to run naked around the pool, in short strides, raising his knees very high. The little boy's laughter echoed through the galleria. Marking time, he began to imitate Crassus, and his laughter increased as Crassus came nearer. Crassus passed in front of him. Without slowing down, he said in a threatening voice, "You think that's funny, Sicinio!" Still laughing, with the robe and sandals in his hands, the boy started to run behind Crassus, aping his stride. Crassus suddenly turned around and grabbed him by the wrist. "Aha! Making fun of Lord Crassus, Sicinio!" The child was now laughing as he was trying to break away; Crassus threw aside the robe and sandals and, holding the boy by both wrists, dragged him toward the pool. "No! No! Not in the water!" With one arm, Crassus dangled him above the pool. Through his laughter, the child was yelling, "Not in the water! Not in the water!"

Crassus dipped the boy's feet into the pool. "It's cold, Sicinio." Crassus set him on the edge. "Go get some lemonade for me from Mamita." The child ran off. Crassus picked up the robe and put it around him. Then he started running again, under the arch, onto the long L-shaped terrace which extended beyond the pool and turned behind the villa; he leaped over several stone benches, came back under the great white arch erected in honor of Flora and lay down on some cushions in front of which Sicinio had placed a jug of lemonade and a goblet.

Galba was coming up to him, looking gloomy. Crassus smiled at him. "What's wrong, friend Baebius?" he asked. "Did you see a monster?"

"Some gladiators escaped, milord."

"Weren't you able to stop them? Sit down."

Galba was not ready with an answer. "I saw Baliatus," he said, "and I . . ."

"Who's that? The lanista?"

"Yes, milord."

"Go on, Baebius. And sit down, you're blocking out all my sun!"

"But . . . I had also hoped to see the praetor! I . . ."

"He had too much to eat last night," said Crassus, with a look of disgust. "He's sick. Go on with your story."

"According to Baliatus, there were guards everywhere; in front of the gate, in front of the refectory, on the training field, and along the fences. I'm familiar with the gladiators' school, milord; it is well guarded."

"If you're trying to tell me that the lanista has nothing to gain from an escape, you're wasting your time; I know that. It costs a lot to train a gladiator. So—what happened?"

"He doesn't know a thing about it."

Crassus gave a hard, impatient laugh. "I'm not interested in his explanation. I want yours—as commander of the Capuan guard!" He laughed. "As the one responsible for maintaining order."

"But I don't know a thing about it, either, milord! I wasn't at the lanista's when the gladiators made their break. I was in my quarters, preparing for today's exercise, when I heard shouts. One of my men came in to tell me that the gladiators had escaped and that they had massacred about twenty guards in the marketplace."

"When did they escape?"

"A little after noon."

"Hmm! Where were your guards? Off drinking and making love?"

"Some in the palace quarters and others in the garrison."

"Did you go after the gladiators?"

"Immediately. They left by way of the South Gate and seized a weapons convoy belonging to another lanista; before that, they looted a cookshop."

"How many men did you take with you?"

"Two hundred."

"Every man you had, eh?"

"Yes, milord. Just about."

"How many gladiators escaped?"

"According to Baliatus, seventy-three, plus two women."

"Did you catch up with them?"

"Yes."

"I can see from looking at you that you're not . . . Do you have many wounded?"

"Many dead, milord."

"How many?"

Galba hesitated.

"How many dead, commander?" Crassus repeated sharply.

"A hundred and fifty, milord."

Little Sicinio came back with some fruit and another goblet. Crassus took a piece of fruit. Galba was sweating under his tunic, looking yearningly at the cool pool. Crassus poured himself a goblet of lemonade and resumed his pacing. He suddenly turned around. "Seventy-three men plus two women . . . Stop making such a face! If you're thirsty, help yourself. A hundred and fifty militiamen killed! Hmm! I realize they were up against gladiators, but . . . where are they now?"

"They headed in the direction of Mount Vesuvius. I sent some men that way last night; I should know where the gladiators are as soon as I get back to town."

"Do they have a leader?"

"I don't know. My men recognized a gladiator they call Spartacus; the fugitives have . . ."

Crassus was no longer listening to him. "Spartacus! The mirmillo! . . ." Crassus took another piece of fruit. "Of course, he was the best of the lot. Brave, clear-headed, determined. He didn't salute the praetorian box before the fight. A leader . . ." Suddenly, he stopped. "Toward Mount Vesuvius, you say?"

"Yes, milord."

"In that case, they went by my farms!"

"I don't know, milord."

Crassus motioned to Sicinio, who came running up. "Tell the praetor I want to see him at once." He started pacing again. "Keep the city gates closed, Baebius. Day and night."

"I've already seen to that, milord."

"Well, good. Very good. Absolutely no one is to leave the city without a written permit from the praetor. Send a brief report to Rome. As short as possible. But clear! Very clear! The senators get lots of reports; they appreciate them short and clear."

"Yes, milord."

"They should be informed simply. Escape, date, time. Number of gladiators . . . As for the guard, let's skip embarrassing details; let's say . . . the local guard was dispatched in pursuit of the fugitives, but . . . but the gladiators succeeded in getting away. Leave that part as vague as possible. Uh . . . in view of the uneasiness of the notables—they'll know that means me, but you never know what hands these reports fall into—in view of the uneasiness of the notables, you urgently beg the senators to send you reinforcements at their earliest convenience. Will you know how to make out that report?"

"Yes, milord."

"I want to see those dogs butchered."

"Yes, milord."

"Quick!"

"Yes, milord."

Since Sulla's abdication, the Senate theoretically held all police powers. But, the dictator having methodically carried out the demilitarization of Italy, the consuls no longer had any legions at their disposal. The wars, against Lepidus at home, Sertorious in Spain, and Mithridates—who had started acting up again in Asia at the beginning of the winter—had virtually exhausted the best manpower available through conscription. The Senate therefore held all the police powers, but could not exercise them, since Sulla and the immediate needs had taken all speed and efficiency away from their repressive action.

When Galba's message reached the Senate, the supreme council could therefore dispatch only three thousand men recruited among the very young of the city and the unemployed, to be led by propraetor Claudius Glaber. These mercenaries were not frightened by a fugitive-slave hunt. They were in for a march of several weeks, but as long as they were paid and fed . . .

Hearing the news in Rome, Alexander immediately left the bathhouse, took four Nubians and a dozen porters from Crassus' and left for Suessa Aurunca. As soon as he saw Crassus, he asked him who had sent the call for reinforcements to the Senate.

"I did. That is, I virtually dictated it."

"That's what I was afraid of. It's a serious mistake, Marcus."

"Why?"

"Because it gives too much importance to this escape."

"Too much importance! They burned one of my farms near Nola!"

"That's a great loss, Marcus, but, if they had been left to their fate, the gladiators would merely have become a few more individual bandits roaming the country. In having them chased down, you force them to remain together, to fight as a body. You were not thinking of the example they . . ."

"What example? They're runaway dogs! They have to be butchered, that's all."

"It's not that easy."

"Glaber, the propraetor, has three thousand men."

"Your Galba had two hundred guards."

Crassus laughed. "That makes twenty-eight hundred more."

"No, Galba had guards. Glaber has only idlers, unemployed, Roman street loafers."

"But there are only seventy gladiators, Alexander."

"How do you know?"

"Galba told me, my friend."

"He told you there were seventy of them when they left Capua. But how many are there now? News gets around fast among the slaves, especially in the South where they've been kept in groups. Today, all of Latium, all of Campania know who Spartacus is and where he is. News grows as it travels, from mouth to ear, at each step. All slaves more or less dream of escaping, but now there is a new fact: Spartacus and his gladiators made it. They are an example of success; a chance to be free now appears possible to the slaves."

"Oh, be quiet, professor; you've never understood our system. Let's go to dinner and . . ."

"I don't accept oppression, because I've been subjected to it!"

"Precisely. Having spent your childhood in slavery has made you too subjective. You see many necessities with the eyes of . . ."

"Say it, Marcus. With the eyes of a slave."

"Well, that's the fact."

"That's also why I understand the state of mind of the runaway slave. To say nothing of that of the gladiator."

Crassus burst out laughing. "As if there were any difference!"

"A great one, Marcus. The gladiator makes a break because his fate always dangles from the point of his sword, if he's lucky; it can also often be at the mercy of a whim, dependent on which way the praetor's thumb points. He breaks out because he can no longer stand the suspense of the unforeseeable, but as soon as he decides to escape the unforeseeable disappears. Suddenly, he has a destiny—of his own choosing. The escape may cost him his life, but its loss will no longer have been in vain. All he has is his life, but now it belongs to him. For the ordinary slave, it's quite another matter. It's probably much more difficult for him to make up his mind than it is for the gladiator, because his life is not daily in jeopardy in the arena. Once he does escape, he has something: his life is no longer the property of a master. It leads somewhere. He may not know where, but he heads straight for it, master of his own steps. That was all he had been missing."

"Such subtleties! Let's go to dinner and forget the whole thing."

Alexander kept talking about it all during dinner, and Crassus had to listen to him. When Alexander, in his excitement, said, "This dispatch of reinforcements may have the most far-reaching consequences in the history of Rome," Crassus roared with laughter.

"You've been drinking too much, Alexander. You no longer know what you're saying."

"And suppose the gladiators were to hold their own against Glaber?"

"Seventy of them against three thousand?"

"Yes. Assuming there still are only seventy of them."

"Impossible. They don't stand a chance."

"That may be. But just suppose they do crush Glaber."

Crassus smiled. "If seventy gladiators can defeat three thousand men, we'd better send them against Mithridates. You've had enough to drink, let's go to bed."

"You didn't answer me."

"There is nothing to answer; you're drunk."

Alexander stood up, a goblet of wine in his hand. "You know perfectly well that I can drink a barrel of wine and still recite Aristotle until I'm stopped."

"That's true, the more you drink, the better you recite. Which means you're crazy."

"All right. I'm crazy. And drunk, if you like."

He came and stood before his friend and looked at him solemnly. "Promise me one thing, Marcus."

Crassus smiled. "Anything you want, but tomorrow. Right now, I'm going to bed."

"No. You don't go to sleep until you've promised."

Crassus got up. "Let me through. You're no longer amusing."

"No. You're not getting through."

Crassus looked at him. Alexander set the goblet down. "You won't get through, I'm stronger than you are. Promise."

Crassus laughed nervously. "Very well, I promise. What do you want?"

"Do you . . . solemnly promise?"

"I solemnly promise."

"Good."

Crassus waited a moment. "Now, what do you want?"

"I forgot."

"Well, then, let me through, Alexander."

"No. Wait . . . It's coming back to me. I want you to promise me that you'll keep out of this gladiator business."

"Yes, yes, I promise."

"Because, you understand, Marcus, my pupil . . . Marcus Licinius, I'm proud of you."

Crassus smilingly took his arm. "Come on, Alexander, I'm exhausted, and by tomorrow you'll have forgotten all about it."

"Exhausted? What have you done? I'm the one who travels, and you get all tired out!"

"Alexander, you've been talking to me about the same thing all night long without any objectivity whatsoever. Come on, it'll soon be daylight!"

"Already!"

Crassus sighed. "Come on, I'll take you to your room." As he was about to leave, Alexander stopped him again. "You promised!"

Crassus yawned his reply. "Yes, yes, I promised."

Alexander let go of his robe.

ARENA

VII

Propraetor Claudius Glaber derived no pleasure from the mission he had been given. His men were soldiers in appearance only. After the first day's march, for want of training and discipline, they had covered no more than five leagues. The burning sun did not make the march any easier, and the troop reached Capua several days late with bleeding feet and demoralized.

Glaber was not without military ability, nor ideas, but what could he do with so wretched a lot! When Galba informed him that there were no more than seventy fugitives for him to fight, he felt relieved. He announced to his men that they outnumbered the enemy forty to one and granted them two days' rest.

They had been gone from Rome for two weeks when they reached the foot of the steep slopes of Vesuvius. Head-on assault would probably be costly, so Glaber decided to lay siege to Spartacus and his men. The indications were that it would be an easy campaign. Confident in their numbers and physically restored, the soldiers sang as they took up their positions. The sky was clear, the sea blue, rations arrived regularly. They gaily set up their tents at the foot of the only accessible slope. The other mountainsides being considered too steep to be used by the fugitives, Glaber conscientiously posted sentries at the foot of the slope, a hundred yards from the entrance to the camp. Torches were lit and wine, illicitly bought in Capua, was passed from group to group, bringing song and laughter to everyone's lips . . .

From the top of Vesuvius, the fugitives looked at the camp. Spartacus sat dreamily beside Polla, watching the little lights of the torches dancing in the distance, all the way below. The wind wafted up the sound of laughter or a snatch of song. The siege had begun. Spartacus' war, too. The fugitives gradually went back to their bushes. Polla and Spartacus had remained with Gannicus and Capito, gazing at the camp. They were engulfed in the inhabited silence of the Campanian night, redolent of olive groves and fisheries, brought by the mingled winds from the coast and the interior. Polla was lying on her back, her head resting in Spartacus' lap. The regular breathing and the surrender of sleep lent a swollen pout to her lips, perhaps reinforced by her detached expression of confidence. Her sleep, her mouth, the curved, raised line of her lashes underlining the darkness of her eyelids, betrayed a sensual longing, an expectation of sexual discovery, a secret desire for fulfillment. The knitted brows alone, perhaps, suggested some anxiety, some frailty.

"What are we going to do?"

Capito had whispered. His hands were flat on either side of his thighs, his legs dangling, his head tilted a bit forward and hunched into his shoulders; his words did not express his thoughts as much as did his whole body. Gannicus was standing between Capito and Spartacus, legs spread, hands clasped behind his back, forehead creased by a deep, round furrow. "We'll have to fight." The Celt had tossed the words out as he might have kicked a pebble with the tip of his foot, but his frown suggested questions that were not answered by his contempt for the battle.

"They don't want to let us get away," said Spartacus. Capito turned his head. "What?"

"We have to get away," Spartacus said.

"How?"
"I don't know."

From Nola to Capua, from Cumae to Pompeii, everyone knew that three thousand soldiers sent from Rome were laying siege to the Capuan gladiators on Mount Vesuvius. Tradesmen had pitched their tents around the camp, taking advantage of the siege to sell food and drinks. Pimps had sent in their women for whose favors the soldiers gambled away their pay while awaiting their turn among the whores' tents.

Two days went by. Up above, hunger was setting in. The fugitives spent their days sitting at the top of the slope, watching Glaber's camp. On the third day, a group of them decided to venture an attack that evening. "There are more than two thousand of them!" said Gannicus.

"There won't be any less tomorrow!" someone retorted. "Nor the day after!"

For his part, Spartacus was walking about, trying to find a solution that continued to evade him. He had crossed Vesuvius from one steep edge to the other more than a hundred times in every direction. On the other side of the peak from Glaber's camp, the rock sheered off perpendicularly to a wooded slope leading right into the sea. Immersed in thought, Spartacus caught his foot in a tangle of vine shoots and fell forward. Picking himself up, he released his foot by cutting several stems; he took one of them and tried to break it by tugging at it with both hands, but the vine shoot would not give. He then looked around him; wild vines covered the entire surface of the top of Vesuvius. He ran back to camp. The group who had decided to go that night were not interested in listening. Spartacus explained his idea to Gannicus, Capito, Alba, and Polla. They cut the most flexible vine shoots they could find and set themselves in a circle, placing the stems end to end. About two hours after sunset, the group that were planning to try the breakthrough came toward them. "Are you with us?"

"No."

They were not interested in waiting for the rope to be finished, and began their descent on the camp. They advanced cautiously, but this descent, dangerous enough in broad daylight, proved impossible by night. One of the fugitives made a misstep on what he had taken for the shadow of a rock that turned out to be a hole. Without a word, he rolled like a stone, gaining speed, hurtling into a branch here, banging against a rock there. A sentry raised his eyes at the noise; others had also heard it and ran over. The fugitive was falling like a lead ball; he crashed into a tree, unconscious. He was slaughtered on the spot. Another came down in the same manner, but he put up a good fight for his life, killing two men and wounding three others with his sword. Now, the camp was on the alert. When the other runaways got down, they were crushed by sheer weight of numbers. One of them had succeeded in stopping halfway down the slope, against a rock. He tried in vain to climb back up. At daybreak, one of the sentries saw him and shot him with an arrow. The soldiers spent the whole day celebrating, and Glaber, certain now of easy victory, did nothing but eat, while soaking his feet in water.

Despite the heat and the thirst which had gotten the better of the weakest ones, the runaways worked all day long. By the evening of the third day, they had completed a long rope, on which they made knots about a foot apart. Taking advantage of the fact that the moon was lighting up the other face of Vesuvius, they made their descent and reassembled in the wood at the foot of the volcano, then skirted around it. All the sentries were dispatched without their making a single sound.

Going forward in silence, the fugitives got close to the tents. In the first, they slaughtered six men while they slept. In the second, a well-aimed trident nailed an officer to the woman he was embracing. Thus surprised in the middle of the night, the besiegers succumbed in large numbers and their tents went up in smoke. One of them, unable to sleep and tossing on his pallet, saw Capito come at him, wild-looking, spattered with blood. The man screamed before dying from a mace-blow that smashed his skull. His yell awoke the camp and precipitated a panic. The soldiers came running from their tents, practically naked. The fugitives ran about, screaming as they struck, egged on by the soldiers' terror.

Claudius Glaber did not even try regrouping his men; the

attackers were coming on much too fast and giving no quarter. Seeing their leader run away, followed by his officers, the soldiers took to their heels after them, running as fast as they could through the night and the confusion. The tradesmen's tents were looted and the prostitutes who fell into the hands of the victors were forced to submit without a word; the fugitives ate and drank to their hearts' content among the burning tents and the fallen standards. Before daybreak, they had salvaged the best of the tents and bagfuls of food and clothing. The drunken men regrouped as best they could, dragging the whores behind them. In order to be able to keep a lookout on the surrounding country, they decided to go halfway up the slope, on the accessible side of Vesuvius, where they pitched their tents.

Contrary to all expectations, the fugitives had won. The news of their victory spread rapidly and had considerable repercussion. It was related in Capua by Glaber, who, in his discomfiture, had to exaggerate the number of runaways in order not to appear utterly ridiculous, and when it reached Rome the praetor Varinius set out at the head of an army of six thousand men, consisting of young recruits and veterans. At the same time, hundreds of escaped slaves from all over Campania came and joined the former gladiators, along with cowherds and shepherds from surrounding estates, and gladiators who had been encouraged by the example of those from Capua. Their leaders marched ahead of them: two Celts, Crixos and Oenomaos, and two Germans, Magnus and Leo.

The question of command had never arisen among the Capuan escapees; Spartacus, Gannicus, and Capito seemed to enjoy the confidence of their companions, who followed them without questioning their decisions. All the more so after the victory over the besiegers. Therefore, when the new group of gladiators joined theirs and the Celt, Crixos, asked to speak to their leader, they quite naturally turned to Spartacus the Thracian, Gannicus the Celt, and Capito the Samnite.

"Where do you intend to go?" Crixos asked Spartacus.

"We want to leave the country," Spartacus replied.

Crixos turned to his lieutenants and they discussed the matter at length.

"Where do you intend to go?" Crixos repeated.

"I can only answer for myself," said the Thracian. "I want to go back to my own country."

"And the others?"

"To theirs, I suppose."

Crixos held another parley with his followers. He was as tall as Spartacus, but much heavier. His very long red hair was tied behind his head and reached down to the small of his back. A bushy mustache, lighter than his hair, merged into the double-pointed beard that Crixos curled and smoothed as he spoke. This seemed to be a habit of his whenever he was thinking. Such was the case at the moment. Magnus, Oenomaos, and Leo having left the final decision to him, Crixos turned to Spartacus and signaled to him to step aside. The others remained there, facing each other, waiting without mistrust, yet on their guard, for the outcome of the talk between their leaders.

"How many of you are there?" Crixos asked.

"With your people, close to seven thousand."

"Now that we're alone, tell me, where do you intend to go?"

"Everyone to his own country . . . I'm going back to Thrace."

Crixos sat down on a rock and smoothed the points of his beard; Spartacus remained standing.

"I heard about you in Pompeii, after you beat Blamma the Samnite."

Spartacus was gazing into the distance, toward the sea. He did not reply.

"But I don't know you, Spartacus."

"No, you don't know me."

"Is Thrace far away?"

"Yes, very far."

"When are you planning to leave?"

"Tomorrow night . . . maybe tonight. First I want to find out what's going on in Capua, Cumae, and Pompeii."

Crixos stood up, surprised. "You mean to go back to Capua?"

"No. I plan to send one or two men there to bring back the news."

"And . . . you'll wait here for them?"

"They'll find us easily enough, wherever we are."

"In other words, you have no plans?"

"We can't make any, Crixos. I want to go back home. By what route? How? I don't know. I'll have to go up north, cross the mountains. But in between, I don't . . . Look!" A troop was advancing toward the volcano, raising a cloud of dust as it marched. "Who among your men is familiar with Capua?"

"I don't know."

They ran back to the others. Magnus and Leo were familiar with Capua, having long been employed there in the perfumeries and at cleaning the circus. Spartacus pointed out the troop to them; the sun was glinting on its weapons. "Go into Capua, Cumae, and Pompeii. Find out what's going on. Try to find out what they're planning."

The two men set off at once; Spartacus and Crixos decided on their battle tactics. They split their army into two parts. One of them went deep into the woods between Vesuvius and the sea, while the other moved toward the north and deployed into the woods. The tactics were simple: when the advancing troop had gone by, the fugitives would attack it from the north on one flank and at the rear; the troop would then fall back toward the sea and be attacked from the south by the other group of fugitives. The Romans would be surrounded and have to fight with their backs to the sea. In case of a setback, the fugitives could quickly take cover in the woods.

Praetor Varinius was approaching with his six thousand men. In his haste to avenge the defeat of Claudius Glaber, Varinius, unaware that the runaway forces had grown from seventy to seven thousand in a few days, made a serious mistake: he split his army into three columns of two thousand men each.

The first group, the one that Spartacus had seen marching up, was under the command of the legate Furius. Like Glaber, the legate came head on, confident because of the number of his men. They were surrounded and, with their backs to the sea, hacked to pieces.

The second detachment was led by the legate Cossinius who, since the sun was setting, halted his men along the coast; while the tents were being set up, the legate went for a swim, convinced that the runaway slaves would never dare attack them, and equally sure that Furius had already put them to the sword. While he was bathing, the fugitives in the twilight attacked his soldiers, who were exhausted by the forced marches in the sun and had almost completely undressed. This second detachment suffered the same fate as Furius', but even more rapidly. The faces of the dead reflected amazement, as if something they had never dreamed possible had suddenly materialized before them.

The seven thousand slaves, now wild and covered with blood, continued their offensive by attacking the praetor himself. The battle was joined in a great clash of swords and one overwhelming yell. Varinius' horse stepped back too quickly, reared, and threw its rider. Terrified by the melee, the horse ran away, knocking men down in its path. Varinius had lost his horse, but he was still surrounded by his lictors. Seeing him move to the rear, the Celts under Crixos rushed in pursuit, scattering the praetor's army as they went. Varinius succeeded in getting away with his quaestor while his lictors were killed one after the other in front of the little defile through which he had decided to go and which his officers defended to the death. Harassed, the small groups of isolated soldiers had to take their chances trying to flee. Some of them dived into the water; many more ran off into the woods. Dispersed during the fight, they never regrouped, and deserted by the hundreds.

Varinius and his quaestor Thoranius stopped at Cumae, where the praetor hoped he would be able to regroup his army; he waited all night long. A few hundred veterans reported in, but by dawn it was evident that the young recruits had deserted.

ARENA

VIII

Ashamed of such a defeat and fearing the sarcasm of the senators, Varinius preferred to send his quaestor to Rome to explain the seriousness of the situation. Thoranius set out immediately, but instead of going straight along the coast to Suessa Aurunca he decided to run the risk of going through the woods to Capua, where he asked to see the praetor. This magistrate was away at Crassus', in Suessa Aurunca. Thoranius waited all day for him. The praetor did not come back until very late in the evening; he received Thoranius at once. He was dumbfounded by the news. "But . . . how could you have been beaten? There were six thousand of you against a bunch of slaves! . . . If only I had been kept better informed, I would have asked Varinius to come to see me at Suessa before the battle, my young friend; we could have studied the situation with General Crassus and devised a plan of campaign! Now, it's too late; there is nothing more that I can do for you."

The praetor signed a written pass for Thoranius and assigned two men to him. "Leave at once, you can be at Suessa before daybreak; the General will see you right away. I don't understand! I just don't understand! There were six thousand of you, and . . ." He threw up his arms and turned his back on Thoranius, who left, followed by the two praetorian guards; he showed his pass to Galba at the North Gate, and from there set off at top speed for Suessa Aurunca . . .

After the quaestor left, the praetor sent for Galba. He held the young commander responsible for Glaber's and Varinius' defeats. Why did he bear such a grudge against Galba? Because the commander had not succeeded in massacring the gladiators when there were still so few of them. As a result, all the troubles that now beset the municipium of Capua were the fault of Galba's original mistake. The mere thought of the upcoming elections made the praetor groan. Capuan merchants could no longer carry on their trade with surrounding cities without worrying over the safety of their shipments. All forwarding of perfumes to Rome had been suspended. Loads of meat coming from the Campanian farms had been intercepted; others had begun to rot by the time they finally arrived after lengthy detours. These consequences of the slaves' revolt frightened the praetor because of their immediate effects on the population and his own future in office.

During the day, the rumor spread in Capua that sacks of grain had been seized the day before by the runaways; yet, the slaves could not have fought Varinius and, at the same time, stolen the grain. Finally, to crown the exasperation of the Capuans, the woods, the Volturno, and the coast, where they usually cooled off during the summer months, had all been placed off limits since the closing of the city gates.

The heat, the interrupted trade, unemployment, the cancellation of the games, the successive defeats of the praetors, all aggravated the inhabitants of all the cities of Campania, who, by way of reaction, took out their anger on the slaves; and not only on their own. Those who had faithfully remained at their tasks were, in their masters' eyes, nothing but potential runaways. Blows rained on them without reason and the rage provoked by such injustice grew steadily greater among the slaves . . .

Guards were patrolling the streets. Robberies, and arson

became more numerous. Before the gladiators' school, a hundred-odd praetorian guards, paid for by Baliatus, kept the ludus shut to the furious mob, which would indiscriminately have lynched the coaches, the lanista, and the new gladiators . . .

Moreover, the tribunes of the plebs kept minds at a boil. Gatherings in public places being an inviolable privilege, they took advantage of every incident, every emergency decree, to press their protests. The measures taken by the praetor became political levers these orators were able to make good use of. The general chaos favored them. "Look," they would say, "they don't give a damn about us! They claim they've closed the gates to protect us from the runaway slaves, yet every day the praetor mobilizes a century to go and bathe at Crassus' villa! Why can't the same century escort the grain shipments?" The crowd screamed, fights broke out, the tribunes withdrew, and the guards charged the mob . . .

"Look, they don't give a damn about us! The Senate first sent an army of three thousand men against the gladiators; it was beaten. Slaves went and joined the gladiators. So the Senate sent an army of six thousand against the runaways; it was beaten. But what does our praetor do? Instead of using his guard to protect food shipments, he makes part of it available to the lanista to protect his gladiators and keeps the rest to take him bathing!" The crowd screamed, fights broke out, the tribunes withdrew, and the guards charged the mob.

The praetor, surrounded by his family, received Galba at the dinner hour and did not invite him to sit down. He just asked him three questions: "What will happen tomorrow, commander? Are the victorious fugitives about to attack Capua now? That is a possibility that Capuans will be thinking about. How will they react tomorrow? That is all, commander. Good night!"

Galba was pacing madly back and forth in his quarters when a guard came in, carrying a torch.

"Well? What's going on now?" barked the commander.

"Lord commander, there's a merchant who wants to go through."

"The gates are closed!" Galba thundered.

But the guard stayed where he was, head down. Galba picked up a whip and walked toward him. "Did you hear me? The gates are closed!"

"But . . . milord. He says General Crassus is expecting him!"

"Does he have a pass?"

"No, milord."

"Then let him see the praetor."

"But . . . the General is waiting for him, milord."

"He has nothing else to do! Let him wait!"

Thereupon, Galba resumed his pacing, whipping the walls as he went; his tunic was stuck to his skin with perspiration, his face drawn with heat and fatigue. It was almost in a whisper that he finally said, "All right. Show him in."

The guard went out and came back followed by a very old man with rosy cheeks who looked inquisitively about him; he was carrying a sack and had a flask strapped across a light toga of very fine material.

Galba helped himself to a large cup of wine, which he drank in one gulp. He poured another and downed it just as quickly. He waved and the guard moved away. The old man took a few steps forward; he tilted his head as if to get a better look at something, then evinced a bit of surprise.

"Where are you going like this in the middle of the night?" Galba said, as he poured himself another cup of wine.

"To Suessa Aurunca, to General Crassus."

"Your name?"

"Vetus."

He took another few steps forward and said with a smile, "I made the tunic you are wearing, lord commander."

Galba looked at his tunic, then looked up. The old man was still smiling.

"Are you satisfied with it?"

"Yes, of course, I like it. . . . I'm wearing it," said Galba.

"I wanted to make you . . ." the merchant began.

"You know very well that the city gates are only open during the day, and only if you have a written pass," said Galba, drinking in large gulps.

"I know that, milord. I know, but . . ."

"So . . . Why are you asking to go through now?" Galba plumped himself down, another full cup in his hand.

The old man wiped his forehead with a spotless handkerchief. "It's a long way to Suessa, that's why I . . ."

"Do you have a letter from the General?"

"I have an order . . ." said the old man, searching in the folds of his toga.

Galba leaned back against the wall. "An order? An order from Crassus?"

"Yes, milord."

He held the papyrus out to Galba, who merely glanced at it. "Yes, yes, that's an order; but it's not a pass."

"I never thought of applying for one, milord. It was almost dark when the General's order was delivered. A praetorian guard brought it to me. You can see that it all has to be at Suessa tomorrow morning."

This time, Galba read the letter, while the old man explained. "I had to wrap the materials, get out the chariot, harness the mules, cross the city. Won't the General's order be enough?"

"The regulations are explicit: no one leaves the city without a written pass."

The old man looked at Galba, anxiously fidgeting with the strap of his flask. "Oh! I have to have a written pass, a written pass . . . But I also have to be at the General's tomorrow morning!"

Galba started to laugh quietly and got up to pour himself some more wine. He grumbled, "I have the whole population and the praetor on my hands, but General Crassus has to have materials delivered!" His sentence had ended in a nervous laugh. He reeled slightly as he came over to Vetus. "The praetor didn't make that regulation for his own enjoyment, but to protect you . . . you and all the Capuans." Galba sipped a little and dashed the cup against the wall. "All the Capuans!" he repeated. Suddenly, he laughed. "The General will understand your delay when you explain the reason to him. He was the one who insisted on written passes from the praetor. Not me!" He came closer and put his hand on the old man's frail shoulder. "The roads aren't safe; wait for daylight."

The old Capuan looked up. Galba had the expressionless face

of a tired man. Vetus smiled. "Oh, I'm not particularly afraid; I'm not carrying anything the valiant gladiators would care about."

Galba was now leaning on Vetus' shoulder. The old man went on, "The poor wretches! They're probably looking for something to eat! What would they do with my silk goods?"

Galba answered in a neutral tone, almost mechanically, his eyes blank. "Watch your words, merchant. Those slaves are not valiant men. . . . They're mad dogs!"

The old man made a slight gesture. Galba looked at him, continuing in a low voice, as if telling him a private story: "And the day isn't far off when they'll all be slaughtered . . . as they deserve!"

Vetus gave a short laugh. "Yes, I know. They'll be slaughtered, like the pigeons and squirrels of Capua were killed off! But, however close that day may be, I hope I don't live to see it!"

Galba was now looking down at Vetus; the old man's head barely came up to the commander's armpit. They looked like two old friends, whispering to each other, exchanging confidences.

"What kind of talk is that, Vetus? Do you mean because you're so old, or because you sympathize with the rebels?"

Vetus tossed his head. "Yes, I'm old, it's true. . . . No, milord, it is not because I smile at my impending end that I hope not to see the day of that massacre. Nor is it out of sympathy for the runaways. . . ."

Galba pushed Vetus aside, picked up a cup and filled it with wine.

"Well, then, merchant! Why do you hope not to see those dogs punished, huh? Here, drink this!"

"No, thank you. Wine is treacherous in this heat."

"Why don't you want to see those dogs punished?" Galba thundered.

"Dogs . . . rebels . . ."

"Answer me!" Galba shouted.

"I'm twice your age, milord; three times, perhaps . . . I've seen lots of men die, executed, assassinated . . . Today's patriot is tomorrow's rebel. . . . Look, that's what happened to poor Caius!"

"What are you talking about?"

"Oh, a friend."

"What was that name?"

"Caius."

Galba now had a stubborn pout that made him look adolescent and stupid. "Which Caius?"

"Caius Gracchus."

"Who's he?"

"You never heard tell of him?"

"No. Is he a Capuan?"

"No," said Vetus. "Caius was not from Capua."

"Is he dead?"

"Murdered. Before you were born, milord. A long time ago."

Galba raised a finger and shook it. He opened his mouth to speak, thought better of it, and drank a mouthful, shook his finger again, and said, making an effort to stick with his thought, "What . . . does his story have to do with the questions I asked you about the rebels?"

"I've seen so much punishment. . . . It's a convenient word the authorities use to justify their crimes. . . . Now all these murdered men float in the same bloodbath in my memory."

Galba was staring at Vetus. He walked to the merchant and grasped the strap over the old man's shoulder; he drew him closer with one finger. "Your Caius must have been a traitor to deserve to die. . . . He must have been a traitor!" he shouted into Vetus' face.

"Traitor, milord! Who knows where the right lies? The Senate honors a man today, then closes its doors to him tomorrow. Poor Caius!" Vetus smiled sadly. "How easy it is to judge the dead!"

Galba shook the old man's strap violently. "They are judged by what they leave behind them, aren't they?" Galba started to laugh quietly, but Vetus was pale.

"Caius' mistake was to leave behind a prejudice that outlived him. He fought against a party that hasn't been out of power since he died!"

Galba let go of the strap and pushed Vetus away with the back of his hand.

"A man has to know how to choose," he said with a hiccup.

Vetus tossed his head. "The places allotted by posterity are subject to the whims of fortune!"

"Oh, I don't understand what you're talking about, merchant. But . . ."

"It's quite simple," Vetus cut in with passion. "If Caius had defeated his enemies, he would be a hero today and his tomb would be honored!" His hands were trembling. He clasped them and bowed his head.

Galba put down his cup. He was looking at his feet, and said in a neutral tone, "You should know that it's dangerous to treat the enemies of Rome as victims."

"Caius! An enemy of Rome!" Vetus had blanched. "If it should rain until the end of time, if the thickest fog should cover the earth, no rain could wash away, no darkness could hide man's shameful ways toward man. Have patience, Caius. The clouds pass in front of the mountain. They hide it from us for a while, but the mountain is still there."

A short laugh shook Galba's shoulders. With his chin on his chest, he looked at the merchant. "In your friend's case, the clouds seem to be taking their time."

"Time works for the dead; it tidies their houses."

Galba hiccupped. "You're toying with your life, merchant!"

Vetus stood his ground pluckily. His white hair fell on his forehead, evenly trimmed. He had a haughty look. He gave a little laugh. "Well, it's about time. Life's toyed with me long enough." And, suddenly angry, he went up to Galba till he was standing right under his nose. "Anyway, so what? It's the privilege of the old, my little captain!"

His hands flat on the table, his legs crossed, his head sunk into his shoulders, Galba was looking at him. Vetus had calmed down, but he remained close to Galba. "You made me lose my temper." He laughed briefly. "Maybe it's because I've seen too much of the blood of those wretched slaves. They never stop dying!"

"Their blood keeps our men going."

"Today, milord, the runaway slaves are probably making just as light of the blood of Varinius' soldiers."

Galba straightened up. He was pale, uncomfortable with the wine and the heat. His head to one side, undecided, he peered at Vetus as if he were wondering what the old merchant was doing there.

"You're lucky you're as old as you are.... You've got a lot of courage.... Do you want to go through?"

"Yes."

"Go ahead . . . And may the god of merchants protect you."

"Thank you, milord."

"Just a minute . . . When you see Crassus, watch your language."

Vetus smiled. "Oh, I wouldn't surprise him. He knows the position of the council of merchants about all this mess since the gladiators escaped. But I'm touched by your interest, milord. Don't forget my shop, near the perfume stores, when you come by the market. I'll be pleased to present you with a tunic."

But Galba was no longer listening to him. Stooping a little, walking heavily, he led Vetus outside. "Let him through!" he shouted to the guards, who understood his gesture better than his words. Galba watched Vetus' chariot jolt away in the moonlight over the broad stones of the Appian Way. "Old fool!" The old man was long out of sight before Galba stirred.

He lay down on his bed and fell asleep at once. A guard came in and waited a moment; as Galba did not move, he poured himself a cup of wine, which he drank quickly, and started to tiptoe out. The sword ran through his body, and the mace smashed his head, stifling the cry in his throat. Magnus and Leo, the two scouts Spartacus had sent, went into Galba's room. His sleep saved him. The two fugitives left Capua without so much as a glance at the two guards lying dead under the arch of the North Gate. Hidden behind the little lemon and orange trees that bordered the road, Magnus and Leo ran over to Vetus when he came into sight in his chariot. The men jumped agilely into the chariot and lay down under the materials.

The sun was high in the sky when Vetus went through the gate of Crassus' estate. Some guards stopped him for a moment. Under the materials, Magnus and Leo were ready to strike. The mules started up again. After a while, the two men jumped off; they immediately disappeared into the shadow of the trees on the driveway, as the chariot made its way toward the villa.

ARENA

IX

After his victories over Varinius and his legates, Spartacus regrouped his men at mid-slope on the accessible side of Vesuvius, leaving scouts on the roads to Pompeii, Naples, and Nola, and sentries at the top of the volcano. When he got back to his tent, everyone in camp was asleep. Polla was not there. He left his tent and crossed the camp. He knew she had not been wounded: she had fought alongside him and they had gone back to Vesuvius together. Spartacus went through the camp again, more slowly this time, and returned to his tent. Polla was lying there, her arms under her head. He lay down beside her. She waited a long time before speaking.

"Were you looking for me?"

"Yes."

"Aren't you . . . aren't you wondering where I was?"

"No."

"You want to know?"

"Only if you want to tell me."

"I was up on a rock; thinking of you."

Spartacus waited, his eyes closed.

"Ever since I chose you, you . . ."

She turned toward the Thracian. He lay still, his eyes closed, breathing regularly. He seemed asleep.

Polla got up nervously and went out. A light rain had begun to fall; the air was much cooler, almost cold. Polla ran off, barefooted, bare-legged. Spartacus got up and went out, too. Polla had a good hundred strides' head start. She was running with half-open mouth, straight ahead, uttering a one-noted, nervous, waspish sound. Though she ran faster and faster, Spartacus could easily have caught up with her, but he seemed only to want to keep her within sight. Turning along the edge of the wood, Polla began climbing the slope; suddenly she was in the full light of the moon, toward which she appeared to be running between jonquils and wild jacinths.

Spartacus lost sight of her behind a large rock; he quickened his stride and followed her around the rock. There was a large empty space covered with heather, stretching above him to the left. Spartacus took a few steps forward and leaned over; Vesuvius sheered off to the dark woods below. Behind the woods, the sea was breaking against the rocks in long silvery lines. Polla was familiar with this face of the mountain for having descended it on the vine shoot rope before the surprise attack on Claudius Glaber. Since the moon was lighting it, she could not have failed to see it, to recognize it. Spartacus turned around. The steep slope rose toward the summit, hidden now by the overcast sky. He returned to the big rock and started to climb toward the left. While sidestepping a shallow hole, he heard a sob. There was Polla, sitting with her head on her knees, her arms around her legs. He jumped into the hole, picked her up, and carried her to the rock under which he laid her down. He stretched out beside her. Polla was sobbing, her teeth clenched, her face shining in the rain. She was cold. Spartacus ran his hand several times over the upset face of his mate, brushing back her hair. He placed his mouth on her wet chest and blew on it at several spots, warming her with his breath. He lay on top of her, resting on his elbows, just close enough so she might feel his warmth without choking under his weight. The rain, running down off the rock, fell on Spartacus' back. He took Polla's face in his hands and whispered in her ear, "You put up a good fight. . . . you weren't scared

. . ." She was no longer sobbing, though she was still weeping, with her mouth half-open. He stroked her face and put his cheek against hers, waiting for her to calm down.

The warmth of his body, his tender fingers over her eyes, his cheek against hers—and Polla breathed evenly again. The night around Vesuvius was heavy with the scent of resin. The rain made a dull little plopping sound against Spartacus' broad back. The Thracian did not move. He was tender. And warm. His breath went down along Polla's neck, reached her shoulder, her breast. Above Spartacus, the crest of the rock, the dark sky, starless. Far below, the lazy sound of the sea. The passionate impatience that had driven Polla out of the tent seemed to have vanished. All she could feel now was the warmth that was pervading her body, and with the warmth the relaxation of tension, of the state of alarm. Then she could feel her nakedness. She did not move. Spartacus' fingers were fondling her hairline and tenderly coming back to her eyelids. His belly rested on hers, hard, heavy. Yet light. She could feel the weight and the lightness.

And then Spartacus' belly no longer had any weight; it was only a sweet warmth. The man's fingers ceased their caress. Polla opened her eyes. The hand was pressing on her cheek and its thumb was on her lips. Spartacus raised his head and looked down at them. His thumb was caressing them, tracing their outline, pressing here, flicking there. Polla was looking at Spartacus. She was breathing through her mouth now. The warmth of her belly was irradiating. Her blood beat faster. Polla was waiting . . . Spartacus' hand passed over her breast, then came back to stop there. The broad nipple of her free breast swelled out hard. Spartacus took one of her lips between his own, then the other. He backed away a moment and her two breasts reached up as if calling to him. Polla opened out. Her arms and legs went around his rain-soaked neck and waist. Spartacus raised her on one arm; his other hand slipped under her armpit and took her by the neck. They stayed like that a moment; Polla's body trembled in the aching expectation of her taut breasts as they grazed his chest. Her lips were swelling, heavy, moist, over her bared teeth. A warmness overcame Polla, who opened her mouth wide, without breathing, her nostrils dilated, her eyelids almost closed. Her head held up by Spartacus' hand, her legs and arms tight about him, she was nothing more than a proffered, open shell. She was nothing more than a belly. Together, they chose this moment to cleave with long strokes. In Polla's throat, a slight, long, muffled rattle. She grasped his head and her rattle burst into his mouth, raucous, violent, while they plunged into a passionate, burning swell.

Spartacus carried her back to the tent. They fell asleep in each other's arms. There was a smile now on Polla's broad lips; with her head on one side, a new expression had come to her mouth. The line of her eyes was still raised in the arch of discovery.

Polla did not say a word all the next day. She did not open her mouth until Spartacus came to her in the tent, at evening. She took off his tunic and sandals and then undressed herself. She got on top of him and covered him with her kisses and caresses. They did not fall asleep until much later. This time, Polla's smile was merely a sign of gratitude; sleep laid bare her sensuality; her lips still showed her enjoyment. Just as in the damp, cold pit of the prison at Brundisium where they had slept side by side, her hair was spread over Spartacus' shoulder and her long, dark fingers looked tiny on the Thracian's broad chest.

A few days later, Spartacus was informed that the praetor was reconstituting his army. Varinius' soldiers had already killed several scouts who were covering Cumae and Naples. As soon as he received this news, Spartacus broke camp. Marching all night, he took refuge on the heights separating Campania from Samnium and Lucania; looking down on the Silarus flowing calmly toward Paestum, he could thus be ready for any attack. He spent the first days inspecting the terrain, posting guards at strategic points, setting up tents, fencing in the meager stock that the shepherds and cowherds had brought with them when they came up on Vesuvius. Knowing that Varinius would soon be on his tracks and stimulated by his recent victories, Spartacus made a smashing raid on three little cities off in the Campanian hills: Abella, Nola, and Nuceria Alfaterna. He brought back some grain, a small herd, a few horses, some clothes. And in order to keep open these routes into Campania, he posted three detachments of Celts to guard these cities' gates.

After Spartacus' earlier victory over Varinius, slaves of both sexes had set out for Vesuvius, from where news of his exploits had spread to the neighboring provinces; these new runaways were prompted to flee by the injustice and irritability of their masters, who now looked on each slave as a potential enemy. When they found no one on their arrival at the foot of Vesuvius, they followed the tracks left by the passage of the seven thousand men. After the capture of the three cities by Spartacus, slaves ran away in still greater numbers to head for his camp.

Once the camp was fully set up, the fugitives found themselves split into two groups: the Germans and the Celts with Crixos; the rest, all the rest, Thracians, Samnites, Greeks, Cilicians, Asians, with Spartacus. Following the lead of their chiefs, the two groups had entirely different ways of life.

The tents in Crixos' camp had been set up without plan, some too close together, some too far apart, in a basin with northern exposure that rang out in the night with the noise of the orgies taking place in it. Bones, old baskets, and excrement piled up between the tents. Everyone went to sleep late and got up late; they drank a lot, ate their whole day's rations at one meal; and the women gave themselves to the men promiscuously. Fights frequently broke out; the rest would then gather around and egg the fighters on. Several men had already been killed in these quarrels. As Crixos never interfered, the men in his camp took greater and greater liberties, leaving the camp without permission and devastating the countryside and small defenseless villages. Learning of these doings in the middle of the night, during his revels, Crixos would join in the fun with the marauders back from their murderous raids; his brigands never failed to bring him back wine or women, often both, and Crixos shut his eyes to the excesses of his people.

Spartacus' camp was divided into two parts: women and children on one side, men on the other. As Alba and Polla had escaped with the first group of gladiators, they had the authority of leaders, both in battle and in ordinary routine. Their camp was well kept and Spartacus often sent to them for rations to replenish his men's supplies. Each one spent his time as he had seen his old masters spend theirs, within the limits of the clandestine possibilities available to fugitives. The women did the washing and took care of the children, something most of their former

Roman mistresses had never done; they did each other's hair and gossiped together. They found it hard to talk at first. But, little by little, since no one forbade their communicating any longer, the women got into the habit of walking around the camp with their husbands who had come over to join them, alone, or sometimes with their children, and they talked for the pleasure of hearing themselves talk, just to be saying something.

The main activity was battle training. The runaways got together in groups of a hundred; each gladiator, in charge of several of these combat groups, organized sham attacks suited to day or night time, mountains, valleys, general skirmishes, hand-to-hand engagements, and individual fighting. Like the men, the women and children were part of these training groups; relations of equality grew up between them. The pregnant women and the oldest fugitives of both sexes watched these maneuvers, either commenting on the action, or in silence, according to their make-ups, the moods of the moment, the interest the fight aroused. Spartacus, like his former fellow gladiators, also trained several of these groups of a hundred. Polla and Alba were in one of them. Since their escape from Capua, Alba had changed a great deal. Life in the open air, the passion aroused by battle, the delirious joy following the successive victories had brought a new erectness to her shoulders, new light to her eyes. The marches, the sorties, the work without a slave driver, the battle training, and especially sleep, free sleep, sleep without terror, out in the open, confident, relaxed rest had filled out her body, firmed up her shape.

She discovered hidden desires brought to the surface by a new sap rising within her body, swelling her bosom, giving her walk a troubling bounce that her astonished mind tried in vain to control. Alba, listening to the calls of her flesh, looking about, talking, but never seeing herself as she had become, struggled against this sensuality that enveloped her, invaded as she was by new needs, never before experienced. The sun had given a golden glint to her skin; air and sleep had brought life back into her dark-red hair that shone and fell in heavy waves. Polla, who had followed this rapid change with affectionate interest, was one day alongside Alba, sword in hand, in the main street of conquered Abella, when she caught the look Crixos was casting on her companion. Crixos, his mouth open beneath a large flask, was sitting with legs spread, his mustache and beard ambered by the liquid. When the two women went by, he had swallowed noisily and placed the flask between his legs. Alba had glanced briefly at the Celt and Polla had seen her blush, then suddenly turn pale and run away. Polla had found her again just outside the city; her head on her arms, Alba was weeping against a tomb along the side of the road.

Another time, Polla had come upon Alba leaning over a tub of water, peering into the dull mirror which reflected a distorted image of her. This time again, Alba had cried, lying back on the rock, her hands clenched over her bosom.

At Nola, Polla had found a mirror. That very evening, she had taken Alba by the hand and led her into her tent. Having done her hair, binding it on the top of her head with a green ribbon, she had suddenly thrust the mirror before her face.

"This is for you, Alba. See how beautiful you are."

Laughing and crying, Alba had looked at herself in the mirror until it got so dark she could no longer see. From that day forward, self-confidence was hers, and she grew more and more popular in the women's and children's camp which she ran with Polla, and even more so in the men's camp. It would have been easy for her to spend long evenings with the groups that formed at nightfall, separated into couples, and strolled away from the tents. She confided in Polla. She no longer wanted to bear the humiliation of the brutal possessions to which all her life she had been forced to lend herself. Yet, if her newfound self-confidence made her feel free and alive in terms of her sex, it also tied her desires in with a young girl's pride, the pride itself forever bound to a resolve never again to fall into the trap of an unexpected and later humiliating enjoyment. Thus her memories and her hopes forever intermingled and opposed each other. The woman once degraded, humiliated in her sex, now resisted the calls of a mature, healthy body seeking the path to sensual relief, as well as the mind of the girl she had never been, but who had come to life in her newfound freedom. And the little girl could feel a wave of desire and sadness rising within her womanly body, a score of times raped but never satisfied. It was this satisfaction, this fulfillment that her body was demanding, and that left her on certain evenings panting, naked, her breats taut, her belly hollow, her nails digging into the earth, craving a weight upon her outspread legs, hoping for a wound through which she would have loved her body to discharge itself. On those nights, she would moan. When day returned, an unbearable, exasperating sense of modesty invaded her, taking its place among the desires of a sad and irritable Alba. She could feel that, once she overcame this proud modesty, she would give her body to the first handy male in the camp. If she were not then to achieve the satisfaction of her desires, she would at least suffer no humiliation; the man and the time would have been of her own choosing.

Spartacus' forces had now grown so large that it was impossible to keep them regularly supplied. Therefore, helpless, the Thracian was forced to put up with the raids of the Celts and the Germans, who never brought in more than the skimpiest of food supplies, as they were more interested in women and drink. Those among them who were no longer strong enough to run such risks without the help of the main body of the forces either perished or stole what the marauders brought back to camp; violent quarrels would then break out and their outcome was often fatal.

Having no intelligence of Varinius' doings and being unaware that the praetor had been unable to muster an army large enough, Spartacus decided one day to break camp. The underfed fugitives having become too weak, regular training had broken off several weeks before. Spartacus kept them busy distributing skins as clothing for the constant stream of new arrivals; others tended fires used to harden sticks that could serve as lances; still others fashioned shields from basket bottoms and vine shoots. As their bodies grew weaker, a cold, determined anger set in.

On his way over to Crixos' camp, Spartacus made a stop at a rock overlooking the valley to watch the fugitives who kept arriving in uneven, though uninterrupted groups. Twenty feet below him, Capito was lying on his stomach. The Samnite was watching the newcomers, too. Carrying a basket of skins, Gannicus stopped near him to catch his breath. Neither of them had seen Spartacus. Gannicus said, "Still they come!"

"Hasn't let up since last week," answered the Samnite.

The Thracian was about to leave, but Capito's tone of voice caught his ear.

Gannicus was laughing. He lay down on his stomach alongside Capito. In the valley, the fugitives were approaching from all sides. They came from everywhere: from Apulia, from Lucania. That very morning, a hundred German gladiators had come in; coming from Etruria, they had had to bypass Rome, travel by way of Samnium and cross almost its entire length. The closer the fugitives came to the camp, the faster they walked. Some of them were even running. Women, children, entire families. A hundred here; two hundred there; over there, a thousand. A veritable army.

"They're coming from all sides!" Gannicus exclaimed.

"Look at them," said Capito.

"That's all I've been doing."

"Take a good look at them."

"I am taking a good look," said Gannicus.

"Don't you notice anything?"

"Yes, I do."

"What?"

"They're shouting. They seem happy."

Capito got up, raging mad. "Don't you see they're empty-handed?"

"So what? Weren't we empty-handed when we left Capua? They're joining us, they're increasing our forces! We're getting stronger and stronger!" Gannicus got up, too. "Let them come empty-handed! At least, they had the courage to leave. No more whips! No more masters, no more humiliations, no more . . ."

"No more regular food supply."

Gannicus looked at the Samnite. Astonishment had opened his mouth.

"What are you saying?"

"I say there's no more chow. I wonder . . ."

"I know!" Gannicus said. "I know what you wonder." He strode up to Capito. "I'm not hankering after the Romans' starvation rations. And you'd do better not to talk to the newcomers; they might think that . . ."

"They might think what you know as well as I: we can't fight on empty stomachs."

Gannicus went on as if he had not been interrupted. "They might think we're fighting among ourselves." He had hammered out those last words, staring hard at Capito, who broke out laughing. "They wouldn't be wrong! Is there anything we all agree on, anyway?"

"One thing, at least: freedom."

Capito laughed one tone louder. "Freedom! What freedom? To go back home, maybe?"

"To go back home, first we have to get out of this country."

Capito angrily threw a pebble down into the valley. "Get out of this country! That's fine for you. Where can I go? Don't forget, I was born here. And I'm not the only one in that boat!"

Capito was at the very edge of the rock jutting out over the valley; his back was to Gannicus; his face was somewhat downcast, with an expression of despair breaking through. Gannicus put his hand on his shoulder. His voice was warm, friendly. "You'll get out of this country with us, Capito. We'll find another place where we can all settle down."

Capito remained silent for a moment, gazing at his feet. He laughed briefly. "We'll find another place, huh? Just as easy as that! Like Sertorius on his dream raft, we'll go looking for our Fortunate Isles. Look, you see, you make me laugh . . . But you're real nice."

"You're wrong to laugh. In the place we're going to, you won't earn your keep under the lash, with death dogging your footsteps. You won't have been born there, but it'll be your own country."

Capito's face looked distraught. "You're crazy, Gannicus! No more lash! What makes you think that other countries are the Land of the Blessed?"

Spartacus had heard enough. His brow furrowed with concern, he resumed his way up to Crixos' camp.

"Nothing," Gannicus was saying. "But I do know that, far from Rome, I'll no longer be a hounded slave, a living dead man."

Capito laughed a bitter laugh. "Oh, Gannicus! Far from Rome, you think you'll no longer be a slave!"

"That's right."

"Be still! Why wouldn't you be a slave any more? There are Romans everywhere! *Everywhere!*"

Tears mixed with his laughter. When he realized he was crying, the tall Samnite ran off, yelling, "Everywhere! They're everywhere!" Gannicus watched him go. He looked back at the valley and picked up his basket.

At the camp of the Celts, Spartacus did not find Crixos. He went slowly back down to his tent. Polla was sleeping. He lay down, his hands under his head.

Crixos was in Alba's tent. Night had fallen, he was waiting. When Alba got there, she stopped near the tent and then went on. She walked out of the campsite. Crixos followed her and backed her up against a rock. Instead of fighting as she had seen a girl do whom he had taken at Nola, she let him find her mouth. When he tried to caress her, she took his face in her hands. With a smile, she said gently, "Crixos! When you drink, you slop the wine over your beard and stomach. . . . You don't kiss any better." Furious, Crixos set her on the ground and lay down on top of her, mashing her breasts. Stifled under his weight, Alba managed to grab Crixos' braided hair and make him raise his head. He looked down at her, the points of his beard shaking in his furious openmouthed laugh. She exclaimed, "Why are you trying to take me like a Roman girl?" Crixos let go of her, nonplussed. He got up and suddenly burst out in a loud laugh. He looked at her. Alba was still lying on the ground; she had turned her head toward the valley. The torches of the approaching fugitives could be seen in bunches, shimmering like stars. Crixos walked away without a word, heading for his camp. Alba watched him a moment and threw her head back; she closed her eyes and called as loud as she could, "Crixos!" Crixos turned around. "Crixos!" The Celt came back to her. Alba looked at him, lustful and maternal at the same time. She opened her arms to him, spread her legs slightly, breathing in short gasps. "Take!" Crixos crushed her under his weight. Stirred by her own desire and bruised by his violence, Alba's back flexed. She clutched at Crixos' broad shoulders and her nipples rubbed brutally by the coarse goatskin made her moan with pain, further exciting her eagerness. Crixos responded to her appeal. Shaken by a furious joy, a searing call echoed her desire; she was unconsciously repeating in a voice growing more and more hoarse, "Take! . . . Take! . . . Take! . . ." Suddenly her legs spread wide open, then scissored around Crixos' waist; she threw her head back and opened her mouth; a slow moan rose from her lips . . . And she felt the full weight of Crixos collapsing on top of her, spent, bathed in sweat.

Alba was shattered. Her legs had spread and fallen, her hands clutched at the earth. She could scarcely breathe, her mouth smothered by the Celt's heavy chest. Suddenly, she became conscious of another distress which gripped her at the roots of her hair, pressing her head with a thousand icy spikes. Her stomach contracted. The nauseating smell of the goatskin, further enhanced by the sweat of the Celt, overcame her. An acid taste burnt her tongue. Alba shoved Crixos off with all her strength, freeing herself only enough to turn her face away, covered with a cold sweat, vomiting in quick spasms, her forehead resting on her arm, her nails dug in under her breast. Her eyes closed, curled up, a final tremor shook her. She rolled over on her side, gasping for breath, her chest bloody. Crixos was sitting, mouth open, his belly naked and satisfied. He slowly got up and readjusted his clothing. He called, "Alba!" She opened her eyes. "Say, Alba!" Her teeth clenched, her cheeks hollow, livid, she was looking at the Celt without seeing him. Crixos called to her one more time. Getting no reply, he went back up toward his camp.

ARENA

The next morning, Spartacus informed Crixos of his intention of breaking camp.

"That's crazy," said Crixos. "Where do you expect to go?"

"No. It would be crazy to stay here."

Crixos tugged furiously at the points of his beard. "Why?"

"We'll talk it over with the others."

Spartacus got up. "Coming?" Crixos followed him without answering, a sulky pout on his lips. They reached the plateau from which they could look down on the newcomers' camp some twenty feet below. Seated around the fire, their entire general staff was waiting for them: Alba, Polla, Gannicus, Capito, Oenomaos, and two recently added members, Velox and Valens.

"There are more than ten thousand of them," said Crixos.

"Yes," said Spartacus. "Almost all the latest come from Campania. How many horses have we, Oenomaos?"

"Two thousand, not counting the Celts'."

"Call up one of the Campanians who has seen Magnus or Leo."

Oenomaos picked up his mace and went down among the

newcomers. Spartacus was pacing silently. Capito got up and deliberately stood in his way. "What are you going to do, Spartacus?"

Spartacus looked at the Samnite. Capito seemed worried. As always, his pale, lashless eyes gave him a lackluster look.

"Continue toward the North."

"And . . . how do you expect to feed our people? With sticks? With basket bottoms?"

With sad face and downcast eyes, the Thracian answered, "I've called everybody together this morning to let them know what I have in mind." He turned toward the valley, where the newcomers were mixed in among the veterans. A cold wind was blowing on the camp; the sky was overcast to the north. Awakened too early, the Celts and Germans were in a nasty mood; they were swearing as they took their places among the others. Alba and Polla were sitting behind Gannicus; the Celt was staring at Spartacus as he rubbed his big flattened nose. Spartacus climbed up on a small rock. A movement forward immediately ran through the camp.

"Capito has been asking me some questions that affect all of us: he wants to know how I plan to keep us all fed."

A murmur arose from all three of the camps. "Good question," some said. "Who's that?" asked others.

Spartacus took advantage of a moment's silence. "Listen! . . . Shepherds, cowmen, gladiators . . . What did we do? We revolted at the same time at Cales, Caratia, Nola, and Capua. So what happened? . . . We joined forces and defeated the praetors' armies by surprise. By surprise . . . and against all expectations!"

The cheering kept him from continuing. He turned toward his general staff. "Look at them! Still they come! They have dared!"

It was quiet again. The Thracian went on.

"Through our little victories, we made your oldest dream possible! You dared!"

Before going on, Spartacus looked at Crixos and Capito and turned his head toward the valley. "When we fled from Capua, we weren't quite sure how we'd do it, but there was only one thing we wanted: to go home to our own countries—some to Gaul, others to Thrace. How did we eat? When a herdsman ran away, he brought a few head of cattle to us. An animal always finds something to eat; not much, but enough to go on looking further. And then further still. We did the same thing. Yesterday, there were forty of us; today, there are forty thousand!" Spartacus glanced around at Capito.

"So, how am I going to keep us fed?" he shouted. He turned to the valley: *"I have no idea!"*

There was a stir in the crowd massed at his feet. He continued in the same vein. "I did not ask you to come and join me! You're hungry? So what? We're all hungry! I did not escape in order to pillage and wage war! I ran away in order to go back home to Thrace. All of you, Germans, Celts, where were you going when you ran away? You were headed back home! Have you changed your minds?"

He looked at Crixos who was tugging at his beard points. A few voices rose, weakly, "No, no, no!"

"You want to eat?" Spartacus went on. "Well, you'll eat when you get home! If you want to get there, we have to march north."

Crixos got up and joined the Thracian. "Why? Why to the north?"

Spartacus turned to him. "Because the Romans will not follow us once we've crossed the mountains. We took them by surprise. That's how we got this far." Turning toward the valley: "We only have half the road left before us. A few days' marching, a few days' patience, and you'll be eating. But the most important thing now is to get over those mountains!"

Capito now went up on the rock.

"The most important thing is to eat! Always!"

A long cheer went up from the camp of the Celts. Spartacus turned toward them. "If you want to eat in this country, you have to fight the Romans!"

"Why?" asked Crixos.

"Because forty thousand men who kill those who stand in their way and steal anything they can lay their hands on are no longer simple runaways. Was that what you had in mind when you fled from slavery?"

Spartacus was looking in turn at Crixos, Capito, and the Celts assembled down in the valley.

"What are you proposing?" Capito asked.

"Let's get across the mountains together and reach the out-of-the-way places. There, if we still want to stay united and work together, we'll build our own city."

Crixos burst out laughing. "We'll build our own city! What city? They'll never let us build anything!"

"Who will stop us?" said Spartacus.

"The Romans!"

"Always the Romans," Capito chimed in.

In the valley, the women grasped their children to them. Capito's words ran from mouth to mouth, spreading consternation. Spartacus lifted his arms, to restore a bit of calm. "There are no Romans in the out-of-the-way places we are going to!"

Capito got off the rock. Spartacus looked at him with concern. The Samnite started to laugh. He was speaking in a low voice, to himself. "Out-of-the-way places! Out of what way? Away from the Romans? There are no places out of the way of the Romans. They are everywhere! Everywhere!" He started to laugh, going from one to another. "The Romans are everywhere! Everywhere, you hear me? Everywhere!"

Spartacus jumped quickly off the rock and grabbed him by the shoulders: "There won't be any Romans where we're going!"

Capito laughed twice as hard. His big yellow teeth in his bloodless, hairless face made him look animal and pathetic. "They'll come there some day. They go everywhere! There's no place in the world without Romans!" He looked at Spartacus, desperately. "They'll get to the city you want to build, just like they go everywhere; they came and grabbed you at home in Thrace, didn't they?" He freed himself from Spartacus' grip and laughed again. "They'll come and we'll become their slaves! Just like before . . . The same as always!"

"We haven't been their slaves since Capua, Capito."

"As long as there are Romans, all we will be to them is slaves. And there will always be Romans."

"Then there will always be runaway slaves who will join us."

Solemnly, Spartacus, looked around at all his companions. "We will not always run away. I give you my oath that if the Romans attacked us in the land of our choice, I would defend it to the death without giving an inch."

An enthusiastic shout arose from the ranks of the runaways. Spartacus went on. "But it has not yet come to that. We're still in their land. First, we have to get away. Fast. As fast as possible. Does everyone agree?"

"Yes! Yes!"

Capito ran up to Crixos and took him by the arm. "Do you agree, Crixos? Tell him how your men feel! Tell him what they're doing!"

Spartacus turned to Crixos. The Celt still had his sulky pout. He looked at Alba who was beside him, but she had eyes only for Spartacus. Uncomfortable, Crixos looked up at the Thracian. "They refuse to leave the South."

"Why? What do they expect to do here?" Spartacus asked.

"They want to go to Apulia and spend the winter there."

"You must keep them from it, Crixos! You must!"

"I can't. They've already taken two little towns . . . for a food supply."

Spartacus started. "Two towns? What towns?"

"Nares Lucanae and Forum Annii."

Capito began to laugh, watching a dumbfounded Spartacus repeating the names. "That's right! Oh, yes, we're all agreed!" the Samnite sneered.

Spartacus was staring at Crixos; he was going to say something, but Crixos said, "They won't listen to anything else, Spartacus."

Spartacus remained silent a moment, looking from Crixos to Capito, from Gannicus to Alba, to Polla. . . . All of a sudden, he went back up on the rock and stretched out his arms to command silence. "We break camp tonight. Get ready!" The Thracian turned; those below were silently dispersing.

"We had decided to leave this country; to go back home," Spartacus said, as if talking to himself. "Get this, Crixos. If the Celts spend the winter in Apulia, they'll be forced down to the sea in the spring and massacred."

"They don't want to hear your reasons, Spartacus. First of all, they want . . ."

"To drink," said Alba.

"No, to eat and drink," Crixos laughingly replied.

Spartacus started. "And, in order to eat, they steal! They kill! And they don't only kill soldiers!" Spartacus started to pace up and down the small plateau. "Eat! Well, we eat. Poorly, I admit, but we do eat!"

Crixos raised his voice. "Not enough!"

"Enough so we can march!"

Crixos shouted even louder, "Not enough so we can fight!"

Spartacus lowered his eyes. "But how can I make you understand? If we crossed the mountains, we wouldn't have to fight any more."

Capito shook his head. "How do you know?"

"He doesn't know," Crixos replied. "How could he know?"

"I'm sure of it! They won't be for long, but right now the Romans are routed. We have to take advantage of that to . . ."

Oenomaos appeared on the plateau, followed by a tattered, bloody Celt. He was a small man with broad shoulders and very powerful arms. A sword stroke on his shoulder had slipped along the bone and ripped away an inch-wide strip of flesh; he had lost a lot of blood. Spartacus went up to him. "What's your name?"

"Castus."

"Have you seen Magnus? Leo? Any of the gladiators who . . ."

"Magnus has been . . ."

Castus was leaning against the rock, near Alba. "Are you . . . Spartacus?" The Thracian nodded. Castus raised one arm and embraced him. He was short of breath and spoke in broken phrases, so low that Spartacus had to bend over to hear him. "The guards caught up with Magnus. He had an arrow in his thigh, just above the knee. We . . . we did our best to carry him, but the militiamen were getting closer. . . . So Magnus asked for a sword and propped himself up, with his back to a tree, to face the soldiers."

"Didn't you see Leo?"

"No . . . I think he was the one who set fire to Crassus' farm, but . . . the guards were arriving from Capua, so he probably couldn't get away from them." Castus shook his head.

"Do you think that . . ."

Castus raised his hand, interrupting Spartacus. "I don't think anything. I am sure about what happened to Magnus, because I saw the soldiers surround him. But I can't say for sure about Leo."

Crixos came over. "How did they get in to Crassus'?"

"In the chariot of a Capuan merchant who was delivering some silk goods to Crassus."

Spartacus smiled at him. He said gently, "Did you live at Crassus' very long?"

"I was born there . . . I guess. I've never been out of the place except to come here."

Spartacus turned to Oenomaos. "Help him to the camp. Give him something to eat."

Oenomaos put the little Celt's arm around his shoulder and took him by the waist. As they were going off, Castus stopped. He turned. "Spartacus!" The Thracian ran over to him, followed by the others. Castus was very pale; he could hardly be heard. "When we . . . we got away . . . Crassus was getting ready to go to Rome."

Spartacus helped Oenomaos sit Castus down. Alba and Polla began to bandage his shoulder after covering it with herbs.

"To Rome? How do you know?" asked Crixos.

"He said so in front of me, to Quaestor Thoranius."

"What else did you hear?"

Castus turned his head toward Spartacus. "Thoranius explained why . . . Praetor Varinius . . ."

"Isn't that one dead?" Crixos interrupted.

"He withdrew to Cumae. That's what Thoranius was saying . . . He was telling why Varinius lost the battle he fought against you."

Crixos burst out laughing. 'That, I would have liked to hear!"

"He said that Varinius ought not to have split up his army. . . . That he shouldn't have made it march so fast. . . . Crassus was furious when he heard you had surprised Cossinius while he was bathing." Crixos snorted. Castus went on: "And he laughed when he heard Varinius had lost his horse in the fight. Crassus had offered him ten times its value for it, but Varinius had always refused . . ."

"Fine," Spartacus said. "Now go and rest."

Castus raised his hand and inhaled deeply. "Thoranius," he said as they all leaned over him, "asked Crassus to help him explain to the senators about why the new recruits deserted from his army."

Crixos gave Capito a big slap on the back. "Roman soldiers

desert when they face gladiators! Well! What did Crassus say when he heard about that rout, huh?"

"He was furious with Varinius and the Senate, but . . . he promised to help Thoranius. Crassus was yelling, 'Spartacus has it easy, with those weak-kneed senators! What we need is soldiers running the country!' I think that was when he decided to leave for Rome. . . ."

Spartacus made a sign to Oenomaos, who helped Castus to his feet; Gannicus went to the other side of the wounded man and they started slowly down to the camp, followed by Alba and Polla. When they had covered a fair stretch, Spartacus came back to Crixos and Capito.

"You heard that as well as I did. Crassus is going to Rome with Thoranius to tell the senators that the police cohorts are not strong enough to beat us. They've been routed."

Crixos had lain down on the rock near Capito who was whittling a branch. He clasped his hands behind his head. "What are they going to do?" he asked Spartacus with a smile.

"I don't know . . . I don't know what Crassus is going to do, but he's going to take action; one of his farms at Suessa has just been burned down and some of his slaves escaped! As for the senators . . ." Spartacus shrugged his shoulders. "They'll have to talk, to come to an agreement. . . . We have plenty of time to get across the mountains, if we leave without delay." He stopped in front of Crixos. "If the Celts stay behind, it'll be open war with Rome and they'll be massacred by the legions in the spring."

Crixos laughed. "Legions! Come now! The Romans are not going to send legions against slaves! Some police forces, at the most." He sat down and began to smooth the points of his beard. "And what if they did? My men are right; they want to kill some of them. I do too. I'd like to show those Romans a thing or two."

Spartacus was listening to him, his thumbs in his belt, his eyes on the valley. Crixos got up and started to walk, avoiding Spartacus' eyes. "I followed you wholeheartedly, but look . . . since I've been with you, I haven't had a chance to enjoy my freedom."

Spartacus turned around. Crixos looked sidewise at him. "It's true. We go to bed early, we get up early, we . . ."

Spartacus smiled. "Not you, Crixos. Nor your men, either. You go to bed late and you get up late."

Crixos opened his mouth comically, feigning offense. He went on as if Spartacus had not interrupted him. "We fight and we never stop marching. To go where? Huh? Where are we going?"

Spartacus was still looking at him and smiling. Crixos glanced at Capito and went on, aware of his own bad faith. "Well? Where do you expect to go? The Romans are everywhere." He emphasized his last words with a gesture toward Capito, inviting the Samnite to come to his rescue.

"It's true," the other said. "They are everywhere!"

Crixos gave his head a comic little twist, but Spartacus' smile had frozen. Crixos paced around the Thracian, making broad gestures, stepping aside and coming back to him. "The Celts are having a good time. They eat, they drink, they bring women back to camp; in a word, they're living!" Crixos stopped in front of Spartacus. "Well? Haven't you got anything to say?"

"What would you expect me to say? If it's living you want. . . . If it's war you want. . . . Eat! . . . Make love! . . . Drink! . . ." Spartacus flung his arms out in a helpless gesture. "Go celebrate the Saturnalia!"

Crixos looked furious. "What? What are you saying?"

"It looks like the coming of the calends of January is affecting your senses, Crixos. . . . In a few days, the slaves will be putting on togas and pretending to give orders to their masters. And the masters will pretend to submit. The slaves will be allowed to do whatever they please! Anything! They'll roam the street. . . . *Free!*" Spartacus laughed briefly. "And their mistresses, those noble whores, will even let themselves be whipped before giving themselves to them." Spartacus looked up at Crixos. "If you want to have your slave's vacation, you'd better leave now! Alone, you can get yourself purchased anywhere! By anyone! Go ahead! Leave, Crixos, the Saturnalia are at hand!"

Crixos turned and walked off, then came back again, furious that Capito was there to hear. Spartacus changed his tune.

"Crixos! Crixos, look at me. Remember . . . when the guards led you to the arena, did you ever see the eyes of the people on the street?"

"Sure," said Crixos in a fury. "They were scared."

Spartacus looked sorry. "Scared! Scared of what?"

"Of us, the gladiators."

"No, they weren't scared, Crixos."

"And I say they were scared!" Crixos hammered stubbornly.

"Why should they have been scared of us? We were surrounded by guards, Crixos. There were guards everywhere: in the streets, in the squares, in the shops; and the people who watched us go by felt safe, precisely because there were so many guards."

Crixos was now beside himself.

"They were scared of us!" he shouted.

"Maybe they were sorry for us, but not . . ."

"Sorry for us!" Crixos yelled. The Celt paced around in a circle, boiling mad. Spartacus went on calmly. "There were some who didn't even see us. Others, on the other hand, were interested in us only because they had bet on us. But some were sorry for us, I think. They were thinking that we were about to die. . . ."

"All right. So what?" asked Crixos in a constrained voice. He had stopped his mad circular pacing. Now, true anger had taken hold of him; he was livid.

"Today, those very same men, who were not scared of us and who perhaps even pitied us, are going to hate us because the Celts are taking their women, their daughters, their harvests."

"So what? I don't need their pity!"

"Neither do I, Crixos! But they're going to turn against us. They're going to close the gates of their cities."

"They're doing that already."

Spartacus came near Crixos; he took his arm. "At this moment, men are crossing the whole country to come and join us. They believe in us. They are sure their lives took on meaning the minute they found the courage to run away. And it's true, their lives now do have a meaning, a future: they have made a choice. But they expect something from us. They're not coming here to eat and drink. The slave who does his work in the fields, and lives within his own family, has something more than the gladiators; death doesn't threaten him every day. He doesn't run away so he can make war on the Romans. He comes to add his strength to ours so as to make something of that new life he has discovered."

Crixos was looking at Spartacus with a mocking smile. The Thracian looked him in the eye. "After all, Crixos, what have you got left after you've eaten a sheep and raped three women?"

Crixos' smile froze. He opened his mouth, but Spartacus went on, "Oh, I know you! I've seen you. You don't make love. You rape!"

"And you . . . you, . . ." Crixos began, trying to find something offensive to say. "What do you have when a thousand more men get here and you have nothing to give them to eat?"

Spartacus shrugged without answering, but Capito pressed on: "What more do you have when you march toward the North?"

Crixos and Spartacus sought out Capito as one looks for an insect, and then stared at him. The tall Samnite became confused and got up; he looked at the two leaders, shrugged, and walked slowly away. Spartacus returned to the question of the Samnite by pointing in the direction he had gone. "By going north, Crixos, I won't have to fight any more. I can promise that to all the new arrivals. Try to understand; they're not looking for immediate pleasures that they can't even picture. They come here to feel stronger because they're all together. In order to do something. They still don't know what, but they feel things will be better for them."

"Well, do you know what they are going to do?"

"Yes. They're going back to their homes. If the Romans are there, they'll assemble farther on, elsewhere . . . and they'll build a city without gladiators and without slaves."

"They can't build anything."

"They can do anything! They've built a hundred cities! All the cities!"

Crixos burst out laughing.

"All right, laugh, Crixos! But show me one city, one monument in this country that wasn't built by slaves. And our numbers are increasing; you were here almost from the start. . . . Tonight, there are forty thousand of us."

"No, Spartacus! Thirty thousand! There are ten thousand

Celts you can't include in your forces. We'll pick up as many again on the way."

"Don't count on it. The runaways won't join you; they've had enough bloodshed. Your men are even more brutal than the Romans in enemy territory. They sow terror wherever they go. You can be sure that the slaves who might escape won't dare do it if the whole country is up in arms against us."

They spent the afternoon and part of the evening talking this way; when it grew dark, they were still on the small plateau. Gannicus came up to them, carrying a torch. "There's nothing left to give them," he said. In the plain, they could still see the same scene; clusters of torches were coming toward the camp, from all sides at once. "They keep coming!" Gannicus said. "A woman came in with two children in her arms. She had a nanny goat, for milk for the children." Gannicus lowered his head. "They stole the goat from her! They're hungry!"

"Kill fifty horses," Spartacus said.

In astonishment, Gannicus looked at Crixos, then at Spartacus. "But . . . you forbade me to touch them!"

"Do you have any better solution?"

Gannicus shook his head. "We'll break camp tonight," the Thracian said. Gannicus wanted to talk, but thought better of it. There were two apples left in his basket, he gave one to each of the men. Crixos devoured his in a trice; Spartacus put his hand on Gannicus' shoulder. "Take the oldest ones."

"Of course," said the Celt. "And . . . what about the goat?"

"Yes, the goat, . . ." Spartacus thought for a moment, eating a piece of apple. He observed the fruit, at length. "Exchange a horse for it. . . ." He looked at Gannicus. "Do something," he said impatiently. "If you find the ones who stole it, send them to me."

Without a word, Gannicus went off with his torch and the two men were in the darkness again. Spartacus ate a piece of apple and sighed. Crixos came very close to him. "I'm hungry, too, Spartacus. But I intend to eat."

"You've never been hungry so often."

"Maybe. But now, I have time to think about it."

"Be sensible, Crixos; gladiator, slave, freeman, legionary, senator, or consul, everyone has to eat. Until they die. But you don't live only to eat! Have a little patience, Crixos, you'll soon have enough to eat."

Crixos was facing Spartacus, one hand on his hip, the other tugging at his beard. "I can't wait. I intend to eat every day and just as often as I feel like it. . . ." The Thracian observed his apple after each bite. "Well, I'm not like you," Crixos went on. Spartacus looked up. "Aren't you ever hungry?"

Spartacus answered in a murmur: "Sure, I am. All the time."

Crixos started to urinate. "Bah! You're never hungry," he said.

Spartacus shrugged. Crixos went on: "If you were like everybody else, you wouldn't eat like a baby."

The Thracian gazed at the apple; he took another bite.

"How do you hold out?" asked Crixos.

Spartacus had finished his apple. He spat out the pits and joined Crixos, pissing with him down into the valley from the rock. He said, "Crixos, I'm nothing but a belly." Crixos laughed. "For everything," Spartacus went on. "For hunger, for love, for fighting. I've reached the depths of slavery. Instead of fighting against hunger, in order not to be a slave to my belly as well, I gave myself to it. Completely. I took care of it. I thought only of it. Instead of waiting for it to call, I anticipated its wants. I trained it to take a little at a time and at rare intervals. Long since. So it closed up. It got tough." He turned toward Crixos, with fist upraised. "Tough as this. That's what's saved me, always. I was hungry a long time, a very long time. Now, that's over. I feel hungry the way I breathe, but I don't ever think about it any more."

"No? Well, I do; I think about it all the time."

Spartacus was looking at Crixos. "You are going back into the arena, Crixos. Without any guards, or anyone else, forcing you to."

"I can't follow you any more," said the Celt. "In the life that you want, I miss certain things. Hard, violent things. Even things that hurt. I miss injustice itself; it's what sustains my anger for me. With the Celts, I have everything I want. No problem. With this, . . ." Crixos raised his fist, "and with this," as he patted himself on the crotch.

"You have too many things to lose, Crixos. You expect too much out of a life that hasn't even started yet for us."

Spartacus had his back to him; Crixos went and grabbed him by the shoulders. "A little while ago, I laughed when you said you'd build a city without gladiators and without whips. Maybe I was wrong. I think that . . . I think it's too late for me because I'm . . . I think I'm still a gladiator."

"You had become my friend, my brother. What's happening to you, Crixos?"

"I don't know!"

The words faltered in their mouths like the torches in the valley. Since Spartacus had not turned around, Crixos let go of him and turned his back on him, too, watching the torches come up toward the camp. "I don't know," he repeated. "It's like when I'm too hot and the rain falls on my head; something happens somewhere, but I don't know what it is. I can feel it but I don't understand it!"

Crixos stood a long time watching the valley. The two men were back to back, lost in their thoughts. Suddenly Crixos murmured, "Maybe I'm just a born gladiator!"

"They made you into one."

Crixos turned around. "In your city, there won't be room for any." He tried to laugh. "I've talked too much. I never before talked so much, I think. Good-bye, Spartacus!"

Spartacus turned, his face expressionless. Crixos quickly embraced him. "I'll send you my men's horses. They'll come in handy!" Crixos moved away, his long braid swinging from one shoulder to the other. When he turned to look back, they both raised their arms at the same time. Crixos managed to laugh. "You'll be far away before they realize they don't have any horses. . . . And besides, we'll be able to steal some more!" He laughed. Spartacus was looking at him. He murmured, "Good-bye, . . ." as Crixos disappeared into the night, ". . . gladiator!"

Spartacus kept looking in his direction for a long time. Polla was coming up behind him, on the other side of the rock. She went to the Thracian and put an arm around his waist. With her head on his shoulder, she said, "You're far away. Come back.

Talk to me. Why are you so far away?" Spartacus did not answer immediately. Polla looked up. She ran her hand over his face.

"I'm watching Crixos," he said. He put one arm around Polla's shoulders and stroked her hair, his eyes still lost in the direction Crixos had gone. Polla nestled against him. They walked for a while, close against each other, and stopped at a turn in the path. There, twenty thousand torches were lighted beneath them, but a silence hovered over the camp, broken only by the whinny of a horse, the response of another. The fugitives were ready to leave. In the silence, a hammering could be heard, quickly increasing in volume; soon it swept through the whole valley. Lighted at its base by the torches, the mountain seemed even higher in the dark sky. Its sides echoed the rumbling, multiplying its strength. Several hundred torches quickly moved about, forming up in two lines. Now the noise of hooves could be distinguished in the mad scramble falling on the camp. The fugitives who had formed the two lines threw their torches into a pile and ran back to the main body of the camp. Behind them, above the torches lighting up the defile, the Celts' horses burst into the scene, shouldering each other, foaming at the mouths. A cry of terror rose from the camp. The fugitives flattened themselves against the mountainsides in a quick, violent rustling. Up above, the brown herd was charging. Suddenly seeing the wall of fire in front of them, the first horses reared and the following ones crushed into them. The lead animals went down. A few others jumped over them and tumbled down into the flames, their legs broken. The dust raised by their galloping followed in while the animals crushed into a wall of burning flesh, its awful stench filling the defile. Behind, the hoofbeats had died down, giving way to a long wave of neighing. A shout of victory rose from the camp and the men rushed forward, led by Gannicus.

"Crixos has sent us his horses," said Spartacus.

"Is he leaving?"

"He's left."

"Why?"

"He can't help it; time is crushing him. . . . He'll never see our city!"

"Hold me tight!"

He stroked her hair. She had put both her arms around his waist. "What is there after death?"

"I don't know . . ."

Looking tiny as she nestled against Spartacus, Polla whispered, "Yes, you do. You know everything."

"I think that after death there is nothing, but life goes on everywhere."

"How do you know there's nothing?"

He stroked her face and hair. "I know that life goes on because I have seen death. I have seen men fight. Nothing, no sign indicated that one of them would stop living a minute later. Then, all of a sudden, one of them fell. Then there was a kind of silence, a darkness in the silence. Nevertheless, the sky would still be blue. Some place, even, children would be singing. But the others were there, their bellies open, their mouths in the sand. So, I loved them. And I understood. All that silence, all that cold, that was life going on. . . . The more uselessly I risked my own life in the arena, the more precious it became to me. Since we got away, I've been dreaming of a warm, happy life. If I had to fight tomorrow, it would be against those who want to take that dream away from me. It's my only reason for living. I'll devote my whole life to making it come true, or die fighting for it. It's the same thing. . . ."

Polla trembled and squeezed tight against him. He stroked her hair and put an arm under her shoulder. They walked back down to the camp that way.

Gannicus had dispatched the wounded horses and men were busy around him cutting up large quarters of meat. The horses still standing were retrieved and spread around the camp. As soon as Spartacus arrived, Gannicus went up to him. Castus had been put on a stretcher drawn by a horse. The torches had been damped. Spartacus raised his arm and set out toward the north. Behind him, thirty thousand runaways began to move. Farther away, in the valley, other fugitives were still arriving in larger or smaller groups. Seeing that the others had broken camp, they fell in behind them without stopping.

ARENA

XI

The sixteenth of the calends of January was the start of the feast of Saturn; it lasted two days or three, according to the cities. During the Saturnalia, all commercial activity was suspended. The circuses being closed, people either visited relatives or friends in small groups, or else stayed home for family gatherings. Everyone received gifts and joined in the general good mood of the period. Even the poorest found a way, several days ahead, to set aside some of the food distributed more generously by their patrons at this time of the year so as to be able to organize the traditional feast. By the light of the lamps, mothers told their little ones how Saturn, having devoured his children, had been driven from heaven by Jupiter; how, once on earth, he had hidden in Latium; how he had been welcomed there by Janus and had taught the Romans the art of agriculture; how he had brought them peace, plenty, and justice—the Golden Age.

In Rome, the men of certain powerful families gathered merrily at the foot of the Capitol, at the temple of Saturn in which the public treasury was kept, before going home to their own tables. After the feast, the youngest slaves, eager for enjoyment, ran through the streets dressed in their masters' togas. Provided with money, they drank in the shops, sang, knocked over urinals, and carried on a great uproar until the small hours without fear of the guards, who laughingly allowed themselves to be molested. Women called in their favorite slaves and gave presents to them; others took advantage of their husbands' absence to run out with their girl friends and meet the slaves released in the City. Some of them even locked themselves in their homes with their slaves and the orgy lasted as long as the master, himself consorting with other slaves, did not recall his people. Or, quite simply, until everyone fell asleep, exhausted.

But, that year, slaves and citizens did not look forward to the Saturnalia in the same manner. For the stranger arriving in Rome, Brundisium, or Capua, it was impossible to detect the tension prevailing in the city; people were getting ready for the holiday as in previous years; but no longer in the same spirit.

For more than six months, slaves had been fleeing from homes and farms to go and join Spartacus, wherever he was. When the Thracian's name happened to be spoken by their masters in their presence, some of the slaves became aware of the look they were given and they went on with their work tensely, ill at ease; others would smile, reassured by the length of time they had spent in the service of a given household and the familiarity their masters tolerated. It was not uncommon, however, for slaves to have a relative among the fugitives or to be the remaining few servants in a house deserted by the majority of its personnel. But, whatever the length of service, the deepest mistrust now prevailed in the relationships between masters and slaves, and the greatest goodwill of old servants who had remained faithful, devoted to their masters' families, was of no avail. Instances were cited of slaves who had fled, carrying off their mistresses' jewels, or after murdering their masters. Idleness helping, tongues wagged on in the days preceding the Saturnalia of 72, magnifying the theft of a chicken into a jewel robbery, the purloining of a cloak into the murder of a master. Taking advantage of these feelings on the part of the citizens, brigands looted shops after having knocked out their owners, set fire to the establishments of patrons they considered to have been ungenerous, and intercepted shipments of silks or perfumes. The slaves of masters thus robbed or attacked ran away, since they were sure of being accused of these misdeeds.

By following the rumors, it would have been impossible to reconstruct the itinerary of Spartacus and the runaways in terms of the offenses and crimes they were accused of, because, throughout the country, everyone claimed to have seen them or to have been their victim.

That winter, parents would threaten their disobedient children that Spartacus would get them, if they did not eat their soup or go to bed without tears. Even slaves who were in charge of children, or teaching them, used the Thracian's name in order to be obeyed.

In a few months, Spartacus' name had become the symbol of a terrifying legend. The earlier uprisings led by Eunous or Athenio were also referred to. Some even went so far as to confuse the names and facts, blaming Spartacus for crimes committed by Marius or Cinna—among others, the opening of the doors of the prisons of Etruria. Others, in order to appear interesting at dinner or in the baths, "had heard from an unimpeachable source that . . ." and recounted stories going back to Hannibal, that everyone had heard a hundred times, but that never missed their goal: to attract attention. And yet, even though the misdeeds attributed to Spartacus were generally false, the citizens became convinced of them, made them the basis of their daily lives, even if they did not believe them. These misdeeds were the news, the event of the day. And one might almost have said that those who never mentioned them were looked at askance, as if they were suspect themselves. Thus, as the tongues wagged, Spartacus' barbarian hordes were said to threaten the countryside and the cities and to be at once at Brundisium and at Capua, or in the North and in the South; and Spartacus, at the same time wind and pollen, a knife between his teeth and bespattered with blood, revived the terrible and the marvelous, according to the social standing and the imagination of the "unimpeachable source" spreading the rumor.

And thus it was that that year the Saturnalia were celebrated throughout the country in a totally different manner. Inflamed by the lies and the secret libations, young minds dreamed up the most horrible kinds of reprisals. Taking advantage of the general relaxation of supervision within their families and within the cities, young men came together at nightfall, armed with daggers and swords hidden under the folds of their cloaks. They had mutually inquired, several days before the festival, into the comings and goings of their parents, the visits they planned to pay or receive during the festivities. Although distrust prevailed in the slave families and many of them had decided not to celebrate the day of Saturn, many of the younger ones allowed themselves to be tempted by the recollections of earlier feasts which had been evoked so often in front of them; some agreed to go out as messengers or litter carriers while others went, on the express orders of their young masters, directly to the meeting place of the plotters to whom they themselves belonged.

All these slaves were massacred. Some of the plotters went so far as to go into houses where they knew they would find mistresses giving themselves to their slaves. There, the most horrible scenes took place. While the masters were celebrating in neighboring rooms, the slaves were murdered in the arms of their mistresses or the beds of their masters. Those among the citizens who put up a fight were either beaten to death or stabbed, and their houses were sacked.

Such scenes took place in several cities of Campania and Latium, where the guards, either out of complicity, or because they took the dying cries for sounds of revelry, did not intervene.

In Rome, the discovery of the murdered slaves plunged the citizenry into a murderous frenzy; groups of "vigilantes" joined with the plotters and a slave hunt ensued. The guards closed their eyes to it all, having little desire to enter into open struggle against these wild gangs who were threatening to set fire to homes and tenements if the masters did not turn over their slaves; but, well before dawn, by themselves or in groups, the stronger of the slaves had fled to go looking for Spartacus. The plotters, afraid of encountering organized groups of runaways outside the City, did not venture beyond the gates, but they left men posted there and went carefully through every house, every shop, every tenement, until every slave who had remained in town had perished. They considered whether a ludus with sixty remaining gladiators should be stormed. But that would have meant at the same time depriving themselves of the promised games, and this plan was abandoned for that reason and also because the local lanista kept a personal guard almost as numerous as his gladiators. And, as the day moved forward, the plotters succumbed to fatigue; they got drunk and at nightfall went home, singing, stepping over the corpses of their victims. So ended, that year, the feast of Saturn.

ARENA

XII

At the beginning of the year 72, the Senate was informed that the body of fugitives had been split, the Celts making their way through Apulia toward the Adriatic and the rest of Spartacus' troop going up toward Picenum. The senators immediately decreed mass levies of legionaries; in a few weeks they had six legions which they divided among the two consuls of the year, Gellius Publicola and Lentulus Clodianus, and the propraetor Quintus Arrius. With these six legions, the Senate now had a total of eight, including the two normally assigned to the Cisalpine proconsul, Cassius Longinus, which were stationed north of the Rubicon. This then was no longer merely a police force, but a veritable army of forty thousand men.

In a combined action, the consul Publicola and the propraetor Arrius set out with ten thousand men each in pursuit of Crixos, while the other consul, Clodianus, also at the head of two legions took up the trail of Spartacus, with the intention of avoiding any actual engagement, but following him until a favorable moment for attack.

Crixos, for his part, convinced that Rome would never send

legionaries after him, was taking advantage of his freedom. Having attacked several Apulian cities, he spent the best part of his time in orgies. With Oenomaos, he had surrounded himself with two thousand Celts who sacked cities, securing considerable booty which they amassed in a cave outside Luceria. At first mistaking Crixos' troops for Spartacus' and determined to make the most of their freedom, some ten thousand runaways joined the Celts and gave no further thought to joining the Thracian, thus through their numbers further increasing Crixos' confidence.

After a few days of this proximity, the citizens of Apulia wished for nothing more than the arrival of the Romans. They were not long in coming. Outside Luceria, where they had spent the night in orgies, Oenomaos and his men were surrounded by Publicola and Arrius; none of them escaped the massacre. Immediately, consul Publicola sent scouts in all directions to locate Crixos' camp. But the Celt, warned by his marauders of the presence of legionaries, decided on the simplest of tactics: he retreated to the heights of Mount Gargano. Out of training and weakened by their excesses, the Celts climbed the first slopes of the mountain with difficulty, and by the time they reached the summit they were exhausted. This tactic, which had nearly proved fatal to Spartacus when he was besieged by Glaber on Vesuvius, provided no more than a dead-end retreat. Harried by the legionaries, the Celts continued their retreat, but after having traversed the mountain top in its entire length, they had to face the fact: they could retreat no farther for Mount Gargano was none other than the spur, the jut of the Italian coast out into the Adriatic. With their backs to the sea, battle was inevitable.

Made cautious by the lightning victories of the fugitives, Publicola and Arrius were sparing with their men; they set up their camp at the foot of Gargano and posted a strategic line of guards from Sipus to Teanum Apulum. The Celts were poorly equipped to withstand the cold and hunger which immediately gripped them. The second day of the siege, it began to rain. Crixos said to Capito, "Spartacus was right. . . . Rome sent its legions after us!" He checked his weapons. His men were silent, like gladiators before the fights. Crixos looked at them. Each one was going to fight for himself, without the enthusiasm that sparked Spartacus' troops.

The third day of the siege, the rain which had been falling since the day before had not stopped. Crixos received word that the legionaries had come closer to the camp during the night. Gloomily, Crixos took up his helmet and his weapons. He crossed the camp without saying a word. As he went by, the men got up, took up their weapons, and fell in behind him. At the top of the slope leading to the Romans' camp, Capito was next to Crixos. "Spartacus was right, . . ." the Celt said to him. "We're back in the arena! . . . With him, I had the feeling I was fighting for something. . . . You know what he asked me?" The big Celt smiled tenderly as he asked this question. "He asked me what I had left after I had eaten a sheep and raped three girls!" He laughed. "That's something Spartacus will never understand! I'm dying of hunger! Aren't you hungry?"

"Yes, I am," said Capito.

Crixos turned around. All the men were looking at him. He raised his arm that held the mace, without saying a word, and started down without looking back.

When they were out in the open, the Romans greeted them first with a hail of arrows. The Celts advanced in a straight line, fighting with desperation, without any discipline, morally defeated before they started. There was a hecatomb. Immediately surrounded, Crixos whirled his mace to terrible effect, but a velite leaped from his horse on to the Celt's back and buried a dagger in his neck, beneath the queue that Crixos had been so proud of. The Celt had time to grab the velite's head. He broke his neck with one arm, quickly, against his shoulder. A lance went through his chest and it was all over. Crixos was dead before he hit the ground. The men and women who had followed him suffered the same fate.

Only one man escaped the massacre: Capito. He had fallen into a hole from the first moment of contact with the legionaries: his trident had remained stuck in the ground. A legionary who had seen the Samnite fall grabbed the trident at the same moment as Capito, who was getting back up. Off balance, the legionary fell on Capito, who was holding his sica point upward; the dagger went right through the young Roman's belly. Above them, the battle was joined; Capito made no further move, the legionary lying bleeding on top of him. Two men fell on them and fought each other there. Capito got a mace-blow on the arm during that fight. A legionary and a very young Celt rolled on the ground; Capito released his arm and did not even have to swing his sica; the legionary rolled onto it. The young Celt was already out of the hole, continuing the fight. Capito spent the day there, without moving. In the evening, a decurion came to see who had fallen there; he jumped into the ditch and turned the corpses over. He saw Capito covered with the legionary's blood and took him to be dead. Capito stayed there all that night and the next day. When night came again, he freed himself; the legionaries had struck camp. The moon lighted the thousands of bodies of his companions fallen there. He took a legionary's tunic and dressed in it; he thrust the sica through his belt and came out of his hole. There he stood, alone, on this desolate slope of the Gargano, covered with corpses. Very far below, torches were going by on the road to Teanum Apulum. Capito fell to his knees, exhausted. He had had nothing to eat for four days. His tall body moved loosely inside the legionary's tunic. His arm that had been hit by the mace hung straight down, as if dislocated. His features drawn, his lashless, pale eyes half-closed, his bald pate shining in the moonlight, the Samnite's head was weaving above his broad shoulders. He collapsed, his head on his knees, right beside a dead man's thighs. The Samnite stayed in this position a long time, unable to move. It was well into the night when he was finally able to pull himself together. Barely conscious, he took his sica and crawled on his knees, dragging over the bodies of his comrades until he reached the covered spot where the Romans had camped. He found a stake he could lean on to get up. Clenching his teeth, he went staggering down the Gargano; at dawn, he was found, inanimate, near the road leading to Teanum. Seeing the legionary's tunic, a citizen fed Capito and helped him up into his cart, in which the Samnite fell asleep. The man took him straight to the camp of propraetor Quintus Arrius, near Teanum. When Capito awakened, he was inside a tent, surrounded by sleeping Romans. He felt his belt; his sica was no longer there. He got up and took his neighbor's sword. There were nine legionaries in the tent; going from one to the next, without haste, he plunged the sword into their throats. Under the bloody head of one of them, he found a quarter of a mutton, which he ate on the spot, amidst his victims. He stole a large cloak and went out of the tent. He shivered in the cold; a light snow was falling, covering the ground and the tents. Avoiding the town, he walked straight forward, toward the North, looking for Spartacus.

Walking by day, hiding by night, Capito one morning reached a small lake on the shores of which a troop had recently been camped. Following the tracks left in the snow, he walked uphill under the fir trees all day and part of the night, and suddenly found himself before a legionary standing guard, leaning against a rock. His helmet was shining in the night. The man turned his head and saw the silhouette of Capito clearly outlined against the snow. He drew his sword and spread his legs, covering the entire path. Capito quickly looked around him: to his right, the rock rose in a gradual slope under a mire of leaves covered with snow; to the left, the fir-covered terrain fell off almost sheer. The legionary took two steps forward; he was as tall as Capito, young, with a black beard framing his face. Capito, tired by his long walk and still weak, did not feel up to doing battle; besides, the clash of the swords might attract other sentries. His heavy blade in his hand, Capito stepped off slightly to the left. The legionary took two more quick steps, his sword raised, and made a great swipe with it from left to right. Capito had to dodge toward the right and duck to avoid it, then he struck in his turn. The legionary dodged it by jumping sidewise, turning his back to the ravine. Capito tried one more weak blow, which the other evaded without trouble, and in an almost slow move he raised his sword. Doubled over, Capito quickly went over to the edge of the chasm, thus forcing the legionary to execute an about-face. His sword raised, he brought it down on the shoulder which Capito was practically presenting to him. Capito rushed forward under the blow, which came down on a stone, leaving a string of sparks between the Samnite's heels; Capito seized the soldier's legs and quickly stood up, carrying the full weight of the man on his one wounded arm. The legionary, dragged forward by the violence of his own blow, found himself chest forward over the abyss. Capito let go of his legs and quickly turned around. The legionary fell without a sound, almost docilely, as if he had dived this way into the ravine a hundred times. Capito went up onto the slippery leaves between the rocks and found an opening through which he long observed the plateau.

Legionaries on the march always camped, even if only for a single night, as if they were settling in for a six-months' siege. Their camp was surrounded by a trench ten to twelve feet deep and by a rampart surmounted by a palisade. The tents were lined up on the whole length of the plateau, all facing the center of the camp, where the trophies, eagles, fasces, and standards stood. The center lane was the widest; halfway down it, the tents formed a circle around the trophies. On either side of this central lane were four parallel lanes of the same length. At the four corners of the camp, the horses. At every tenth tent, up and down and across, three long stakes tilted in to form a tripod holding the water rations. Between each two groups of ten tents, clearly separated from those of the men, stood the centurion's red tent. Taller and broader than the others, near the trophies in the center, were the tents of the consul and those of his quaestors and lictors.

Capito suddenly stood up. A man had just come out of the camp, heading toward the spot where the other legionary had been standing guard. Capito quickly went down and waited for him behind a tree.

When the other went by, looking for his companion, Capito knocked off his helmet and struck him down with a blow of his sword pommel. He put on the helmet. With the tunic and the cloak, Capito looked like any veteran legionary. He turned the legionary over with a kick. He then put his knee on the man's chest and waited for him to regain consciousness. When the man opened his eyes, Capito grabbed his hair and pulled it back, stretching his neck against which he was pointing his sword.

"How many legionaries in the camp?"

"Two legions," the man whispered.

"Ten thousand men?"

"Yes."

"The leader? Who?"

"The consul."

"What consul?"

"Clodianus."

"Where is Spartacus?"

"Who . . . who are you?"
"Saturn. Where is Spartacus?"
"Ahead . . ."
"Far?"
"Above Bovianum."
"When's the attack for?"
The man hesitated. Capito pricked his throat and a bit of blood oozed up under the sword's point. "When?"
"Don't know! . . . Tomorrow, I think . . . I don't know! . . ."
Capito slit his throat and pushed the body down into the ravine. Wrapping himself in the legionary's cloak, he went up to the camp, which he crossed from one end to the other, passing before the tents at a steady pace. Reaching the end of the lane, he went straight up to the two legionaries guarding the horses.
"Consul's messenger . . . A horse."
A man went and untied one. "Where are you going?" the other asked.
"Rome."
Capito took the reins that were held out to him.
"You wouldn't catch them sending me to Rome!" said the second legionary. Capito did not listen any further. Pulling the animal, he quickly went down the path on the other side of the plateau. After he had passed the last sentry, he put his sword back through his belt and disappeared into the night in search of Spartacus.

ARENA

XIII

Since Crixos had left, Spartacus' troop had made hardly any progress. After the bloodbath of the Saturnalia, many more fugitives had swollen the Thracian's ranks and multiplied his problems. He no longer spoke except to give the command for departure, and sometimes he merely signaled it by raising his arm.

On the heights, the troop moved forward, compact, silent, determined. For the first time in their lives, these runaway slaves found themselves part of the body of a movement of revolt. Their numbers reassured them. They had often been tempted to escape, but they knew of no others who had succeeded, for one isolated slave had practically no chance of getting away. At night, he is locked up; he can therefore escape only by day, but since he cannot run in the open without attracting attention, he has to hide out all day and await the night. But before night comes, guards—or trusty slaves—have noticed his disappearance and set out to find him. The runaway slave is generally killed on sight, because the master has sole responsibility before the law for his slaves, whether they be captive or fugitive. The runaway is therefore relentlessly pursued, lest he give vent to acts of vengeance against his masters or their property. In escaping, the slave loses the confidence of his masters and, despite the monetary loss his death means to them, he is either killed on the spot or chained until death to a mill, along with criminals, old horses, or oxen. The pack sent out to hunt him down knows where to look for him and generally finds him very fast, huddling, trembling, between two bushes, under a pile of leaves, in a hole. An entire family can escape more easily from a city than a resolute man from a farm.

Escape itself was thus a process of selection among the slaves; those who left had made a choice: they understood the fatal outcome their undertaking might have. The success of the escape was a second process of selection; it was proof that the slave had been able to hide and bide his time without panicking at the sound of the footsteps or shouts of the pack hunting him down. The third process of selection was a moral and physical test: to get to Spartacus' camp wherever it might be. On arrival, the runaway still had the eyes of a hunted man, but a deep joy quickly pervaded him; he had finally joined forces with those who were fighting for their freedom. Having won one first great victory over himself and the oppressor, he arrived and mingled with the others as a river flows into the sea. And, like the river, the flow of fugitives knew no letup.

It was not rare that several fugitives, shortly after their arrival, asked to see Spartacus. They had conjured up a Roman image of him as the great leader, living apart from the rest, in a larger and more comfortable tent than all the others. Then someone would point the Thracian out to them, seated, with a child on his lap, or cutting branches that would be turned into lances. They went to him, embraced him, thanked him for being there with his troop. Spartacus would listen solemnly and, according to the circumstances of the escape as they were related to him, congratulate soberly or remain silent. And the newcomers would stay within the ranks, a bit disappointed at times, but at any rate taken aback by the welcome tendered them by Spartacus and the others.

One day, in a group arriving from Lucania, there was a pregnant woman, and her pregnancy was in a very advanced stage. Alba had known her. She took Polla to this group. The woman was about to give birth when Spartacus gave the departure signal at nightfall. Polla ran up to him, asked him to wait. "We have to leave right away," he said. "We can't stay here any longer." A stretcher was made and slung between two horses. The woman gave birth on it without delaying the march.

That was the evening when Capito got back to the troop. As soon as they heard his horse's hoofbeat, the former gladiators who were guarding the rear hid in a thicket. One of them jumped on the Samnite as he came by, with raised dagger. Capito recognized him. "It's me, Capito!" The man held himself back in time; blood was already begining to ooze on Capito's neck. The gladiators recognized him and let him go; he gave his horse to Alba as he went by and went up through the troop as far as Spartacus, who was walking alongside Gannicus. They marched all night, separated from the others, listening to Capito report Crixos' words and relate his defeat and death. When he had finished, it was day. Spartacus, who had listened to Capito without interrupting him, asked him, "Why did you come back?"

"Because I'm not a gladiator any more, but . . . there are Romans everywhere."

Breaking with the usual routine, Spartacus did not halt the march during the day. The troop reached a particularly narrow defile; Spartacus immediately raised his arm. To the left of the entrance to the defile was a small spring. Capito ran to it and drank in long gulps. As he swallowed, with his head back, he spied a spot of sky in the middle of the rock. He closed his eyes and opened them again; the spot was still there. He jumped over the spring and spread some of the branches. After a few paces forward, he found himself in front of a rock. Going on toward the spring between the rock and the branches, he found himself at the foot of a narrow mountain pass at the summit of which he again saw the spot of sky that had surprised him. The pass was difficult to go through, covered with round slippery stones. Capito alerted Spartacus who in his turn came to inspect the terrain. He made up his mind immediately. After several hours of climbing, they reached a slightly inflected plateau, covered with heather and rocks; farther on, the mountain shot up almost vertically at that point. Spartacus turned around. All along the pass, and far, far behind, his troop was following, worn out by this long march ending with the crossing of this slippery pass. Night had fallen by the time the gladiators in the rear reached the foot of the pass. The last of the fugitives, the oldest and the children, too exhausted to climb up, had stopped on the stones on either side of the pass. Spartacus went down the pass with those who had reached the plateau first and slept there all afternoon. He himself placed the sentries at the approaches to the cave in the foliage which concealed the entry to the pass and sent some hundred men to spend the night even farther down, almost in the valley. The Thracian climbed back up the pass between the prone bodies and took a dozen men with him; they followed him up the rock at the edge of the plateau. At the top, Spartacus stationed a first team of six men to keep a watch on the defile and left the other six to relieve them. To the south, the entry to the defile was practically at the level of the cave hiding the opening to the pass. The defile broadened toward its center, allowing six or eight horses to go through abreast; at that point, a rather steep rock-and-vine-shoot-covered slope came down from the plateau. The defile narrowed again at the north, leaving just enough space for a chariot or for two horses abreast.

The day after Spartacus' troop reached this plateau, the first marauders sent into the plain the day before came back to camp bringing intelligence. They had located Clodianus' two legions half a day's march away. With the marauders, there was a limping man who had been wounded in the thigh and asked to speak to Spartacus, but the Thracian had been gone since morning with Capito; they had gone up to the summit where the teams of six men were watching the defile.

On the plateau, beside a small fire, Castus and Gannicus were lying with their hands behind their heads when Polla and Alba arrived with the marauders and the wounded man.

"He wants to talk to Spartacus," Alba said.

Castus looked at the man. He shrugged. "Everybody wants to talk to Spartacus. Let him wait."

The wounded man fell to one knee and warmed his hands, blue from the cold, over the fire. "He has to know right away," he said.

"Where is he?" Polla asked.

Gannicus indicated with his chin. "Up there."

Castus rose up on one elbow to look at the wounded man. "What does he have to know?"

The wounded man turned his head away. He was very pale. Alba leaned over him and gave him something to drink.

"First of all, where do you come from?" Castus asked with a distrustful scowl.

The other was leaning against Alba's legs. He was breathing with difficulty. "From Rome . . . Clodianus, the consul, is coming with two legions! . . ."

"That's true," said one of the marauders. "We saw them last night. They're half a day's march from here."

They all looked at the newcomer in silence.

"What's he doing up there?" Polla asked Gannicus.

"He's walking, he's talking . . . A little while ago, he yelled," Gannicus said. He shouted, imitating Spartacus, "Crix-ooooos . . . Crix-ooooos! . . ."

"Is he alone?"

"With Capito and the watch."

"I followed them," the wounded man went on. "Last night, I strangled a sentry and . . . I slipped into their camp . . ."

The man looked at his thigh, slit down to the knee. "He put up a good fight! He was guarding a centurion's tent. I heard someone talking, one they called Carbo—he must have been a centurion. He was saying that Publicola, that's the consul, and the propraetor Arrius were coming from Apulia with four legions . . ."

"The ones that killed Crixos and all the Celts!" said Castus. The little Celt got up, restlessly.

"Four legions!" Alba exclaimed.

"And to think Crixos used to say that Rome would never send its legionaries against slaves and gladiators!" said Castus. "And Capito believed him! They sent twenty thousand of their legionaries against them! . . . What else did your centurion have to say?"

"Publicola and Arrius are going to attack Spartacus from the rear while he is facing Clodianus' two legions," the wounded man said. He took Alba's hand and she helped him up. "Spartacus must . . . He must know right away! . . . Right away! . . ."

Quite a few others had by now surrounded the little group.

Everybody had heard and stayed there, thinking, their eyes glued to the little fire. Farther on, to the rear, people were shoving each other, to see, to hear better.

"He needs me," Polla said, looking up toward the rock.

Gannicus went up to her. He said softly, "And you need him. You can be more useful to him when he comes back down. For now . . ."

"He's hurting," Polla said.

"Yes."

Gannicus took the arm of a young mirmillo. "Velox. Help Castus hold up the wounded man; he has to talk to Spartacus."

Castus and Velox placed the wounded man's arms around their shoulders and moved off. The others remained around the fire, silent. All that could be heard was the crackling of twigs in the embers.

"We didn't march fast enough," said a big red-headed Samnite wearing a black skin that came down to his knees. Polla, who was next to him, looked at him, absent. He went on, addressing her: "If we had marched faster, we wouldn't have to fight any more."

"Maybe," said Polla, still vacant.

But the other persisted, raising his voice. Everyone looked at him. "We weren't supposed to have to fight any more . . . Spartacus said so!"

A murmur ran through the ranks now pressed around the little fire. Gannicus looked in the direction Castus and the wounded man had gone. They were almost at the foot of the rock. The climb would be hard with that man to carry. Gannicus turned to the big Samnite. "If we have to fight, we'll fight, Valens."

Valens looked at Gannicus as if he had said something outrageous. He turned toward the others to answer, hoping they would stand behind him. "Against the legionaries? They didn't take a single prisoner! Capito was the only one out of ten or fifteen thousand to get away!"

"Crixos was bound to lose," Gannicus said calmly.

"Why aren't we?"

Everybody waited for Gannicus' reply; he realized the importance of what he had to say and weighed his words.

"We're not in the same fix as the Celts; they couldn't move! On one side, the sea, on the other, the mountain. So they took refuge on Mount Gargano. The legionaries didn't have to hurry; they just surrounded them and waited. . . ."

Gannicus was sweating. Alba was looking at him as if she were seeing him for the first time, her mouth half-open, her head lowered a little. Gannicus caught her glance; Alba's eyes smiled to him as her mouth opened a little farther.

"So what?" Valens shouted. "What's to keep them from surrounding us?"

"Crixos had no rations in reserve and the legionaries knew it. The Celts were weakened by . . ." His eyes met Alba's again, and this time he had to lower his. "By . . . women and orgies," he went on in a less assured voice. He coughed. No one seemed to notice his embarrassment, since they were no more used to talking than he was. "The legionaries knew all that. When they attacked, the Celts weren't able to resist."

This time, Valens bounded up.

"Capito never said all that. How do you know Crixos didn't have any reserves?"

"I know because I knew Crixos. He gobbled everything up on the spot. I could see that on his face the very first day."

It was very cold on the plateau; fires had been lighted here and there. Everybody being still exhausted from the long march of the day before, the group gradually broke up. Soon, around the fire, there was only Polla looking up at the rock, Alba—who now seemed to be breathing only through Gannicus' mouth—Valens, and Gannicus.

"You could see it on his face? What do you mean?" said the Samnite, raising his thick red eyebrows.

"He wore his death on his face by his way of life. . . . And the Celts did too. Spartacus predicted everything that happened to them."

Valens took a long look at the Celt, visibly making a great effort to comprehend. He said, "All the Celts were not gladiators like you."

"That's true, but they lived like gladiators," said Gannicus. He was speaking with bowed head, gazing fixedly at the embers. "They ate, they drank, they did everything . . . as though it were their last time. As though they were going to their last fight the next day. You can make love like that . . . because . . ."

Valens was looking at Gannicus, openmouthed, frowning. As for Alba, her nostrils dilated, she had lowered her head and was looking at Gannicus with eyes a little lost under her now half-closed lids.

". . . because . . . the end of love is like the end of life: your body goes away but you stay there, eyes closed, with your belly oozing away. . . ."

Valens looked at Alba and Polla to see whether they were paying attention to what Gannicus was saying. Raising his arms, he said, "There he goes, talking about love again!"

Alba smiled strangely; her mouth had never been so wide. Without taking her eyes off Gannicus, she asked, in a muffled voice, "Does he talk about it often?"

"All the time. He can't say a thing without talking about love."

Gannicus smiled, gazing at the embers. "That's because love challenges everything—takes up everything anew."

"He needs me," Polla said.

"It all comes back to love, all the time," Gannicus said, going on with his thought.

"We were talking about Crixos," Valens cut in, "not about love!"

Gannicus, listless, looked at Valens. He said, as if to himself, "You can't spend your whole life dying!"

Her hands clasped over her stomach, her eyes on the rock, Polla mumbled, "You can't spend your whole life making love!"

Valens looked at Gannicus and Polla. He shook his head and left them, going over to Alba. "Alba. Don't you think the legionaries are going to surround us?" Alba, with a start, stared at the Samnite without seeing him. Valens eyed her for a moment and walked off with a sigh.

"We won't let ourselves be surrounded, Valens, not now that we've been warned," said Gannicus.

"We're lucky," Alba said.

Valens suddenly turned his head. Alba walked toward Gannicus; she gave a small laugh that seemed to come from her nose. She went right near the Celt, her upper lip slightly pulled back over her teeth. "Don't you think we're lucky, Gannicus?" she whispered. Gannicus had lowered his eyes to look at her. She was so near him now that he could feel Alba's breasts against his chest. His eyes left hers to look down at her breasts. Although Alba was covered by a thick cloak held at the waist with a military belt, the broad points of her nipples stretched the material, drawing between them a horizontal line that hollowed and tautened with her breathing. "Your eyes aren't blue today. . . . They're green," said Alba almost without moving her lips.

Gannicus looked back up at her and said, "Why?" Alba was not moving any more. "Why are we lucky?" he asked again.

"Because the wounded man warned us the legionaries were coming."

Gannicus looked at her a long time. "Yes, very lucky, Alba." He smiled at her. She moved away a bit, looking at his mouth.

Valens sat down near the fire, making showers of sparks by throwing in twigs that caught fire as soon as they touched the embers. He had been talking to himself for a bit; suddenly, his voice rose. "And I say we didn't march fast enough!" His hands clasped in front of his knees, he leaned back a little and looked at Polla, standing with her back to the fire, opening and closing her hands above the low flames that bent beneath the wind and roared as it went by. "What do you think about it, Polla?"

"Maybe . . ."

Valens took out after Alba again.

"If we'd marched faster, we wouldn't have to fight any more!"

Thinking he had still been talking to her, Polla replied, as vacantly as ever, "Maybe not! . . ."

Alba had squatted on her heels, her arms resting on her knees, her hands dangling over the fire, her hip against Gannicus' leg.

"That's what Spartacus said!" Valens snorted.

Alba looked up at Valens. "We have enough time to prepare a surprise attack."

"Spartacus didn't say that!" said Gannicus, who seemed to have lost some of his calm. Valens looked at him, swaying back and forth now, his hands crossed over his knees. "He said," Gannicus went on, "that once we were over the mountain, we wouldn't be bothered so much and we would build our city."

"If we left without waiting! If we left without waiting!" Valens said.

Gannicus spoke a little louder. "Yes."

"But we did wait! And we're waiting still!" Valens shouted.

"We set out the very night Crixos left!"

Valens shouted again, "And we didn't march fast enough on account of him."

Gannicus' growing irritation suddenly seemed to drop off. "Because of Crixos?"

"Yes," said Valens, jumping to his feet. "Because of Crixos, 'cause Spartacus was hoping he'd come back."

"Maybe we didn't march fast enough," Gannicus conceded, "but Crixos didn't have anything to do with it."

Valens had not listened. "Well, what was he doing while we were waiting for him?" he asked, pacing back and forth in front of the fire. "He marched twice as fast as we did in the opposite direction."

"That's right, the Celts covered a lot of ground. But why? They were eating and their road was downhill toward the sea."

Valens suddenly stopped, facing Gannicus, on the other side of the fire. "Spartacus was hoping that Crixos would come back and join us, I'm sure of that."

Alba got up and went and put her arm around Polla's waist. The wind was getting stronger and Polla's hair was sweeping over her shoulders, blowing into her face. Alba sat down with her friend and started to braid Polla's hair.

"I don't know what Spartacus was hoping," said Gannicus. "But I do know the Celts were going downhill," he went on, following the movements of Alba's hands in Polla's hair. "And the legionaries were on their heels."

"What about us?" Valens cried. "The legionaries aren't only behind us; they're in front of us, too!" He flung out his arms, doubling the spread of the great black skin he was dressed in. "But we don't move! The wounded man warns us that six legions are marching on us and we just stay here while Spartacus goes up on the rocks and calls to Crixos as if he could see him in the sky!"

Her head thrown back, her hair pulled to the sides stretching her great green eyes even further, Polla said with a sigh, "If Spartacus hasn't moved, it's because he has his reasons."

Valens walked up to her. Gannicus stopped him with a question. "In Spartacus' place, you would have had us march faster?"

Valens turned toward the Celt. "That's what we should have done to avoid disaster."

"And how would you have gone about it?" asked Polla.

Valens turned around. "To do what?"

"To march faster," Alba explained.

Valens shrugged. "To march faster, you march faster. As simple as that."

"No, it's not so simple," said Gannicus. Valens looked at him. "The only day we put in a good day's march," Gannicus went on, "yesterday, half the troop arrived here half a day late—exhausted. Today, they can't move."

"Half the troop!" Valens exclaimed. "What half? The old people, the children? Talk about a troop! It's their fault. If we hadn't waited for them, we wouldn't be in this fix."

"Well, we had to wait for them; we're all together," said Gannicus.

"They're with us. That's not the same thing. And they slow down our march!"

This exchange seemed to bore Gannicus. He squatted, watching Alba's brown hands braiding Polla's red hair.

"They slow down our march!" Valens insisted more loudly.

Gannicus' jaws contracted. He looked at the heather between his knees, trying to regain his calm. "We can't help it. . . . Neither can they," he said.

Valens looked at him a moment. An idea came to him that made him smile. He quickly went over to Gannicus and squatted beside him. He said in a low voice, "If we set out now, we could get a day's head start on the legionaries."

"We can't set out now any more than we can march faster."

Valens sneered, "Because of the old people?"

"Yes. Because of the old people. They're tired."

Valens got back up, furious. "Not only do they keep us from making time, but they're also going to get us massacred. And they don't even fight: they complain! They know how to do that, all right! They can't march, but they sure have strength enough to complain!"

Valens picked up a big stone and threw it angrily into the defile.

"I can still hear Spartacus," he said. "The runaways won't join the Celts, they'll come to us, . . ." he began with emphasis, making broad gestures. "The Celts are even more savage than the Romans to their enemies; they sow terror wherever they go. The legionaries will slaughter them." Valens sneered and went on, "The legionaries . . ."

"We did everything to avoid . . ." Gannicus began.

"*Everything!*" Valens interrupted. "Don't tell me that. Tell it to the legionaries! We didn't loot," he said, clapping his hands. "We didn't eat," he punctuated with his hands again, "we even spared the fields by going around them!" Now, Valens was shouting. "But today, thirty thousand legionaries are marching against us!"

Gannicus decided to cut the matter short. "If we have to fight, we'll fight," he said in a noncommittal tone. And he walked off toward the defile without waiting for an answer.

Velox, the little mirmillo who had helped Castus accompany the wounded man, was coming back to the small fire. When he saw the young Samnite, Valens ran to him.

"Did he say anything?"

Velox shrugged. "He listened to the wounded man and asked us to leave him alone."

Valens growled. "Good. As for me, I've had enough of it!" And he walked quickly toward the pass.

Little Velox caught up with him. Running alongside Valens, he asked, "Where are you going?"

"Away."

"Away?"

"Yes."

"Where?"

Valens stopped and looked at the little mirmillo who smiled mischievously at him.

"Where?" said Valens. "What do you mean, where?"

"You say you're going away. I'm just asking where you're going. No need to get sore about it. Where are you going?"

Valens pouted sulkily. Embarrassed, he looked at his feet. "I don't know."

"*Listen to me! All of you!*"

Spartacus' voice surprised everybody. The Thracian was above the plateau, at the edge of a recess, halfway between the camp and the top of the rock.

"*Listen to me!*"

Everybody got up, came out of their tents. From every part of the plateau, the runaways started moving toward the rear, toward the foot of the rock.

While they were gathering beneath him, Spartacus walked around compulsively in the recess; at one point, he disappeared toward its rear but came back right away. He looked at the camp. No one was moving. Everyone was looking up, waiting for him to speak.

For the first time since Crixos left, Spartacus was going to talk. Many of them had never heard his voice, did not even know him. Spartacus stopped pacing. He came to the edge of the recess and raised his hands, palms toward the low, heavy sky.

"We have tried to get out of this country as quietly as possible, without disturbing anyone. They want to stop us! *They're forcing us to fight! Rome just keeps sending us back into the circus!* Gladiators or slaves, Rome just watches us die. As fugitives, Rome won't let us leave, but sends its legionaries after us. *Why?* Because Rome has decided to give us only one choice: *To live under the lash or die in the arena!*"

Spartacus stopped for a moment. His voice came back, echoing off the wall of the defile: "*. . . Or die in the arena!*"

His faded tunic merged into the reddish-brown moss of the rock. Some of the fugitives were climbing toward the top of the pass to get to see him. But, from the top of the pass, he could be heard but not seen. Now, no one could move on the plateau any longer, each one pressing below the recess from which the Thracian was speaking. His voice lashed out all of a sudden:

"The legionaries are coming! We will beat them!"

Heads wagged with surprise and anger. Spartacus had to wait for silence to be restored. "Clodianus will have to come through this defile with his two legions. We will split up into three parts: the rear and the flank will attack at the same time when the smoke signal rises from the top of this rock. At the front, the north exit of the defile, our third part will come down to close in on the Romans only after we have engaged them."

Spartacus raised his left arm.

"Arrius' and Publicola's four legions are coming through the valley, from the north. I still don't know when we'll meet up with them, but the Romans don't know where we are. So we'll have the edge of surprising them."

Enthusiastic shouts greeted these last words.

"Watch out! Only a few among you have ever fought the legionaries. But the gladiators know them well: Rome sent the legionaries into the gladiators' schools to learn defense against certain weapons; they became the gladiators' pupils! The legionaries are tough. Strong. Their work is never done. They refer to themselves as Marius' mules; not without reason. In a campaign, they act at the same time as bricklayers, ditchdiggers, engineers, and fighters. They never go to sleep at night without having set up a fortified camp. On the march, they carry more than eighty pounds of equipment. Weapons, armor, cooking utensils, hatchets, spades, saws, baskets, tent pegs, and two weeks' rations. At the end of the day's march, they cut down trees and surround their camp with a deep trench surmounted by a palisade. The legionary carries arms that are more powerful and heavier than those of any other soldier. The legion's cavalry is dangerous. Its velites are young, lightly armed; at the least signal, they swing from the horse's rump or fight on foot. . . . Do you know why the legionary loves war? . . . Because he has never lost any! To him, war is an object lesson; peace is a study and practice period. He learns in peacetime what he has seen during the war. By waging war, he has learned the best things to wage it with: Spanish swords, Numidian horses, Cretan archers, Balearic slingers. . . . The legionaries are so strong there's no difference between a charge of horses and the thrust of their lines. I know, I've fought in the Roman army."

A murmur ran through the crowd of fugitives. Spartacus raised his arm.

"There are soldiers from all over the world in the legion. They would be unbeatable if it weren't for one fault, *one serious fault: they don't know what they're fighting for!* And they never will know! . . . In this country there are only two kinds of people: those who suffer and those who make others suffer for their own private interests. Rome trains its legionaries to defend its privileges with the sword. . . . What have the Romans been doing since we ran away and came together? . . . *They've been scared!* . . . In order to fight us, they have to make up reasons. . . . *They pretend to hear a threat in what is only a cry of suffering!* They sic their legionaries on us like a weak man uses a big dog to protect him! . . . They don't know, these legionaries, that Rome looks on them as gladiators . . . but trained gladiators—trained like a big dog to kill anyone his master sics him on. We're the ones they've sicked them on. . . . We have always been the intended victims *because Rome will not tolerate our freedom any more than we want to live as slaves!*"

A long roar of anger rose from the plateau; Spartacus waited a moment for them to calm down.

"If you just remember that you have nothing but life and that they are trying to take it from you, you'll know how to defend it! After that, we will continue up north."

Spartacus quickly went down to the plateau and took ten thousand men with him. They went down the pass and through the defile. They marched on straight ahead for several leagues and Spartacus called a halt. Then, going back up the length of the column, he had everyone do an about-face and, being very sure of going back in exactly the tracks they had made as they came, they returned to the north exit of the defile. There Spartacus divided the troop along the slopes leading up above the defile and posted sentries at their summits in such a way that each one could see the central plateau from which the signal to attack would be given. He left Gannicus at the head of this troop and took the steep way up to the camp, studying the terrain as he went. He had all the baskets emptied and placed along the heights overhanging the defile; after which, the entire camp was mobilized to fill them with stones. When they were all full, Spartacus assembled a further ten thousand men in the funnel at the bottom of the pass and left them under Capito's command.

Once these measures were taken, the Thracian went back up to the plateau to sleep a little. He was walking toward his tent when Valens came up to him. The big Samnite walked alongside the Thracian for a moment without saying a word; he was taking long strides, setting his feet down heavily in front of him, flatfootedly, his knees flexed and his head bent forward. Spartacus looked sidewise at him. Valens was hesitating, as if he did not know how to broach the subject which he had apparently decided to thrash out once and for all with Spartacus. For his part, the Thracian did not seem to feel like talking. His dark skin shone on his emaciated face. The only trace of fatigue might have been the fixedness of his gaze, the slower blinking of his eyelids; perhaps also the fact that he was not helping Valens to come to the point. He looked at him once again. A deep furrow creased the Samnite's forehead in his effort to concentrate. Spartacus sighed briefly and stopped a few paces from his tent, before which Alba and Polla had built a small fire. Spartacus looked at the fire.

"You want to talk to me?"

"Yes."

"I'm listening."

Polla gave Spartacus a smile, but he did not see it; he was almost dozing. "I'm listening," he repeated.

"You said we wouldn't have to fight any more."

"No. I said if we could get over the mountains, we wouldn't have to fight any more."

"All right, if you like."

"That's what I said. Now it's too late to back out. Why? Don't you want to fight?"

"What would they do if we didn't fight?"

"Don't you know?"

"Maybe they . . ."

"No. There's no 'maybe' with the legionaries. They kill."

"I'm sick and tired of fighting."

"So am I."

The two men were talking while looking at the fire. His head bent, the Samnite looked sad. He talked in a low voice and when Spartacus spoke he listened to him with raised eyebrows, pursed lips. "But we never stop doing it," said Valens. "We never stop fighting!"

"We're being forced to."

"But . . . what if we stopped?"

"If you don't fight, you die. If you do fight, you have one chance out of ten of staying alive. Haven't you understood that yet?"

"Sure. It's because I have understood that I'm sick and tired of it. I'd rather go away."

"We're all trying to get away."

"I don't want to stop to fight any more."

"We don't either! Nobody wants to stop to fight!"

"And yet you are willing to fight."

"What else would you do?"

"Go away."

Spartacus smiled sadly. "Like you? Each man for himself?"

"Yes."

"You can't always go away. . . ."

"I won't always go away!"

Spartacus looked at Valens. The Thracian's eyes were almost closed; he raised his eyebrows very high to keep them open. "You escaped in order to join us, but you want to leave us because you don't want to fight any more. You'll never stop running away."

Valens raised his voice. "I won't always run away!"

"Sure. The day you won't run away any more, it won't be because you decided to stop. You'll be dead."

"What if we all left separately? We could get together again farther on, and we wouldn't have fought!"

Spartacus shrugged. "Separately? In fifty thousand different directions? Why should we meet again farther on if we can't stay together when there's trouble?"

"You said we'd build a city!"

Spartacus shook his head. He took Valens by the arm. "You don't understand . . . The ones who build that city will first have to go a long way together. You're not talking about our city, but only about a city." Spartacus let go of his arm. He raised his voice, impatient. "It's not just a question of putting up walls! The city we want starts right here. It started the day we all came together. That city, first of all, is the struggle to keep alive."

Valens raised his voice in turn. "I understand very well, on the contrary. The struggle to keep alive, huh?"

"Yes."

"What about Crixos?"

Spartacus blanched. Polla and Alba got up, looking at the two men. "What about Crixos?" said Spartacus in a very low voice.

"He struggled to keep alive, but he died."

Very gloomy, Spartacus answered as if to himself, "That's a bad example. Crixos didn't have anything to keep. He had a life, like everybody else, but he didn't use it to live. . . ."

Polla was crying. Spartacus went on. "Crixos measured his life by days and nights. By the passage of time. Life didn't owe him anything, but he expected something from it. He kept running after it, losing his breath . . ." Valens, Polla, and Alba were looking at Spartacus. He ran his hand over his face; his head was tilted slightly, his eyes staring at the fire, at the women's feet. "He ought to have stopped! You think Crixos struggled to keep alive?" The Thracian shook his head. "No. He counted the waves. The waves that will never stop! Each one of them struck a blow at him! So, he went into the sea. He'd already been dead a long time when he left us to live his life!" Spartacus turned his head slowly toward Valens and said, very softly, "You want to leave?"

"Yes."

Spartacus looked at him a moment and something hardened on his face. His voice was drier when he spoke. "Go!" he said.

"We could meet again! And maybe . . ."

"Your way would be too long around! You're going backward and you think you're getting away. How do you expect us to meet again?"

Valens wanted to say something, but Spartacus was no longer listening. The Thracian went off and disappeared into his tent. Valens looked at Polla, Alba. Then he saw Velox who must have been listening not far away. Alba went off toward the women's camp. Polla followed Spartacus into his tent. Valens turned toward Velox, but the little mirmillo had already turned his back on him, walking toward the defile with a big stone on his head. The Samnite shrugged his shoulders and briskly set off toward the pass with a dozen of his fellow countrymen.

In his tent, Spartacus had lain down. His hands behind his head, he had closed his eyes. Polla knelt beside him; she covered him with a cloak and bent over him, placed her lips on his mouth. "You remember," she breathed, "at Capua, you said that after the escape everything would be easy, so easy."

"I remember."

"See, it's not as easy as you thought!"

"At Capua, there was only you and me. . . ."

Polla had barely heard his answer. She leaned over a little farther, so close to his face that she could feel his breath on her cheek. "They don't want to let us get away!" he said again, and he fell asleep.

ARENA

XIV

Spartacus was awakened in the middle of the night. The scouts had come back: Clodianus and his two legions were camped two hours' march away from the defile. This mountain corridor being the only negotiable passage in this part of Samnium, the consul would certainly take it at dawn to join Arrius. Spartacus immediately sent word to Gannicus' troop to the north of the defile and to Capito's at the foot of the pass, repeating his instructions to each of them. Behind each basket of stones, the Thracian placed the strongest women and children, and went down the slope of the plateau that led to the defile at its widest point. He crossed it with a thousand men armed with daggers, lances, and tridents, and posted them on the other slope under the command of Castus, behind every rock, halfway up the slope, or at the very edges of the corridor. Once these measures had been taken, Spartacus climbed back to the plateau. Followed by several men carrying wet vine shoots, he undertook the ascent of the steep rock. The summit was swept by an icy wind. To get maximum protection against it, the men on watch had lain down. The six relief men were sleeping under the wind, huddled against one another. Spartacus found a hole several feet deep in which he piled the vine shoots. He lighted them under the cloaks and skins, and the watch began, the night watch under the wind, on the rock or on the earth hardened by the cold.

All of a sudden, surprising everyone, the gallop of several horses could be heard from the defile. The corridor was still dark even though the sky for a while had begun growing lighter in the east. No one moved. From the noise, Spartacus counted about twenty horses. They were velites sent as scouts, Spartacus knew, but in the van of what legions? Those of Arrius and Publicola, from the north? Those of Clodianus, from the south? From the distance covered by twenty animals, even if they were two abreast, the sound of their galloping echoing from wall to wall and filling the entire defile, it was impossible to determine in which direction they were going. For a moment, the Thracian looked first north then south to try to tell which way they went out. The velites had come up to the defile noiselessly and galloped into it to avoid an ambush. On the other slope, Castus let them go by without flinching. The velites emerged to the north, therefore in the van of Clodianus' legions. The Thracian then tried to detect the main body of troops to the south. Very far away, a glow was approaching: the helmets and shields of ten thousand legionaries. Spartacus looked back at the velites, who stopped a few hundred feet beyond the defile. The mixed-up tracks left by Gannicus' men led them to believe that the troop of fugitives had gone through and continued toward the north. The velites split up: one half continued on their way to meet Publicola, the other half came back toward the defile, through which, this time, the horsemen went more slowly.

Clodianus had stopped to await the reports of his scouts. When he resumed his march, the sun was up. Now it was possible to make out the color of the uniforms. Helmets, shields, weapons shone. The velites were in the van; behind them came the lictors, carrying fasces and entirely surrounding the consul's horse. Behind Clodianus came another handful of velites; farther on, marching in step, ahead of the eagles and standards, the foot soldiers. To the side, each centurion went back and forth along the flanks of his century, clearly detached from the following one by several paces. An hour later, the velites entered the defile.

Spartacus' rock stood out clearly against the gray sky, a sky heavy with snow, as it had been the day before. The Thracian and his men were lying down, observing the march. One of the watchers threw a pebble in front of Spartacus to attract his attention. The Thracian turned his head. The other raised his arm toward the north end of the defile; two or three velites were galloping back toward the legions. They had probably reached the end of the tracks left by Gannicus' troop and had not needed much thought to realize where the fugitives were: to the north, Publicola and Arrius; to the south, consul Clodianus; and in the middle, this defile.

In a few moments, the velites would be telling Clodianus where the fugitives were! Publicola would certainly be informed. Of Clodianus' two legions, only a few hundred men were in the defile; there were still more than nine thousand outside. Besieged by Publicola on the north with twenty thousand men and by Clodianus to the south with ten thousand, with no way of bringing in food supplies, the fugitives were doomed.

Spartacus was about to give Capito the signal to attack in order to close off the defile and get out to the north, when the velites fell from their galloping horses, brought down by arrows shot by Gannicus' men some fifty paces from the defile. The Celt had reversed the situation. The watch continued. From the depths of the defile, the centurions' commands could be heard. They had been forced to reduce the breadth of their centuries to six men abreast, then to four. They were shouting now, trying to keep order in their ranks, which they could no longer freely monitor on the flank. Their orders, far apart at first, now mingled with those of the following centurions as the latter came into the defile. With the echoes of orders bouncing back three or four times off the canyon walls, the legionaries no longer knew whether they were obeying their own commanders or other centurions. Finally, after two hours of orders and counterorders shouted and constantly bounced back by the echo, the velites in the van emerged at the north end of the defile. Spartacus suddenly pulled the cloaks away. The smoke played among the stones for a moment and then suddenly shot up, thick, dark, immediately swept off by the wind at the level of the rock. Spartacus then held up a blanket between the wind and the smoke; two men came to his sides, with a cloak stretched between their arms. Protected, the smoke rose more than six feet, visible from everywhere: the signal had been given.

Simultaneously, the defile is blocked at the north and south ends while the baskets of stones tip over. All the legionaries look up; the stones are rolling faster and faster, raising a cloud of dust in a terrifying rumble magnified by the echo. The cries of the first victims of this avalanche sow panic among the legionaries unable to escape being crushed. They try to make for the rear, for the van, but the defile is too narrow and the baskets continue to loose their murderous hail of stones. A cloud of gray dust rises from the defile. From the plateau, it is now impossible to see the legionaries; beneath the uninterrupted rumble of the avalanche, the cries of the wounded mingle with the orders shouted by the centurions. One of them, a young Roman who towers above all the ranks, succeeds in getting some twenty men to follow him. He rushes to storm the other slope in order to avoid the rain of stones, hoping that everyone will follow him. Well sheltered behind their rocks, Castus' men massacre them as they go by, and resume their watch. To the south, Capito's troop has surrounded the seven or eight centuries which have not had time to get into the defile. His sword in his right hand, his sica in his left, Capito is cutting, crushing, decapitating, at the head of his men. At the north, Gannicus has had the velites struck down by a hail of arrows and retrieved their horses. Waiting for the avalanche to end before going more fully into action, his men cut down the legionaries coming out of the defile in small groups. A few wounded horses have fallen at the exit of the corridor; other heavily harnessed animals have come and toppled over them, now blocking any exit from the passageway. Beneath the rumble of the stones, the defile has turned into one single uproar. After the last baskets have been emptied, the legionaries still alive are subjected to the simultaneous assault of Castus' and Spartacus' men.

The snow had been falling for a long time when the battle ended. Clodianus' two legions had been cut to shreds. More than five hundred horses fell into Gannicus' hands. Spartacus methodically set about salvaging weapons, clothing, and food supplies, and, giving his men no time to lose their heat, he harried them until all the distributions had been completed and the corpses lying in the defile pushed aside.

Night had fallen. The heavy-flaked snow now covered the plateau and the defile, hiding from the victors the crushed or gutted bodies of the legionaries. Losing no time, Spartacus set his still-hot troop in march toward the north to meet the legions of Arrius and Publicola. After two hours' march from the defile, Spartacus halted. The twenty thousand legionaries were camping there, at the edge of a wood. If the Thracian had not marched out of the defile, he would have been besieged there at dawn or forced to leave it by the southern end and fight in the open.

First disposing of the sentries, Spartacus surrounded the camp and struck before dawn. Followed by ten thousand men filled with confidence by their complete victory of the day before, ordering absolute silence, he attacked on foot into the central lane of the camp, straight toward the intersection where the tents of consul Publicola and propraetor Arrius had been set up. As he went along, Spartacus turned at intervals and signaled to his men to move upon the tents in the cross-lanes. When he was within about a hundred paces of the intersection, he saw three centurions come out of the shadow of the propraetor's tent with swords drawn. Almost every tent was now surrounded by the fugitives. Galloping on a little horse with a long black mane, Gannicus was coming down the center lane, from the opposite direction, followed by five hundred horsemen. The centurions turned around at the noise. Around the intersection, the comings and goings of legionaries carrying out orders the day before had hardened the snow. Suddenly coming to the end of the powdery snow at the outer stretches of the camp, the gallop of the horses led by Gannicus ended in disaster; the quivering animals were charging straight into the intersection, their nostrils steaming, their necks shining with sweat in the icy night. One of them slipped on the hardened snow, dragging down all those that followed. To avoid falling, one horseman made his horse jump, but it crashed to the ground as it came down with a crunch of broken bones. Sliding on its belly, its legs waving like ribbons, it cut down the center pole at the top of which the standards of the four legions were snapping in the wind. Here and there, tents were beginning to burn.

A man came out of the propraetor's tent, bareheaded, shouting orders. It was Arrius. A group gathered around him. As he opened the door of his tent, inside which lamps were burning, a flash of light caught a lance set up before it; atop the lance, Crixos' head. The jaw pulled down by the lance had opened the mouth; the swollen black tongue hung out on the chin. The Celt's long mustache was unmistakable, still falling in awesome arcs far down into the red beard. The head was illuminated only for an instant. Just as Spartacus saw it, someone let out a great cry. It was as if Crixos, in death, were yelling an order to the Thracian. The next instant, the tent door fell shut, leaving around it only the glint of the snow.

Spartacus ran to the three centurions who were between him and Arrius. Castus and two thousand men were behind the Thracian. One of the centurions fell immediately, an arrow in his throat; the other two looked at Spartacus for an instant and then ran toward the group around Arrius. Spartacus continued forward, hatchet and sword in his hands. He rushed furiously into the fight; men fell before him like severed branches, with a curious expression of bewilderment, like the legionaries in the defile.

Horses freed of their riders, others out of their fetters, now run down the lanes of the camp, galloping madly, their manes waving in the wind. Spartacus rushes at Arrius. Four centurions still protecting the propraetor fall under the Thracian's blows; helmetless, armorless, Arrius grabs at a mane and leaps on a horse dashing between the tents. Spartacus watches for a horse and jumps on it in pursuit of the propraetor who is yelling orders as he goes by. Arrius has rushed into the middle of a melee on the right flank of the camp. Stimulated by the powerful whirlwind of his blade, his men repulse the assailants and make for the intersection. The camp has turned into a torch, a furious roar, a death rattle.

Spartacus is by himself for a moment, rushing toward the legionaries led by Arrius who are now charging him. The Thracian pulls up his horse and throws his hatchet, which hurtles, lashing the air in the darkness. Spartacus turns his mount around and heads it toward the intersection where Gannicus' men still have their legs caught between the flanks of the horses that fell under them. The hatchet catches Arrius right in the middle of the forehead; he falls from his galloping horse, in the midst of his men, but he has restored the chances of one part of the camp. Spartacus jumps off his horse and rolls on the ground against Arrius' tent that has begun to burn, now lighting up Crixos' head—hideous, crushed, green.

Spartacus pulls up the tall burning centerpole and knocks it down across the lane; Arrius' horse gallops, dragging along the propraetor's body connected to it by one foot, followed by three or four centuries of velites. Seeing their path barred by flames, the horses rear and crash against each other in a melee that their speed makes even more terrible. Spartacus jumps on a horse and rushes toward the left flank, but by now the legionaries are resisting only in isolated groups. At daybreak, the attackers have won the battle. Out of four legions, only four centuries survive. Spartacus has them tied together, four men to a group, and gives the women the task of guarding them.

The camp had now turned into an immense pile of ashes, melted snow, and mud. In the gray dawn, men and horses emitted their death rattles beneath a dark sky still heavy with snow. Wolves were howling in the nearby wood. Here and there, groups of exhausted fugitives were throwing tent poles into the live embers, and the pale flames added still further to the sinister sight.

Spartacus rode his horse, chin on chest, gloomy, closed. He found the place where Arrius' tent had been pitched. Still on the tip of the lance, Crixos' head had fallen down. Spartacus dismounted. He took the head in both his hands, under the ears; with one foot on the lance, he pulled. Crixos' mouth snapped shut. The red hair was hard, matted into long dark locks; the cheeks were slashed, crushed. The nose had no shape left. With Crixos' head under his arm, Spartacus got back up on his horse. Near a fire, he saw a squatting Samnite busily roasting a horse's foreleg; he asked him for some water. The man did not know the Thracian; he pointed to a stack of spears supporting a brown bag. Spartacus washed the Celt's head and got back on his horse.

Necessity imposing its own discipline, the salvaging of rations, weapons, and horses had begun, but not everyone was working; many just sat and ate where they were, without concern for the others. However, on the whole, troop spirit prevailed. Beside a fire, tending the wounded, Polla waved to Spartacus as he went by. He did not see her; he was going over to the prisoners.

The legionaries were looking at their conquerors. Weary, the women had lighted fires; they stood guard in grim silence. Tied up off to the side, the prisoners said nothing as they looked at the smoking ruins of their camp. This was the morning they were supposed to have set out after Spartacus, to surround him with Clodianus, to massacre his troop!

The rattle of the dying men and horses with still-steaming entrails, the howling of the wolves, the tense and somber silence of the victors, the anger that could be seen in their eyes when they met those of a prisoner, emphasized the defeat of the supposedly invincible legionaries far more than if the fugitives had displayed unbridled joy, lighted an immense bonfire, and celebrated their victory with excesses. This state of affairs especially worried one centurion who seemed quite disturbed.

When Spartacus came near him, the man called out: "Hey, you, horseman!"

Spartacus pulled up his horse and looked down at the centurion.

"I want to talk to your leader."

Spartacus went on looking at him without moving. A woman came up with raised whip. Spartacus looked at her; the woman lowered her arm.

"Go bring your leader to me!" the centurion ordered Spartacus.

"What do you want to say to the leader?" the woman said.

"Talk," said Spartacus.

"Go bring your leader to me, dog!"

The woman lashed the centurion across the face. "He is the leader. He's got nothing to say to you."

"Talk," Spartacus repeated.

The centurion and his companions looked at Spartacus, surprised, curious. How could this skinny creature, with the hollow eyes, with his hair down on his shoulders and merging into his beard, almost naked on his saddleless horse, how could he—like a general—have been able to lead this wretched herd of slaves to victory? Out of the four thousand horses harnessed for war, out of the twenty thousand men equipped and trained, only four centuries remained. The propraetor was dead, the consul had fled, Spartacus had once more upset destiny.

The Roman looked into the eyes of the Thracian for a sign of the fear inherent in the slave condition, but Spartacus was slowly moving away as he went around the square of prisoners; he came back in front of the centurion who had called to him.

"So, you're Spartacus?"

"Talk."

"Get that bitch away from here."

Spartacus leaned over the woman; he stroked her cheek, straightened a lock of her hair. Despite her wild look, there was fear in the depths of her eyes, but there was also anger, seething, salutary, which in the end would certainly overcome the old inherited fear that, for the moment, she could do nothing about. Spartacus smiled at her. In her hollow cheeks, the smile she returned to him could not be seen; but, in the fold of her eyes, at the slight trembling of her lips, the Thracian could read the smile. He sat up. "If you don't want to talk in front of everyone, I'm not interested in what you have to say."

The centurion lowered his voice, but his companions heard him.

"I promise you your freedom if . . ."

"Freedom? I am free."

Spartacus stared intently at the man; he had given him a simple answer, but the usual sadness in his voice had disappeared. He had spoken quickly, in a toneless voice.

The centurion smiled. "But . . ."

"There is nothing you can promise me, Roman. Nothing you can give me. Nothing you can say to me."

The centurion insisted haughtily, mincing his lips, raising his chin. "We are soldiers," he said, "we obey orders. . . . Look, I have six slaves in Rome. They are happy with me; they will never think of leaving me."

"They'll never think, . . ." Spartacus began. He stopped, unable to find words. He looked again at the centurion, as if regretting there was nothing he could tell him, and then went slowly away, no longer listening.

"Dog!" the prisoner shouted. "Come back here!"

Spartacus turned. "Use your whip as you see fit," he said to the woman.

"What are you going to do with us?" called the centurion.

Spartacus pulled up his horse. His back was to the prisoners. He looked at Crixos' head for a moment and turned slowly toward the legionaries. "What do Romans do with their prisoners?"

The man did not answer. Haughty, but uneasy, the officers were looking at Spartacus. The centurion watched the eyes of the Thracian as they rested on Crixos' head.

"That's the head of the man from Gargano," he said. "He wasn't tortured, he was wounded in battle! . . . That's war! . . . The propraetor . . ."

"Yes, that's war," said Spartacus. "What do Romans do with their prisoners?" he repeated.

"You have no right to touch us!" the centurion cried. "You're slaves!"

"We won't touch you," said Spartacus. The Thracian had spoken very softly, but the centurion heard him. He turned to his companions with a haughty, conceited air. There was a ripple of laughter.

"No!" Spartacus thundered. "We won't touch you!"

In the camp, everyone looked up. Those who were asleep opened their eyes, listening. The centurion had turned around. Spartacus was brandishing Crixos' head above his own. When Polla started running toward the Thracian, the whole camp followed.

"*Crixooooos!*" Spartacus shouted. "*Crixos, hear me!* . . . This morning, at the foot of this mountain, there was a great battle. I fought for you . . . and we won."

From the farthest corners of the camp, everyone came running up. Those who were closest to Spartacus and who had known Crixos exclaimed at seeing the Celt's mutilated head.

"*Crixos!*" Spartacus thundered. "Since Roman blood was always the best dittany for your wounds, I have kept some prisoners who are going to fight the way they used to make us do: two by two, to the death!"

A wild shout went up in the camp. Immediately, a great circle was formed in the middle of the fugitives. Spartacus leaned over; he took a sword from the hand of one of his men and with one stroke cut the bond of the first four prisoners. The centurion who had just been talking started to scream as he was being dragged off, "Dog! You don't have the right!"

Without a word the fugitives pushed the legionaries toward the improvised arena; at the same time, a corridor cleared, leading from the square of prisoners to the arena.

"You don't have the right!" screamed the centurion.

Women armed with lances, maces, lashes, came forward in the circle. A first pair of contestants were pushed into the center; each one was given a sword and a sica. Around them, silence; the solemn silence of immolation. Spartacus raised Crixos' head in his hands.

"The Romans are going to fight the way they used to make us do," he repeated. "Two by two, to the death!"

In a gloomy voice, Spartacus went on, "I dedicate these fights to the memory of our . . ."

"Dog! You don't have the right!"

A woman who was close to the centurion struck him violently across the mouth with the back of her hand.

Spartacus resumed, "I dedicate these fights to the memory of the men who died in the circuses merely for the pleasure of the Romans! I dedicate these fights to the memory of the fugitives who died at the hands of the Romans . . . In their name, we will overcome those who stand between us and freedom! . . . I dedicate these fights to the memory of Crixos and his comrades who fell in their flight to freedom! Crixos! The Romans will die like gladiators. Without understanding why. And their cries will be heard in Rome, carried there by a messenger blinded with blood!"

Spartacus got off his horse and sat down among his comrades on the hard, frozen earth, Crixos' head in front of him facing the arena. Somber, Spartacus raised an arm and the women whipped the first two contestants, forcing them to confront each other.

Two men stood ten paces apart, a centurion and a simple legionary. Believing he could gain an advantage because of his rank in such circumstances, the centurion went toward his adversary, very erect, ready to strike, sure that the other would never dare raise his arm against him. The legionary looked at him. In that instant, he crossed all the distinctions; an entire life of military endeavors would never have allowed him to achieve a footing of equality with his superiors. But he too had heard Spartacus. It was no longer a question of obeying, but of fighting for his life. No one henceforth would be able to punish him; he sprang quickly backward, supple, leaning forward with arms outstretched, observing his opponent. It was all over. There were no more ranks, no more legionaries, no more Roman army, only two animals ready to strike. The centurion had dropped his arrogance. Like the other, he was turning, leaning forward, arms outstretched. There was a very quick move forward and the men were once again ten paces apart; under his tunic, slit from the shoulder to the belt, a long red line crossed the centurion's chest.

Spartacus looked at the next prisoners who were to be pushed into the arena. The horror of the fight they were about to engage in had seized them. They were not talking any more. Their lips were pressed tight, their eyes hardened; their faces were tense, livid.

The fights went on into the night.

Into the night, under the torches surrounding the arena, the four hundred legionaries were pushed forward and fell one by one. The closer they got to the last ones, the more savage, the more desperate the fights became. The winner of the previous fight waited, weapons in hand; another fighter was then sent in to face him until one of them went down. There was no chance of winning. For a bit, strength, skill postponed the fatal moment; but the strongest, the most skillful, after having brought down two or three opponents, fell exhausted before the blows of a man perhaps weaker, less skillful, but fresher.

There was only one man left in the center of the arena, wounded on the arms and chest; he was standing, erect, completely naked, covered with sweat, blood, and mud. His face was deeply furrowed, the upper lip drawn back over his teeth, the lower split in two down to his chin and opening in a V over his gums; his eyes had lost almost all expression under his eyelids nearly closed by blows, while his chest heaved rapidly, gasping for air with a hiss through his teeth. Under the uneven light of the torches blown by the wind, the man took on frightening proportions—his body was one steaming wound in the cold night air.

Spartacus got up. Everyone imitated him in silence. The Thracian took a few steps toward the man, who retreated.

"Go back to Rome," said Spartacus.

The Thracian's voice had lost all anger. "Go back as you are, with death in your eyes and your head." Two women came up to the man and took away his weapons, sticky to the hilt with blood. "Go back to Rome as a gladiator. Let someone give him a horse and escort him to the middle of the defile. Roman, in that defile, you will find legionaries' tunics. Ten thousand tunics. Don't be tempted to put one of them on, you would risk being beaten to death on the way by runaway slaves; the roads are not safe for isolated legionaries. Naked, or in an old cloak, you may pass for a slave and be arrested, but you'll be able to explain. Before you tell your leaders what you saw, don't forget to go and watch a gladiatorial contest. Afterwards, you'll be able to answer all their questions."

ARENA

XV

The cold and hardships of the last months had taken their toll of the troop. Despite the crushing victories they had just won and the food supplies that had fallen into their hands, the fugitives were in no gay mood. Spartacus granted two days of rest to his men. The news of his triumph made its way across the provinces; from all sides, the wildest, most desperate slaves marched toward the Thracian's camp. On all the roads of the peninsula, from Bruttium to Picenum, even from Cisalpine Gaul, runaways were going forward toward this man who—like Hannibal, but even more swiftly—had beaten the legions at the gates of Rome.

Before resuming his exodus toward the North, Spartacus had sent scouts up the Adriatic coast, up the heights of Picenum, into the Marches, and as far as Spoletium, in Umbria. The first scouts to get back to the camp at the prearranged meeting place, above Corfinium, brought two extraordinary pieces of news: the road was clear; Rome had no more legions to send in pursuit of the fugitives.

These items very quickly spread through the camp. Groups gathered here and there and delegations came to ask Spartacus whether he intended to attack Rome.

This question surprised Spartacus, who postponed his answer to the next day, but during the night, with his hands behind his head, he said to Polla, "Today, I was asked whether I intended to attack Rome."

"What are you going to do?"

"I don't know."

When Spartacus was speaking to her in the tent, Polla squatted beside him; she stroked his face, rubbed oil over his body, massaged his feet. She raised her head, surprised. "You always know what you're going to do; why don't you know tonight?"

"I don't know. Tonight, I don't have to strike camp. Rome has no more legions to send against us."

"Since Capua, this is the first time you don't know what you're going to do."

Spartacus drew Polla against him. He ran a finger over her forehead. "You have lines on your forehead. . . . You didn't have them in Capua."

"I don't know."

"You are beautiful!"

Polla pressed the Thracian's lips between her own, then said, "Why don't you know what you ought to do?"

"I don't know. Habit, maybe!"

"Habit! I . . . I don't understand. You always used to say we didn't run away to make war on the Romans, but to go back home. You don't have to attack Rome to get back to Thrace."

"No. But we are not alone. . . ."

"We never were."

"Precisely. It's just because we are not alone that we have been able to stay free."

"But . . . You wanted freedom to get back to Thrace, not to make war."

"The Romans want war. They don't understand. I tried to talk to one of the prisoners the other day; but dialogue is impossible. The Romans are sure of everything; even the thoughts of their slaves. That centurion was sure that his slaves would never think of leaving him. . . . They are always sure of everything. They are always right. . . ."

They were speaking softly, slowly. They looked for their words and, after having spoken, did not seem sure they had said precisely what they were thinking. Long silences went by between their exchanges.

"This is the first time you don't know what you ought to do."

"Maybe it's . . . It's the first time I have time to choose. Since Capua, we never stopped except to fight. Tonight, no one is threatening us. We're really free. So, all of a sudden, I don't know."

"Maybe, now, maybe we can leave the others."

"No."

"Why?"

"Slaves are running away all over the country."

"You can't help that."

"They're trying to join up with us."

"They can go back to their own countries. They don't have to be together any more. . . . They don't need you any more, or me. We don't need them any more!"

"Maybe . . ."

Polla lay down against Spartacus. "We don't need them any more, Spartacus. And they don't need us any more."

"Then why do they keep looking for our camp?"

"I don't know. They can go back home without us. There will be runaways as long as there are slaves and masters. You can't help that!"

Spartacus quickly answered, "If there were no more slaves, there wouldn't be any more fugitives."

Polla got up on one elbow and looked intently at the Thracian. "But there are slaves, Spartacus. And you can't do anything about it."

"We have beaten the legionaries. Rome has no more army here; we could free all the slaves!"

"But all slaves aren't thinking of freedom, Spartacus."

"Maybe! Living in slavery became a habit with them before thinking did, but their bodies rebel against the torture, the fact of being slaves. Those who think run away the first chance they get."

"Those who run away have known something else, a different life; they are the most desperate ones. But you forget those who were born slaves, on a small farm; the ones whose masters work the same as they do, eat the same as they do, sleep with them, among the stock; I've known some of them. Why should they run away? Where would they go?"

Spartacus looked at Polla a moment before answering. He seemed a bit surprised. "They would have no need to leave if staying had been their own decision; but they never had the freedom to choose. They didn't choose their way of life."

Polla snuggled against Spartacus, her head on his shoulder. She said softly, "You can't help it, Spartacus. The world would have to be changed. You can't change the world."

Spartacus' eyes were closed; he was stroking her hair. "Sure, Polla, we can change the world. We beat the most powerful armies in the world, us, the slaves, the gladiators."

Polla turned her head, he opened his eyes. She was looking at him, as if slightly embarrassed, without reproach in her eyes, but some astonishment.

"Don't look at me that way, Polla," said the Thracian. "When we ran away, all I wanted was freedom." Polla dropped her eyes. Spartacus took her face in his two hands to look into her eyes again; he spoke in a tender, passionate voice. "Tonight, for the first time, I really feel free; the Romans have been beaten and forty thousand slaves are free, victorious. The world is changed, isn't it? To change the world sounds like something fantastic, words that are impossible to speak out loud without the woman you love looking at you as she never has before, as if she didn't know you. But the world changes, Polla. It changes every day, a hundred times, a thousand times. When a slave decides he's taken all the lashes he will, he changes the world; when the gladiator decides he won't go back into the arena, he changes the world; when the little girl repulses her master's caresses, when she slips under a legionary's horse and cuts one of its legs, she changes the world. The world! What ever is the world? The world of the Romans is first and foremost the world of slaves; they built the Roman world. In any weather, they build the roads, the marketplaces, the circuses, the houses, the cities; they plough the earth, gather the harvests, pluck the grapes. Their deaths aren't even noticed. 'Well, I don't have so many left,' the master thinks, 'I'll need some more for the fields.' And then, there are the fisherman, the perfumer; there are the painter, the sculptor, the architect, the scholar—who are the master's pride, who teach his children, decorate his house, design his city, his temples. . . . There are a lot more slaves than Romans, and all Romans don't have slaves. There are a thousand, ten thousand times as many slaves as Romans. . . . That centurion who kept saying I had no right to send him into the arena was not defeated; he was the master. An old habit. To him, we were nothing but slaves. He only really felt beaten when he was in the arena, confronted with a gladiator's pointless death. . . . The Romans don't understand anything but victory and defeat. When they take a country, they turn its people into slaves; they call that the right of conquest. That's the Romans' world for you! . . . And since that way of life has been going on for a long time, the conquered think as they do; they really believe no other world is possible. They never even think of a different kind of world. Emancipated slaves who make a little money only have one goal: to live like Romans, because they have nobody to imitate but the Romans. They are often tougher on their own slaves than their old masters ever were on them. There are also freed gladiators who run the betting in circuses, others who buy gladiators and make them fight. Habit! If the Romans haven't reached a country yet, they're expected there; when they get there, their reputation has gone before and people are all ready to do their bidding. Habit! Those who fight are killed, the rest are sold in the markets of Delos or Rome. In Capua, after we escaped, the lanista counted up his money and bought some more Capitos, some more Spartacuses. The world, Polla, is your world, too. The world of Alba, Castus, Gannicus, of every one of us. If I don't know what I ought to do, it is not because I'm wondering whether I ought to attack. Maybe it's the habit of thinking that Rome is unattackable. . . . And anyway, you don't attack Rome, you take it. That can be done. There are no soldiers left in the city; at most a few cohorts, and there are forty thousand of us. We can take Rome and turn all its slaves free from its markets, from the whole country. All we have to do is occupy it and, as the Romans do wherever they come in as victors, set up new laws: no more slaves! We decree that there will be no more slaves. We decree that there are only citizens free to stay or to go back to their own countries. . . ."

Spartacus was silent for quite a while, stroking his mate's hair. He went on very softly, talking to himself, "For the first time, I am able to choose. To go away or stay. Take Rome or go back to Thrace. But, in both cases, it means fighting against a force more powerful than all the Roman legions and all the fugitives put together: habit."

Polla raised her head. "Habit?"

"Yes, habit. Habit in general. The habit of everything, of the Romans, of slavery. The habit men have of thinking of a Roman as a master and of the men he treats as slaves as garbage. By force of habit in the Roman world, the gladiator dies to entertain, the slave under the lash, and the Roman rules. The habit of those who have always been defeated, who spend their slaves' lives in trying to save them by complying with all their masters' caprices. The habit of the Romans who are so sure of themselves that they never even chain their prisoners to go through a town. They sell them by entire shiploads, they count them out in lots of tens and their prices are low in the marketplaces. You were saying that all slaves do not think of freedom. That's true. The Roman has so long been in the habit of attaching no importance to the thoughts of a slave that the latter, by force of habit, doesn't even allow himself to think. But the one who stops a moment and does think at once gets outside the Roman world. His condition becomes unbearable to him. He can no longer bow and scrape; he can only refuse and flee. We fled. Forty thousand of us decided to flee; we beat the legionaries and Rome has no legions left. So, we have changed the world, Polla. In spite of habit."

Polla stroked the Thracian's face. She ran a finger over his lips. "Good, we've changed the world. What are you going to do now?"

"I don't kn . . ."

Polla had taken his mouth.

Spartacus' tent was almost in the center of the camp. Here and there, some fires. Beside one of them, Alba and Gannicus, silent, looking at the flames. Around the camp, the white mountain, the howling of a wolf, the trees frosted, spiky, shining, under a moon that was well defined and very close, on that evening.

Spartacus the next day announced his intention of resuming the march toward the north. Going now in broad daylight, without haste, the troop was constantly increased by the arrival of numerous runaways encouraged by the repeated successes of the Thracian. The danger constituted by the presence of the legions seeming finally eliminated, a general slackening occurred within the ranks and hunger reappeared, extended itself and occupied its full place, at the same time weakening resistance to the cold. At one evening's halt, a woman discovered the child she had been carrying all day was dead in her arms. Impatience was invading even the most sensible.

Assured by his scouts that the roads were safe, Spartacus brought his troop down to protect it from the cold of the heights, crossed the Rubicon and had to stand by, powerless, while farms and towns were pillaged. Despite his decisions, he too had to eat, and he was forced to accept a share of the plunder. One farm, ten farms, the very reserves of several cities were hardly enough to satisfy the needs of a troop of a hundred thousand runaways who now threw caution to the winds as they advanced upon larger and larger cities. On the road to Modena, Cassius Longinus, the Cisalpine proconsul, tried to stop them with ten thousand legionaries whom he, like the other consuls before him, believed to be invincible. The fugitives routed the two legions in a battle in which the women participated furiously. It concluded so rapidly that the main body of Spartacus' troop never even had to fight, arriving on the site after it was over. Cassius Longinus safely survived this crushing defeat and made haste for Rome, surrounded only by a few lictors.

After this sixth brilliant victory, the fugitives advanced on Modena, which closed its gates to the victors. Spartacus, refusing to attack it in spite of the impatience of his men, turned his troops toward smaller cities which bravely followed the example of Modena—brave or unaware of the danger they were running by thus defying Spartacus. He could have invaded all of these cities without trouble and satisfied the needs of his troop by cutting into the huge concentrations of victuals amassed for the winter. He refused to do this. The encounter with Longinus' two legions had surprised him, had upset plans which were already shaky. He had heard Capito say to Gannicus, "See, there are Romans everywhere." Since the threat of the legions had been eliminated, Spartacus had become gloomier, spoke even less, spent long periods by himself, marched off to the side. The troop having fallen upon the legionaries' horses for food, Spartacus rebuilt his cavalry with stock he rustled in the Po Valley plains.

He had halted for a few days between Verona and Modena when, very early one morning, Gannicus woke him. The overflowing of the gray waters of the Po flooded a stretch of country as far as the eye could see. Upstream, to the west, the masses of sand carried by the river further raised its bed, making all navigation impossible. When Spartacus broke camp, he was asked why he was returning south. The Thracian explained. "There are a hundred thousand of us and we have nothing to eat. I cannot attack cities that shut their gates in order to protect their stores, because I do not want to act like legionaries against people who never did anything to us. Since we have to eat, let us feed off the Romans."

"But you wanted to get out of the country," said Polla.

"We'll leave it later. I cannot keep the troop supplied here, nor can I make everyone swim. We have to go back to the cities we know."

No one having a better solution to offer, none held out any further, and the troop took the road back to the Rubicon.

ARENA

XVI

Alexander arrived at Suessa Aurunca under an overcast sky toward the bath hour. Crassus was in the kitchen; little Sicinio was on his lap. At the moment, the child was raising his big blue eyes and a serious face toward his master.

"Your daddy was the one who asked me to take you away," Crassus was saying.

"But he always asks you to when he's making cakes."

"Yes, because you eat the raw dough while he . . ."

"No, no!" the child protested.

"What! You don't eat the raw dough, Sicinio?"

"No. I taste it."

"Oh, you taste it."

"Yes, I really have to taste it if I want to be a baker, like daddy."

"And what does your father say when you tell him you're not eating the dough, just tasting it?"

"That's the trouble. I think you ought to explain it to him, because I have the feeling he doesn't understand."

"Why do you think that?"

"Because . . . he always asks me what's the difference between eating the dough and tasting it. 'I can't see any!' he says. 'And you taste so much of it that there's not enough left to make the cakes.'"

Crassus laughed and shook Sicinio's curls. "That's it. You taste too much of the dough. You taste too much of it."

"But you'll explain it to daddy, won't you?"

"I'll try."

"Promise?"

"I promise."

Mamita came in through the courtyard door, followed by an ageless bondwoman carrying logs; she noiselessly set them down near the fireplace. Mamita was holding two plucked chickens by the legs.

"Those aren't very fat chickens, Mamita," said Crassus.

"There's only two more left. These are the fattest of the four."

"Only two more chickens? Why, there were over twenty dozen of them a few weeks ago!"

"Yes. But the others went off with the runaways and it isn't . . . Sicinio! What are you doing here? You were supposed to chop some wood!"

Crassus laughed. He let go of the child, who ran off, and then he got up. The bondwoman gave him a jar of milk and a jar of honey. He heated the milk and the honey separately, added a spoonful of orange marmalade and a handful of rose petals. Then he sat on the edge of the table to drink, gazing at the flames in the hearth in which, at the end of a poker, Mamita, squatting, was grilling some peppers. He was so absorbed in his thought that he did not hear Alexander come in. Alexander came and sat down beside him and waited. The huge kitchen was now lighted solely by the flames. In the middle stood the long rectangular stone table on which the two men were sitting. Along the walls, long poplar shelves were covered with trays, plates, knives; in the cedar chests there were the spices, fruits, jars of honey, milk, flour, and various vegetables. A good aroma of grilled pepper spread through the kitchen. Alexander watched Mamita. When she felt her peppers were sufficiently toasted, she put them beside her on a tray, placed some others on the grill, and turned them over to keep them from burning.

"You'll be having peppers for dinner, Marcus," said Alexander.

Crassus turned to him with a smile. "When did you get here?"

"A few minutes ago."

Mamita turned around.

"Hello, Mamita."

"You want some milk?"

"No, thanks."

"How did you find me?" Crassus asked.

Alexander smiled. "I know your habits." The two men were watching the flames as they talked.

"No, the pepper isn't for dinner," said Crassus. "Tell him what you're doing with it, Mamita."

"Once they're toasted, I put them in olive oil with spices and leave them there till next spring."

"They must be tender, prepared that way."

"Help yourself," Mamita said without turning around. "There are several jars of them in the middle chest."

"Not now, Mamita. I'll come back tomorrow."

"Tomorrow, tomorrow. What tomorrow?" Mamita scowled. She turned. "Eat now!" she ordered. "Tomorrow's still a long way off."

Alexander looked at Crassus who raised his eyebrows with a slight smile. "You heard Mamita. Eat now, tomorrow's still a long way off." Alexander took several peppers and came back to sit on the table. Crassus took one and said, "How is life in the dirtiest city in the world?"

Alexander smiled. "I've finished, Mamita. May I take some more?"

"Eat, eat, son. Tomorrow's a long way off."

Alexander helped himself to a plateful of the black preserved peppers that sparkled with red reflections. "Oh, they are so good! They have their own pepper taste, and behind it, just pungent enough to be felt, a little touch of almond. A dream!"

"Eat, eat!" said Mamita.

Alexander set the plate down between Crassus and him. They

ate for a while without talking. "Long live life away from Rome!" Alexander exclaimed. "Living there is the worst torture I know."

"It's a city full of rats," said Mamita.

"And full of contrasts," Alexander went on. "It was built by men to make them suffer. Its area is ludicrously small, but half a million people crowd into it; its streets are too narrow to walk four abreast comfortably, but its tenements are absurdly high."

"Well, if the city doesn't spread, it has to rise."

"But when there's a fire . . ."

"Rome is always on fire some place," said Crassus with a smile.

"Yes. Three or four fires a day. And if you live on the fourth floor . . . or above . . . you're sacrificed. You climb higher and higher and then you can't jump any more. You either burn to death or get eaten by the rats. Insects swarm everywhere, rats run through your room, but all that wouldn't matter if you could only sleep. You can't sleep in Rome, there's too much noise. Day and night."

Crassus smiled. "Poor Alexander!"

"People are either too hot or too cold. Or else there are too many of them in one room and the insects, the snores, and the smells keep them awake. So what do they do? They get up early and go to bed late. Tradesmen open their shops before dawn, take over half the street with their displays. Since it's still dark, passersby trip over the merchandise and yell, and carts circulate all night from one part of town to another because they can't get around during the day. When the sun comes up, the great daily battle of the crowd begins. Bricklayers and carpenters arrange for the transport of enormous beams, stone slabs as big as this table, to build—like you—palaces between the side streets or to rebuild tenements that are about to collapse. Blows rain, shouts never stop, the uproar is uninterrupted, day and night. To say nothing of the smells!"

Crassus laughed. "Ah, the sweet smells of Rome!"

Alexander went on, "Sweet! At every street corner, there's a receptacle for the citizens' urine. A crazy idea if you live next door; excellent if you live far away."

Crassus could not stop laughing. Alexander picked up again:

"But what do they do with that receptacle when it's full?"

"They empty it."

"Sure. They try to do it outside the city walls but they never get there. It's tipped over, on your robe, or you fall into it. And the smell of urine mixes in with all the other, the smells of warm bread, roast dormice, honey cakes, stale fish, men, and animals. And Rome," Alexander went on emphatically, "whose name alone brings shivers to kings in every corner of the world . . . who polices almost the entire earth . . . all-powerful Rome smells bad by day and bad by night . . . Rome is noisy . . . Rome is disgustingly filthy . . . Rome is tiny . . . Rome is overrun with vermin, rats, and beggars with running sores!"

"Those are the splendors and miseries of our times, dear Alexander."

"Well, long live Suessa! Long live the aroma of Mamita's peppers! Long live the sound of the sea, the birds, the wind! Long live space and fresh air! Long live life away from Rome!"

"When I'm consul, I'll set up a schedule for cartage and I'll get traffic under control. I'll see that building is done outside the city and I'll name a superintendent for every tenement. If . . . "

"If Spartacus hasn't surrounded Rome before that."

Crassus smiled coldly. "I'm not joking when I talk about becoming consul, Alexander."

"Nor am I when I talk about Spartacus."

"But . . . where is he? What do the senators say?"

"The senators are in full panic."

Crassus leaned toward his friend. "Then the situation is excellent for me. I'm listening to you, Alexander, I'm listening to you," Crassus said delightedly, taking another pepper.

"So is Mamita," said Mamita.

Alexander laughed. "Why didn't you run away with the others, Mamita?"

Crassus smiled. Alexander looked at him gravely. "Did you already ask her that?"

"A long time ago."

Mamita turned her head and looked at Alexander. "Mamita didn't run away because she carried little Marcus in her arms right after he was born," said the bondwoman as she got up, "you know that very well." She took a pepper from the plate.

"And because Mamita is old," she added, straightening the folds of Crassus' robe over her master's knees.

"Otherwise, you would have gone?"

"Maybe. I don't know." She went back to her fire and her peppers and said, "What's the gladiator doing?"

Alexander told them about the immolation of the four hundred legionaries, the defeat of Longinus, and the countermarch of the fugitives toward the South.

"Tongues must be wagging," said Crassus.

"The tribunes are making the most of the situation."

"They'd be stupid not to. What are they saying?"

"Oh, they go back to the senators with their same old demands at the time when farmers, tradesmen, and middlemen mix with the patricians and even with former members of the Senate Council to ask the senators what they plan to do."

"And the consuls?"

"That's just it. The senators were overwhelmed and they ordered the consuls to go out and intercept Spartacus to interdict his access to Picenum, but all they had left was a few hundred guards. The consuls had to impress men by force as they went. Result: the hundred thousand fugitives didn't . . ."

"There are a hundred thousand of them!"

"At least. They didn't even have to stop to fight Longinus. They massacred his army and continued on their way. Now everyone is afraid that all the consuls can do is die if they confront them."

"And leave Rome undefended! Where are these fugitives heading?"

"They alone know."

"That's fantastic. They've beaten all the consuls, all the legions, all the praetors, and the road to Rome is practically wide open before them." Crassus got up. "Let's go and bathe before dinner."

During dinner, lying down across from his friend on the stibadium cushions, Alexander analyzed the situation and came to a conclusion. He said, "All the praetors and consuls have been beaten. There are no more legions. Lucullus is in Macedonia at the instruction of his uncle Sulla; Pompey and Metellus are in

Spain at the instruction of the Senate. Today, the nobles are so frightened that they are hiding their sons to keep them from being dragged into this murderous war. There is no one left to stand in Spartacus' way."

"So I'm alone. . . . The situation is perfect. I've been waiting for this moment for years, Alexander."

"I know."

"This is the ideal time for mentioning me to the senators. They have no legions left; I have money enough to raise fifty of them and maintain them for several years."

"Yes. It's the right time to reappear on the scene. You're the richest landowner in the country. It's proper for you to rise up and defend your interests. That's very good. No one will think you have political motives, since you've practically not been seen in Rome since Sulla's proscriptions, over ten years ago."

The two men looked at each other. Crassus sat down, then got up. He took a few steps, then came back and stood before Alexander. "We have to have a very serious talk about this," he said as if he had just understood how serious the situation was.

"That's what we're doing, Marcus. . . . There's no point in mentioning you to the senators. Your return to Rome will be enough to spread your name around."

"What could that lead to?"

"To your being asked to take up the pursuit of Spartacus."

"Fine. That's all I want: a pretext for raising legions before Pompey comes back. What do you think?"

"You either succeed or fail. If you fail, there are still Pompey, Metellus, and Lucullus, who haven't finished their wars in Spain and Macedonia. If you succeed . . ."

"What can keep me from succeeding?"

Alexander smiled skeptically.

"Why are you smiling?"

"All those that Spartacus beat must have said those same words to themselves, 'What can keep me from succeeding?' "

"I'm asking myself the question out loud, that's all. I'm thinking of what, actually, might lead to defeat. Or, if you prefer, I am wondering about why the others didn't succeed. What do you think?"

"You are thinking of the problem in a way exactly opposite to the way the people in Rome are. There, everyone will ask you, 'How could those dogs have crushed our legions?' But you're the traditional Roman soldier. You wonder why the legions didn't succeed."

"Isn't that the best way to avoid their mistakes?"

"The only way. I think everybody set out against Spartacus with the assurance of praetorian guards chasing tramps four steps away from the palace."

"Probably."

"How many times have I heard it said, 'After all, they're only runaway slaves.'"

"That's a fact."

"No, Marcus. They are runaway slaves . . . and rebels . . . and several times victorious . . . and there are over a hundred thousand of them."

"Their numbers don't change the fact that they're runaway slaves. Up to now they've succeeded in escaping the punishment they deserve because they are desperate."

"You have understood."

"They have nothing to lose, they are scared and hungry. Result: they fight like lions."

"You have understood perfectly. It's a deathtrap if you don't know that before you set out against them."

Crassus got up. "Let's go to sleep; we'll leave early tomorrow morning."

Alexander poured himself a goblet of wine which he downed in one gulp. "That was what I was afraid of. What a filthy city!"

Crassus smiled. "If everything happens as I expect, we won't be there more than two days."

Before retiring, Crassus woke the commander of his guard. He had him select twenty men, whom he dispatched posthaste to the consuls, saying, "I will be in Rome in a few days. Come back, two by two, and report to me about the location of Spartacus' troop, day by day. When you go through Rome, let the Prince of the Senate know the purpose of your journey. You will report to him, and to him alone, in case I am not yet there."

ARENA

XVII

By the early fall of 72, the little escape from Capua had assumed the proportions of a national disaster and the situation for Rome had become tragic. No one dared to venture out on the roads, where bandits, sure that Spartacus and his men would be accused of their crimes, plundered convoys and attacked travelers on the way to their winter residences. In normal times, there would have been little mention of these attacks, rapes, robberies, and fires, since they were so frequent, but now they took on increasing importance as they closed in upon Rome, where all such crimes were attributed to Spartacus. All commercial transactions were henceforth endangered. The great slave owners having lost virtually all their people, farms and fields were lying fallow; their shops having been ransacked, tradesmen had nothing left to sell. When the population has nothing to eat, the rats come out in the street.

The dismal prospect of economic collapse therefore impelled the holders of Roman wealth to harass the senators who, bereft of an army, were unable to insure the safety of citizens, crops, and transport. The specter of Hannibal returned to haunt the streets of Rome, in which the shops were closed and the odors—those odors of the small stores so characteristic that people claimed they could go through Rome blindfolded provided their noses were uncovered—were disappearing, taking away with them the identity of a street, a square, a neighborhood. Street calls had also lost their symbols. Deliverymen in a hurry, difficult customers, bustling retailers were now merely Romans who had grown irritable with their unaccustomed leisure—perhaps even more than with the news of robberies and massacres—whose irritation had finally calmed down to make room for collective fear. With idleness and deprivation, armed assaults grew more numerous each day. The usual hubbub of the city had therefore not abated; it had simply changed its character. The discomfort of their dark, constricting lodgings, the cockroaches, the rats—whose daytime daring increased proportionately as the reserves diminished—sent the citizen out into the streets before daybreak and offered him no incentive to return. He went back home only to collapse on his bed, drunk with wine or exhaustion, but his body found a little relaxation only at bath time, a break that he extended on the least pretext.

For the Senate, the alternative was simple: money had to be found to raise some legions and—an equally difficult problem to solve—a man to train them and lead them. Who? How? The answers were not easy. The Senate already owed far too much money to the richest citizens.

Such questions were being raised in the curia when a young quaestor one morning came to inform the senators that the Prince of the Senate was calling a meeting for that very evening. The quaestor walked about, going from group to group, listening to the crisis created by the servile war. Nearly everyone seemed convinced that Spartacus was returning southward for the sole purpose of besieging Rome. A minority held that Spartacus was only in a hurry to get out of the country. "If he had wanted to march against Rome, Spartacus would not have crossed the Rubicon merely to crush Longinus' ten thousand men. He would have attacked the City after his victory over Publicola and Arrius." Those who followed this line of reasoning seemed sure that the report of Spartacus' return was a false rumor. Finally there were those who complained of the poor state of Rome's defenses. "No army! No army!" the oldest ones grumbled. "This danger is nothing new! We ought to have revived Cato's old idea of a standing army of two thousand horsemen to protect the City."

From one group to another, senators sounded each other out, took one another by the arm to step off a bit to the side, gravely bowing to some notable or peer as they went by. All in all, being too uneasy to wait until evening without further news, they decided to send their doyen Lucius Philippus to see the Prince of the Senate "to make arrangements for the meeting." In reality, they were sending him to see what he could find out. Alexander, who had discreetly spread the rumor that Crassus was in town, then called upon the Prince of the Senate to inform him that his friend requested an audience.

Along the way, the palatine quaestor recognized the tribune Lollius Macer whom doyen Philippus had taken aside; they separated after exchanging a few words and Philippus motioned to the quaestor, who came over to him. Speaking with the same emphasis as if he had been addressing the entire Senate in plenary session, old Philippus said to the quaestor, "The Prince of the Senate must now be informed that the tribune of the plebs, Lollius Macer, will be with me when I come to the palace." Then, in a confidential tone, the old diplomat added, "That way we'll find out. . . ." But suddenly Philippus changed his tack. He raised his voice and shook a yellowed finger in the direction of Lollius Macer. "That way we'll find out, the better to forestall it, what position the tribunician opposition will be taking tomorrow. We have known their arguments for a long time, but do they have a solution for the crisis?" Macer, who was walking away, smiled without turning around.

On being informed by his quaestor, the Prince of the Senate exclaimed, "Philippus, that old rascal! How does he get about now? On a stretcher?" He added, "When will they be here?"

"Any minute, milord."

"Good, good . . . The old rascal! A fine idea he had, to think of Macer. Did you walk about the curia? What are the senators saying?"

"Most of them fear that Spartacus is coming back to attack Rome."

"Most of them! Most of them! Did you count them? Hmmm! What other nonsense did you hear?"

"Others were saying that the report of Spartacus' return is a false rumor."

The Prince of the Senate walked a few steps toward the terrace and pulled aside a drape; the sun suddenly lit up the audience chamber. With mincing steps, the Prince came back alongside a stibadium, smoothing his mustache as he went. He sank down on the cushions and closed his eyes. He seemed to be sleeping. He remained that way for quite a while. The quaestor watched him, not daring to move.

"I can hear them," the Prince of the Senate grumbled without opening his eyes. "And I can see them, too! A false rumor . . . Our messengers are the only ones who can tell us where Spartacus is right now. Send in the first one who gets here. . . . Whenever he comes."

"Yes, milord."

Another young quaestor of the palace staff came in. "Milord, noble Lucius Marcus Philippus has come to inquire after your health."

"Hmmm . . . show him in, show him in. I'm feeling quite well," said the Prince as he got up.

Old Philippus, bent, dry as a stick, made his entry on the arm of a young slave. He was wearing an old laticlave much too big for him, whose purple stripe had long since faded to pale pink. "Ah, my friends! What a mess! What are we going to do?" He stopped and looked at the Prince of the Senate for a moment. Philippus' eyes were still very blue, but his yellow hands, distorted by arthritis, bespoke his age more than his scarcely wrinkled, amazingly pink face. Perhaps it was the color of that face, the still-smooth skin, the man-child's head on the worn-out body, that were so irritating. Or perhaps it was the ridiculous noisy walk, the knee raising the material as if to take a great stride, then falling back down in a dry sandal sound, moving forward barely a few inches per step. "We have to do something, friends, we have to do something!"

Behind him, slim, young, dark, dressed soberly in a straight robe tied at the waist, Lollius Macer came in. Beneath the bushy eyebrows, his pale face, tired black eyes, and red lips were set off by the brilliant white of his teeth, his mustache, and his short black beard. He went straight to the Prince of the Senate and greeted him.

"Welcome, my friends," said the Prince. "Greetings to you, Lollius," he added, laying his hand affectionately on the young tribune's shoulder.

Puffing and groaning amid the noise of his sandals, Philippus sat down. "What a fall! For a heat wave like this, you have to go back to . . . well, well, the summer of Sulla's abdication!"

The Prince of the Senate held out a cup of orangeade to him. He said, reminiscing, "Sulla! Cornelius Sulla! . . . Yes, what a summer that was!"

Philippus took the cup and started to drink in small sips. He motioned to the quaestor. "You're the one I saw this morning, aren't you?"

"Yes, milord."

"Come a little closer."

The quaestor took a few steps forward.

"Ah! You must be a Metellus."

The quaestor smiled.

"Your father should soon be back among us, now that Perpenna has settled things in Spain with Sertorius."

The quaestor smiled again and looked at the Prince. His mind elsewhere, Macer was walking toward the terrace. "Speaking of ghosts," Philippus kicked the quaestor's legs, "I mean Sertorius, not your father, do we have any news of Spartacus?" Macer stopped without turning around, but the Prince did not reply. "And you, over there . . . Yes, you," said Philippus, addressing the other quaestor, "didn't you marry little Cornelia, Cinna's daughter?"

"Yes, milord."

Philippus gave him a long stare, with raised eyebrows. "Your troubles are over. . . . Sulla now is dining with the gods." The quaestor looked at him calmly, and did not answer, deliberately. "You must tell me some day how you got away from the pirates of Rhodes." The quaestor looked at the Prince of the Senate and then slowly back at Philippus, insolently sizing him up. The old senator grumbled something and repeated his question to the Prince. "Well, do we have any news of the gladiator?"

"We are expecting some, Lucius," said the Prince.

Macer walked on toward the terrace and leaned against a column. Old Philippus was fidgeting on his cushions. "You know I came for news at the senators' request. Do you have anything to tell me? . . . We are not going to allow the slaves to attack Rome, my friend; something must be done."

The Prince of the Senate went up to the two young patricians; smiling, he answered Philippus. "We are doing our best, Lucius." And, turning to the quaestors, he said to them very softly, "Stay over there and open your ears. You'll learn more in a few hours than from twenty official meetings. Go sit down in a dark corner." The quaestors were walking off as Philippus went on, "We have to make a special effort, my friend, a special effort."

"But, look, Philippus, haven't we done everything?"

Macer turned his handsome, tormented face. "Have we done everything, milord?"

"Yes. The consuls tried to stop Spartacus wherever they could."

"Like Longinus!"

"Yes, like Longinus. All of them have done their best."

"And now?"

"Well, as you probably know, we have sent the consuls and praetor Manlius into Picenum, to head Spartacus off."

"Do we have any news?"

"We are expecting some from Crassus."

Philippus became excited. "From Crassus! Licinius Crassus?"

"Yes, my friend. Is there any other Crassus in Rome?"

"Why would Crassus be informed before the Senate?" Macer cut in.

"Because he offered to send messengers to the consuls for us. We should have daily reports as soon as the fugitives are sighted."

"But your consuls have no armies," Philippus exclaimed. "They'll be crushed like flies. . . . We have to get a move on, my friend. . . . How long are we going to put up with such a series of defeats at the hands of a bunch of slaves? . . . Our young tribune is right to question what our consuls can do. . . .

I don't doubt that they have done their best, but the result is rather pitiful. . . . We must do better than they. . . ."

"We are all agreed on that point, Lucius," the Prince said patiently. "Do you have a suggestion?"

"Well, to begin with, why can't we stir up a reaction against this gang of bandits? Huh?"

"Because," the Prince began, and his thought made him smile, "we'll never know whether Crassus or his friend Alexander said it: there can be no glory in a victory over runaway slaves, whether there be fifty or a hundred thousand of them, but there is unspeakable disgrace in defeat."

"So, they have to be exterminated!" said Philippus in a tone of finality.

"There is no military solution to servile wars," said Macer. "That was true for the last two, and it is true again for this one."

"Listen to those steam-bath statements! You can do better than that, Macer. How will you maintain order if you don't quash all ideas of rebellion in the country?"

Macer smiled. Philippus misinterpreted this, and went on emphatically, his finger raised: "We have to set an example. Only by inflicting severe punishment on Spartacus and the runaways can we make the other slaves stay where they belong." And in the same gesture his raised hand gently came down to stroke the cheek of the little Black who was waving the fan at his side. Turning to the Prince, Philippus went on, "We must not let this get the better of us, my friends. After all, they're nothing but a wretched bunch of slaves. We tend too often to overlook that."

"I am not overlooking anything," said the Prince in a glacial tone. "You are the one who is losing sight of the fact that a hundred thousand slaves who cannot afford the luxury of the slightest defeat are virtually invincible."

Philippus had opened his mouth long before the Prince had finished; he shouted, as if addressing all of his peers assembled, "It is no concern of ours to know what the slaves can or cannot afford! Our prestige is at stake! The prestige of Rome!"

"Prestige, indeed!" thundered Macer. "Are you out of your mind? In its first clash against the legions, that 'wretched bunch of slaves,' as you call it, had no more than thirty thousand naked men against our twenty-four thousand Roman legionaries . . . the best soldiers in the world . . . the best fed, the richest, the best trained. . . . Spartacus wiped them from the face of the earth as easily as he might have blown out a lamp. . . . Powerless, our consuls virtually had to stand by while Spartacus forced four hundred legionary prisoners to fight each other like gladiators! . . . That 'wretched bunch of slaves' captured the arms of six legions. . . . They picked up enough fugitives along the way to double the number of their fighters. Starting at Capua, which they left a year ago, that 'wretched bunch of slaves' one after the other has crushed the cohorts of Glaber, Varinius, Furius, and Cossinius. They crushed the legions of Clodianus and Publicola and crushed those of Longinus. . . . Forty thousand Roman soldiers . . . forty thousand . . . have already been sent against that 'wretched bunch of slaves'! . . . Crushed in a few months! . . . That is almost three times as many men as Pompey and Metellus needed, over five years, to try to reconquer Spain from a Sertorius in league with a Mithridates! And you still talk about prestige! . . ."

"What do you want me to talk about? Negotiations? Capitulation?"

Philippus was suddenly very pale, but with a waxen pallor which now gave its true age to his unwrinkled face. He turned to the Prince. Without a gesture, without emphatic pause, without tone in his voice, he said, "The senators assembled a little while ago delegated authority to me to assess the situation with you." The Prince was listening attentively. Macer, too, but without looking at him. In the dark corner of the audience chamber, the two quaestors were following the discussion, each according to his own makeup: Metellus with the relaxed expression of the well-bred young patrician who has listened attentively at his father's dinner table; Caesar with the brow of the conscientious student, whose color changed, revealing the intensity of his impulses, his preferences. Philippus had gone on: ". . . and we must find a satisfactory solution this very day. Our hot-headed tribune reminds us that we had to mobilize many more men for this affair than against Sertorius. Of course, we could cite other figures that would further bear him out: Sulla in Asia, Lucullus in Macedonia. . . . But what does all that mean? Does it mean that our experienced consuls and proconsuls are not as good as the gladiator? All we have to do then . . ."

"How good our consuls are is not the question," Macer interrupted. "The point now is how strong Spartacus is."

As if Macer had not spoken, Philippus went on in the same restrained tone, addressing himself to the Prince alone and weighing each word, "All we have to do then is to find another Pompey."

"You speak of finding another Pompey as you would of another chariot, as if it was something that could be manufactured! Our consuls are capa . . ."

"Oh! They've shown their mettle! We can really do without them!"

"Once again," Macer shouted, "how good the consuls are is not the question. That is all Lucius Philippus for you, all of yesterday's Senate. . . . They forget legality in their panic. Result? Pompey was given absolute military power and now Philippus wants to give the same power to someone else. Can you imagine what these generals might do if one day they were to march on Rome with their armies?"

"Oh, Pompey is young; he's a soldier worthy of our trust." The old senator turned to the Prince with a wily smile. "You always have to promise rewards to generals, that's the only way to keep them muzzled."

"So be it," said the Prince. "Whom do you propose? What other Pompey do you have in mind? I would like to meet him."

"I am not thinking of anyone in particular," said Philippus quickly. "But . . . we can all . . . it ought to be easy . . . we have something of a choice, don't we?"

"No."

"No?"

"No. No choice at all, Lucius."

Philippus looked at Macer, then back at the Prince, who went on with this thought: "If our consuls fail once more, I see no one we can send against Spartacus in so disastrous a conjuncture. Our most eligible officers have been spirited away by their families for endless vacations, and the healthiest, most vigorous youth of the country seems to be plagued by disease. I have no friend whose eldest son does not have a weak heart or feverish lungs.

". . . That is because, as you know," added the Prince with a quick smile, "there is no future in hunting down runaway slaves, but only serious risks."

"The man who will march against Spartacus today," said Macer, "will be the one whose interests are most threatened by the rebellion."

Philippus was fidgeting in his seat, staring at the folds of his laticlave. The Prince of the Senate smiled. "You have someone in mind, Philippus."

"Well, yes, I do have someone in mind. Everyone has had him in mind since he arrived in Rome, but no one dares suggest him."

"Who?"

"Crassus."

Macer was quickly very close to Philippus. "Who?"

"You heard me very well. I suggested Crassus. He does not enjoy the favor of certain influential families, but . . . he is very rich. In fact, he is the richest Roman I know of. . . . Our treasury is practically empty; as a result, we have no more army and . . ."—he pointed a finger at Macer's robe—"since the plebs are on strike against conscription . . ."

"They are absolutely right," said Macer. "This war is no concern of theirs: they have nothing to lose by a slaves' rebellion. They never owned any. There are even a lot of citizens who are delighted by it: this is their revenge against the rich. If the plebs are mobilized, they want to be fed and paid. The Senate will never get their cooperation with convicts' rations."

Philippus looked delighted. "Yes, yes, yes! Agreed!" he said, clapping his hands. "This is precisely why it is imperative to select Crassus. With his fortune, we could finance the enlistments. He could quickly have several legions on a war footing—legions drilled through his efforts, since the flower of the youth of our country is behaving so shamefully. We ask nothing more of him. Do we?"

"But what will he ask?" said Macer. "That is the question."

"Oh, we have not come to that yet, my friend," replied the old senator. "For the moment, I would rather concentrate on this question: Is Crassus the best man? In the present circumstances, he is. His slaves have left him in droves, his estates have been burned; none of this can be to his taste. His self-interest therefore assures us of his zeal and determination to free us from this plague."

A silence followed this last remark of Philippus', each one weighing, in the light of his own responsibilities, the importance of the decision to be made.

In the street, Crassus and Alexander were making their way slowly toward the palace. Recognized as he went by, Crassus had to shake hands, acknowledge greetings, ask after families. The two men were tall and might easily have made haste by clearing a way for themselves, but Crassus did not seem in a hurry to arrive. Alexander had announced his intention of calling upon the Prince of the Senate and he knew the latter was now consulting with the delegates of the two extremes: patrician reaction and plebeian opposition. "When I get there," he told his companion, "I'll soon know what they decided."

"Yes."

"Philippus is for me, Macer is against. So the decision will be up to the Prince."

"He will have to choose you, Marcus, because he cannot recall anyone from abroad. Only conditions prematurely spelled out could make him hesitate. As for Macer, if you don't lose your temper, he'll let you know the opposition's temperature."

"Oh, I know it. The tribunes' demagoguery will never change. . . . Don't forget to hurry the cooks, I want to see the nobles this evening. I want to know who is ready to follow me."

And the two men separated a few steps from the palace. Some senators immediately surrounded Crassus—a smiling, skillful Crassus, who handled all personal questions amiably, and all those relating to the crisis cautiously.

"Crassus can be useful to us, that is certain," the Prince of the Senate was saying. "After all, his banishment at the hands of Sulla may be what held back his political ambitions. . . . This would be a splendid opportunity to make up for lost time."

"And since he is envious of Pompey's career, he, . . ." Philippus added mischievously.

"All soldiers are," the Prince cut in.

"Yes, but not the way Crassus is. In fact, his feelings about Pompey should make him the more devoted to us. The more maneuverable, anyway."

The Prince looked at Macer. "I confess," he said, "that, for the time being, Crassus is almost the ideal man. The ideal man," he quickly added, "considering the circumstances, needless to say."

"Almost! Why do you say 'almost'?" Philippus asked.

"Because Crassus has not as yet proved his worth as a soldier, Philippus."

"Bah! Even without great military ability, he has the qualities we need in times of crisis. He is proud, bold . . . Remember how he handled the situation at the Porta Collina the time when Sulla . . ."

"Yes, yes, he certainly has qualities of that kind," Macer sneered. "And he also has that complete lack of sensitivity which spares you any remorse over what our generals call necessary cruelty. Remember the proscriptions."

"He was rightfully avenging himself on the murderers of his father and brother! That is the most positive side of his character, my dear tribune. As far as repression is concerned, I think we can really count on Crassus."

With irony, Macer replied in the same tone, "We are sure of that, my dear senator."

"That is what bothers me most about Crassus," said the Prince.

"I suggested Crassus because I do not see anyone else in Rome, today, who has the money, the pride, and . . . Oh, anyway, you seem to forget that Spartacus must be eliminated without bothering for the moment about . . ."

"I am not forgetting anything, Philippus, especially not Spartacus. But we are taking a big risk with Crassus."

"So is he, if he accepts," said Macer.

Philippus raised his eyebrows and opened his eyes as if Macer had just completely astounded him. "Him? What is he risking? And why should he not accept?"

"Because everyone has ducked out, that's why. He will want to feel there are at least some supporting him. He can't do it all without any officers. What does he risk? Being defeated, like all the others. There's cause enough for hesitation between political preferment and the very real danger involved in going to war against Spartacus."

"Those are his problems, not ours," said Philippus. "And if . . ."

"They are ours, too," the Prince of the Senate interrupted, "because he will lay down some conditions."

"All right, all right . . . so be it. He will lay down conditions. Let us first obtain his consent and see how he sets to work. Afterwards, we will make our decision. Where is he today? Right now?"

"He is due here any minute."

"Good, excellent."

"Have you thought about the consuls?" Macer asked the Prince.

"Yes."

"How do you expect to get them to share their authority with Crassus?"

It was Philippus who replied. "If the senators endorse him by a simple majority, the consuls will not have to share their command with him." Philippus looked around and went on almost in a whisper, "We will be obliged to relieve them of it."

"Again!" exclaimed Macer.

"Of course. What else can we do?"

Macer's face had grown even paler, which had not seemed possible. He said in a restrained voice, "Lucius Philippus . . . You were curule magistrate when the Senate restored the military authority to overthrow Lepidus. You were still in office when this consular power was granted—illegally—to Pompey. Today, we see you panicking for the third time and proposing to invest Crassus with absolute authority. That is a heavy responsibility, Philippus. You are quick to commit the future of the Republic!"

"Quick to commit! . . . Quick to commit! . . . Just a minute, my little Macer. Forty years of experience taught me how to commit, quickly, the future of the Republic. We had no more choice in the case of Lepidus than in that of Sertorius: both of them were threatening Rome. We had to make a decision. Quickly. The consuls and Pompey got absolute command, true enough, but Lepidus and Sertorius are now just unpleasant memories. We have no more choice today than we did then;

there is no one but Crassus and . . . Carthage must be destroyed! As for the demands that may follow . . ." Philippus raised his eyebrows, lowered his eyes, and straightened the folds of his garment. "As for the demands that may follow, let us recognize that Crassus' nobility is a safeguard."

Macer laughed harshly. "Stop recognizing, Philippus, and consider facts. Crassus' plebeian nobility does not safeguard us against the use that generals make of their absolute power any more than Sulla's patrician ancestry did."

Philippus looked at the Prince, seeking support. "But, really, the nobility of . . ."

"Nobility! But what is nobility after all, senator?" Macer thundered. "Hereditary wealth . . . Hereditary public office . . . The latter protects the former, supports a clientele, bribes the electorate, and deceives the people. . . . That is the true face of nobility. . . . Just like Sulla, noble Crassus will serve his own ends without truly serving ours, and we will have to pay the price of the repression of Spartacus—if indeed he is defeated, which has not yet been accomplished—by a new dictatorship."

The Prince laughed like a young man. He swallowed a long gulp of fruit juice and said, with his eyes closed, "You're amusing, my friends. To protect our frontiers, you would have invincible leaders, men of granite who, as soon as peace is restored, would suddenly turn into timid, humble citizens. You are asking for the impossible. We can't change human nature."

Philippus, delighted, took up where the Prince had left off. "Anyway, we have nothing to fear from Crassus by way of a test of strength. Pompey is only in Spain."

"Haven't your forty years in the Senate and the lessons of history taught you any more than that? If Crassus, all standards awave, one day arrives at the gates of Rome as the great conqueror, whether Pompey is in Spain or in the middle of the Forum, we will be exposed to every kind of power grab and will have to bow before exorbitant demands."

"If Crassus is victorious!" said the Prince.

"It is our duty to anticipate how far his demands may go."

Still smiling, the Prince was following his thought with closed eyes. "He still has not gotten the better of Spartacus. And . . . he has not even accepted our offer yet."

A guard came in and bowed. "The . . ."

Macer, icy, very stiff, interrupted him. "In the name of the people of Rome, I formally object to the selection of Crassus."

The guard resumed: "The praetor Marcus Licinius Crassus." The Prince got up, waved, and the guard went out.

Philippus, who had gotten up hurriedly, almost fell as he went over to the Prince. "Well, what are you going to do? We have to have some legions, my friend."

Turning first to Philippus, then to Macer, the Prince said quickly, "Let everyone act according to his conscience and his responsibilities. Crassus did not make the trip across the City in this heat just for the pleasure of seeing us." And he walked solemnly toward Crassus who was coming in.

"Noble senators, greetings."

Macer and Philippus greeted him.

"Good afternoon, Licinius," said the Prince. Taking him by the arm, he led him over to the others and poured him a cup of fruit juice which Crassus downed in one gulp. He set the cup down and turned to the Prince. "Spartacus has defeated Manlius and the consuls in Picenum."

"Where is he?" Philippus asked.

"Coming south."

"Where is he this evening?" the old senator insisted.

"He must be at the border of Picenum and Campania."

Philippus looked at the Prince, but the latter was pacing slowly, his chin on his chest, his hands behind his back. He stopped in front of Crassus. "Why did Spartacus come back? He must have good reasons. I think those reasons are the key to our victory. What is he planning to do, Licinius?"

"We will find out: several of my men are following him. He is now at the head of a hundred thousand fighters; we might just as well call them twenty legions."

"Does that include women and children?" Philippus said nervously.

Crassus answered over his shoulder. "Yes."

Shocked at Crassus' less than courteous attitude toward him, the senator looked at the Prince, who motioned to him, urging calm. But Philippus was not easily satisfied. He said drily, "If you are including women and children, Spartacus does not have a hundred thousand fighters, but only half that many."

"The women and children fight, too."

"Come now, you can't mean that."

Crassus looked at Philippus a moment and mustered a smile. "Oh, yes, I very much mean it."

Philippus burst out, "I will never understand anything about the strength of those dogs!"

Turning to the Prince, Crassus explained, "I have looked carefully into the details of our legionaries' battles. Two facts, that at first seemed unimportant to me, today assume great importance, for they are repeated every time. The legionaries are overconfident. The fugitives arouse their curiosity, because they don't believe that slaves will dare put up a fight, but it is too late when they realize they are up against determined fighters. Because, while two soldiers may see each other, they don't have time to look at one another. I have come to the conclusion that our soldiers are no longer learning the lessons of the previous battles."

"It is up to great generals to do that for them, Licinius. I was sure that you were getting valuable lessons from this war, even though not directly involved in it."

"Perhaps distance made it easier. Had I been involved, I might not have understood the over-all pattern, either."

"What tactics would you use, knowing what you have learned, if you were to fight Spartacus?"

Crassus gazed at the Prince for a long time. He opened his mouth to answer, thought better of it, and with a gesture indicated he did not know. Philippus could not resist his desire to express his opinion. "We ought to surround those dogs' camp in the middle of the night and butcher them in their sleep like animals. It's as simple as that."

The Prince of the Senate smiled. "That's too simple, perhaps. What do you think of it, noble Crassus?"

"Nothing."

"Hmmm. I'm not surprised," said Philippus.

Crassus turned around sharply. The Prince laughed. "Our friend Lucius often uses the prerogative of age to manhandle us a little."

"The prerogative of experience is enough for me," said the old man in a fury. "With a well-disciplined army, it ought to be easy to put an end to this wretched drove of stinking cattle."

They looked at him for a moment without answering. Turning toward Crassus and Macer, the Prince resumed. "If it is still possible to understand Spartacus' intentions, I do not believe he will try anything at all against Rome. At least, I hope not. What do you think, my friends?"

"I have no idea what Spartacus may or may not do," Crassus answered.

"Spartacus will not march on Rome," Macer stated. "His clandestinity prevents him from laying formal siege to any city. He has no reserves. All the cities have closed their gates to him, and his army is increased daily by the slaves who join it. Before attacking Rome, Spartacus must first see to his food supply. That is his real problem, I am convinced. Once that is solved, perhaps! . . ."

Crassus retorted nonchalantly. "He solves that by stealing horses from the landowners."

"I don't believe that is anything like a systematic plan. After all, you are one of those landowners. You must know that the slaves run away with whatever animals they can take with them. As for the horses, I don't believe Spartacus uses them exclusively for food, because . . ."

"No? What does he use them for, then?"

"For cavalry. He needs horses."

"That is a conjecture."

Macer turned to the Prince. "No, it is a deduction. Everyone," he insisted, "says that Spartacus' cavalry is perfect. That is the proof that he . . ."

Crassus interrupted him again. "Naturally, most of his horses were taken from the legionaries."

"No. Only part of them. It seems to me Spartacus has been used as a scapegoat a little too often in the past year. Have you already forgotten the scandal of the legionaries selling their horses to landowners? According to all reports, Spartacus' men are undernourished." Macer broke out in a short laugh. "They wouldn't be if they ate all the horses they are alleged to have stolen! The price of wheat coming from Sicilia has just gone up considerably. Is Spartacus responsible for that increase, too?" In the icy silence that followed, Macer helped himself to a full cup of fruit juice and drank it in long gulps. He went on more calmly: "But it was not intended for this meeting to discuss problems that existed before the slaves' revolt." Macer continued, as he walked, "I think I know why Spartacus has not left the country. Think about it. It is late in the season; harvesting is finished in the fields and the vineyards. Spartacus cannot venture into the mountains because he has no reserves. And how could he have any? He has a hundred thousand mouths to feed! So he comes back to Lucania, toward the cities he passed through last year, in which he may have kept contacts." Philippus made an abrupt arm movement, but Macer went on with a smile, "Sympathizers . . . or contacts . . . as you wish, Philippus."

Philippus was now so excited that his little feet were beating out a quick march. "Contacts! Reserves! Sympathizers! What I want to know is how half-starved, half-naked creatures can stand up to our well-fed and marvelously trained legionaries. It's unbelievable!" he concluded, hammering out each syllable.

"But not new to history," Macer retorted.

Carried away by the polemics he had hoped to bring about in inviting Macer, Philippus had straightened up. He no longer looked his age. He walked with quick little steps toward the young representative of the opposition. "But what is this tribune saying? The history of Rome has no place for slaves!" And the wily senator, without moving his head, observed Crassus' reaction after that remark. Seemingly impassive, the rich landowner was listening attentively: they were talking about his manpower, his problem. Philippus appeared to be sure of this, for a smile passed over his lips, which he quickly dissembled, but Macer's reply obviously delighted him.

"Then it will have to make a place for them," the tribune was saying. "Our daily lives are full of slaves, why should we not find them in our history?"

Philippus became calmer and more relaxed as Macer played into his hands; turning to Crassus, he continued his thrust, since the tribune was now speaking without restraint. "Does it not sound like our tribune is defending these dogs?"

"Oh, we are well aware that the demagogy of the tribunes sometimes leads them to forget certain basic facts, or to pretend they have forgotten them: in this case, the fact that a slave is not a citizen. A realistic politician never forgets this. Nor does he forget that the citizen of Rome is the strongest, the richest, the freest in the world. The slave serves him, entertains him. His escape, his death represent a financial loss, nothing more; he has no more place in the history of Rome than do dogs or parrots."

Philippus seemed delighted; apparently, Crassus was reacting to Macer as the senator had hoped. But the young tribune, who probably had never had so splendid an opportunity to address the cream of the aristocracy—at one and the same time, the Prince of the Senate, the most powerful Roman financier, and the doyen of the Senate—did not seem inclined to yield an inch of ground. "The people Spartacus encouraged to escape will find their place in history, Crassus. We are no longer talking about slaves as chattels, but of those that Spartacus has raised against our society. . . . I admit it, what Spartacus represents is a mystery to me. To you, too, but none of you will ever acknowledge it. Do we even know what kind of enemy we are up against? Servile wars are silent; they are shapeless; our consuls say they are not . . . 'conventional.' No one dares say they are the most difficult ones, but everyone talks about them with passion. To the people, troubles in Sicilia or isolated uprisings are events of no consequence; yet the Senate ought to understand that this affair, looked at as a whole, is part and parcel of the same phenomenon; yes, they are all one and the same war, continual, interminable, even if, in putting an end to it, we do not try to remedy its true causes . . . or even simply to study it in good faith. But, since this war is a monster peculiar to us, as his arthritis is to Philippus, or the storm is to the sky, does it not behoove us to find out why it is always threatening somewhere and continually keeps coming back? The solution to this problem would then become self-evident."

Philippus frowned and quickly turned his head toward the Prince.

"My friends," said the Prince, "the character of emergency of the situation demands that we proceed as quickly as possible to a realistic conclusion of this . . . meeting. We cannot afford to waste another minute in debating the phenomena that lead to servile wars. We would have to consult with one another, draw preliminary conclusions, put the question on the agenda, give everyone the right to speak, hear all the senators . . . in short, have a peacetime debate. But we are far from peacetime. Instead, a state of national emergency has been proclaimed, all our consuls and proconsuls have been defeated, all our lines of communications between cities have been broken, and . . . we no longer know what to do to solve this problem. The senator was delegated to me by his peers to discuss the matter. He fortunately took it on himself, in order to save time later on, to bring with him the most eloquent representative of the opposition, with the express purpose of avoiding a long public debate that might aggravate the situation by arousing tempers and, in any case, would delay the essential goal: to find a solution quickly. Have you found a solution, my friends? That is what we must talk about right now."

As no one answered, Macer said, "You have not told us why the presence of noble Crassus is indispensable to this discussion." And he added politely, but without haste, "I do not doubt that his participation will be invaluable to you when you have to decide on a course of action, but there are notables in Rome who might take umbrage at his presence here today. While his visits to Rome are rare, they never pass unnoticed. So, what is the reason for his presence here?"

Crassus had blanched at Macer's first words. Very erect, he now eyed the Prince of the Senate, who had to counter the tribune's question, this very minute. "If I did not know you to be so conscientious in your work, so devoted to the well-being of our citizens, so concerned with justice and so little interested in personal gain, Lollius, you would not be in this audience chamber today and your question would be offensive. But in it I see on the contrary only the expression of your admirable frankness and your fine devotion to the Republic. It is therefore in the same spirit, with equal frankness, that I am going to answer you: If noble Crassus is here with us now, it is because his experience and certain circumstances can be of great service to us. I hasten to add," said the Prince, with a smile at Crassus, "that he had sent me his request for an audience even before I knew of your coming here or the senators' decision to send their doyen to me. The situation being what it is, when I later learned that the senator and you were coming, I did not postpone our noble friend's audience because, as I said, his experience can be of service to us. Let us not forget either that the rebellion had its origins in Campania, the province in which he has his greatest latifundia. That is also the province in which he lives, knows the praetor, and sponsors his games. On these farmlands, Crassus maintained a large labor force which abandoned them to follow Spartacus; he is therefore directly affected by these mass desertions, but his interest as a landowner alone would not concern us if, for many years, the Romans had not been supplied by him with all the farm products they consume, whether wheat, milk, meat, or poultry. For a year now, our reserves have withstood the halting of transport only through his generosity and also, one must add, his public-spiritedness, for he has not yet been paid! You know as well as I, Lollius, the state the public treasury is in. Were it only because Romans no longer eat except thanks to Crassus—despite the rationing we are forced to impose upon them at the moment, since no new stocks at all are arriving now for our reserves—I should have made a point of receiving him without delay. But there is another reason. It is now known in Rome that he is here and, as you justly said, his presence never goes unnoticed. In this crisis we are going through, people's minds are at work. His arrival at the palace has been noticed. I do not yet know why he asked to see me, but I know that his mere presence among us will have a reassuring effect. Even if the general uneasiness is not abated, the man in the street will know that we are deliberating, that measures are being planned, that we are not letting things take their course. . . . I think it is useless to explain any further the importance of our friend's enlightened and ever-generous participation. But, at the same time, I am grateful for your frank question, Lollius, because it gave me a chance to pay tribute to him, while still looking forward to the pleasure of doing this publicly when opportunity arises. . . . And now, allow me to repeat my question: Have we found a solution? Do we have any ideas, any suggestions to offer?"

"I have a solution," said Macer, "but I know it is pointless to submit it for your approval, because it has been lying idle in the Senate for months, officially recorded, but left to the fate of forgotten files." The tribune went on calmly, "In that bill, I proposed that Spartacus and his entire troop be freed; they thereby acquire the right to decide for themselves what they want to do. If they choose to stay in this country, we grant them naturalization."

"Lollius Macer," said Philippus, "you are the most entertaining tribune in all the republics."

"Rome would emerge with greater prestige from this useless war," Macer argued calmly. "Her prestige thus enhanced, she would be twice as respected and influential." Everyone laughed. "Our worst enemies could not help but admire us. . . ." Everyone laughed. "Only the most powerful country in the world can afford such a gesture. Such magnanimity would shine through history like a sunbeam in the centuries to come. . . ." Everyone laughed. The tribune eyed them one by one. A bit of color had returned to his cheeks, making his face look much younger; he brushed aside a lock of hair and smiled. "It is obvious that I will not be able to come to agreement with you on the decision to be taken and, since I am not an insider, I am not interested in knowing before the crowd whatever you will decide. You wanted to know what opposition you would find in the streets tomorrow. Now you know. Allow me then to take my . . ."

"Wait, Macer!" Philippus cut in with a laugh. "Don't you want to have Spartacus appointed military tribune?"

"To grant him a triumph?" added Crassus, smiling condescendingly.

"To allow him to present his candidacy for the next consulate?" Philippus went on. "After all, once freed and naturalized, he would not have to stop at anything, would he?"

Macer, who had gone toward the Prince to take his leave without turning to face the sallies that had crossed his path, stopped short. He turned slowly, with a smile, made somewhat scornful by his haughty manner.

"General!" he said. "Spartacus has proved ten times since the beginning of this war that he deserved that title as much as Pompey. Laugh, citizens. Your lack of imagination appalls me; but, at the same time, I am used to it. It is my greatest enemy among my contemporaries. If we showed as much imagination in our politics as we do in the art of war and the enslavement of conquered countries, this country would be an example to the rest of the world until the end of time." Turning to Crassus, he said with the same smile, "A triumph for Spartacus? . . . Men have been awarded triumphs for much less great feats of strength. Out of fear, perhaps . . . but is not the return or the arrival of victorious generals always awaited with fear? . . . The populations of a good many towns have greeted Spartacus as a victorious general. Tradition dictates that we grant a triumph to generals who have served their country well. In Spartacus' case, with a little imagination and a lot of good faith, he has, in his own way, done the country a service by bringing it face to face with the increasingly serious problem of the continued import of slave labor into our territory. As for the consulate," he said, turning to Philippus, "if all the slaves . . ."

"We have laughed long enough," Crassus interrupted in a loud voice. "As long as a hundred thousand slaves are loose in the country, there can be no security here, either for farming or for commercial transactions. We must . . ."

Macer interrupted him in his turn. "May this prospect of economic collapse give the holders of Roman wealth the courage to save it."

"Meaning what?"

"Those who, like you, have everything to lose in this war know very well what an economic collapse means. The slave is the free manpower over which the master has the right of life and death. When he escapes, it means that all the manpower is gone. Farms, tanneries, fields, all stop working. What is left to the master? Nothing. He is ruined. That is what the economic collapse of the country is, Crassus: your own."

"Macer, your attitude is unspeakable. It proves your sympathy for Spartacus and I shall publicly accuse you of treason."

"Why? Because I don't see any military solution to this war?"

"Because you do not condemn Spartacus. Worse than that, you look for reasons for him."

"I don't have to look for reasons for the gladiators; I know them."

"Do you hear him?"

"And I don't condemn them."

"Aren't you going to call your guards?" said Crassus to the Prince.

But Macer was launched. "What do they have to lose? Their lives? They were condemned to die in the arena! . . . Can't you see? We have the best and oldest form of government in the world, but is that enough? Is it as good as it could be? Our history is peppered with foreign wars and power grabs, revolts at home . . . to say nothing of the scandalous assassinations that go unpunished. We have naturalized so many foreigners that we scarcely have any identity left. Roman blood is by now so mixed with that of all these new citizens that, if we added Spartacus' hundred thousand fugitives to theirs, we wouldn't even notice the difference. And don't talk to me about an inborn love of one's country; not everybody has it. It isn't something that is handed out like a wheat ration. Whether newly naturalized or citizens for several generations, men react to every injustice, to every mistake of the government, which by reaction produce opposition, resistance, revolt. . . . Our passion for gladiatorial contests has grown even further with the influx of prisoners on our markets. They have brought about the appearance and flourishing of the most abominable—and, as we are finding out, dangerous—of industries: gladiatorial schools. They all prosper because, as long as people are diverted by the games, they don't think about anything else. . . . We are responsible for the revolt of Spartacus and his hundred thousand men, because we allowed the lanistae and injustice to thrive among our citizens. . . . The slaves' uprising is like a balance trying to establish itself on our social scale. . . . Today, we see estates that lose their entire manpower in one swoop. To reach Spartacus, the runaways sometimes have to cover several hundred leagues out in the open, but the danger doesn't hold them back because, to them, Spartacus represents what they want most: the right to choose their own fates. That's all they have when they link up with Spartacus, but all of a sudden they are alive, their lives begin, they take on a meaning: they have made a choice. Those, Crassus, are their wretched reasons."

"The reasons of slaves do not interest us."

"More's the pity, because slaves are the weak point of our Republic, and gladiators our chronic disease. By refusing to die for our amusement in the arena, by rejecting the injustice of their condition as slaves, the fugitives upset the balance of our country's forces. Think of what such uncontrollable spontaneity could mean if it occurred simultaneously in Greece, in Spain, in Asia. . . . That is why the reasons of the slaves interest me."

"The Republic can replace them at the rate of a hundred to one. It . . ."

"Today, yes—and with your money."

"We are their absolute masters!" Crassus thundered.

"Well, then, master Spartacus!" said Macer calmly. And he went up to the Prince of the Senate and bade him farewell. The Prince accompanied him to the door. "Lollius Macer," the Prince said to him, "you are of the breed that gets assassinated."

"I cannot shut my eyes to the shortcomings of our government," Macer answered. "If everyone kept still, who would know anything? As for assassination," he added, smiling sadly, "I have illustrious predecessors!" Macer walked off in dignity, without haste. The Prince watched him as he went, solemn, thoughtful. He remained motionless for a while, with his back to the other two. Crassus was waiting haughtily, still scowling with anger. The old senator could no longer hold still; followed by his fan-boy-slave, he went over to the Prince. "Well, my friend, what do we decide?" Philippus had to repeat his question, for the Prince did not seem to have heard it.

Without turning, he answered slowly, as if thinking aloud, "I think it is time to recall Pompey. It is not good to leave our generals abroad too long; they forget the true spirit of the government and acquire bad habits." Crassus turned his back on them abruptly and helped himself to a drink. As he turned to the old senator, the Prince noticed Crassus' reaction. "What do you think of it, Philippus?" he asked.

Crassus set the goblet back down without drinking and turned to face them. "Noble senators, allow me to take my leave. I have a few messages to send and some friends coming to supper." He walked toward the door, close to the Prince.

"Good-bye, noble Licinius," said the Prince, and he sighed. "I would gladly exchange my evening for yours."

Without smiling, Crassus answered, "Perhaps you will be able to join us after the special meeting of the Senate. And perhaps this supper will be a farewell party if the noble Senate honors me by entrusting me with the defense of the interests of Rome. It was to ask you that that I requested this audience."

The Prince smiled. "An excellent idea, Licinius. Excellent idea. I have no doubt the Senate will receive your proposal favorably. Personally, I shall not fail to support it; we are really very fortunate in having you at our sides in this distressing business. As for the supper, I accept your invitation with pleasure, and look forward to drinking to your success."

After Crassus left, Philippus laughed for a long time. "For once, Macer was clumsy; he did all my work for me. What a pity he's so impassioned and so unrealistic. Too bad, really."

The Prince, his chin on his chest and his hands behind his back, looked at Philippus out of the corner of his eye and went over to the stibadium. He let himself down on the cushions, and heaved a long sigh, his eyes closed. Philippus had followed him with tiny steps, his sandals beating a dry rhythm. "Macer is a rare man," said the Prince, his eyes still closed, to the senator who was standing, bent, beside the stibadium. "His great qualities could be useful to the Republic, Philippus, but his emotional excesses, like the one he just had, play into the hands of factions that know how to exploit them . . . somewhat as you did tonight. Well . . . you wanted Crassus, my friends, and you've got him."

"You were able to play on his envy at the proper time, my friend," said Philippus. "This is a historic day . . . Come, come . . . Let yourself be a little more optimistic; your face is as long as a piece of yard goods."

The Prince indeed looked overwhelmed and suddenly very old. He opened his eyes and looked at the senator. He slowly clasped his hands behind his head. "I can't be optimistic, Lucius. In fact, I tremble for the Republic at the thought that one day Pompey and Crassus might become reconciled. And I wonder whether, even now, we must not start trying to set them against each other, to divide them, to exploit everything that stands between them. . . ."

"Their discord obviously is a guarantee of security. But if there is to be a reconciliation between them one day, we will no longer be here, my good friend. We will be long dead by then."

"But the Senate will be alive. And I loathe the idea of seeing it embark on the path of compromise. That is a slippery policy. In order not to fall, you have to grab hold of the generals' blade: it cuts easily. . . . We overcame Lepidus and Sertorius, but it cost us our hands; I fear that in subduing Spartacus we may lose both our arms and our head."

"It will be understood that we had no alternative."

The Prince sighed. The two men spoke in lowered voices as if they answered each other's innermost questions, guessing the responses before they quite heard them.

"Will it also be understood that at one and the same time we had to be on guard in Spain, Macedonia, Mauretania, and Transalpine Gaul, and still maintain order here in the streets? Because there's trouble there, too. . . ."

"Yes, yes, of course, it will be understood."

"Will it be understood that we had no more troops available?"

"Oh, they will be able to see that we could not stand up against the whole world and maintain still more powerful military reserves at home to fight rebellious slaves."

"And Spartacus? How will he be explained?"

"Oh, that one! . . . Anyway, with Crassus on his heels . . ." —Philippus made a gesture of utter obliteration—". . . he should not be bothering us much longer."

"I've been hearing that tune for over a year now. . . . And Crassus! Will it be understood, Lucius, that we all owe him money? Money that the treasury can't pay back! A debt he never mentions! . . ."

Philippus looked tired. The two men eyed each other for a moment without speaking. Philippus affectionately put his hand on the Prince's shoulder. "I'll see you later at the meeting," he said, and he went off with little mechanical steps, held up by his fanboy-slave.

"It will be short," said the Prince, closing his eyes again. "Very short," he breathed, and fell asleep.

The quaestors, who had remained standing all that time in the darkest corner of the chamber, came over to the Prince. Seeing he was asleep, they sent away the slave who had come in to fetch the cups and went out without a sound.

ARENA

After stripping the consuls of their supreme power, the senators formally conferred it upon Crassus. The magnate was overjoyed. The senatorial decision not only allowed him to take part as absolute commander in a war which threatened the fruit of his rapine, but also presented him with a superb entry on the political scene, an ambition delayed by his running afoul of Sulla, sickened by his greed during the proscriptions of 82. And Crassus, who, for ten years, had enviously stood by, helpless, as Pompey rose to prominence, now had the unhoped-for good fortune of seeing himself entrusted with the same proconsular authority, thus making up for all the time lost.

Alexander had erased the last cloud to reassure his friend, trying at the same time to put him on his guard without discouraging him. "People won't even be able to say that Pompey had to face up to a soldier like Sertorius while Crassus was confronted only with runaway slaves, because in only a year Spartacus has shown the dimensions of his military genius. The news of his brilliant victories has spread beyond borders and over seas. It is therefore just because the gladiator is so dangerous an adversary that the Senate stripped the consuls in your favor. A victory over him could be spectacular and therefore the more glorious for the victor."

"And we will never know where Pompey would be today if Perpenna had not murdered Sertorius," Crassus had added.

"Hmmm. He fought Sertorius without too much success, true enough, but you should leave disparagement to the mediocre; it is their only weapon."

Although Crassus had done his utmost within the curia, in Rome and throughout the country, to gain the favor of the Senate so that they would think of him when the time came—being affable, acting benevolently toward people in need, distributing presents, sponsoring games, supporting entire cities with his gifts—this plutocrat had, nevertheless, accepted his powers with clear mind and conviction. Conscious of the enemy's strength, to be sure, he was yet convinced that their chains must be quickly put back on the slaves. He never ceased repeating that this was a war because the enemy was threatening the country, but, the enemy being a troop of slaves, this war retained the character of a punitive expedition. Slaves had to remain in their places: at the feet of their masters.

These ideas, shared by the nobles whose estates had been looted and then deserted, brought Crassus the devotion of the holders of Rome's most handsome fortunes, that is to say, the nobility, both patrician and plebeian. The name of Crassus had been coming up so often in conversation since his arrival in Rome that no one was surprised at seeing the Senate confer upon him absolute power with the title of proconsul. Some conservatives, faithful to the memory of Sulla, did not approve of the choice, but somebody had to be sent against Spartacus. They therefore met at the home of one of them on the very evening of his assumption of power and agreed on at least one point: the urgency of the situation had allowed no better choice to the senators at bay. After which, though only for the duration of the servile war, they decided to throw their support behind Crassus.

Within the twenty-four hours following the Senate's decision, Crassus announced that he would need ten legions. He reconstituted four of them rather easily, by regrouping the soldiers who had returned unscathed or only slightly wounded from the previous encounters with Spartacus. Seeing that the mere mention of his name was not enough to imbue the citizenry with a confidence that Spartacus' lightning successes had seriously shaken, Crassus then spent a night with Alexander in figuring out what ten legions would cost him during a six-months' campaign. At dawn, he announced that he would triple the pay of enlisted men. Marching under the banner of the richest of all Romans appealed to the most youthful, the unemployed, the isolated bandits. Within a week, after rigorous selection, Crassus had forty thousand men. As commander in chief of the armed forces, minister of national defense, principal source of finances for the State, and now enjoying the support of the conservatives, he was a man whose decisions were carried out without delay. He spent a fortune on armament, another on cavalry, and twice as much again to establish supply lines and dependable transport.

To prevent Spartacus from reaching Lucania, below Campania, he set out in quick time, sending ahead two legions under the command of his legate Mummius. The latter had been given formal instructions to follow the Thracian's forces without attacking them, and to keep Crassus periodically informed of their position. It was Crassus' intention to interdict the fugitives in Samnium, surround them, or push them back to the Adriatic.

As Crassus subjected his soldiers to stringent drill before each daily march, the eight thousand men who were to follow Mummius were not sorry to be detached from the main body of the army. Like the other generals Spartacus had defeated, Mummius, seeing the wretched horde of runaways before him, estimated that he would easily be able to dispose of them with his two legions. But Spartacus, informed of the presence of Mummius by his scouts—ragged beggars stationed along all the roads surrounding the Thracian's troop, with their horses waiting behind a hill or in a forest and ready to fly like arrows to advise their leader as soon as the Romans had gone by—had placed forty thousand fugitives on the heights on his right flank, the same number on the left, and marched in the open with twenty thousand men. Deceived by this simple tactic, though aware of the fact that there were now a hundred thousand fugitives, Mummius attacked head-on in spite of Crassus' orders. The first arrow had not yet fallen to earth when the pincers of the eighty thousand fugitives closed in furiously on Mummius. It turned into a run-for-your-life rout. Several hundred soldiers fell in less than an hour. Trying to keep from being surrounded, the legionaries left weapons, rations, and tools on the battleground in order to escape faster. Spartacus had no one to send after them as his famished men threw themselves on the legionaries' supplies. The legate regrouped his men a league away and returned to Crassus.

Hearing of Mummius' disobedience and what it had cost him, Crassus slapped the legate in front of all of his officers. The next day, Crassus ordered his entire army assembled in companies of five hundred lined up in fifty files of ten and announced a disciplinary measure. On horseback in front of his army, his face pale, Crassus revived the punishment of decimation long since fallen into disuse: each decurion chose a victim in his group of ten men and make him kneel down. At Crassus' signal, four thousand heads fell; an entire legion had just died in a few seconds. After which, Crassus ordered his army to move forward a few hundred feet and announced that no one would receive his pay. It would be held as security for the weapons each legionary had been issued and would be paid after the campaign only to those who returned their weapons intact. Two hours of concentrated drill followed this calling to order. That afternoon, Crassus decided to attack Spartacus himself, relying on the legionaries' fury to make them fight without yielding an inch of ground to the enemy.

After the brief encounter with Mummius, Spartacus had made a short halt. Certain now that he could reach the South without again being engaged, Spartacus decided to make a few sallies for provisions while the women and children continued their march under the command of Alba and Polla. To protect them on the way, he left five thousand fighters headed by several former Capuan gladiators. When Spartacus returned two days later, all of his men and many of the women had been massacred. He spent a whole day looking for Polla and Alba among the victims. No one could find them. They had been taken prisoners along with the pregnant women and the children. Young mothers and pregnant women were particularly valuable: travel was difficult for them, and they would hardly think of running away again, being only too happy, perhaps, to have escaped death.

Spartacus deliberately set up camp out in the open and sent out scouts in all directions. Crassus, he was told, was now in south Samnium; soon he would be in Lucania! When the Thracian also learned of the punishment of four thousand men by decimation, he understood that he too would have to shake up his men if they were to face an enemy so savage that he had not hesitated to wipe out an entire legion in order to stiffen the discipline of his army. To gain some time, he quickly marched to the outskirts of Thurii, on the Gulf of Tarentum. The proverbial indolence of the inhabitants of this region was well-known to him, and he knew that here he would have time to think without being harassed. So he subjected his troop to intense daily exercise, for the first time insisting on strict discipline: reveille, drill, supervised distribution of rations, more drill, lights out.

Gannicus told him one evening that some men from the East were asking to talk to him. They were two pirate leaders, Cilicians whom Spartacus had met seven years before at Byzantium, and with whom he had spent a year in captivity in the quarries of Mount Paryadres. He had escaped with them. Recaptured, they had been sold in the slave markets of Rome. Spartacus recognized them as soon as he saw them. They sat down in his tent and asked him what his plans were. The Thracian was still uncertain and hesitated to reply; the pirates then suggested that he attack Sicilia with them. They would furnish the ships to embark two thousand fugitives and the bulk of the troop would follow after capturing several towns. It would then be much more difficult for the legionaries to attack them on the large island, because, once they were masters of Sicilia, which was overflowing with wheat and cattle, the fugitives would be able to fortify the coast where it did not have natural defenses. Then, Rome would sooner or later have to negotiate. Spartacus accepted their offer. Leaving Castus at the head of a line of sentries along the whole width of the isthmus, he broke camp and struck out into Bruttium as far as Regium.

When he heard of this, Crassus lost no time; breaking camp in the middle of the night under a heavy rain, he advanced rapidly.

Spartacus now being locked on the isthmus by the sea, Crassus deployed his men along the whole width of the tip of the boot, from the Tyrrhenian Sea to the Ionian. He was getting ready for the night when a quaestor about thirty years old, whose father had been a censor with his own some twenty years before, a patrician by the name of Julius Caesar, requested an interview. Crassus agreed to see him. Young Caesar came in, elegant, handsome, slim. With young Metellus, he had been present during the entire discussion that had taken place in the palace of the Prince of the Senate. Crassus looked at him. The quaestor's tunic was impeccable, although the marches decreed by Crassus had been as hard on the officers as on the men. Crassus smiled. The young man's reputation had reached the provinces when Sulla had asked him to repudiate his wife Cornelia, daughter of Cinna. Caesar, then nineteen, had refused and fled, while Pompey, not daring to disobey the dictator, had agreed to separate from his wife. When Caesar's friends had come to plead the case of the young man, then known only for his dissolute youth and his extravagances, Sulla had made a statement that had remained in Crassus' memory: "Beware of this adolescent with his ill-fitting belt; there is the stuff of several Mariuses in him." A libertine, beloved of women, rich, handsome, lettered, gifted with an amazing memory and splendid energy, the young man now stood at a respectful distance, waiting to be spoken to.

"What do you want, my friend?"

"May I be allowed a suggestion?"

"Sit down. I am listening."

"The fugitives are surrounded by the sea to the west, north, and south. The isthmus at this point is only thirty leagues wide: a trench barring their route would keep our men busy for a few weeks and . . ."

"An excellent idea. We could avoid a night attack, surprises . . . and the army would be kept in good condition . . . a sentry every hundred feet, relieved at four-hour intervals. . . . An excellent idea. Winter is coming. Spartacus will run out of supplies and try for a breakthrough with reduced forces."

Crassus congratulated his quaestor. They talked about this plan far into the night and Crassus had his men awakened. Tired though they were, the legionaries were not fazed. In a few days, they built a palisade about thirty leagues long, from one sea to the other. In front of the palisade, along its entire length, they dug a V-shaped ditch fifteen feet deep and just as wide. Behind the palisade, they set up watchtowers. Anticipating the battle to come, Crassus subjected his men to rigorous daily exercise, awaiting the enemy with confidence.

From the top of the sheer cliffs overlooking the Strait of Messina, Spartacus waited for the pirates. Looking out to sea with Gannicus, watching for the arrival of the boats promised by the Cilicians, Spartacus grew gloomier from day to day. Having sent some intrepid swimmers across the strait at its narrowest point, he had learned that the governor, Caius Verres, had had the Sicilian side of the strait fortified to make it inaccessible to pirates. Without the help of the Cilicians, it seemed impossible for the Thracian to undertake such a crossing. He would have needed several dozen ships, all manned by sailors.

After waiting in vain for three weeks, the Thracian spent one more day with Gannicus on the cliffs. By evening, he had given up the plan of taking the fugitives across the strait.

"Impossible to go north, impossible to cross the sea here, this country is like a great prison!" Spartacus said.

"We're trapped like flies in a bottle," Gannicus answered.

Spartacus looked out to sea a last time, his face closed, hard. "Maybe," he said, "but no one's been able to put his thumb over its neck so far. Let's go see what Crassus is doing."

They crossed the camp. The fugitives stood up as they went by and the troop resumed its march toward the Gulf of Tarentum. After short daily marches, they arrived one evening at a height a few leagues from Scylacium, where Spartacus had left a line of sentries. He was pitching camp for the night when Castus arrived. He drew Spartacus and Gannicus aside. "Crassus has dug a trench and built a palisade from one sea to the other."

"Well, he's a cautious fellow. Let's go see it," said the Thracian.

Very late in the night, the three men came close to the ditch. As if hoping to discover a chink in it, they walked along it for a moment. Everywhere, behind the ditch, there rose a palisade twelve to fifteen feet high. Toward Scylacium, it was too dark to be able to see, but it was possible to locate the siege line from the sounds of shovels and picks. Castus, who was walking in front, stopped suddenly. His companions came up to him in silence. Apparently the legionary thought he was far away from the enemy, free of all danger, for he was humming as he crouched, defecating. He died with the tune on his lips: Castus' mace had smashed his head. Farther away, an invisible legionary was on guard in a tree; his arrow grazed Spartacus' neck, leaving a streak of blood behind. The three men headed back for their camp without a word. Gannicus stopped before his tent. "Like flies in a bottle!" the Celt sighed as he bade good night to his companions.

ARENA

XIX

On one of his numerous estates, near Consentia and only a few leagues from the siege line, Crassus was entertaining a young magistrate, a friend of Alexander's, Marcus Tullius Cicero, who had just completed his quaestorship in Sicilia and was returning to Rome. As some slaves served the two diners, others were trimming their toenails, massaging their legs, perfuming them. Cicero sat up, very straight, on a cushionless corner of the stibadium; he looked like a long piece of pale glass. The quaestor was thirty-four years old. Thin, his hair cut short and combed forward, he was watching the relish with which his host ate the magnificently prepared appetizers. To do honor to Crassus' table, the quaestor from time to time took an olive, a pepper. He sighed. "The pressing demands of the digestive system take disturbing priorities over the brain!"

Crassus, who at that moment was slicing into a fowl in aspic covered with orange slices, raised his eyebrows, surprised, but did not look at his visitor. He took a mouthful. "You are a welcome guest at my table," he said.

"And with the bad habits of the body, the mind builds doctrines from all the rubbish of the intellect," Cicero continued.

"Bad habits? Which?"

One course followed another. At a sign from Crassus, musicians had taken their places at some distance from the diners. Slaves came and emptied baskets of flowers on the white mosaic while Oriental bondwomen served them with cool wine and then went to dance near the musicians.

"It should be possible to get along without eating," the quaestor explained.

"If you had a good stomach, you would appreciate the pleasures of the table." Crassus raised a tall goblet. "I drink to your health, Marcus."

Cicero laughed briefly and picked up his cup. "Thank you," he said, and he drank in small sips. "I envy you, noble Crassus."

Crassus took a bunch of grapes, which he dipped in a cup of water. "Consider yourself at home here, and do me the honor of staying as long as it pleases you."

Crassus had heard about Cicero from Alexander, who saw a great deal of him when they were both in Rome. Cicero had the reputation of being a "Greek," a "schoolman," terms of abuse in the mouths of Romans, but this magistrate had been able to gain the ear of the notables and must have displayed true proficiency to obtain a quaestorship when he had no fortune.

"I have had an urge to be nasty to someone all day. . . . At sea, when I heard that this sumptuous villa belonged to you, I decided I would like to meet you, noble Crassus, and I felt Rome could certainly spare me a day's rest. But I still have that urge to bite someone, in spite of your charming hospitality."

Crassus shrugged and said, while eating, "If that can help you digest better . . ."

There was a long silent moment. Crassus ate his grapes without looking up. He said, "Excuse my lack of zest, Marcus; I've had a long day. . . . I'm tired."

"What reward are you going to ask of the Senate after you defeat the slaves?"

Toying with his grapes, Crassus looked at Cicero with a polite smile. "Reward? What do you mean?"

"You were granted a proconsulate with full military powers, weren't you?"

"Yes."

"Once you are through with Spartacus, you will come back to Rome with your legions and nothing will prevent you from exacting your own reward. Isn't that what all generals dream of?"

"Since you say so, I suppose one can look at it in that way, but I must say that the thought never entered my mind."

"Yet, it is a logical military conclusion to the campaign of a victorious general."

"In case of a civil war, perhaps. . . . As for Spartacus, he is only under siege, not defeated yet. But tell me, is your quaestorship in Sicilia ended?"

"Yes."

"How long did you stay on the island?"

"Three years. Why?"

"Because you were only a few leagues away from the country, and yet you speak of Spartacus as if you came from another world. Many things have happened in the past year, as you will very quickly realize. . . . You know Verres well, don't you?"

"As one knows his superior. Why?"

"I do not understand how he was informed of Spartacus' plans to cross the strait."

"Verres was lucky. That's all."

"What do you mean? Was Spartacus betrayed?"

"Perhaps. I had not thought of that. But Verres was merely lucky. He wasn't warned of anything—he did not even know that Spartacus was in Bruttium. As I understand the matter, Spartacus had planned to cross over to Sicilia with the help of pirate boats that were to carry his army. At the same time, Verres blocked the strait and fortified the coast as protection against the pirates for some shipments of wheat he was sending to Rome." Cicero laughed and accepted another cup of wine. "You see, he was lucky. You, too. Everyone will think that the rascal blocked the strait to help General Crassus besiege Spartacus, but we know the truth of the matter."

"It's your word against his. Verres is a very powerful governor."

Cicero laughed wholeheartedly. "His only power is his money. I will not contradict him about Spartacus. He may take in the Senate with his misrepresentation of so trifling a detail, but when I cross his path with my charges of extortion, there will be nothing left of Verres. Nothing."

"You speak of him as if he were an enemy."

"He is behaving like an enemy of Rome in amassing his fortune."

Crassus gave a smile, the meaning of which was not misinterpreted by Cicero. "He made his fortune from stolen money, Crassus—money stolen from Rome."

"Ah! Where is he at the moment?"

"In Sicilia. He is still useful there as long as his fleet keeps Spartacus from crossing the strait. By the way, have you ever seen him?"

"Who?"

"Spartacus."

"From a distance, in the arena."

"How does he fight?"

"Wonderfully. You have the feeling he always knows ahead of time exactly what his opponent is going to do next."

"I do not understand the success of this uprising. Who was commanding the Capuan guard when the escape took place?"

"Baebius Galba, who today is one of my best lieutenants."

"Your man is either an incompetent or a traitor."

Crassus smiled. Cicero went on harshly, "He had a cohort at Capua, why didn't he put a quick end to the whole thing?"

"He says he could not do anything against the gladiators with a single cohort. As for me, I never express an opinion about any action in which I was not personally involved."

"You know as well as I what happened at Capua."

"Perhaps I do not know what you know," Crassus replied, still smiling.

"It's simple. Fifteen soldiers here, twenty there, some whoring, others busy drinking or sleeping. In short, there were none left to maintain order."

"You are unaware that at the time I was only at Suessa. And besides, I have full confidence in Galba." Cicero was examining a gold statuette set off on a high black-marble pedestal. "How did you surround Spartacus?"

"I didn't surround him. I simply had a trench dug and put up a palisade between his army and mine. He surrounded himself by going into Bruttium."

"He'll try to get out."

"Probably."

"When?"

Crassus shrugged. "Tonight . . . Tomorrow . . . I don't know when, but soon."

"And what if he has supplies?"

"He doesn't. His men are hungry. If he had been able to keep them supplied, he would not have split them up when he came south. In fact, it's because of that mistake that I killed six thousand of his men and recovered a thousand slaves."

"To replace the ones who had left you?"

"Yes."

"Did you get any of them to talk?"

"Yes. They were so glad to be fed every day that they forgot the very existence of their leader."

Cicero laughed briefly. "The belly, as always."

"Yes, the belly; that's the place to get them."

"Didn't even one of them remain faithful to Spartacus?"

"A few. They're hoping for I don't know what miracle. They believe in him. If you think it'll be fun, you can talk to one or two women who followed him from the start. I'll send them to you. I keep them for my own entertainment, to make them talk about Spartacus."

"That's interesting. What do they say?"

"I don't understand their blabbering and I have no time to waste on them at the moment. They do their work well, which is all I ask of them."

"Why do they consent to work at all?"

"Because they're prisoners. And besides, the reasons that slaves have for working do not interest me. Their work is all that counts."

"Do you have them guarded?"

"I now have the best guards in the world. The ones I call the privileged slaves. They're anxious to keep their advantages and do their work better than any militiamen. I selected them myself."

"How many of them have you?"
"Two hundred."
"Two for every eight; that's a lot."
"Yes, but my mind's at ease."
"Isn't that an expensive solution?"
"No. The slightest escape would cost me ten times as much."
"That's true."

Crassus got up. "I have to go. Let me repeat, Marcus, this house is your home. I may be back tomorrow; perhaps in three months, depending on . . ."

"On Spartacus."

"Yes. Depending on the time he takes to die . . . or to kill me!"

Crassus walked a few steps away and then turned around. "Is it true, what they are saying about your name?"

The quaestor seemed flustered, a blush came into his cheeks. "What are they saying?"

"They say that in Sicilia you made offering to the gods of a silver vase on which you had had your two names engraved: Marcus Tullius and, in place of Cicero, they say you had a chick-pea drawn."

Cicero laughed good-naturedly. "In the same way a Fabius or a Lentullus might have signed with a bean or a lentil. But you reassure me. Here I was, afraid that my name had gotten lost in Rome, like a chick-pea in a garden. . . . No, Crassus, that story is not true. Not yet! But I owe it to myself to make it so quickly."

Crassus smiled politely. "Since your urge to bite me seems to have disappeared, will you allow me to make a suggestion?" Cicero smiled his consent. "If you are to take a hand in public affairs, why don't you change your name?"

The quaestor drew himself up. "People who change their names do it before they are famous, and then regret it afterwards. I intend raising mine as high as that of Scaurus and Metellus." A thought made him laugh. "Marcus Tullius Chick-pea!" He laughed lengthily.

Crassus smiled. "Good-bye, Cicero!"

Cicero bade him farewell, still laughing. "I'll see you again in Rome, Crassus, after your victory!" said the quaestor. Crassus waved his thanks to him as he left.

ARENA

XX

After Crassus had gone, young slaves of both sexes came in humming and poured cool-scented water on Cicero's hands while others brought in desserts. Between the trays of iced preserves and other fruit jellies, a tower of delicate semolina cakes rolled in almonds rose on silver grills. A bondwoman came and poured hot honey over these cakes and placed long gilt tongs between slices of pomegranate laid out to look like flames rising beneath the cakes. A tray of fruit, cut up and mounted in transparent jelly shaped like a large duck, drew a cry of admiration from the quaestor. The humming slaves left the room, walking backwards and scattering flowers on the mosaic as they went.

Left alone, Cicero picked up the gilt tongs and cast a greedy eye over the table. Here spearing, there pressing, he sampled everything, drank a little, and then lay down on the cushions covered in brightly colored fabrics. He was about to doze off when he heard someone go by, and he turned. This woman seemed to come straight out of a long sunbath: with copper-colored complexion, her hair rolled into a heavy braid down one side and falling between her breasts, she was wearing a straight, simple white dress tied at the waist by a thin cord of the same material. Her beauty had a surprising effect on Cicero. He got up and took a few steps toward her, but then thought better of it. The tables being between them, he pretended to be looking for a piece of fruit. The woman was walking slowly on the terrace, her head turned to the sea. Cicero stopped her. "Who are you?"

"Alba."

Cicero lay down again on the cushions and propped himself up on one elbow. "Come a little closer so I can see what you look like." Alba came toward him and stopped two paces away; she calmly rested her large green eyes on Cicero's.

"Where do you come from, Alba?"

"I don't know."

"Have you been here long?"

"No."

"Where were you before serving your present master?"

"Crassus is not my master."

Cicero stood up abruptly. Obviously, he thought for a moment that he had taken a woman of high rank for a slave. But then he smiled and sat down: he had not been mistaken, since she did not know where she was from.

"What are you doing here, if noble Crassus is not your master?"

"I am a prisoner."

Alba talked low, her deep voice multiplying her presence, adding to her charm that of mystery.

Cicero swung his arm out toward the sea. "Why do you stay? There is the sea!"

"The sea . . ." Alba murmured. She walked a few steps toward the marble columns and leaned against one of them. Cicero's face hardened. "You might regret the liberties you are taking if I were to tell your master about them." Her gaze lost out to sea, Alba did not move. The quaestor could barely hear her reply, "The whip is under the blue drape, to your left."

"I . . . I don't understand," said the quaestor, suddenly looking very young.

"It doesn't matter," said Alba, coming back toward him. "If you want to go for a walk, call Laetitia; she'll show you the gardens."

"And suppose I don't want to go for a walk, what do you suggest?"

"Nothing."

All of this strange beauty and detachment exasperated Cicero. He asked in an authoritative tone, "What are your duties, Alba?"

"To get you anything you ask for."

"I don't need anything. I want to talk to you a little, to look at you. You are very beautiful." He stretched out a hand and touched her hair. Alba looked at him blankly. Cicero was disconcerted. He let go of her hair and looked behind her. "The sea is restful when the sun is not dancing on its waves." He looked at Alba, who was staring at him, absently. "Don't you think so?"

"The sea is always beautiful, with or without the sun."

"But not always restful."

"Oh, yes. Always."

"Why?"

"Because it is strong. And clean."

"Are strength and cleanliness restful to you, Alba?"

"Yes."

On the face of the young quaestor, the liveliest interest seemed now to have replaced irritation. "Well," he said nonchalantly, "then Crassus should also be restful to you."

"Crassus is neither strong nor clean."

Cicero was relishing this moment. The play of this dialogue had put a light in his eye and, with the help of the wine, color in his cheek. "Do you know anyone who is?"

"Yes."

"Who?"

"Spartacus."

"Do you know him well?"

"I know him."

"But do you know him well?"

"How does one know anyone? You know or you don't know."

"But one may not know well."

"Then one doesn't know at all."

"What is he like?"

"Why do you want to know?"

"Because he is strong and clean," Cicero said eagerly.

Alba looked at him for a moment and then turned toward the sea. "If something hurts you, he puts his hand in the right place, and . . ."

"It doesn't hurt any more?"

"And you take your suffering."

"You take your suffering?"

"Your suffering takes everything, your belly, your legs, the light, noise. Spartacus puts his hand where it hurts and you take your suffering."

"How does he know where to put his hand?"

"He has suffered everything; he knows where everything hurts."

"You talk of him as of a god. Isn't that a lot?"

"If the power of a god begins where Spartacus' ends, he doesn't have much left."

"Fortunately, there are gods for those who have no Spartacus."

For the first time since they met, Alba smiled. The thought of the Thracian was lighting up her face. She went on speaking, softly, calmly. "Spartacus fights, he shouts, he cries, he is hungry, he makes love. The gods the Romans worship do not bleed."

"That is why they are gods."

"That is why you can't see them and they don't interest me."

Cicero helped himself to a goblet of water and lay down on the cushions. "So—Spartacus is a god?"

Alba was looking at the sea. "Spartacus is a man. The kind of man that a god who loved men would want them all to be."

"Do you know any other man like him?"

"No, but there must be many, surely."

"Why?"

"Because it is not hard to be like him. He is simple! So simple!"

Cicero got up and dropped his voice after making sure that he was alone with Alba on the terrace. "All right, very well, then, Alba. Tell me: with Spartacus here on this terrace, what would he do that I have not done, that would make the difference between us?"

Alba smiled.

"Why are you smiling?"

"I can't picture him on this terrace."

Insistent, Cicero came very close to her. "Imagine him here. Is it so difficult to give him proportions—for me, who does not know him?"

"Spartacus, here . . ."

Alba went over to the table and touched the pitcher Cicero had used to pour his drink of water. "You drank, a little while ago."

"Yes."

"Why?"

"I was thirsty."

"Do you know why you're thirsty?"

"Because I am warm, I suppose."

Alba's finger was on the pitcher, tracing its edge, its handle. Slowly, her eyes went back up to Cicero. "You are warm, so you drink?"

"Yes, naturally."

"That is why you are not like him."

"I don't understand."

"You are warm, you are thirsty, you drink . . . It's like a dream! . . ."

"That's pure logic, it's human."

"Yes. When you are alone."

Cicero blushed. "But . . ." He went over to the table and took the pitcher to pour her a goblet of water; he looked about him as if he were afraid someone might come in.

Looking straight at him, Alba broke into a hard little laugh. "I'm not thirsty," she said. Cicero hesitated, put the pitcher down, and spread his arms in a comically helpless gesture. He smiled embarrassedly. Relentless, Alba said, laughing, "You have one thing Spartacus doesn't have." Cicero stiffened. "What?" Alba looked at him for a moment without answering, then emphasized each word: "The gift of making people laugh." She laughed at length, louder and louder, without looking back at him.

She laughed in long waves, her mouth wide open, her head thrown back. Her throat was round, long, and full, with a slight beat along the right side, barely noticeable, pushing life ever so gently under the tanned skin. Cicero was close enough to notice it. He must have been quite caught by the rhythm of that beat because he shivered when the laugh stopped.

Pretending to have been humiliated in order to disguise his discomfiture, Cicero said almost kindly, "Well, that's something."

"Yes . . . It is something. But, when you're thirsty, it's not funny."

"Oh, you're not always thirsty."

"Of course not, when you can drink!" Alba shouted.

Cicero looked at her as if groping for something scathing to say. "You talk just like a slave."

Alba raised her arm. "And you talk with what's behind the drape!" she shouted. She drew the material aside, took down a whip, and held it out to him. "Here, take it! Teach me your Roman truth!"

Tense, pale, Cicero stared at her as if suddenly confronted with a creature from another world. He had something of the expression of the legionaries who had fallen before the onslaught of the runaways, as he looked alternately at Alba and the whip. Alba burst into a prolonged laugh, her head thrown back. She dropped the whip at Cicero's feet and, turning her back to him, walked toward the sea and called out: "Spartacus! Oh, Spartacus!" He looked at her, nonplussed, her silhouette neatly cut out between the columns against a hazy moon. Hearing the sound of footsteps, he gathered up the folds of his toga and quickly left the terrace.

It was Polla. She came running up and stopped on seeing Alba alone and the table still spread for a banquet. "You're calling him, too? Oh, Alba!" She ran to her friend who clasped her in her arms. "I want to go away!" said Polla in a breath against Alba's cheek. "Impossible," said Alba just as softly.

"Why?"

"If we ran away, Crassus would have fifty slaves crucified."

"Did he tell you that?"

"Yes. Why do you think he leaves us alone like this? He knows that we won't run away."

Polla hid her forehead against Alba's shoulder. "I am ashamed of my thoughts."

Polla raised her head. Her face covered with tears, she took Alba by the shoulders and shook her as she spoke. "But even the slaves think we're crazy, Alba. They jeer at us! This morning, they told me Crassus had never been so hard on them. They say it's Spartacus' fault!" Polla said these last words in a sob, as her head fell back on Alba's shoulder.

"Not all of them, Polla. Only the weak ones. The ones who don't say anything are with us."

"We have to try to convince the others. Spartacus did it at Capua."

"We'll try if Spartacus breaks through Crassus' siege."

"Is there a hope? Have you heard anything?"

"They're hungry . . . They'll get cold. They'll try to break out! . . . But the legions are lined up behind the trench."

Polla moved away. With her back to a column, her face in the wind blowing in from the sea, she shouted into the sound of the waves breaking against the rock a little lower. "I need him! So much!"

Alba had come close to her. "He needs you, too."

"Yes, that's what he used to tell me. . . ."

They stayed there a long time, silent, in the sound of the wind and the water against the rock. A light rain had begun to fall. All of a sudden, Polla went to the marble parapet at the edge of the terrace. Beneath her, the waves were carrying on their monotonous assault. . . . Alba followed her; she heard her say, "I feel that I am closer to him, all of a sudden. Oh, Alba!" Polla turned and found herself up against Alba, who took her in her arms. "It's strange, Alba. Why?"

"It's the sea."

"The sea?"

"Yes."

"Would the sea bring me closer . . . to him?"

"It brings together separated lovers. It carries to the living the messages of the departed."

"But, why, Alba? How?"

"Because the sea is the last confidant of those who love . . . and will never see each other again."

Polla roughly broke out of Alba's embrace. With the rain and tears mingling on her face, she shouted the Thracian's name.

"Spartacus! Spartacus!"

"The last confidant of those who shriek . . ."

Polla fell to her knees.

"Of those who implore . . ."

Polla was weeping, her mouth open, her hair clinging to her face.

"Of those who weep . . ."

Polla gasped amid her sobs.

"Of those who suffer . . ."

Polla sobbed for a long time, then calmed down. She got up. Her hands flat on the shiny, icy marble, she said fervently, "I will see him again! I will see him again! I will see him again!"

"The last confidant of those who hope. The sea keeps all secrets. For a long time . . . For ever . . . It carries love messages to those who are waiting for them. The sea is all love . . ."

"Can he see me cry?"

"The sea sees your tears, but does not carry them to him."

"Talk to me, Spartacus! I don't hear his voice!"

"The sea has not received your confidence. You have not given it your love!"

Slowly, Polla undressed, offering herself to the wind and the rain. Motionless, her arms along her body, she looked like another dark polished marble statue glistening in the rain. Her voice rose like a plaint. . . . "I loved him right away because he did not look at my body. I gave myself to him because I had nothing but myself to offer him. For him, my fingers trembled and my body flowed for the first time. My mouth seeks him. My skin craves his hands. I love him because he made me love life and love love. He made me all love for all things . . . and my shoulder misses his hand. I was hard, cold, withdrawn. He happened! He opened my hands, my eyes, my body! I was cold; he hollowed the ground, covered me with his body, and on his back the rain fell. I was afraid. . . . He explained the reason for my fear, and I lifted up my head. I was alone. . . . He showed me the little flower that closes up at night and I multiplied into as many little flowers as my eyes could see. He made me see as I had never seen before. He taught me to look at men, to understand them, to love them. He showed me life . . . everywhere! He gave me everything I have, yes, everything I have belongs to him, yes, and I save myself for him because I have nothing but myself, yes, yes, yes . . . Alba says that you receive the prayers of lovers who will never see each other again. If . . . if I were never to see Spartacus again, I would cling to my life because I owe it to him. I owe him my true birth. . . . He has given a meaning to everything I do. Bring him, yes, bring him all my love! . . ." Polla passed her hand over her eyes and over her lips and slowly lifted it, palm up, as if giving a very gentle thrust to her kiss.

On a rock, a few leagues away, Spartacus and Gannicus were watching the sea beneath the rain. Near them, a gull rustled by with a harrowing cry. "It must be a relief to be able to cry like that," said Spartacus. The Celt looked at him. Since their escape from Capua, eighteen months before, this was the first time his leader showed a trace of weariness. But, in the next moment, the tone of Spartacus' voice erased that impression. "We must try to get out of this bottle!"

ARENA

XXI

In the woods of Bruttium, twelve thousand fugitives moved forward through the rain toward the trench the Romans had dug. As Spartacus could no longer feed them, their leader Velox had decided to separate from the Thracian without telling him. Lying a few feet from the trench, the young Samnite was observing the movement of the sentries behind the palisade. The guards were visible only through the faint reflections of their wet helmets. Velox was surrounded by a few of his compatriots, selected for their agility, who had served with the Romans in auxiliary corps. There was even one young legionary among them, a Samnite deserter from Clodianus' army who had fallen before Velox when Spartacus had attacked the consul, and the young mirmillo had spared him when he pleaded for mercy in his own language. Since then, the deserter had fought bravely at Velox' side in the march to the Gulf of Tarentum where Spartacus had been awaiting his detachments. Covered with leaves and branches, Velox crawled to the edge of the trench and slid into it. Between the sentries' rounds, he climbed to the top of the earth wall and lay down against the palisade. Between two posts, he could see a camp of some twenty tents around which Crassus had not bothered to have another ditch dug. Velox slipped a rope of vine shoots around six posts and made a slipknot as high as possible. He went back down into the trench and motioned to his lieutenants to join him. Working between the sentries' rounds, they filled in the trench to half its depth and climbed the other slope, where the fugitives were now grouped; the vine-shoot rope was immediately seized by a hundred impatient men. Velox checked each one's position and went back toward the palisade with a dozen men. At his signal, they climbed over it and moved away. Lying in the mud, they waited for the sentries to come by, and killed them. On the other side, the men tugged at the rope and the palisade fell with a brief snap, opening a four-foot gap. Staying at the foot of the palisade, Velox sent his twelve thousand fugitives through, and they regrouped on the other side. Rushing the tents, they found them empty! It was too late to reverse their field: the legionaries slaughtered them to the last man and rebuilt the palisade where it had fallen. They impaled two wretches on it by way of warning.

Informed at dawn, Spartacus and Gannicus deliberated. The food problem was getting worse and their discussions did not help to solve it. Within the camp, overcome by cold and hunger, the weakest ones went to sleep, never to awake again. The women, no longer able to feed their children, sent a delegate to Spartacus, who asked her for one more day's respite. That day, the Thracian had to make a decision, whatever it might be. Gannicus was for attacking, but his reasoning did not seem to convince Spartacus.

Between Terina to the west and Scylacium to the east, the high ground constituting Bruttium falls in steps to the Tyrrhenian Sea and in a more gentle slope toward Scylacium. Over a short distance, the high ground splits into two high, wide spurs that stretch along the coast. This was where Crassus had blocked the isthmus, forcing Spartacus up on to the wooded heights of the Sila, covered with pine forests. This part of Bruttium is the coldest of the whole region. In such weather, Crassus knew that, if they were to attempt a breakthrough, the fugitives would have to avoid the heights so as to move rapidly; he had therefore deployed his troops in the open between the two spurs.

In his tent beaten by the snow and the wind, only a few leagues away from Polla who was calling to him every evening before the sea, Spartacus lay with his hands behind his head, long, brown, lean as a wolf. Beside him slept his faithful Celtic companion, athletic and hard. Behind and to the sides, the plateau was covered with snow and whipped by the wind whistling through the pines. In front were the deep, wide trench, the high palisade and, behind it, Crassus and his thirty-six thousand legionaries.

Spartacus wrapped himself in a long centurion's cloak and went out. Not everyone was asleep. In front of the tents, some were warming themselves around fires, drinking a soup of herbs and melted snow; here and there, two men were trying to keep warm by wrestling. Everywhere, they recognized the Thracian and smiled at him with confidence. Spartacus turned back toward his tent and stopped before a small grotto in which the snow was swirling. He stayed there, watching the snow, his back to the wind, the cloak slapping his legs. Daylight came, gray, beneath a sky clogged with snow. Spartacus awakened the tall Celt. "Come on, Gannicus." When they were within a few hundred feet of the trench, where his outposts took turns guarding the camp, the Thracian stopped. "We have the numbers, Gannicus, but we are growing weaker and weaker. We ought to avoid a fight. I am going to try to negotiate with Crassus."

"Negotiate!"

"Yes."

"Negotiate what?"

"Our freedom."

"With Crassus?"

"Yes."

Gannicus ran his hand over his broad broken nose, blue with cold. "But we are besieged, Spartacus. What can you offer him?"

"Not to attack him."

"Not to attack him?"

"Yes."

"You will double his self-confidence, Spartacus."

"Why?"

"After his victory over Velox, you ask to negotiate with him, that's why. The one who asks to negotiate is the one who feels he's weaker."

"Not always. He can be stronger but want to spare human lives."

Gannicus looked at him a moment. "Do as you wish, Spartacus," he said finally. "I am with you."

"I know that."

"Only remember what human life means to Crassus: nothing! Remember the decimation of his own troops."

"I remember . . . But at least I'll have tried to avoid a massacre, whether victor or vanquished."

"How are you going to go about starting these negotiations?"

"I don't know. . . . We'll have to call some legionaries, attract their attention, ask to see their leader."

"Do you think he'll accept?"

"I don't think anything. If he accepts, the preparations for the meeting will make the men forget their hunger. If he refuses, their anger at the legionaries will stimulate them and we will try for a breakthrough. . . ."

That afternoon, Crassus was in his tent with his officers when he was informed of Spartacus' offer to negotiate. This news was so unexpected and gave him such pleasure that he gave a drink to the young decurion who had brought it to him, asked him his name, and immediately had him transferred to Baebius Galba's command. Crassus turned to his lieutenants; he was flushed with joy. "That dog is the height of impudence! Now he wants to negotiate!" He ordered drinks for everyone and his good mood was such that he asked his two quaestors their opinion. Caesar and Galba suggested that Spartacus' offer be rejected with scorn; the officers endorsed this idea. "So be it," said Crassus, delighted by their reaction. "But why not have some fun? Let's get a close look at the dog's face. Give him a chance to talk. Let him tell us what he expects to get from us, which, in any case, we are going to reject."

"Isn't that doing him too much honor?" asked Galba.

"Of course, Baebius, but there is a lot to learn from looking at the enemy, listening to him . . . And, besides, this siege may last a long time, and opportunities for fun are not so frequent." He turned to the young decurion. "Tell Spartacus we agree to meet with him. We will let him know later . . ." Crassus turned to his lieutenants and smiled. "We have all the time we want, while they are dying of cold and hunger in their holes. . . ." He turned back to the decurion, and went on, "We will let him know later what arrangements we have made for this . . . interview." The decurion went out, and Crassus said, laughing, "And now for the fun! Let's plan the protocol of this meeting."

After receiving Crassus' reply, Spartacus communicated it to everyone. As he had foreseen, since each one had an opinion about the proposals to make to the Romans, hunger and cold were less painfully felt during these animated conversations. While all the tongues were wagging, the Thracian, together with Gannicus, Capito, and Castus, got his camp ready for the meeting. He had two watchtowers built to a height of more than sixty feet, from which the guards could observe the comings and goings of the Romans while remaining out of range of their arrows. About fifty feet in front of each of the towers, two catapults were put up and a supply of big stones placed beside them. Under cover of the woods, two lines of archers were drawn up under the command of Capito.

On the Roman side, they had cut the walls of a red cloth tent in such a way that Crassus and Spartacus would be sheltered from the snow, but visible from a distance. The two leaders were to report unarmed to the enemy's lieutenants. The red tent was set up about a hundred feet from the palisade, but equidistant from both camps. At the prearranged signal, Gannicus and Castus came forward. A section of the palisade was lowered, and they met Galba and Caesar in front of the tent. While the two quaestors were going up to the palisade where Spartacus was to be searched, the two fugitives walked toward Crassus, who, like Spartacus, was waiting for the quaestors to arrive. Having made sure that the two leaders were unarmed, the four lieutenants turned toward the tent; with their backs to the enemy camp, they each raised an arm.

Crassus came forward first. Behind Gannicus and Castus, two ranks of archers less than a hundred feet away; at their sides, two groups of fifty horsemen ready to rush to the aid of their leader. The proconsul walked with dignity, his cloak thrown back, held at the shoulders by the buckles of a resplendent breastplate outlining powerful pectoral muscles, and beneath it, falling to mid-thigh, a white tunic ending in gold-edged stripes. Crassus was wearing comfortable leather sandals and hammered copper leg armor, attached behind the calves and the ankles by leather bands. Knotted around his neck, a gold muslin scarf floating down his back made an elegant contrast with the red cloth of the cloak. Beneath the old combat helmet that he had already worn in Spain, in Mauretania, and in Sulla's army, Crassus' face was calm but pale.

Spartacus, for his part, walked like an athlete going into a stadium, his breathing even, his body relaxed, thrifty, his step supple.

Watching the Thracian move off toward Crassus, Galba had said to his companion, "So there's the gladiator who beat all our legions!"

"Without knowing him, we could have known he was the one, among a hundred thousand slaves."

"I've never seen a man so strong! What a body! Hard, warm . . . I could have gone on searching him for hours!"

"He walks like a lion."

"Did you ever see a handsomer fellow?"

"No. But he sure stinks!"

"Yes. He ought to be perfumed and . . ."

Galba had suddenly stopped. The two leaders were no more than a few paces from the tent.

"What a lousy mug!" Castus had said after Crassus left.

"I don't know what kept me from choking him during the search," Gannicus had answered.

The two leaders had reached the tent at the same time and stopped. And, as if the hundred and twenty thousand men of the two armies had simultaneously realized that the slightest gesture, the shortest word might seal their fates, there was a silence over this desolate space between the two camps, the silence of crowds before an event, as if each one had stopped breathing. The earth turned up by the digging of the trench, the comings and goings of the legionaries between their camp and the palisade, the daily exercise, rain and snow had turned this valley into a vast field of cold mud, hardened in spots and covered with snow. From the low, closed, snow-laden sky, there filtered a yellowish gray color covering everything with a stiff, indifferent sadness, adding to the desolation of the place an impression of something irremediable, something absolute, about everything that might be done or said on that day. The cry of a gull cut itself into that silence, lingering within the minds a long time after the bird was gone. It was like a signal: the two men went into the tent.

A joke of Galba's? Or Caesar's? An order of Crassus'? . . . Right in the center of the rectangle formed by the tent posts, a high, succulent plant spread its spines. From either side of the plant, the men looked at each other.

In front of the Thracian shepherd, soldier of the Roman army, deserter, slave, gladiator, Marcus Licinius Crassus, the richest man of the Roman world, owner of three-quarters of the tenements in Rome, of more than five hundred carpenters and masons, fertile lands, silver mines, several thousand slaves of every origin and specialty—readers, copyists, metallurgists, stewards, perfumers, masseurs, table servants, chambermaids, kitchen help, and painters, sculptors, architects, . . . Crassus, who regularly tithed his income to Hercules, annually gave a banquet to all the inhabitants of Rome by distributing to each citizen wheat enough for three months . . . Crassus, who had studied Aristotle, who knew hundreds of humble citizens by name and would stop in the street to speak to them . . . Crassus, who owned his army and had had four thousand of his men decapitated for the sake of discipline . . . Crassus, who had gained his fortune through arson, delation, and assassination . . . Crassus, whose manners and affability were praised on every lip . . .

The vertical eyelashes that veiled the Roman's glance momentarily bothered the Thracian who was trying to meet his eyes, while the other, his head proudly thrown back, was looking at him severely.

Two camp beds had been set up for them. Crassus sat down. He crossed his legs, covered them with his broad cloak and leaned back on the cushions. He had had a large pitcher of wine and two goblets placed on the table between the beds. Turning his head toward Spartacus as if the Thracian had just come in to be granted an audience, Crassus rested on one elbow. He waved to the Thracian to help himself, but Spartacus did not move.

"What do you want, Spartacus?"

The Thracian had never seen a great Roman leader from so close up. In his mouth, the name of the fugitive had cracked like the snap of a whip. His eyes on Crassus, Spartacus took a few slow steps between his bed and the table. He was wearing a thick brown skin that fell halfway down his thighs and high leggings tied in the Celtic fashion with vine-shoot strings. He had kept, rolled over one shoulder, his long centurion's cloak. Spartacus stopped in front of Crassus and answered, "To leave this country without trouble."

"You are runaway slaves, Spartacus, and you must be punished," Crassus answered rather severely, but with a worried face, as if he were sorry he had to be severe.

"We are no longer slaves."

"Since when?"

"Since we escaped."

"You are runaway slaves and you must be punished," Crassus repeated.

"They tried to punish us, but they did not succeed."

Crassus slowly helped himself to a goblet of wine. He drank in small gulps, looking into the bottom of the goblet as if something were happening there. "Why did you ask for this meeting? Are you afraid of losing?"

"I am not afraid of losing, I have beaten all the Romans. But what about you? Why did you agree to see me?"

"To find out what you want."

"To leave this country without trouble and avoid another massacre."

Crassus raised his eyes from the bottom of his goblet to look at the Thracian.

"You deserve the punishment that awaits you, Spartacus," he said severely. "You left your master Baliatus, at Capua, after having sworn the gladiator's oath. Your life belonged to him, he had bought you. You took with you a hundred evil characters and you did not submit to the police forces sent after you. You accepted into your troop runaway slaves who had fled with goods belonging to their masters. You have plundered estates and set fire to them throughout the country. No town, no village has any security left. Your dogs arrive; they rape, they plunder, and they kill. With all the wretches who joined you, you dared to face up to the legionaries. Because of your numbers, but mainly because you were lucky enough to come up against badly led legionaries, you beat them. That gives you no right, Spartacus. You brought the greatest part of your troop back to this region of the country where I have besieged you, and you cannot come out of your hole without being slaughtered as you deserve. Cold and hunger are beginning to take their toll of your pack of disobedient dogs. When you saw there was nothing you could do about feeding them, you brought about this meeting. To get what? To ask me to let you leave this country with impunity, after you sacked it?"

"To avoid a useless war, a mass . . ."

"This is not a war! Wars are fought against soldiers! But against dogs that upset the smooth running of a whole system of government through their uprising, there are only punitive expeditions!"

"But, up to now, I am the one who has punished the legionaries. . . . Your system is a slaughter machine. In your system, slaves do not . . ."

"This system has gone on for a long time, Spartacus. I am not responsible for it and I do not have to discuss it with you."

"Yes, you do. Because instead of learning a lesson from this drive for liberation, instead of turning it to the advantage of your system, you rush after us to try to slaughter us. How long are you going to keep running, Crassus?"

"As long as it takes, because your pack is a threat to my country. There is no limit to your impudence! You not only want me to let you go, but you also want to call into question the established order!"

"Your order established on the massacre of slaves by generals, landowners, and lanistae, does not interest me. Have you not understood that your established order is called into question every time a slave escapes? In the last few months, it has been called into question a hundred thousand times! And this is not the end!"

"It is clear, you want something beyond your freedom."

"No. I only want to get out of this country of masters and slaves where the master treats his slaves like units of a monstrous system . . . in which human life does not count."

Obviously, Crassus had now decided to have some fun. He agreed to go along, but the tone of his voice retained its paternal severity. "The master must govern his home through his slaves and his slaves by himself. If economic science is applied only to objects, only to the inanimate, it is no more than trade! But, when applied to human beings, it becomes part of the science of government." Crassus calmly helped himself to a goblet of wine. He drank a few mouthfuls without looking at the Thracian, who was now clearly making an effort to control himself. "It is a system that has stood the test of time," Crassus added with a smile, "since we rule over a large part of the world."

"Your system holds on only so long as men accept slavery. It collapses as soon as they revolt. Today, a hundred thousand of your dogs are jeopardizing it because they want to live as free men. Tomorrow, what will become of your punitive expedition when all the dogs in the Roman world decide that your system does not suit them? The wealth of all the Crassuses in the world will not be enough to buy the police forces and the legions needed to fight them. Then you will really have a war on your hands and, for the costs involved, the senators will never find a Crassus rich enough, or legionaries in great enough numbers."

Crassus smiled. "You are dreaming of impossible tomorrows, Spartacus, because the fortunes of princes also enable them to . . . create certain needs that keep in their places both slaves and the citizens of conquered countries."

"I don't understand."

"I know," said Crassus with a laugh. "You cannot understand . . . because you do not know the power of money. It is one of the great strengths of our system."

"Crassus . . . slaves will not forever accept being dogs in your service. That day, your system will have run its course, and your Senate will not stop engaging in endless punitive wars."

"In order to reach that point, the slaves will have to find other Spartacuses. That is why you are a danger, gladiator. And that is why," Crassus promptly added, "all runaway slaves have to be quickly punished, without any mercy."

Spartacus was pale. He paced a bit and said, "I was sure this meeting would lead to nothing. But now I can tell my men that there is no point in trying to negotiate with the Romans. We have to rip them open until they understand and die rather than serve them." And, without haste, just as he had come, Spartacus left the tent. Crassus got up, disconcerted by this sudden departure. For a moment, he watched the Thracian walk off, wrapped in his legionary's cloak. "Dog!" said Crassus between clenched teeth. And, his head thrown back, he quickly returned to his camp.

ARENA

XXII

After crossing the trench, Spartacus waited for Gannicus and Castus. The Romans closed the section of the palisade, the siege went on. Spartacus and his lieutenants went back to Capito's two lines of archers under the cover of the woods. They all followed the Thracian, leaving only the four catapults and the two watchtowers in front of the ditch. Going up the length of the trench, Spartacus had his lieutenants and the archers walk a good part of the day; when he stopped, he had found what he was looking for. At nightfall, he went up close to the trench. Over one short section, it was not so deep, the rock having prevented further digging, and, on the other side, the wall was also not so sheer below the palisade. "This is where we will break through," he told his men. "But we have to make the Romans believe that our camp is still down there, at the same place." He returned to the main body of his army during the night and spread the word that he planned a breakthrough requiring everyone to make ready for combat. He raised their morale by having all the horses slaughtered and distributed for food. After they had eaten, there was still one day's rations left, and Spartacus decided to set out at once. Leaving fires burning here and there in order to deceive the Romans about their position, the fugitives got under way despite the snow, under the command of Gannicus and Castus, while Capito brought up the rear and urged the laggards to hurry. During the course of the morning, the snow became even thicker and a strong wind came up. When they got to the spot the Thracian had selected, Gannicus and Castus waited for their leader. The fugitives had gathered under the firs, along the trench. Spartacus had the last meat ration distributed and joined his lieutenants. "We are going to fill in the trench tonight and you are going to leave with a third of the troop. You will have to march as fast and as far as you can without fighting. Crassus does not have enough men to maintain his siege against us and still go after you, but, being afraid of being surrounded, he will give chase to you so as not to find himself besieged in turn. Then we will be able to come out and link up with you. We will come up on him from the rear, in case he should join battle with you."

That night, thirty thousand fugitives crossed the trench. The legionaries having concentrated their forces facing the fires left by the fugitives, Gannicus and Castus did not even have to avoid battle. They marched until the evening of the following day without affording themselves the slightest halt. As Spartacus had foreseen, Crassus went after them, thus freeing the Thracian and the bulk of his army to march on Crassus.

Alarmed, Crassus set up a fortified camp on a height, from where he sent two decuries to Rome to ask the Senate to recall posthaste the Macedonian legions and those of Pompey. Two other decuries were dispatched to Brundisium to await the troops from Macedonia and direct them to his camp.

Seeing that Crassus was avoiding combat, Spartacus slowed down his march a little and turned it toward the Gulf of Tarentum, where he found only a part of the troop commanded by Gannicus and Castus—the others had gone on to Metapontum. The Thracian would have liked to go and join them, but he could not induce his troop to do this. Tired and hungry, the men first wanted to eat their fill along the coast. After a few days spent in fishing, food was no longer an immediate problem. Informed by his patrols of Crassus' position, he made ready to link up with Gannicus.

For his part, Crassus marched cautiously toward Brundisium, avoiding the gulf coast. North of Heraclea, he heard from his patrols of the arrival at Brundisium of the reinforcements under the command of Lucullus, the proconsul of Macedonia. Encouraged, but furious at having had to call for help, and knowing that the fugitives had not yet regrouped, he marched straight on Metapontum, where the thirty thousand men led by Gannicus and Castus were laying over. He gave chase to them as far as northeast Lucania, where Castus and twelve thousand men were surrounded; the rest managed to rejoin Spartacus and informed him that Gannicus was a prisoner. Castus and his men were massacred and Crassus retrieved the legions' trophies that they had carried away: eagles, fasces, and some twenty standards.

When he heard of the sizable reinforcements that had arrived from Macedonia, Spartacus drew back toward Petelia, in the gorges of Bruttium. Their morale shaken by Castus' defeat, the Thracian's men were marching in easy stages when one evening Spartacus was informed that one of Crassus' legions, marching slightly in the van of the Roman army, was very close behind him. The fact was that, wanting at all costs to put an end to the campaign before the arrival of Pompey, Crassus had sent his legate Quinctius and his quaestor Scrofa at the head of a legion to sound out the enemy.

Taking ten thousand volunteers with him, Spartacus did an about-face and fell on the legion's camp in the middle of the night—night attacks had always been successful for him since Vesuvius. Under their tents set afire by the torches of the fugitives, the Romans, surprised in their sleep, lost half of that legion and the rest were routed. Quinctius was barely able to carry off young Scrofa, who had been wounded. In this rout, the Romans left behind more than three hundred horses and all their supplies. Gloomier than ever, Spartacus returned to his camp without pursuing the legionaries.

Crassus was momentarily disconcerted by this setback but, on hearing that Pompey had just crossed the Alps, he decided to unleash his entire army against the Thracian. With his quaestors about him, he carefully studied the terrain while scouts came and went ceaselessly between their camp and the fugitives' to keep their leader informed of Spartacus' position. After two days of deliberations, Crassus decided to attack Spartacus from the south just as the Thracian would reach the Silarus river, which broadens there before flowing into the Bay of Paestum. Blocked by the mountains to the east and the west, the fugitives would have no way of escape.

Fearing an attack in force and encouraged by the return of spring, Spartacus wanted to continue northward. But the fugitive's lightning victory over Quinctius and Scrofa, their replenished food and rest had given them a wild confidence. Wanting neither to retreat before the legions nor to obey the Thracian, who spoke rarely and then only to Capito, the fugitives one morning surrounded their leader's tent.

"What do you want?" said Spartacus.

"To finish off the legionaries!" shouted the most excited of them. "We don't want to retreat."

Seeing Spartacus alone and surrounded, Capito picked up a trident and easily made a way for himself to the Thracian. With his hairless face, his tanned skull, his pale, lashless, browless eyes, the retiarius had always inspired a certain superstitious fear among even the boldest. The two leaders were several inches taller than the tallest of the others. Capito took his trident in both hands and with the handle began calmly pushing back those in front. Wanting to get close so as to be heard, two fanatics, twins, silently resisted Capito. The two men grabbed the metal handle of the trident with both their hands and tried to push Capito back near Spartacus. The Samnite's neck and head grew red; he paused for a moment, but the two men had to give way: Capito was moving forward. When he had shoved them far enough away from Spartacus, Capito came back to the center to start the same maneuver over again, but the fugitives moved back without his shoving them. A small child made his way through the legs of those in front. Capito picked him up under the arms and looked at him. His legs and arms bare, he was wearing a cutdown old legionary's tunic. Capito sat him up on his shoulders and went back to the Thracian.

"Who wants to retreat?" Spartacus asked.

"You! You!" some of them said. "You're getting ready to break camp!" said another.

"Avoiding battle is not retreating!" Spartacus retorted.

"Why avoid it? We're the strongest!"

Since the escape from Capua, Spartacus had spoken only to say what was necessary. After Alba and Polla had been taken prisoners, although the Thracian regularly visited his camp to see what shape his troop was in, he had nevertheless lost all communication with the men. For it was Polla who used to ask him the questions that were circulating in camp, thus forcing him to think about what was being said around him. Since his return to the South, his troop had grown even bigger. To make his decisions known, Spartacus had had to delegate Gannicus, Castus, and Capito, who spread them through the camp; sometimes they had had to answer questions without consulting the Thracian. Moreover, a large number of the fugitives had never had any personal contact with him; many had never even seen him. One day, a man had taken his cloak and occupied his tent; when Spartacus came back, the other had attacked him. Thanks to Gannicus' presence, a fight had been avoided. Those who saw the incident had laughed about it; a year before, they would have felt personally offended by it. And besides, there had been a general relaxation for several weeks during the first stop before the Gulf of Tarentum, immediately followed by the siege, the winter, the hardships. After the long march toward Sicilia, those difficult months had further accentuated the lack of communication between the Thracian and his troop.

"You're never the strongest before the battle," Spartacus answered. "Only afterwards—if you've won."

"The legionaries were defeated the other night," replied a young Celt, whom his companions called the Sculptor because he was always playing with a knife and a piece of wood.

"A few legionaries," Spartacus corrected. "Just a legion of scouts. There are a lot more left."

"They'll end up the same way," said the Sculptor, talking to his knife. The runaways shouted their approval.

"What do you want to do?" Spartacus asked.

Capito looked at Spartacus. The Samnite had a pained expression, which on his smooth face took the shape of a sort of pout that made him look much younger. The Sculptor smiled coldly at his knife. Seeing that no one was answering the Thracian, the young Celt felt empowered to act as spokesman. "We want to go back and begin fighting."

He had correctly expressed the general feeling, for everyone shouted with joy when Spartacus said, "Very well. Let's go and fight." While the others clustered around the Sculptor, Spartacus and Capito walked away. The Samnite put the child back on the ground, and the two men watched him scamper away.

"Why did you ask them what they wanted to do? You're the leader," Capito said, making a face.

"The way they feel, I can't tell them a thing. If I asked them to start for the North, they wouldn't listen to me any more than Crixos did. Remember, Capito, you followed him, too."

"Do you think we're going to lose?"

"I think they'll fight better if we're with them."

"But you're not sure of winning?"

"I never am. I just try to be as well prepared as possible. They are encouraged by our victory over Quinctius and Scrofa, by the fresh food supply, by being rested." Spartacus smiled sadly. "And by the return of the good weather." And he added, to reassure Capito, "The battle is half won when the troop has confidence in its strength."

"But you're not convinced. You didn't talk to them the way you used to."

"That's true. I'd rather have an angry troop, but one with discipline. This one only has its confidence left and its vision of immediate satisfaction. . . . Like Crixos."

"But why didn't you talk to them?"

"If I couldn't convince Crixos a year ago, there's nothing I can say today to a hundred thousand Crixoses," Spartacus repeated.

"You didn't try. Maybe it's not too late."

"Yes. I think it's too late."

Capito was no longer pouting. His face and neck had turned pink. "Why? What's changed?"

"I don't know. I think . . . I think we should have kept up their original anger. Or given it back to them. Maybe we would have died of cold and hunger while crossing the mountains to the North, but we should have kept on going, we should have tried to leave this country, not turn back toward the South. Or attack

Rome. That's it, that's what I think we should have done: either gone away or attacked Rome, but not come back to run around in circles. I don't know any more . . ."

Crassus did not seem less anxious than the runaways to put an end to it. If he waited any longer, Pompey's legionaries might twist the outcome of the battles to his rival's advantage. He knew that it was already being whispered in Rome that Pompey would not hesitate like that; he would wage the battle and try to bring it quickly to an end. So Crassus moved as close as he could to Spartacus and waited for night near the Thracian's camp. When night fell, he moved even closer and had a trench dug.

Fearing another encirclement, another siege, the fugitives quickly drew back, but the Silarus stopped them. Then they made an unorganized attack on the legionaries who were working on the trench and massacred them. But the day rose on an unexpected situation that the night had kept hidden from them: to the east and to the west rose the heights that separated Samnium from Lucania, and, behind them, the Silarus. The fugitives were surrounded in a hollow, cut through its middle by the river.

Thus, a few leagues from Capua, where the rebellion had started twenty months earlier, Crassus was forcing Spartacus to fight in broad daylight. For the first time, the Thracian had chosen neither the place nor the time.

Spartacus was sitting on a rock, a sica under his belt, a heavy hatchet placed near him. He watched Capito come up to him with two horses. When the Samnite stopped, Spartacus smiled at him. The retiarius' worried brow made him look sleepier than ever. He was armed with his favorite weapons: the sica and the trident.

"I've set out four lines of archers. The women and children are with the rest of the troop. Everyone is ready to fight."

Capito held his horse's reins out to Spartacus. "No," said the Thracian. "If I win, I'll have the legionaries' horses; if I lose, I won't need any."

"Do you want to talk to the men?"

"No."

Capito was now up on his horse. "I wonder . . . What makes

the Romans always come on a bit farther, a little harder?"

"An old habit."

"Gannicus and Castus told me that, when they searched Crassus, he didn't even look at them. Maybe they think they're creatures of a superior race."

"Maybe . . ."

Capito waved a shy good-bye. Spartacus did not acknowledge it. He watched the tall retiarius move away until he disappeared among a hundred Samnite horsemen. He took his heavy hatchet and got up. A group of fugitives joined him, faithful ones who had fought alongside him in all the battles; only Gannicus was missing that day. Without a word, Spartacus walked toward his troop. Everyone was battle-ready. Spartacus did not stop and more than seventy thousand fugitives started to move off behind him at the signal from his lieutenants, the younger ones in front, the men behind, the women and old people at the rear with the children.

Crassus was waiting for the runaways with eight legions behind the shallow trench his men had not had time to finish. Quinctius and Scrofa had lost about two thousand men in their night encounter with the fugitives, so Crassus had about thirty-four thousand legionaries left whom he deployed by simply doubling the classical table of organization of legions in the field. His lieutenants grumbled that he was lacking in imagination, that he might learn something some day by taking part in one of Pompey's campaigns, that they would prefer to be in the ranks of any other general, . . . But when the four blocks of two legions each were deployed, the officers had to swallow their remarks: the army thus lined up was of impressive power, and Crassus, who had listened without flinching to his lieutenants' grumblings, was not unhappy with the effect produced by his strategy. His face hard, he was looking at his motionless, silent army. Following the classical practice, he had set out four lines of light infantry consisting of a thousand men each, armed with two javelins or arrows, a short sword, and a round shield. Their function was to shoot their arrows and javelins and then get quickly aside. Fighting in skirmishes only, these foot soldiers were to inform the officers of the progress of the battle and carry the movement orders back to the centurions in the line. Twelve hundred cavalrymen had been grouped in four squadrons on the flanks of the next twenty-four lines of heavy infantry; the horsemen carried a small shield, sword, lance, helmet, and breastplate or body armor. The seven hundred and twenty maniples of heavy infantry were deployed in twenty-four impeccable lines, each consisting of thirty maniples of forty men. The first eight lines were made up of young infantrymen and velites armed like regular legionaries: two javelins, a short double-edged sword, a semicylindrical shield four feet long, a helmet, a breastplate, and greaves. Their function: to engage in hand-to-hand combat. The men of the next eight lines were hardened legionaries armed with the same equipment as the young foot soldiers they were to support and relieve. Finally, in the last eight lines, were the pick of the seasoned legionaries, particularly distinguished in past actions—the reserve division from which decurions and centurions were chosen. Instead of javelins, they always carried two lances, in case the enemy should attack from the rear. Equipped for battle, riding the only white horse in his cavalry, Crassus was up on a high ground where olive trees grew. Behind him, his quaestors waited silently, themselves followed by the lieutenants. Crassus was watching the cloud of dust raised by Spartacus' troop, which was coming forward resolutely but without order.

The Thracian's archers have reached the trench. The legionaries start to move out in groups of ten, shield to shield, thus presenting three thousand iron walls to the blows of the enemy. Fifty feet away from the fugitives, all the legionaries turn their shields toward the sun, blinding the enemy and sowing disarray in his ranks; at the same time, four thousand arrows and javelins pierce the fugitives' flesh. Then four thousand more. This simple maneuver determines the outcome of the battle. The four front lines of light infantry move off to the sides, and the two armies are in immediate clash.

Wounded in the thigh at the very start of the battle, Spartacus fights on his knees, hampered by the wound as much as by his own men. A first sword stroke immobilizes his right arm, another goes through his neck. He opens his mouth to gasp for air, to shout, perhaps, and falls back while the young velite who delivered the fatal blow himself dies on his sica. Someone shouts his name, very close by, but the tall Thracian's eyes are already closed. The lowered eyelids now give his face the eternity of marble.

Well protected, methodically sending forward their fresh lines, upsetting the fugitives with their shining shields, the legionaries cracked the enemy lines as a mace might have crushed a nut. The battle did not last long. The legionaries advancing in a pincers movement, the fugitives soon found themselves back to back, then surrounded. Five thousand of them retreated as far as the Silarus and escaped by jumping into the water. For the others, it was a systematic massacre. Sixty thousand men fell. The impossibility of penetrating any further into the fugitives' ranks and the coming of night ended the carnage.

This battle having taken place at the very edge of his estates, Crassus had the battlefield circled by torches set up every twenty feet, and the prisoners were forced to dig trenches into which the victims were thrown pell-mell. Despite Crassus' wish, it was not possible to find Spartacus' body among the corpses heaped on the terrain. For two days and two nights, the six thousand prisoners dug up the earth and buried their comrades. Those who were too exhausted to work were thrown in with the dead. At dawn of the third day, the air was mild, clean, and clear, and beneath the magic light of morning there remained no trace of the battle. Carrying the spirit of enterprise to its highest degree, Crassus had paths laid out on the huge charnel ground along which olive trees were to be planted.

ARENA

XXIII

Crassus was resting at Suessa, calmly resuming the management of his business. On this particular evening, he had invited his officers to dinner, and the slaves were serving the first courses when a guard came in to announce the arrival of Alexander. At hearing his friend's name, Crassus' face lit up. When Alexander came in, Crassus got up as he came near, a signal honor that his peers rarely conferred on even their most distinguished guests. Moved by this mark of esteem, Alexander bowed. When he raised his head, his face reflected the most sincere joy. Crassus was going toward him. "What a happy surprise, Alexander." He embraced his friend and took a step backward while keeping his hands on Alexander's shoulders. "Let me look at you. You've grown thinner and it's very becoming." Alexander smiled, obviously happy to see Crassus again. When he had arrived, the officers had stood up, impressed by the unusual welcome their general was giving this unknown visitor who in turn was now embracing the proconsul.

"I could not wait to congratulate you, Marcus; your victory is complete."

Crassus' smile broadened. Turning toward his officers, with one hand on his friend's shoulder, he said, "Gentlemen, allow me to present Alexander, my friend and mentor." The officers saluted the newcomer.

Alexander raised his arm to return their salute. "Sit down, noble soldiers. As you can see, I am wearing neither the laticlave of the senators nor the ribbon of the tribunes. I am not rich, I have no name, my dress is simple. In a word, I do not deserve all these honors." Crassus led Alexander over to sit down at his right. The word passed among the officers that they ought to go early to leave Crassus alone with his friend. But, as the conversation involved them and Crassus did not get up but—contrary to his usual custom—had more wines and desserts brought in, the quaestors quickly forgot their intention of being tactful.

"What is being said in Rome, Alexander?" Crassus had asked eagerly, without disguising his anxiousness to know how his victory had been greeted.

"They are not talking about anything but your victory. Everyone is very relieved. Normal life will at last be resumed again in this country, thanks to you," said Alexander, eating with good appetite. He raised his eyes. Crassus was waiting with the face of a young author who has just read a poem to his friends. "I had dinner at the home of Philippus, the senator, the very evening of the day your quaestor brought the good news," Alexander went on. "The Prince of the Senate was there, too, although, since the start of the rebellion, he had gone out very little. He was sometimes seen at the baths, but he rarely stayed for long. There were other senators at old Philippus' when your quaestor got there. I've forgotten his name."

"Cnaeus Galba."

"Yes, Galba. Of course, everyone asked him questions, everyone wanted to know how everything had gone from the very start. He went about it very well, answering simply, with composure, presenting the facts without interpreting them. The kind of news that people like, colorful and detailed."

Alexander looked at the officers. They were listening to these flattering remarks with varied sentiments that could be read on their faces. "I am sure, noble soldiers, that your turn will come when you reach Rome, and that each one of you, like your friend

Galba, will be expected to answer the questions he is asked. After all, giving an intelligent report of the development of a campaign, in which one must have participated, of course," said Alexander, bringing smiles to the now relaxed faces, "is part of what the Republic expects of its officers."

Alexander held his goblet out to a slave who poured him some wine which he drank in long gulps. When he set his goblet down again, he immediately fixed his attention on a fowl served under a sauce abundant with eggplant, peppers, and olives. "Hmmm! What a sauce!" said the Greek, whose appetite was catching. "What a sauce!"

Crassus put his hand on his friend's arm. "You are the best of friends, Alexander. With the simplicity and gracefulness that make up your greatness, you have spared the feelings of my officers and I thank you for it."

Alexander raised his goblet. "I drink to the health of our host and to the success awaiting all of you in Rome, noble soldiers."

Everyone joined him in the toast and Crassus, whose good mood was increasing as Alexander talked, seemed now to relax as he had not done for more than six months. The troubles, the severe losses the rebellion had personally cost him, the stringency of his discipline, the months spent with officers who were intelligent but whose youth limited their conversation, had kept him confined in a solitude that had weighed upon him, given him a hard, tight face, which was now melting, thanks to the presence of his neighbor. And this man who never took the trouble to explain his decisions now felt the need in his turn to make his companions of the last months happy.

"I brought you together tonight," he said, "to tell you how much I have appreciated your presence at my side during this punitive campaign. You are proud and noble officers. Each one of you, in the best tradition, gave his men a fine example of courage in battle and during the long marches. One day, the eagles of your standards and the names of your legions will impose respect upon all of our enemies. But perhaps later you will be called upon to govern a province, nearby or faraway, for it is not enough to excel in strategy, to shine only through courage in battle; it is also necessary to organize, to build, to manage, to decide, to impress. In a word, to govern. In your homes as in your campaigns, wisdom, virtue, firmness, and dignity must appear in all of your decisions, however unjust, however hard they may sometimes seem to those closest to you: your families or your comrades in arms. And, speaking of these decisions, let me warn you against hasty judgments of those of your leaders. As my great friend Alexander has just told you, I do not doubt that each one of you, like Galba, could have brilliantly given Rome an account of our campaign. But I chose to send Galba because he was commander of the Capuan guard at the time the gladiators escaped. He was the first Roman officer Spartacus found across his path; he was at the head of two hundred guards ill prepared to fight against determined, armed gladiators. It was he too who at the time informed the Senate of the rebellion and gave me the names of a few of you when I was seeking the best possible cadres for our army. So, as you see, Galba was not arbitrarily selected; he was the one officer to send to the curious senators. And what might," Crassus added with a smile, "seem to you a signal favor is first and foremost, you may believe me, an irksome mission, because the senators always want to know everything; they have to have details, dates, figures, names, explanations." Crassus gave a quick laugh. "And, as no senator wants to be singled out for his silence, each one has a question to ask!" Everyone laughed with Crassus. "There, my good friends, is the explanation of this selection that vexed you a bit because you did not know my reasons. You yourselves will soon have a chance to answer the senators' questions. Your relatives', too, and your friends'; you must be ready for them. You may one day have to choose, to make important decisions, difficult decisions if they are made in the name of Rome. Decisions that you will not always be able to explain to those close to you, either to avoid compromising your goal or because it is not in your nature to explain your decisions. You will then have to face the great loneliness of the leader before his responsibilities. It can be long. And incomprehension may sometimes even survive you . . . until witnesses, your young officers, your posthumous ambassadors in fact, report to our government what they saw and what they understood. And if they did not understand, the incomprehension goes on, survives you—and the greater your responsibility the longer it lasts. . . . So you must be ready, my friends, to face up to your task with serenity and a certain detachment; the detachment that comes from the conviction that one is doing his duty toward his country in perfect accord with his own conscience . . ." Crassus smiled briefly at Alexander, whom he looked at without turning his head, ". . . and . . . taking the situation into consideration." And, without giving his audience the time to react to this last remark, "I drink to your success with your families and with your careers."

They all raised their goblets and Crassus lay back on the cushions, thus bringing his face close to Alexander's. He motioned, and slaves brought in fruit, singing as they came. There was now animated conversation at the tables. Crassus took advantage of this to say to his friend, "If you are not too tired, we will have a talk later on about what is really being said in Rome."

With a smile, Alexander took a fried semolina cake soaked in warm honey and said to Crassus out of the corner of his mouth, "Let's get rid of the young lions as soon as possible."

His hands flat on the cool marble of the terrace parapet, Alexander was watching the sea between the olive trees. Crassus joined him. Slaves were busy in the dining hall, humming as they carried the remains of the dinner, the trays, and the goblets to the kitchen. In the light night air there rose the good smell of the bread ovens which shone from the south side of the terrace when the baker put in his dough or took out a shovelful of loaves or plates of cakes. Everywhere in the villa, and rather far down the other slope of the hillock leading to the Appian Way, the place was alive, preparing for the night or the next day. Some slaves were singing in the distance, busy about the officers' rooms, doing the dishes, working at the baths, while others were keeping up a fire for the master who liked to come and drink warm milk in the kitchen before retiring—he also liked to warm his own honey, to sit alone with the slave on duty, listening to him sing or talk about his family.

". . . new stewards now fully know their way about," Alexander was saying. "As for the carpenters, they have finished the large entrance vault, and the masons were due to start the day after I left. I'll show you the plans tomorrow; you'll be pleased. Your Meneas is an inspired architect when it comes to laying out plumbing and chimneys, and conservative enough to avoid shocking, except perhaps in his conception for the lighting of reception rooms, dining halls, and bedrooms. I won't tell you any more; you'll be agreeably surprised."

Crassus was walking, his hands crossed behind his back. On the hill, below the terrace, two bondwomen went laughing by, pursued by some officers. Crassus kept his eyes on them for a moment. One of the men had caught up with one bondwoman and was pressing her against a twisted olive tree; the other two were lost in the night. Crassus walked calmly. Alexander came up to him, looking worried. He put his arm around Crassus' shoulder. "Marcus, Pompey is back. He encountered five thousand fugitives from Spartacus' troop. He massacred them in an uneven fight, since he was returning with several legions. But you know the senators. When a victorious general comes back to Rome with his legions, they always wonder what he is going to do or demand."

Crassus was walking, pensive. "How far Rome is from Suessa, at Suessa!" he said, turning his head toward Alexander with a warm smile.

"Yes, very far . . . But with your colossal fortune, Marcus, Rome can be far away even in your house in Rome. You don't need the City."

"Agreed, but when I am there, I do what everyone else does. I involve myself in current affairs, I pretend to be concerned about them, I invite the well-placed people who are supposed to know what the tomorrows are made of. All that is a lot of fun. But I don't like Rome any more than you do, Alexander. Yet, its square blue skies create unique mornings, you always have the feeling of getting out of bed in a city that's waiting for you. But how narrow and noisy the streets are! During the day, the tradesmen, the workers; at night, the beasts of burden and their carters, when you don't get both at once, day and night. When I am not there, I am happy to be away. When I am there, I wonder a little what ever kept me away. But that doesn't last long. I know quickly."

"Are you satisfied with your campaign against Spartacus?"

"I believe I'm entitled to be, Alexander. Begun in October, finished in April, it lasted less than six months and I put an end to the rebellion. Why should I not be? No one did it before me."

"So you are quietly preparing to reap the laurels of your victory all by yourself?"

"By myself? What do you mean?"

Crassus had stopped. His eyes still kept a trace of a smile, and he had now lowered his head slightly, looking attentively at Alexander. "And why not all by myself?"

"You asked the Senate to call Pompey to your aid."

"That's true. I also called for Lucullus, but I defeated Spartacus without their help."

"Oh, Marcus. The senators don't reason rationally. They play. They play with words, with ideas, with situations, with passions. They regulate their lives on notions different from ours. For them, Pompey's return calls for a celebration: he defeated Sertorius in Spain."

"Very well. Why not? I don't like that overcautious little general, but he's a nobleman who does a good job on behalf of the Republic. They feel he defeated Sertorius! So be it. But I think of Perpenna and I smile because I really did defeat Spartacus, and without any sort of aid."

"That is not what Pompey is saying."

Crassus stiffened. He was now definitely taller than his old friend. His cheeks had hardened, his wide-open nostrils and his eyes were no longer smiling at all. Alexander had withdrawn his arm from the shoulder of his friend, who was regarding him darkly. "And . . . just what is little Pompey saying?"

"Oh, you must allow for his disappointment. After all, he arrived the day after your victory was announced. There was talk of nothing but you and Spartacus. Pompey had not known the scope of the rebellion, the number of rebel slaves involved . . . He encountered five thousand fugitives: perhaps he thought that was the bulk of the troop. You know, coming from Spain, he didn't realize . . ."

"And what did little Pompey say?"

"When he was told that you had defeated Spartacus in the South, he said, 'Crassus overcame the evil, but I uprooted it.' But you must understand, Marcus, that . . ."

Crassus took a few steps and went to look at the sea. All of a sudden, as if some mysterious trumpet had sounded reveille, all the crickets started to talk at the same time. "Crassus overcame the evil, but I uprooted it," Crassus repeated under his breath, with the expression of a quaestor concentrating on a verbal message and repeating it over and over again so as not to forget a word of it. "And what was their reaction?" he said, turning to Alexander. "The senators do know the scope of the rebellion. They are not just back from Spain."

"Oh, they are reacting the way we did before the Senate entrusted you with the defense of the country's interests. Remember, Marcus, you said it yourself: there is no glory in a victory over slaves, only a . . ."

"Only unspeakable shame in defeat," Crassus ended the sentence for him. "So what?"

"There you are! Those are the very words you proclaimed in Rome, that everyone has taken up since. There is no glory in a victory over slaves."

"Yes, yes, Alexander, those were my words. But you did not answer my question: How did the senators react to Pompey's unjust statement? They know how many runaways there were."

"What are the facts? In the North, a . . ."

"You are not answering my question, Alexander!"

"Yes, I am. I am trying to tell you the senators' reaction. In the North, a Pompey returning victorious from a Spain where Sertorius will give Rome no more trouble. In the South, a Crassus who crushed the rebel slaves and restored peace to the country. Both these generals were given consular command, supreme power, and they are both on their way back to Rome with their victorious legions. The Senate is asking itself some questions. What are they going to do, these two generals? What are they going to demand? What will they aspire to? Will they confront each other before making their claims? Or on the contrary are they going to join forces against the Senate? What is the Senate going to do?"

"Me, join forces with Pompey? Against the Senate!" Crassus gave a short, nervous laugh. "The senators really have time to kill."

"That may be, but for the time being, they are worrying about a seizure of power."

"That's just what I'm saying: they have time to kill. I don't like Pompey, but he is a faithful servant of the Republic. If he had wanted to usurp power, he would have come back six months ago! He would have unleashed an attack on Spartacus! He would have taken Rome! . . ."

Crassus had paused pensively.

"That was possible. We will never know whether the senators did not consider it."

"No. But what we do know is that luck was with them. And with me, too," said Crassus.

"Why?"

"They had no one left to send against Spartacus. They could not recall Pompey without having to fear his subsequent claims: he would have been the only general in Rome, the conqueror of both Sertorius and the rebels. With his legions near the City, he would have been its absolute master!" Crassus smiled. "So they thought of me. Remember, Alexander, the Prince of the Senate was very skillful with me: he knew that I don't like Pompey and he allowed me to believe that he was seriously considering recalling him to send him against Spartacus. *Seriously*. It was that little word, much more than all their arguments, that prompted me to take action. The Prince of the Senate knew what he was doing, all right." Crassus put his hand on Alexander's shoulder. "So, you are right, they are asking themselves questions, but they can try again what worked well before: to use Pompey against Crassus and Crassus against Pompey."

Alexander smiled. "You are my best pupil; you have understood the situation."

The next day, Alexander told Crassus that the Senate had decided to give a triumph to Pompey, and that he, Crassus, would get only an ovation. Crassus blanched. "Why didn't you tell me this last night?"

"So you could get used to the idea that the Senate is indeed going to use Pompey against you and you against him. They have to. It is the only policy possible."

"The only policy possible!" whispered Crassus angrily. "A triumph for Pompey, and for me, charity—an ovation!"

In an attitude familiar to him, even when he was naked, Alexander had his left hand in the crook of his right arm and his chin on his right hand. "The only policy possible," he repeated solemnly.

Pale with rage, Crassus was looking at him intently. "Soon they'll be telling me that my campaign against Spartacus was nothing but a simple police operation!"

"Marcus, there is no glory in . . ."

"In a war against slaves!" Crassus thundered. "I know it! Those are my words! But I also know that my victory has not added any new provinces! Nor any booty! It only brought peace! And the other one gets the triumph for having beaten five thousand fugitives! And I get the ovation for having crushed a hundred thousand of them! I have more prisoners than there were in the whole group Pompey encountered! Ovation! Unbelievable!"

Crassus went off on horseback to inspect his property. He was not seen again all day long. That evening, after his bath, lying on the stibadium of the dining hall, Crassus was the most gracious of hosts. The two friends retired rather early. As he was leaving Alexander in front of the bedroom which was permanently reserved for him near his own, Crassus said, "I have a surprise in store for the Romans; they'll talk about it for a long time. They'll remember their ovation. . . . I'm going to give myself my own triumph. A triumph such as has never been seen before. Good night, my friend."

When Galba came back from Rome a few days later, Crassus kept him at his home. The quaestor took a perfumed bath and had a long massage. Slaves cut his hair and did his feet and hands, and Galba, very handsome, emerged from their hands all ready to go to the table with a fine appetite. Like Alexander, he had kept his bathrobe on for dinner.

"Well, what's happening in Rome?" Crassus said, as soon as his two guests had reclined before the table.

"The Senate has granted a triumph to Pompey. It will be celebrated on the twenty-ninth of December."

"Yes."

"The senators are granting you an ovation, milord. It will take place between Metellus' triumph—which he is receiving for his campaign with Pompey—and Pompey's."

"That is all most interesting," said Crassus, eating without raising his eyes. "Did you hear anything else about me?" the magnate added with a smile.

"Yes, milord. I was continually asked whether you planned to return to Rome before the summer heat."

Crassus' smile broadened, but his eyes remained hard. "Well, now, that's a good question. And what did you answer, Baebius?"

"That you had not spoken to me of your plans, milord."

"Good . . . Very good."

Later, strolling around his lovely swimming pool, Crassus gave a few orders to Galba as they were coming up to Alexander, who was quietly drinking an infusion of mint leaves. "We must have six thousand crosses made," Crassus was saying. "I want them high, solid, impressive." He stopped and helped himself to a goblet of hot mint. "We do have six thousand prisoners, don't we?"

"Yes, milord."

"Very well. I want those crosses as soon as possible."

Galba was staring at him openmouthed. His expression had hardened. He was breathing through his mouth, as if gasping for air.

"Have some nails forged, too. In sufficient quantity. Say, about twenty thousand."

Galba lowered his eyes. He asked in a whisper, "What size, milord?"

Alexander was looking intently at his friend, but Crassus seemed completely absorbed in what he was saying. He outlined the length between his forefingers. "Three to four inches. Ah. Provide cases for the nails and the hammers, too. Don't you want some mint, Baebius?"

Galba was standing very erect, his eyes lowered. "No, thank you. With your permission . . ."

"Yes, of course. You are tired. I'll see you to your bedroom."

Galba saluted Alexander, who returned the salute with a slight movement of his head. Crassus and Galba went off. "Give the carpenters the necessary orders first thing tomorrow." Crassus lowered his voice a little and continued his instructions, while in passing he stroked the cheek of Sicinio, who had come by carrying some logs. "And don't hesitate to punish them. I want all this done very fast." They had reached the entrance to Galba's room. The quaestor raised the drape, but Crassus added, "That red robe over your tanned skin makes a pretty contrast with your fine blond hair, Baebius." His eyes lowered, Galba did not reply. Crassus put his hand on the quaestor's arm. "Why, you're very cold! Are you ill?"

"No, milord."

"You're tired. Do you want something? Ah, I know what will put you back in shape: a massage with hot herbs."

Galba shook his head.

Crassus pressed harder with his hand. "Do you want me to join you a little later?"

Galba slowly raised his eyes; his face was expressionless. "I only need some sleep," he said, but his eyes were not tired.

Crassus was baffled for a moment, but he quickly collected himself and, glancing rapidly from one of the quaestor's eyes to the other, he whispered, as one makes a promise to a child who has just been put to bed, "When you've finished this . . . this mission, we'll have your villa built."

Galba lowered his eyes. Crassus smiled: Galba had blushed. He added, in a voice which had regained its tone, "And you'll choose your own staff, Baebius."

"Thank you, milord."

He gently pushed Galba into the bedroom. "Thank you," repeated the quaestor, who was now smiling again. The heavy curtain fell back behind him and Crassus walked back toward the swimming pool. Alexander was no longer there. Crassus passed beneath the portico along the edge of the pool on the house side. "Alexander!" The name echoed under the vault. He walked very quickly behind the columns as far as the terrace. Far away, at the feet of an Apollo—that Sulla had carried off in his booty from Piraeus and given to him in gratitude for his strong-arm work at the Porta Collina—Crassus made out a seated figure. "Alexander?" he called. Crassus took a few steps more. "Alexander?" The figure moved. It was Alexander, getting up and coming toward Crassus. "Why don't you answer me?" Crassus called. They walked toward each other. Alexander moved slowly, powerfully. Crassus said again, in something of a laugh, "Why don't you answer me?"

Alexander was carrying a broad fold of his bathrobe over his right arm. In the left hand, he held an empty goblet. Crassus smiled. "You're the only one who can drink a scorching infusion while walking. Why didn't you answer me?"

Alexander looked at him. "Let's go and talk close to a lamp," he said in a hoarse voice. "I want to see your face."

They went back into the dining hall and stretched out on the cushions around the table. "Six thousand prisoners. Six thousand crosses. Twenty thousand nails, and hammers . . . Are you going to crucify them?"

"Yes," said Crassus, straightening the folds of his robe. "From Capua to Rome. They will grace my return route every thirty paces."

"Why?"

"I told you the other day. I'm going to give myself my own triumph."

"You are going to commit genocide!"

"Genocide! You forget that these dogs ravaged the country for more than eighteen months! That they massacred consuls, officers, legionaries, citizens! . . . I am being given an ovation for having beaten these hundred thousand dogs, but Pompey and Metellus . . . I want to show the Romans that the number of my prisoners alone exceeds that of the group Pompey stopped in Etruria. And no one will ever dream of repeating little Pompey's words as I go by, . . . 'Crassus overcame the evil, but I uprooted it!'"

"This is not possible! This is not the little Marcus I educated! This is not my intelligent pupil, the excellent orator . . . This is not my friend who is going to crucify six thousand prisoners out of spite!"

"Out of anger, Alexander."

"Out of spite, Marcus. If it were anger, you would avenge yourself on Pompey and the senators."

"I thought of that, Alexander. But I cannot do it without

harming the Republic. And since we are on the subject of roots, I am going to show them that I have six thousand of the roots left!"

Alexander had gotten up. He paced in the space reserved for the servants, between the door and the table. "How can you? Six thousand people crucified! You, the most patient of men, the most understanding toward the slaves! I have seen you help out a slave family when its head was ill. You take special interest in the more gifted children. You have manumitted many of them among your workmen. . . . You . . ."

"He who loves well punishes well."

"You can punish an individual, but not six thousand!" Alexander thundered.

"You never said anything to me about the decimation of my legions!"

"That does not mean that I approved of it! But now, the war is over and you are going to massacre six thousand individuals!"

"Individuals! They are only rebel slaves, Alexander."

"Put them to work."

"I thought of that, too. It is not possible. Every one of them is a menace, another Spartacus! If you don't believe me, it's because you haven't listened to them."

"Cicero told me a great deal about it in Rome. He was startled by the violence of . . ."

"He saw only one of them—and a woman at that! But they are all . . . It's as if you were faced with worshipers of some strange god. To them, Spartacus is a sort of religion. . . . At any rate, they would try to escape. To start all over again. To make them work, I would need as many guards as slaves. It's not possible! They are doomed. And the example will be useful: the slaves will never rebel again."

Alexander had listened to him standing, his face solemn, one hand in the crook of his arm and his chin in the other. Now, he was looking at his friend. The rims of his eyes were red. Crassus looked up at him. "Have you nothing to say?"

"There is nothing to say. I cannot keep you from crucifying your prisoners."

"You are convinced I am wrong."

"I no longer know what I think. You are the richest of Romans, you own the largest number of slaves, the finest lands, three-quarters of Rome, villas everywhere, not to mention your six or seven legions. You are going to arrive in Rome between your six thousand crucified slaves and face wily senators who are caught between two armies: Pompey's and your own. They expect your resentment, they are not afraid of it; but your anger frightens them, because if you were to attempt a power grab, Pompey would attack you at their request. Then there would be a vanquished and a victor. But they do not want a victor; he would subsequently impose his conditions and the Senate would find itself faced with a second Sulla, another dictator. On the other hand, by playing on your resentment, the senators are playing their best card."

"Why?"

"Because Pompey, this very evening, is asking himself the same questions as you. He knows, as you do, that the Senate wants in one way or another to pit you two against each other to consolidate its own position by playing in turn on one and the other, and one against the other. And the more I think of it"—Alexander took a few steps and came back to lie down on the cushions—"the more I think of it, the more convinced I am that the Senate will authorize both of you—you and Pompey—to offer your candidacies for the next consulate. That's logic itself."

"Pompey a consul! He has no right to it; he has never held a praetorship!"

"It is only six months since you finished yours, so the necessary time has not gone by. You are legally eighteen months away from the consulate. But the Senate doesn't care about legality any more. That's become a tribune's slogan."

"I will protest publicly against Pompey's candidacy."

"But why? That would be a mistake, since you will be able to put forward your own for the same consulate."

Thoughtfully, Crassus slowly repeated Alexander's words: "I will be able to put forward my candidacy for the same consulate. . . . But what will the Senate ask? . . . Yes, Alexander, what will the Senate ask in return for the consulate?"

"Only one thing: that you dismiss your legionaries."

"And of Pompey?"

"The same thing. Think about it. By giving you and Pompey

power, the senators neutralize the two of you and retain the reins of government."

"You think that Pompey will agree to dismiss his army?"

"I don't think a thing, Marcus, I can only suppose. Suppose the Prince of the Senate puts this condition to you before putting it to Pompey. What would you do?"

"I . . . I believe that I would agree to it."

"And Pompey?"

"He would be wrong to refuse it."

"There you are. Well, this evening, Pompey is reasoning in the same way. That is, this evening, yesterday, or tomorrow; but he is thinking about it."

"Little Pompey . . . consul with me. . . . He will have had the triumph, I only the ovation, and he'll be consul without having held a praetorship."

"He was a proconsul for five years. Anyway, it is the only policy possible for the Senate."

"Ah! You and your only policy possible!"

"Marcus. Was I wrong when I asked you to join Sulla as quickly as possible?"

"No . . . Of course not."

"When I told you that the moment had come for you, since you wanted to play your part in the running of the Republic, to go to Rome because the senators were going to need you. Was I wrong then?"

"No, Alexander."

"So now you find yourself on the threshold of the consulate after a six months' campaign against Spartacus, whereas Pompey fought for years in Spain. And from being a simple citizen who saw his estates being set afire and his slaves escaping, here you are now a proconsul, at the head of your own legions, holding supreme power over the territory and on the threshold of the consulate."

"You are right. It all happened very fast."

"All of that, thanks to Spartacus. Now you are not only rich and victorious, but you have also made up for lost time and reached the front rank. Like Pompey."

"Like Pompey, that's true."

"You saw how unanimously the nobles submitted to your command for the protection of their endangered estates. They are the ones who got the Senate to strip the consuls of their power and transfer it to you. The senators were not enthusiastic about it—have no illusions about your popularity with them. They still look on you—and Pompey—as Sullans, disciples of Sulla. But, by investing you with power, they became the spokesmen of the general desire of the nobles. You emerged victorious and unscathed from this campaign. Today, your name, like Pompey's, is on everybody's lips."

"At last!"

"Of course. And all that in only six months . . . But you are not satisfied. You stand on your dignity because you get only the ovation while he gets the triumph."

"That's reason enough!"

"No, it isn't. Look at things from Pompey's viewpoint. He had every possible reason to hope to get the triumph. He fought for years while you were amassing a fortune. And don't forget that the Senate stripped the consuls of their power to give it to him five years before they did the same for you. But now here he is coming back to Rome and having to share the Senate's gratitude with a man who carried out a simple police operation."

"A simple police operation!"

"We are speaking from Pompey's viewpoint! To him, that's all your campaign was. He was abroad. He did not see the defeat of the consuls, the officers, and their legions. He did not see the country devastated and did not share the terror of the Romans on hearing that Spartacus was returning."

"That's true."

"So, like Pompey, you are now in the first rank. You . . ."

"And Metellus? Why would they not think of him for the consulate?"

"He's too old. As a reward, he'll get his triumph. No, for the consulate, they are thinking of you, Marcus. You are to be reckoned with. You have become a power."

Crassus smiled. "You've convinced me, Alexander."

"I've convinced you?"

"Yes."

"Then why tarnish your reputation by crucifying your prisoners?"

Crassus sighed. He looked unhappy. "You know the art of analyzing a situation, Alexander. And no one is better than you, nor more succinct, in synthesizing an event. But you grossly exaggerate the importance of certain factors which are nothing to a soldier."

"I am not exaggerating anything. I am projecting my mind into history. It will judge you."

Crassus sighed again. "You remind me of Macer, a young demagogue I met at the Prince of the Senate's. Certain things escape you, Alexander."

"Probably. Which ones?"

"My prestige will not suffer because I have crucified my prisoners. The Romans will even find that reassuring. They will say that I put an end to any idea of rebellion among the slaves, that the example was necessary, that I am a pragmatic man because I avoided a danger by eliminating those prisoners."

"You might some day regret having based your criteria on false values. This will be talked about for a long time, Marcus."

"Oh, I don't think so." Crassus smiled. "Businessmen and senators know too well the cost of manpower. Most senators, as you know, are successful businessmen. They realize well enough that a landowner doesn't sacrifice six thousand workers without due cause. There is nothing to be gotten from these prisoners. They are mad dogs. They have only one idea in their heads: complete freedom. Just look at those two women who lived with Spartacus; they are here. I am going to keep them so they can talk to us about Spartacus, and you will understand. . . . Oh, if this were a case of normal slaves, a few weeks of discipline would make them docile enough. With my legionaries, I had no choice: I lost four thousand men, but I got the other thirty-six thousand to obey. But these prisoners are runaways who would rather die than work for a master. . . . You saw how they fought! It took winter, the privations of a siege, and eight legions, Alexander, eight legions to put an end to them. This has never happened before. Believe me, these crucified slaves may be talked about for a long time—and I'm not even sure of that—but I won't regret a thing. Nor will the Romans."

"And what about history, Marcus?"

This time, Crassus roared with laughter. "Oh, yes, let's talk about history! When people have nothing left to say, they bring up history!"

Alexander smiled bitterly. "Men in power surround themselves with specialists, with thinkers, but they never follow their advice when their pride is at stake."

"I have to make my decisions today, Alexander! I do not live in the future, nor for historians!"

"That is what all men say who commit historic mistakes. But history is made in the present, Marcus."

"History is not concerned with slaves, my dear professor. Neither in the past nor in the present."

"It is concerned with the acts of men. The crucifixion of six thousand prisoners, the decimation of ten legions, are acts of cruelty that are going to besmirch the stages of your career in history and the morality of your contemporaries, because they will bear their share of the responsibility and shame. They let these things happen."

"That is what I was just telling you: you exaggerate the importance of certain military necessities. And since you are speaking of cruelties, let us say that these are useful cruelties."

"The way you deal with human life only gives the measure of your fear . . . and of your weakness at the same time. You are laying yourself more and more open to the judgment of history."

"Listen, Alexander," Crassus said rather curtly. "I remember perfectly well your courses on the politics and philosophy of Aristotle. On the morals of Democritus. You are the one who educated me and I am indebted to you for some marvelous hours. But don't talk to me about history where only rebel slaves are involved, prisoners who constitute a real danger. If history is to judge me for eliminating this danger, let it judge me!" Crassus was now definitely on edge; he was pacing up and down the dining hall. "History! Nothing, you hear, nothing will keep me tomorrow from dictating history the way I want it to be written! In fifty years or two centuries, some wretched little professor will write down what he heard in the street or read in some dictated manuscript. Will you tell me who remembers the Gracchi today? Who mentions Marius? History is the onanism of the impotent. With a pencil! . . . History is not the judgment of the acts of responsible men, professor; it is made up of rumors, of slanders, of planted comments, of the distortion of facts by men and by time. The imagination of a few wretched scribblers does the rest."

"Not all historians are mere impotent scribblers, Marcus. And they cannot all be bought."

Crassus laughed. "History is always written long after the fact, when all the participants are dead. . . . If they are alive, and in power, it is written in their favor and they are panegyrized in the hope of gaining some advantage. If they are defeated, historians are afraid to talk about them for fear of offending the victors. Who is interested in the vanquished? Who cares about the crucifixion of rebel slaves? Come, come, all of that is of no great importance. . . . You've gone pale, professor. Come. I'm going to give you a drink of honey-milk."

In the kitchen, Crassus heated the milk and honey. "My recipe is simple," he said in a playful tone. Alexander was listening to him gloomily. "You heat the milk and honey separately. When your milk is boiling, you pour in first . . . in this order, remember . . . a spoonful of orange marmalade, a handful of rose petals, and the hot honey. In your history, where there's a bit of everything, even rebel slaves, it'll probably be called 'Milk Crassus,' and the doctrinaire demagogues will say that I was not only cruel, but a sybarite as well—'not necessarily an incompatible combination,' the sly little wretches will add. Here, see how this tastes. Watch out, it's very hot."

Alexander, who was able to stand very hot drinks, took a gulp, then another. Proud of his decoction, Crassus was watching the reaction. Alexander smiled. "It's rich," he said. Crassus burst into a loud laugh, his mouth open, his head thrown back. "There! That's what the demagogues will say: rich!"

"And unaware."

"What?"

"They'll say: he's rich and unaware."

Crassus laughed. "That's what the poor always say about the rich. Tell me, didn't that fool Clodianus . . ."

"The consul?"

"Yes. That is, last year's consul. He passed a law that could prove costly to me."

"Which one?"

"The purchasers of holdings confiscated during the proscriptions and sold on credit by Sulla are summoned to make payment of the entire amount to the treasury or have their holdings confiscated. What do you make of that?"

"It's simple. The senators pardoned Lepidus' supporters. They continually allow themselves to be insulted in the streets by the tribunes, who stir up the crowd in order to draw from the Senate the right to initiate legislation. After all, this legislative power is a legitimate revendication. The senators know it, and they retreat further each day before their opponents."

"Why?"

"Because the State coffers have been exhausted by the war. Otherwise, the Senate would not have needed you and your money, and you would not be in the excellent position you are in today. That is why they are going to try to neutralize you by giving you the consulate."

"How do you know all that?"

Alexander smiled. "History. My reading of history allows me to make certain deductions."

"Hmmm. What do you advise me?"

"About what?"

"The law about confiscated holdings."

"If the properties you are paying off in installments are profitable, do as the law says and pay the balance due to the treasury. That will only make you more popular. If they are not profitable, bow to the law publicly and hand over the ownership to the State. You will be considered a good citizen and will not lay yourself open to the attacks of the tribunes. You gain in both cases. But, I repeat, you will probably be consul next year and then you in turn will be able to make it difficult for the Senate if you get together with Pompey to see that certain laws are passed. Isn't it what the consuls always do?"

Alexander put down his empty bowl. "That was very good. I am going to retire. I am tired."

"So am I."

They walked toward their bedrooms without a word. Crassus went on as far as Alexander's door. "You've been gloomy all evening."

"Hmmm."

"The prisoners?"

"Yes."

"Keep up with the times, professor."

"I've run out of arguments."

Crassus laughed. "You? Impossible."

Alexander smiled sadly. "Milord," he said in a voice still hoarse despite the honey and milk, "your name will carry the weight of those six thousand crosses."

"As long as there are slaves on this earth, all those who are not will understand my reasons."

"Now you are talking like a plutocrat. With power at your fingertips, that was inevitable."

Crassus laughed. Alexander went on. "Because you take shelter behind the fact that the prisoners are dangerous and impossible to guard, you think that that's the whole problem and that you are solving it by crucifying. You are mistaken. The problem goes on. It lies in the Roman's concept of his own superiority and the fact that he has a constant need for slaves in his society." Crassus laughed. "Without them," Alexander continued, "his fields, his roads, his houses, his gardens, would be just land covered with weeds, and his children would not learn anything. In truth, his whole society is built upon them. Consequently, it is also dependent on legionaries who must enslave more and more from conquered countries."

"Their lives do not count, professor. . . . The death of the rebel slave is necessary."

"You talk lightly of it now that you have defeated Spartacus, but the slaves are the ones you were all most afraid of!"

"Oh, Alexander, you are most irritating! Keep up with the times, professor, not with a world that doesn't exist."

Alexander sighed. "There is really no means of communicating, is there. . . ."

"I don't understand, professor."

Alexander leaned against the wall, his white hair stuck to his forehead by perspiration. "I know now that you don't. Apparently, you never did. . . . But perhaps there is nothing to communicate. Ever . . ."

"You are tired. Let me put you to bed."

"It's as if," Alexander went on, "men always reached a sort of level of deafness, of impossibility of dialogue, a sort of transparent curtain from which catastrophe always starts. . . . I have the feeling that men will never escape from it as long as pride and jealousy have not departed their hearts. Perhaps, in a thousand years from now, they will have undertood. . . . But what was the use . . . I don't understand what happened to our past. . . . What was the use of the influence of our marvelous philosophers, the plays of our poets, our cult of beauty in all its forms, centuries of civilization! . . . It seems that each time man looks at man he sees the enemy. That each time he moves, he goes faster in his race to nothingness. . . . We go so fast, life leaves us so quickly when we look back, it's as if our mothers had given us birth legs apart over our graves! . . . Perhaps all this struggle is just a quick fall, a simple matter of gravity. . . ."

Crassus laughed. "You are lacking in realism, Alexander."

Alexander breathed deeply and drew himself up. "Go on and laugh, but you will not escape the problem by turning your back on it."

"Well, I don't really see what I am turning my back on!" Crassus said impatiently. "I face up to the problem of the moment as quickly and as well as possible!"

"It's as if we were not living in the same world."

"Look, professor, stop all this nonsense. . . . We are all swept around in the same whirlpool . . . all of us, and no one can change its course. No one! Ever!"

"Oh, yes one can. With a certain state of mind, one can do absolutely anything. Your whirlpool is the event of the moment: what happens now, and now, and now. But what happens doesn't fall from the sky! It doesn't come from the gods! Men create it, you can be sure. Men and men alone. They create the present. So they can also change the course of it."

"Never!"

"Yet, for almost two years, Spartacus effectively changed the course of your whirlpool. And what if he had taken Rome when he had the chance? And if I murdered you tonight, wouldn't I alter your fate? The fate of the six thousand prisoners? The fate of the nation, perhaps, be it ever so slightly?"

"No. There is Pompey. He would see the problem in the same light. He, or another."

Alexander looked at Crassus for a long time without speaking. "Perhaps you are right. Men of your stripe abound."

"I love you too much to feel insulted, professor, but you do upset me. Perhaps I'm not right, Alexander, but you can't try everything! For the intellectual, it is easy: everything takes place in his mind. If his solutions do not work, no one is any the worse off, except him. He becomes embittered. But what about the man of action? The man in power? If his solution doesn't work, the whole country pays the price!"

"Yes, if it's a country without slaves, those convenient buffers. Otherwise, one can always crucify, can't one. . . ."

Alexander suddenly bent forward and brought a hand to his chest. Crassus stretched an arm out toward him, but Alexander turned and went into his room.

"Good night, professor!" Crassus called in an alarmed voice.

Alexander turned and looked at him for a moment. He let the drape fall back without replying.

The next day, a little before dawn, Crassus slipped into Galba's bed and awoke him with caresses and kisses. They spent the morning caressing each other, making love, sleeping, and starting all over again. Toward noon, Crassus said, "You will handle the whole thing, Baebius. I want a dog on a cross every thirty paces, all along the Appian Way, from Capua to Rome. You will set out right away. I'll meet you in Rome in a few days." Galba got up and slipped on a robe.

"When you go out, send Lollius, the steward, to me."

"The fellow who looks like a fat cat?"

"Yes, the fat cat."

"How can you keep such a dirty creature in your service?"

"He does his work well. He has an important position: he is my finance minister. I have to talk to him; Alexander gave me a few good ideas last night. But you're right. Tell Lollius that he has time to take a bath before he comes to see me. He really does stink, the animal."

ARENA

XXIV

On that April morning, a light southeast wind was blowing between Suessa Aurunca and Terracina, bringing a nauseous odor of rotting animal substances. This stretch of the Appian Way runs along the beach, and the Tyrrhenian Sea, never bluer than at this time of day, is always calm there. Between the road and the sea grow olive, orange, bitter orange, and lemon trees. It was before these gently sloping paths going down to the beach in the midst of the orchards, before this dream landscape reserved for the denizens of the neighboring villas, that Galba was crucifying that morning.

The prisoners had been roused from their sleep with strokes of the lash, and, each one carrying his cross, their pitiful procession had gotten under way. From Capua on, two thousand crosses had already been erected, one every thirty paces, and the horizontal rays of the rising sun cast long parallel shadows, cutting across the road at right angles like the unconnected rungs of a ladder fifteen leagues long. Scorched by the sun, the crucified slaves were begging for water, pleading to be put out of their misery, but no one came near these crosses buzzing with flies, covered with blood and excrement. Travelers would follow the procession for a bit, looking on in silence or commenting on the technique of the crucifixion, but then quickly resume their trip to Rome to get away from the stench. Those who were headed for Capua or Suessa covered their noses and mouths with a perfumed cloth, and, lacking perfume, some crushed a piece of fruit under their noses, but all hurried away rapidly.

Carrying his cross, digging the hole in which it was to be sunk, forced to crucify the comrade who preceded him and after that to set up his cross, the prisoner was then laid down on his own cross and crucified by the companion in misfortune who came after him. When a prisoner raised the cross in too shallow or too wide a hole, the cross keeled over, to the jeers of the legionaries, and the crucified victim shrieked with pain or fainted.

Each centurion supervised the execution of a hundred prisoners. On horseback, spurring his officers along, Galba nervously supervised the progress of the enterprise. "At this rate, we won't be in Rome for ten or twelve days!" And Galba shouted at the centurions who, in turn, urged on the decurions and the soldiers. But once the quaestor was gone the hammerblows resumed at a slower pace under the shouts of the legionaries and the stink of excrement discharged by the fainting victims. At the sight, some of the travelers swooned in their turn, threw up along the road, adding their convulsed faces and the smells of their vomit to the scene of torture conceived by Crassus. But it was against the victims that the travelers expressed their resentment, insulting them, spitting on them, throwing stones at them, mocking their agonized groans by mimicking them.

Galba had just left one centurion's group when a commotion arose in the line of prisoners and among the legionaries. A man had let his cross drop and was running toward a prisoner. Two legionaries tried to stop him. There was a short struggle and the man resumed his course, leaving the two soldiers knocked cold behind him. He pushed aside the prisoner who was raising a hammer to nail the hand of the man stretched on the cross and helped the victim to get up. "Capito! Capito!" The tall Samnite, his face swollen by a blow that had sliced away part of his cheek, covered with blood from head to foot, opened his eyes. "Gannicus!" he said in a whisper. Gannicus shook him. "Where is Spartacus?" A legionary came running up and whipped Gannicus. Gannicus let go of Capito with one hand and grabbed the lash that was about to strike him again; he yanked it toward him and ground his knee between the thighs of the legionary, who fell groaning to the ground, clutching his genitals. "Where is Spartacus?" Gannicus repeated. "I don't know!" said Capito. Four legionaries seized the tall Celt; Capito staggered and fell back on his cross. A centurion was coming up; some legionaries stood the Samnite up. The soldiers explained the incident to the officer. A few onlookers gathered around. Aware of his role, the centurion decided to punish the two friends as an example. He gave Capito a hammer and ordered him to nail Gannicus to his cross. Capito looked at the Celt who was struggling. The tall Samnite went feebly toward his companion. Gannicus stopped resisting. He looked at Capito, who was standing before him, thin, pale, bent, with froth on his lips, the hammer in his hand. There was something like a smile on the Samnite's mutilated face. He said, "They will never understand," and slowly turned toward the centurion.

"You heard me, dog!" the officer shouted.

Capito dropped the hammer. "No," he said under his breath.

The centurion ran up to him, threw one hand behind the Samnite's sunburnt head and gouged out one of his eyes. "Nail, dog!"

Staggering, Capito raised his head toward the centurion and spat in his face. The Roman grabbed Capito's head again and gouged out the other eye. As he fell, Capito grabbed the centurion's neck and squeezed. The officer easily broke away and got up. "You think you are dealing with Romans?" said Gannicus.

Galba was coming up. He spurred his horse up to the centurion. "Get to work!"

"They're refusing to nail," said the centurion.

Everywhere the crucifying had stopped. Galba looked at Capito on the ground, then at Gannicus. The Celt, with two legionaries holding down each of his arms, raised his big blue eyes toward the young quaestor. Galba took the centurion's whip and spurred his horse over to Gannicus. Quickly, the four legionaries who were holding the Celt twisted his arms, forcing him to bend over, to present his back. Galba lashed him several times, shouting, "Nail!" at each stroke. The legionaries straightened the Celt up. "No. That's good for Romans!" Gannicus shouted. A murmur ran through the little group of onlookers. A legionary raised his sword at Gannicus, but Galba stopped him with a shout and went back to the centurion. "The general wants them crucified. Call another dog and make him nail him!" A prisoner was immediately brought up, an adolescent who had been watching the whole scene. He looked at Gannicus while Capito was being thrown back on the cross. A hammer was held out to him, but it was too late. Like his two leaders, he refused to nail in spite of the whip. One by one, the prisoners who had seen and heard let their crosses drop, imitated in turn by all the others.

"Another one!" Galba shouted.

A pregnant woman was led up, her feet and knees swollen and covered with blood.

"Nail, bitch!" Galba yelled in exasperation.

The woman was short, deformed by wounds, illness, pregnancy, encrusted with mud—she had probably fallen and dragged herself along under the weight of her cross—and her face was one big running sore under which the eyes and the shape of the nose were barely discernible. And this wretched creature in vaguely human shape, thrust forward at swordpoint by the impassive legionaries, raised what was left of her face toward the handsome, impatient, blond, muscular quaestor, whose pale blue tunic emphasized the color of his eyes and the tan of his skin. The sore in the shape of a face opened somewhere behind the strands of pus: "Go feel your horse, you little snot!"

Laughter rippled among the prisoners and the travelers. Galba blanched. But time was going by, the work was not getting done, and the sun was now very high. Frantic with the urgency of the task at hand, wounded by the laughter, powerless before the inflexible will of the prisoner-slaves, Galba ordered the centurion, "Have your men nail them up!"

The legionaries pushed away some jeering onlookers while the centurion urged his men on. Galba's order was immediately relayed through the prisoners' ranks. They also refused to carry their crosses and started to insult the quaestor as he came by. The legionaries were then obliged to do all the horrible work:

carry the cross, dig the hole, hold the prisoner, crucify him, raise the cross, and fill the hole. Two young patricians came by on horseback, preceding the chariot of two pretty women, very pale, upset by the stench covering the road. "When there are chariots to repair," one of the horsemen said as they rode by Galba, "we'll have to remember Crassus' legionaries; they're not bad at nailing!" One of the two women called out, "Crassus' road stinks!"

The other said, as she looked at Galba as on a parasite, "Crassus has ruined our vacation road."

Capito was unconscious when they crucified him. Then they dragged off Gannicus who screamed, "Capito! . . . Capito! . . ." and his head burst open on the right side. To keep him from moving, they had knocked him out.

Gannicus shivers. He stretches forward like a taut bow and lets out a great shriek. He bounces furiously back against the cross. Several times. His head falls forward; he faints. The wound has lengthened in his blued hands, but no more blood flows from it. During the afternoon, Gannicus opens his eyes. He is sweating profusely. His long black hair falls straight over his face. He throws his head back and he groans: it has immediately struck against the upright of the cross. He painfully turns his head to the right. From his blue, swollen, deformed hand, a trail of dried blood runs along his arm, crosses his chest and goes down to his feet. To the right of the Celt, the pregnant woman is crucified, naked, covered with flies. The flies! A murmur rises in the Celt's throat, pushes at his lips: "The flies!" The words leave a froth between his lips and the flies return as soon as they have come out. Gannicus makes another attempt at thrusting his head back. Behind the moist locks of his black hair, in a silvery fog, very far away, the sea is charging in long, shining strings. In the orchards lining the road, chirping pairs of birds chase each other from branch to branch: the mating season goes on. Other shrieks of pain, other cries burst out beneath the hammerblows, between the sounds of the countryside and the monotonous onslaught of the wave. Groans, shrieks, hammerblows, the wave; groans, shouts, insults, the wave; hammerblows, shouts, chirpings, the wave.

At the top of Capito's cross, a gull is waiting. Beneath it, Capito seems asleep, his eyelids sucked in over useless sockets, his head turned toward Gannicus who is calling him.

A chariot went by, heading for Capua. His head turned to the fruit trees, the traveler held against him a curly-haired little boy who pressed his hands over his ears, his face dug into the man's cloak. In the other direction, rather far away, the metallic sounds of a troop moving forward without haste. It was Crassus'. His skin tanned by the sun, lying on broad cushions, Crassus kept a perfumed cloth under his nose. Resting on one elbow, swaying slightly as the wheels of the chariot passed over the slabs of the road, he contemplated the crucified slaves. In front of him, sixteen powerfully built Blacks pulled the chariot. In front of them, a century was preceded by lictors, the fasces on their shoulders, and, behind, two decuries were followed by about a hundred slaves carrying amphorae, chests of provisions, clothes. Quite far behind rode Crassus' army, bearing its standards high.

When they were out of Capua, Crassus had had Alba and Polla seated between the Blacks and his chariot so that they would not have to walk. Tired with walking, they would not have been up to the little entertainment he had planned. "Look carefully," he said as they went by the first cross. "I don't want to miss him either." To the crucified slave who asked for water, he had had water brought. Only two, until then, had had the strength to make themselves heard. And, as he grew bored, Crassus had had the pace increased, but the swaying of the chariot had bothered him and the slaves had had to resume their earlier cadence. Crassus was dozing off when a shriek that had lost all human tone made him start. Another shout followed, more distinct: *"Crassus!"* He had the chariot stopped. His head on his chest, behind the hair that hid his face, Gannicus had recognized the Roman. *"Crassus!"* he shrieked again.

"Is that he? Spartacus? I don't recognize him!"

He made a gesture. "Lift his head up!"

A decurion rushed up. With the end of his lance, he shoved the Celt's chin and Gannicus' head knocked back against the cross. Gannicus' long black hair fell aside, down to his shoulders.

"Gannicus!" Alba shouted, jumping down to the road.

Polla was looking at the Celt with dull, expressionless eyes.

"Crassus! Curse you!" shrieked Capito, who had heard Gannicus.

Alba turned her head. They had gone by the Samnite without recognizing him. She shivered as she saw him and struggled furiously against the decurions who had stopped her. She was brought back to her place, beside Polla. Crassus waved, the decurion withdrew his lance, but Gannicus' head did not fall back; the Celt was looking at his woman.

Crassus had sat down. "At last something is happening." At a motion from him, a decurion came running up. "Give him a drink and cool his head off."

"Yes, milord."

The decurion took two men and an amphora. Crassus leaned over Alba. "Make him talk! Maybe he saw Spartacus!" Climbing up his comrade's back, a soldier gave Gannicus a drink. The Celt choked a moment on the cool water. He drank a great deal, his head turned to the side. When he stopped, the soldier poured what was left in the amphora over his head. Gannicus' hair was now matted to both sides of his face. The Celt was staring at Crassus. He called out in a clear voice, "Crassus! You will be the shame of men till the end of time!"

His sword raised, a decurion looked toward Crassus, who shouted, "Don't touch him! He'd be too pleased!" And, to Alba, "Make him talk, Alba!"

"Curse you, Crassus!" shrieked Capito. This time, Crassus gave Polla a slight kick. "Come on, ask him where Spartacus is! You think he's a prisoner? Hm? And what about you, Alba, what do you say? Alive? Dead? Wounded? To be crucified?"

"Spartacus!" Polla whispered in a little girl's voice.

"Yes, Spartacus. Tell me, Polla."

"Spartacus!" Polla repeated. "Spartacus is not dead!"

"No?"

"Spartacus! Spartacus!" Polla was whispering as she stared at her fingers.

"Why not us, Crassus? Why are you sparing us?" Alba cried.

"You are beautiful, Alba. You are both too beautiful. You are traders' mistakes. No, not you two. You will live at Suessa. You will go on talking to me about Spartacus."

Crassus motioned, the troop set out again. Alba looked intently at Gannicus. When the Celt opened his mouth, she shouted in unison with him, "Curse you, Crassus!" And their shout was heard by several of the crucified slaves. And when Crassus passed in front of the pregnant woman she found strength enough to insult him. And the next one did, too. And another called out, "Men will dance and sing over your dead body!" And then another, "Curse you!" And soon, the shouts rose ahead of Crassus, greeted him as he came by, continued behind him, and the entire Appian Way turned into one long malediction.

ARENA

EPILOGUE

By nightfall, most of the crucified had fallen into a comatose state. A dense, heavy rain driven by the southwest wind had begun to fall on their feverish heads, chasing away the flies, washing the blood and stains from bodies and crosses. When the rain stopped, the wind kept blowing, and a hazy moon rose into a poorly cleared sky, for a moment casting green shadows on the torn bodies. Somewhere, a cricket gave the signal; all the others answered.

In Crassus' camp, almost everyone was asleep, exhausted by the long march under the sun. A Black, one of the porters, made quickly for the shadow of a tent containing clothing and rations. Not far away, soldiers were guarding the open quarters of the slaves who slept in huddled groups. The Black crawled easily up to them and continued until he had found Alba. He woke her by putting his hand over her mouth. She looked at him without fear, perhaps trying to put a name on his face.

He whispered into her ear. "Listen. You are not far from Gannicus. If you want, I can help you escape. I can get up and start running. Two or three of the soldiers will run after me, and you'll be able to get away easily."

"I could not go far with Polla."

"Go by yourself, she no longer knows what's going on."

"I don't want to leave her."

"Are you sure?"

"Yes."

He looked around, to see if it was safe to leave.

"Come here," Alba whispered. She drew him close to her and stroked his face. "Your friendship . . . You are beautiful. . . . Thank you." She was overcome.

The Black tenderly put back a strand of hair that had just fallen over Alba's face. "You are not alone," he said.

"All those people crucified . . . It's terrible."

"Yes. That's the way Romans are."

"Gannicus recognized me! Did you see?"

"Yes."

Her cheek against her companion's, Alba was whispering into his ear. Her tears rolled down along the Black's face. He took her head in his powerful hand, stroked her face. "Cry, Alba. Cry."

"And Capito . . . Did you see? They gouged his eyes out!"

"I saw, Alba."

Alba wept against him for a long time, even sobbed, her mouth against his chest, her teeth clenched. When she was calmer, but still panting, she said, "What can we do now?"

"We can do everything. Nothing has changed! This is just another day."

"But, everyone is dead! And now . . . the crucifying . . ."

"It's true, Spartacus did not survive what he thought had to be done . . . his ideas . . . But we would be betraying him now if we didn't carry on his fight, our fight for freedom. . . . Besides, not everyone is dead. You're here. I'm here. And the ones over there, they're not dead."

"It's not the same any more. . . . Capito was always saying, 'The Romans are everywhere!' "

"We're everywhere, too, Alba."

"You . . . Are you going to start it all over again?"

"I'm going to carry on—given the least opportunity. Before Spartacus spoke to us, I didn't know, I just felt something was wrong. When I thought over what he had said, up there, before our big fight against Clodianus, I knew better. . . . I knew what was right."

"But they are stronger than we are!"

"Today, yes. But they won't always be, Alba. For us, the most important thing is not to succeed, but to try. Besides, we don't need to hope anymore to carry on the fight. We don't care if we don't survive it. What counts for us, now that Spartacus and all the others have been murdered, is that we know that we are fighting for what is right. They can't kill us all, Alba. Besides, what's the point of surviving, if it's just to be a slave?"

"I'm afraid, I think."

"I'm afraid too, Alba. We are all afraid."

Alba took his face in both her hands. She looked at him a moment and a vague smile came into her eyes along with her tears. She kissed his eyes very tenderly. Several times. And her lips said, "Thank you," but her voice did not come out. "I . . . Maybe I'll be seeing you again. . . ."

"Maybe. And remember, Alba, you are not alone . . . in spite of the dead, in spite of the crucified."

"I'll remember . . . I'll remember. . . . I'm not alone. I'll remember. . ."

He looked around once more. The guards were asleep on their feet, the whole camp was asleep. He turned his head toward Alba. "If I see you again tomorrow, I'll give you a cloak."

Alba watched him crawl away until he was out of sight. The next day, she did not see him again. Crassus had decided to send her back to Suessa with Polla, under the protection of a decury, in a litter borne by four porters, followed by a relief of four more. He had spoken to the decurion. "Tell Lollius, the steward, to see that they are given a good room in the villa and whatever clothes they want. They are to be treated as guests in my house. From now on, you are responsible for their comfort." And the litter had started in the direction of Suessa.

During the afternoon, Alba and Polla passed before Gannicus and Capito again. From the decurion's attentive manner, Alba had understood she could behave as she liked. She asked the officer to see that Gannicus and Capito were given something to drink and walked over to the Celt. Polla had remained in the litter, pale, expressionless, playing with her hands, staring at her fingers, and softly saying, "Spartacus is not dead! Spartacus is not dead!"

The two crucified men could no longer drink. Gannicus did not recognize Alba. "The flies!" he repeated unceasingly in a whisper. "The flies!" Alba walked toward Capito, broken on his cross; his feet now were nothing but a shapeless black lump. A faint groan came from his swollen lips and his massive body was already cold. Alba had cloaks put over them and gave them one last long look. There was nothing more she could do for them.

Suessa was only a league away when night fell on the road. A group of some thirty runaway slaves fell on the decury and lapidated it. Polla died in her sleep, her throat cut by the slice of a sica. A red-headed Samnite tore Alba's dress with a flick of the wrist. He carried her off and laid her down beneath an olive tree. Alba did not try to defend herself. She seemed not to be feeling anything any more: neither her back being bruised against the ground, nor the metal breastplate of the Samnite crushing her. He was jiggling on top of her when she calmly told him that he was raping a prisoner-slave.

"Oh, yes? I've never seen a prisoner-slave carried in a litter by slaves and protected by legionaries!"

Alba whispered the Thracian's name and looked at the crucified slaves. On one cross, a gull was waiting.

"Spartacus, he's dead. You think it's all over?"

The ghost of a smile passed over Alba's face. The Samnite took his lance and plunged it furiously into her breast. Her arms outstretched, her head turned toward the crucified slaves, Alba had not moved. Froth had formed at the corners of her lips, bubbling under the breath that was departing.

A dense fog coming from the sea was rising toward the road, covering all the mutilated bodies, Alba, Polla, the legionaries, the crucified. The gull left its observation post and went into the night with a cry.

Oak Beach, Autumn 1967

GLOSSARY

aedile: municipal officer in charge of public works, games, police, and grain supply
amphora (pl. *amphorae*): jar or vase
Campus Martius: Field of Mars; parade ground; public meeting place
centurion: commander of a century
century: political, administrative, and military unit of 100 citizens
chlamys: large upper garment, mainly for military dress
client: retainer; one dependent upon, or obligated to, a patron
cohort: military grouping; usually, one-tenth of a legion (400 to 600 men)
curia: one of the groups into which the Roman patricians were divided; by extension, the meeting place of the Senate
curule: ivory chair or stool denoting the authority of the magistrate occupying it
decurion: commander of a decury
decury: military squad of ten men
denarius: (pl. *denarii*): Roman coin equivalent to a drachma

dittany: plant deemed to be curative; hence, balm, comfort, appeasement
doyen: senior man of a body such as the Senate or the Diplomatic Corps
fasces: bundles of rods around an axe carried by the Roman lictor
greaves: leg armor
instita: border or flounce on a lady's robe
lanista (pl. *lanistae*): owner of gladiators or of a school of gladiators; promoter or impresario of gladiatorial fights
laticlave: garment with a broad purple stripe, designating senators, equestrian military tribunes, and sons of noble families
latifundium (pl. *latifundia*): large landed estate or domain, often absentee-owned
legion: division of the Roman army, of 4000 to 6000 men, divided into cohorts, maniples, centuries, and decuries (see these entries)
libitinarius (pl. *libitinarii*): servant of the goddess of the dead; those who dispatched the wounded gladiators and disposed of their corpses and belongings after the fights
licium: loincloth
lictor: assistant to a public official
ludus (pl. *ludi*): game, sport; by extension, school for gladiators
maniple: company of foot soldiers; usually, one-third of a cohort (130 to 200 men)
mirmillo (pl. *mirmillones*): gladiator armed with a shield, a sword or dagger, and a helmet; usually pitted against a retiarius
municipium: city administration; the municipality
munus (pl. *munera*): public show, as of gladiators, given by the aediles, or other patrons, for the public
murma: large helmet, worn by the mirmillo, and on which a sea fish is carved
palla: long, wide cloak
pallium: pall cloak, or male outer garment
paterfamilias: head of a household; literally, father of a family
patron: dispenser of largess; sponsor; one to whom others are obligated
praetor: magistrate; leader; chief; the one at the head

propraetor: praetor's deputy; one sent to govern a province, addressed as "praetor"
quaestor: magistrate (judge or prosecutor) in Rome; official assigned as aide to a general
retiarius (pl. *retiarii*): net fighter; gladiator armed with a net and trident, usually pitted against a mirmillo
Scordisci: people from north Macedonia
sesterce: small silver coin, equal to one-quarter of a denarius
sica: dagger; poniard
stibadium: semicircular seat or couch
stola: long dress worn by matrons and musicians
subligar: loincloth; kilt
velite: mobile, lightly armed skirmisher; member of a flying squad